The doe, acting only on he
those with common sense
time to begin running again

The worgen lunged after her. Varian waited for a moment, then stepped from the tree. If Eadrik was here, the lord of Stormwind considered, then his master could not be far.

The bow once again ready, Varian moved in the direction from which Eadrik had come. The worgen hunted as a pack to a point. Being also men, those like Genn would seek their individual kills.

Varian retraced Eadrik's path, moving through the brush as readily as the worgen. His eyes constantly surveyed the vicinity and his ears and nose sought signs of *his* prey.

And at last he saw a worgen who could only be the Gilnean king. Genn flung himself after a massive boar with tusks so sharp and strong that, if the animal turned to face the worgen, Genn would truly risk death. At the moment, though, the boar thought only of flight.

Genn, however, was fast gaining. He ran sometimes on only his legs, but other times used his hands, too. With a litheness that Varian had not even seen from the much younger Eadrik, the veteran ruler closed on the boar.

Having measured the situation, Varian entered the fray. Although without the "benefit" of the curse, he moved with all the skill and pace of one who had survived more critical struggles than surely all the worgen combined. Yet, it was more than merely the reflexes of a former gladiator that served Varian now. Another force guided him, drove him in among the worgen as if he were one of their own and not simply a man. Others in the past had called him Lo'Gosh . . . and, at that moment, that name was more true of him than the one with which he had been born.

Don't Miss These Other Tales in the
WORLD OF WARCRAFT®

THRALL: TWILIGHT OF THE ASPECTS
by Christie Golden

THE SHATTERING: PRELUDE TO CATACLYSM
by Christie Golden

STORMRAGE
by Richard A. Knaak

ARTHAS: RISE OF THE LICH KING
by Christie Golden

NIGHT OF THE DRAGON
by Richard A. Knaak

BEYOND THE DARK PORTAL
by Aaron Rosenberg & Christie Golden

TIDES OF DARKNESS
by Aaron Rosenberg

RISE OF THE HORDE
by Christie Golden

CYCLE OF HATRED
by Keith R. A. DeCandido

WAR OF THE ANCIENTS:
BOOK ONE—THE WELL OF ETERNITY
by Richard A. Knaak

WAR OF THE ANCIENTS:
BOOK TWO—THE DEMON SOUL
by Richard A. Knaak

WAR OF THE ANCIENTS:
BOOK THREE—THE SUNDERING
by Richard A. Knaak

DAY OF THE DRAGON
by Richard A. Knaak

LORD OF THE CLANS
by Christie Golden

THE LAST GUARDIAN
by Jeff Grubb

WORLD OF WARCRAFT®
WOLFHEART

RICHARD A. KNAAK

POCKET BOOKS

New York   London   Toronto   Sydney   New Delhi

Pocket Books
A Division of Simon & Schuster, Inc.
1230 Avenue of the Americas
New York, NY 10020

This book is a work of fiction. Names, characters, places, and incidents either are products of the author's imagination or are used fictitiously. Any resemblance to actual events or locales or persons, living or dead, is entirely coincidental.

First Pocket Books paperback edition June 2012

POCKET and colophon are registered trademarks of Simon & Schuster, Inc.

For information about special discounts for bulk purchases, please contact Simon & Schuster Special Sales at 1-866-506-1949 or business@simonandschuster.com.

The Simon & Schuster Speakers Bureau can bring authors to your live event. For more information or to book an event contact the Simon & Schuster Speakers Bureau at 1-866-248-3049 or visit our website at www.simonspeakers.com.

Cover art by John Polidora.
Interior art by Alex Horley.

Manufactured in the United States of America

20   19   18   17   16   15   14

ISBN 978-1-4516-0576-1
ISBN 978-1-4516-0577-8 (ebook)

For all the adventurers everywhere . . .

ACKNOWLEDGMENTS

I'd like to again gratefully acknowledge those folks who have consistently been there to offer their expertise on the background for this and previous novels. Thank you to Publishing Lead Mick Neilson and Senior Story Developer James Waugh, plus Evelyn, Sean, Tommy, Joshua, George, Gina, and everyone else at Blizzard who's lent a helping hand. Also to Glenn Rane for another fantastic cover!

And how could I not also thank all those who work on *World of Warcraft* in whatever capacity to make it the ultimate online gaming experience? You may be behind the scenes, but without you guys in the trenches, this success could not be possible.

Naturally, my appreciation to Chris Metzen for his creative guidance and for introducing me to Azeroth.

On the publishing side, as ever thanks to those at Simon & Schuster who helped guide the process there— Ed Schlesinger and Anthony Ziccardi.

Lastly, thanks to all of you who continue to enjoy these adventures in Azeroth!

—Richard A. Knaak

PROLOGUE

NORTHREND

Twin rows of straining, green-skinned warriors tugged on taut, broad ropes as they dragged a colossal wheeled cage slowly up the wide ramp leading into the last of the ships. Despite Northrend's eternal winter, the muscular orcs sweated heavily from effort. Their broad-jawed faces contorted with each new heave of the ropes.

Guards stood alongside the ramp, torches in one hand, ready weapons in the other. With steely brown eyes they watched not the workers but rather the great covered cage. The cube-shaped structure towered over them, its outer covering consisting of a great tarp sewn from goatskin. There were no gaps in the tarp, no hint from the container as to just what the cargo was.

But there was a clue, revealed simply in the fact that the orcs themselves maneuvered the cargo. Desolate as the port was, it did have work animals such as the horned, reptilian kodo beasts, strong creatures more than capable of taking the places of the struggling orcs. There was even a trio of mammoths, generally used for transporting several riders at once. Yet, not only were those animals excluded from the effort, but they had been moved decidedly far from the vicinity of the docks. Even there, they stirred anxiously, the kodo beasts flaring their nostrils and the mammoths waving their trunks as all the animals stared in the direction of the ships.

With a tremendous howl, the winds abruptly picked up to storm strength. Weather in Northrend had only one consistent factor . . . that it was foul. But there were many levels of foul, and the docks shook as the waters of the cold sea suddenly churned with great waves. Ship hulls groaned as every vessel rocked hard.

From deep within some of the ships, there came horrendous roars and banging. On deck, crewmembers rushed to the hatches leading down to the holds. Stern veteran mariners and warriors looked anxious.

The last ship also rocked . . . and the gangplank twisted. It dipped to one side, spilling several startled guards and throwing the workers into a tangle.

The cage shifted. At the last moment, the orcs on the teetering ramp kept the container from falling. However, no sooner had they managed that than it began to shake from within. A roar identical to those emanating from the ships but much deeper echoed through the dank port. Something within began pulling at the tarp.

Guards rushed up from the port. Those still astride the gangplank fought desperately to maintain their balance. One failed, instead tumbling into the chill waters between the dock and the ship.

From the shoreline, the fleet captain—a one-eyed veteran mariner called Briln, whose body bore numerous intricate tattoos marking his journeys—raced toward the side of the gangplank and shouted, "Get that cage straightened! Don't let it fall! Get those weapons ready! Where's the powder? If that cage is damaged—"

The cage beneath the tangled tarp rattled. The dim illumination of the wind-blown torches was insufficient to reveal what was happening, but the nerve-scraping wrenching of metal gave Briln enough warning.

"Spears up front! Hurry, you offal! The right side of the cage!"

Two guards either more impetuous or more foolish than the rest moved in closer. From his angle, Briln could not make out everything that happened next, but he saw enough.

The foremost orc prodded the cage with his spear. The next instant, something snagged his weapon and tugged both it and him through a tear in the tarp.

As that happened, the second orc instinctively lunged forward to aid his vanishing comrade.

Something thick darted through the tear.

The orc was too slow to realize his danger. He was plucked from the gangplank as if weighing nothing. Before his fellows could reach him, the massive appendage crushed the guard's torso—flesh, bone, plate armor, and all. The gore splattered those farther back.

The hand threw the limp, ruined body aside, then retreated into the covered cage. From within, there immediately came a cry from the first warrior, apparently left alive for the moment.

Orcs with long, thick spears quickly lunged toward the

spot as Briln raced up to join them. Two guards thrust, but the captain knew that it was already too late.

Shrieks that almost stopped him in his tracks echoed through the Northrend port. The utter fear in those cries could be felt as well as heard. There was little that could shake an orc's resolve or even draw up in one anything resembling terror, but what had been captured at already so much cost was more than capable.

A horrific crushing sound punctuated the shrieks. The orcs near the opening stepped back as something liquid sprayed them. A ghastly stench immediately followed, filling their noses.

"Spears! Spears!" Briln roared again as he neared. The captain looked up. The torchlight enabled him to see the rip in the tarp and the bent bars. Those bars had been forged strong; even with all his might, the gargantuan beast had been unable to do more than pull the bars just a little farther apart. Unfortunately for the two guards, that had been quite sufficient.

"Where's the powder?" Briln demanded to no one in particular.

Another orc finally rushed up with a burlap sack the size of a thick fist. He also wore a coarse cloth over his mouth and nose and handed one just like it to Briln, who used the two strings attached to the piece to secure it to his own face. The mask was merely a precaution. Nothing from the sack should have ended up in either Briln's nose or mouth, but there was no sense in taking unnecessary chances.

The captain was tempted to let the other orc do the task, but then he seized the sack himself. From within the nearby cage, sickening ripping sounds continued.

"Cover me!" The captain positioned himself, then studied the gap carefully. Although he had lost the one eye years ago in battle in Kalimdor against the Alliance forces commanded by the human Admiral Proudmoore, Briln still prided himself on his expert aim.

Taking a deep breath behind the cloth mask, the scarred orc tossed the pouch toward the gap.

The wind gusted, and for a moment Briln was filled with fear that the sack would miss entirely. However, it just barely made the edge of the rip, then fell into the obscured cage.

A moment later the captain heard a small, soft thump. The beast within let out a distrusting rumble. There was the sound of chewing. A slight mist of powder exited the tear, but not enough to concern the orcs. The wind carried away what little escaped, dispersing it.

Inside the covered cage, something heavy and moist dropped. Briln knew it to very likely be what was left of the guard. Despite that, the sound gave the captain more hope that his plan had succeeded.

A confused grunt arose from the shrouded creature. Suddenly, the cage shook harder. Inside, a huge form slammed against the bent bars. Heavy breathing arose near the tear in the tarp, but nothing could be made out clearly in the tear itself.

The breathing became labored, exhausted. The orcs heard stumbling.

Then there came a violent thud. The cage shuddered and almost slipped again. Only the strength of nearly two dozen struggling orcs kept that from happening.

Briln and the others waited several tense moments, but there was no renewed movement or sound. With caution, the captain approached the covered cage. Becoming more daring, he prodded the tarp.

Nothing happened. Briln exhaled in relief, then turned to the others. "Load that thing aboard, then get those bars bent back and that hole covered with something! Better make sure that there's always a sack of that herb concoction the shaman gave us ready to sprinkle on the thing's food! We can't afford this on the seas!"

The other orcs moved to follow his orders. The captain studied the silhouettes of the other ships. Each contained such a cage. The new warchief Garrosh had commanded that this venture be completed, regardless of the cost in seeing it done. Briln and the others here had not questioned that cost, either, for all would have readily perished for the legendary overlord of the Warsong offensive. Garrosh's deeds were epic and retold over and over in the Horde. He was also the son of the late Grom Hellscream and had been an advisor to Thrall, the orc leader who had freed their people from captivity.

Yes, no matter how many lives it had already cost and *would* likely cost by the time the fleet reached its destination, it was all worth it to Briln and the others. The Horde was at last within grasp of its destiny. It had the vitality, the drive, that this altered Azeroth deserved. Those who had held power so long in the world had become decadent . . . too *weak and soft*. The Horde—and especially the orcs—would finally stake its claim on the more lush regions that it needed not only to survive but finally to thrive as it had long deserved.

This recent Cataclysm, so Garrosh had impressed upon his people, was the great sign that this was their day.

The world had been torn asunder, and to survive meant to be able to adapt to its much-transformed lands.

The crewmembers finally had the last cage loaded. Briln watched as they sealed the hull. They had a fair supply of the sleep powder in stock, and there were other threats that were supposed to keep the creatures in line, but the elder orc looked forward to the end of the journey.

Aboard deck, his first mate saluted. "Everything's secured, Captain! All set to sail on your word!"

"Get us going, then," Briln growled. "The sooner we get this cargo to Garrosh, the sooner it becomes the *Alliance's* trouble. . . ."

The other orc grunted agreement, then turned to bellow Briln's command. In short order, the ship pulled away from the dock.

The winds whirled madly and thunder crashed. A storm was brewing, the last thing the fleet needed. Still, the captain thought it nothing compared to what the Horde's enemies would soon face. Briln stared beyond the dark, swirling waters, imagining the fleet's destination, imagining what his cargo would do once Garrosh had it under his reins.

And for a moment, Briln almost pitied Ashenvale's defenders, almost pitied the night elves.

But then . . . they *were* only night elves. . . .

1

THE WOLF

Tyrande Whisperwind knew that the world could never be mended. Deathwing, the great black dragon, had forever changed the face of all Azeroth in a manner even more terrifying in some ways than the Sundering—when the world's lone continent was savagely split apart. The high priestess, who had survived that epic event some ten thousand years ago, had never imagined that she would have to live through anything so brutal again.

To those few who might have been unfamiliar with her race, the night elf, her midnight-blue hair falling below her shoulders, seemed barely more than two decades old, rather than ten thousand years. However, her glittering, silver eyes were filled with the wisdom of so much experience. There were some very fine lines near those elegant eyes, but they were more the result of troubled times during the past ten millennia than from age.

Tyrande strode through the lush Temple Gardens, the

centerpiece—though geographically more west of the center—of Darnassus and composed of several islets of varying size filled with the most exquisite of flora. The light of a full moon shone down upon the gardens and with what appeared particular favor upon her. That it did so disturbed neither Tyrande nor any who happened by the high priestess. After all, it was a normal sight already familiar to those who knew the solemn figure.

She had hoped that out here she would be better able to think, to come to some conclusion concerning the weighty matters upon her. As high priestess, Tyrande generally sought guidance and peace from the goddess Elune, also called the Mother Moon, from a place of quiet meditation in the temple directly to the south. However, even the calm of the perpetually moonlit sanctum of the Sisterhood—the heart of Elune herself, some called it—had no longer proven enough. Thus, she had hoped the tranquil gardens might suffice where the temple had failed.

But although the gardens in some ways embodied the spirit of the Mother Moon even more than the temple, it was not enough to calm the high priestess this night. Tyrande could not keep from constantly worrying about the upcoming summit. The time of the gathering was fast approaching, and already she and the archdruid Malfurion Stormrage—her co-ruler and mate—wondered whether the event would prove worth anything at all.

The Alliance faced a revitalized Horde now led not by the seemingly conflicted Thrall, who might have kept the peace for the sake of both sides, but rather by a new, much more ambitious warchief. Garrosh coveted the great forests of Ashenvale, though he would hardly stop with them should they fall to his warriors.

Despite, as an archdruid, being more concerned with the wilds of Azeroth and having absolutely no ambitions toward politics, Malfurion had done what he could to help maintain unity in the Alliance. However, Tyrande and Malfurion both knew that the Alliance's future did not and could not rely upon him. It was time for someone who could be more dedicated to that goal. That was thus one of the points of this summit Tyrande and Malfurion had put together, to see if through the talks someone would arise who could best guide those assembled forward in this new world.

Of course, the gathering would not matter if not all the members were in attendance, and there were some of significance who still had not sent word of their participation. If they did not join, then no true accord would likely be acceptable.

Among those Tyrande passed during her trek were other priestesses, all of whom bowed low in homage to her. They were clad in silver-white, sleeveless robes similar to her own. Tyrande wore little ornamentation, needing none to mark her as high priestess. All knew her. She acknowledged their greeting with a smile and a nod of her head, but so engrossed was she in her dark thoughts that, in truth, she forgot the encounters immediately after.

The foul vision of Deathwing the Destroyer and what he had caused filled her mind, nearly overwhelming her. Her heart pounded and her blood raced as she imagined the continuing repercussions of his terrifying act.

The summit must prove of benefit, Tyrande thought anxiously. *This is the one opportunity we have to stave off the downfall of our world. If nothing comes of this, there will be no hope of attempting another gathering. It will be too late for all of us by then. . . .*

But they had not received word from three of the major members of the Alliance, including Stormwind . . . and if Stormwind alone did not participate, then—

Around her, the light of Elune grew blinding.

The Temple Gardens vanished.

Tyrande Whisperwind stumbled, then caught herself. Her eyes widened. New surroundings came into view, surroundings not at all even a part of Darnassus, the night elf capital. She now stood in a place far away, a place clearly on the mainland, on the continent of Kalimdor. Tyrande had been transported hundreds of miles in less than a single heartbeat.

More shocking than that, she was surrounded by the unmistakable vision of war. The stench of wholesale death was familiar to her, and darkened mounds roughly the size and shape of bodies—mangled ones—were everywhere.

What had been pristine wilderness—a few ruined tree trunks marked that this had once been forest—had clearly been ravaged by previous battles here. As the high priestess fought to regain her composure, it quickly dawned on her that she knew this place, this time, though whether from memory or because of Elune, it was impossible to say.

She stood in the midst of Azeroth's first climactic struggle against the Burning Legion . . . a battle fought more than ten thousand years ago during the War of the Ancients. That war had culminated with the Sundering and the sinking of the night elf capital of Zin-Azshari into the waters once housing her people's fount of power—the

Well of Eternity. The Legion had sought the end of all life on Azeroth and had come horribly close in achieving that monstrous goal, ironically with the help of the night elves' own queen.

The demonic force surged forward, the fiery infernals at the vanguard. The massive constructs were followed by felguard and felhounds, the former towering, armored warriors and the latter fearsome, toothy beasts. Other demons added to their monumental numbers. The insidious army rushed over the landscape unhindered, contrary to what the night elf recalled of that history. Anything touched by the demons burst into the same horrific green flame that surrounded each of the monstrosities.

Tyrande looked for those defenders she knew should be here, her own people and the many fantastic allies who had gathered to prevent the destruction of Azeroth. However, they were nowhere to be seen. Nothing blocked the destructive forces. The land, the world, was doomed. . . .

But then a powerful howl shook the scene. The high priestess felt her hopes instinctively rise. She felt she should know that howl, for it touched her very soul.

The demons faltered, though only for a moment. As one, they let out a mighty roar themselves, then renewed their push forward.

From the opposite direction, a great shadow stretched across the landscape. Tyrande followed it to its origin.

The wolf Ancient was gigantic, majestic, and so pure white that he all but gleamed. He towered over all else. The huge animal howled again, and this time countless other howls joined in from somewhere behind him.

"*Goldrinn* . . ." Tyrande murmured.

From the dawn of its reshaping by the mysterious titans, Azeroth had been guarded by beings who were tied to the world as no other creatures could be. The dragons had been empowered by the titans, but Azeroth itself gave rise to spirits and demigods, creatures eternal in nature yet capable of ultimate sacrifice. But not until the War of the Ancients had any of these protectors faced a threat as terrifying as the Burning Legion. Dragons had perished by the scores, and among the spirits and demigods there were many who fell in the final battle.

One of those had been Goldrinn.

Yet, this bloody scene before her was not exactly history. Tyrande finally understood that, though her natural instinct was to fear not only for her world but also for the wolf seeking to protect it again. Elune had chosen this urgent scene to tell her something, though the high priestess was at a loss as to what it might be. Was she to watch Goldrinn sacrifice himself once more?

Several demons neared the giant wolf, who growled his challenge to them. But as the attackers came upon him, with renewed cries, a vast pack of mortal wolves leapt from the emptiness behind Goldrinn. They poured over the landscape, sleek, furred hunters already sizing up their individual prey. Though they were not as huge as most of the demons, they charged with ferocity and determination unparalleled.

The two forces collided. The demons wielded blades, axes, savage teeth, claws, and more, and knew how to use all of them well. At first it seemed the wolves had only teeth and claws, but their dexterity and swiftness were unmatched. They darted among their sinister foes, snapping and slashing wherever there was an opening.

Goldrinn stood at the forefront. The huge wolf seized a felguard in his mouth and bit through. Green flames erupted as the beast let the fragments fall. At the same time his claws crushed through another foe.

Two wolves brought down an axe-wielding enemy who had just cleaved in twain one of their brethren. The wolves tore the demon's arms off, then one took out the throat. However, other demons fell upon them, overwhelming the pair.

Tyrande strained to join the battle but could not move. She could only watch helplessly as more wolves perished, and even though they seemed to take more than their number in adversaries, that did little to assuage her fears and regrets for them.

More and more demons focused on Goldrinn, clearly aware that he was what guided the wolves. The demons tried to hack away at his limbs or drag him down so that they could cut his throat, but Goldrinn shook off those near his paws, batting some away so hard that they crashed into their own comrades. In his savage jaws, the gigantic wolf plucked up one demon after another. Some he bit to pieces like the first; others he shook until the sheer force sent their body parts scattering. Goldrinn barreled through the Burning Legion's ranks, his eager pack ever at his side.

Bloody wolf carcasses and dismembered demon corpses already littered the battlefield, but the two sides' numbers appeared undiminished. Another wolf was chopped to pieces, and even more demons attacked Goldrinn. Yet, the enormous wolf was undaunted and continued to claw and bite one foe after another, leaving them piled three and four high in many places.

Mother Moon, why do you show this to me?!? The high priestess strained to leap to Goldrinn's aid, but still could not do more than observe. *Either let me join this struggle, or tell me the purpose of this endless slaughter, please!*

But the fight went on without revelation, and, worse, matters suddenly took a dark turn for Goldrinn. Harassed from all sides, the wolf could not fend off all his opponents. Demons struck him again and again, the growing number of wounds finally beginning to take their toll on the great Ancient.

One of the felguard managed to climb atop the white wolf's back. The fiendish warrior, his eyes blazing green in anticipation, raised his weapon and struck hard at the center of the wolf's spine.

"No!" Tyrande cried out, realizing what was about to happen. She was well aware of this dire event, though she had never known the details.

Goldrinn let out an anguished howl. His legs collapsed beneath him. Demons pushed at him in greater numbers.

From somewhere in the madness to the Ancient's right, a single dark-brown wolf leapt up. Though the height should have been beyond his capabilities, the smaller wolf managed to reach not only Goldrinn's back but the demon who had so terribly wounded him as well.

The felguard turned just as the wolf neared. The demon attempted to slash at the newcomer, but the sleek, lupine form darted under the axe blade. The wolf then bore into the felguard's legs, toppling his towering foe.

Crashing against Goldrinn's back, the demon lost his weapon. The felguard sought to rise, but the wolf was already upon him.

With one ferocious bite, the wolf tore out the demon's throat.

As the corpse slipped off the side, the lesser wolf howled. He glanced down, then jumped. His leap was not without purpose, for he landed atop another demon harassing Goldrinn, then tore out the chest of that one.

Taking the lesser wolf's lead, others of the pack began rending those demons intent on Goldrinn's destruction. The Burning Legion was at last forced to abandon the taking of the wolf Ancient and, indeed, was now pressed back.

But it was too late for Goldrinn. The Ancient managed to push himself up and seize in his mouth a demon. He bit through the armor and sinew, spitting out the pieces. But then the wound took its toll. The Ancient collapsed, crushing a few more of his enemies, and then lay unmoving.

Again, as had happened more than ten thousand years before, Goldrinn died.

Yet, seemingly undaunted by this terrible loss, the dark-brown wolf spearheaded the advance, pushing ahead of Goldrinn's corpse. More and more of the lesser wolves joined their brother, now becoming avengers of their patron.

One demonic warrior after another perished at the teeth and claws of the dark-brown wolf. He howled between adversaries, his cry now as great as that of Goldrinn. He seemed larger, too, more than twice the size of the others.

The Burning Legion began to steer their efforts against him, but that seemed only to encourage the brown wolf. He took on every demon that attacked and

left in his wake their tattered bodies. With so many demons much taller than him, the wolf even began jump-
ing up on his hind legs in order to better snap at an arm
or even a lowered head. His front claws slashed through
armor and flesh as well as any blade.

A helpless Tyrande let out another gasp. The more
she stared at the valiant wolf, the more comfortable he
seemed on two legs as opposed to four. The claws of one
hand clamped together so tightly that they were as one,
and also grew with each successive cut.

This was different from what the high priestess had
heard had happened during the original battle, and she
knew immediately that history had now slipped into
something else. This was what Elune truly wished to reveal to her . . . though what it meant was yet a mystery to
the night elf.

The wolf's claws abruptly became a *true* greatsword,
and the brown wolf *fully* a man . . . an armored warrior
whose face the high priestess could not make out from
where she watched. The pack right behind him, he continued to challenge the Burning Legion. His sword thrust
again and again.

A startling new change followed, but this time among
the demons. They transformed, becoming foes equally
recognizable and far more imminent: *orcs*.

The transformation was swift and happened without
notice by those involved. The wolves tore at the orcs as if
they had always been the enemy.

Felling another opponent, the shadowed warrior
raised his sword and let out a triumphant shout that still
had hints of a lupine howl. The wolf pack surged again,
but now they also stood on their hind legs, and their

forepaws became hands wielding axes, maces, and other weapons. Like their leader, they were now human, albeit even more shadowed than he was.

Disarray overtook the orcs. Their numbers dwindled. The lead warrior once again confidently shouted.

And from behind the line of battle, in the direction the high priestess knew the body of the wolf Ancient lay, there came an answering howl. Tyrande turned her gaze there . . . and beheld *two* Goldrinns. The first was the corpse of the slain animal. The second was a glorious, translucent spirit who once more howled victory.

But though the wolf spirit was like mist, there was something else within him, something more solid and somewhat familiar—

With a start, the high priestess realized that she was staring at the shadowed leader . . . despite the fact that he should have been at the forefront of the battle. Then, blinking, Tyrande noticed that she *was* watching the forefront. Both areas had suddenly blended together. Goldrinn's ghostly countenance hovered over his champion, who seemed to grow taller yet.

An orc wielding two axes swung at the champion. The warrior deflected the first axe, then swiftly did the same with the second. With a whirl of the sword, he then brought the blade between both axes and thrust it deep into the orc's chest.

Blood spurted from the gaping wound as the champion pulled the weapon free. The orc gaped, staggered. His eyes glazed. The axes fell from his twitching fingers.

The hulking orc dropped to his knees. His body shook and blood flowed from his mouth, dribbling over his jaw and tusks.

The shadowed hero took a step back.

The orc fell forward, landing face-first at his slayer's feet. As he perished, so, too, did the last of his comrades.

The battle was over.

The spectral Goldrinn let out a new howl. Then, he and the warrior fully blended together. At the same time, the shadowed champion at last turned his gaze toward Tyrande. His face was finally visible. . . .

And at that moment, the high priestess returned to the Temple Gardens.

Tyrande wavered briefly, then quickly regained her composure. There was no one else in sight, perhaps coincidence, perhaps Elune's intention. Tyrande also suspected that not even a second had passed in the mortal world.

The high priestess did not question being suddenly thrust into the vision. Elune had clearly wished to relay something of such urgency to her that it could not wait. Understanding what it was, Tyrande was grateful, yet a bit confused.

She realized that someone was approaching her. Smoothing her silver robes, the high priestess met the gaze of one of General Shandris Feathermoon's aides. The Sentinel looked a bit flushed, as if she had been running hard.

The female Sentinel—her torso, forearms, and legs protected by light armor—knelt with the utmost deference before Tyrande, not only because the high priestess was their leader, but also because the general was Tyrande's adopted daughter. The warrior was armed with one of the favored weapons of the night elves, a triple-bladed moonglaive.

Keeping her head down, the other night elf said, "The general knew that you would wish to see this immediately, High Priestess."

The Sentinel held forth a small parchment that bore Shandris's personal seal. Taking the missive and dismissing the aide, Tyrande broke the seal and read the contents. The message was short and to the point, as was the general's way.

Word arrives that the king of Stormwind will be joining the summit.

There was nothing more save Shandris's mark at the bottom. The news was significant in one great respect in that if Stormwind was a part of the gathering, then the other holdouts would quickly send word of their coming as well. The high priestess and Malfurion had been hoping that Stormwind would agree to be part, though of late they had been concerned that its ruler might instead decide the kingdom's fortunes were better without its troubled neighbors.

But of even more significance to the high priestess was the timing of this news. She knew that Shandris had only just received it herself a few minutes before and that, as the general always did, Shandris had made certain that her beloved ruler and mother would share in that knowledge as swiftly as possible. Elune had intended for the vision to coincide with the arrival of the missive.

"So, Varian is coming . . . ," Tyrande murmured. "It all makes sense now. I should have seen it."

And the vision now became clear. The night elf had only had a glimpse of the face, but even then she had been certain that the shadowed champion resembled none other than King Varian Wrynn of Stormwind. Naturally, the Mother Moon had known, but could only give her high priestess a sign when there was something that could actually be done with that knowledge.

"Varian Wrynn," she repeated, recalling so much about the king's troubled past in that name. He had been a slave, a gladiator, a man with no memory of his true self. He had watched his kingdom fall and fought to take it back from none other than what had turned out to be the daughter of Deathwing in human guise.

And during those terrible times, when Varian had lost his name and had been forced to fight for his life nearly every day for the pleasure of spectators, he had been given another name by those in attendance, a uniquely important name.

He had been—and still was by many—called *Lo'Gosh*.

Lo'Gosh . . . another name for the ghost wolf, *Goldrinn*.

The two cloaked travelers disembarked from the small boat. That they were night elves like the majority of the inhabitants of Rut'theran Village was evidenced in their build and their ears, which shoved back the fabric of their deep hoods. Their faces remained in shadow.

The port village was humble by night elf standards but exceedingly fresh in appearance, for all the buildings were new. It was actually the *second* settlement by the name, the first destroyed by the sea during the Cataclysm. The second most significant characteristic of the port other than its three docks was the hippogryph breeding area, where eggs of the astonishing winged creatures who acted as aerial transport for the night elves were meticulously cared for and the young were raised.

The most significant aspect of the island was something the pair of travelers had been viewing for quite some time. In fact, they had seen it from miles away on the mainland . . . just as anyone else in this region would have.

Teldrassil was the name given for the island, but only as an afterthought. The island was only an extension of the true Teldrassil . . . a titanic tree filling most of the land and rising so high, the top vanished in the clouds. Its branches were so vast that they dwarfed some kingdoms. The thick crown could have housed an entire civilization—and did.

Indeed, Teldrassil was known as the second *World* Tree. The first, ancient Nordrassil, still lived, but had yet to recover from the violence of the Third War—again, against the Burning Legion—only a few years prior. While Nordrassil had provided immortality, good health, protection from the misuses of the Well of Eternity's magic, and an open path to the Emerald Dream, the second World Tree had served mainly as the new home for the night elf race. Even then Teldrassil had already had its share of troubles. The tree had been tainted by the evil of the Nightmare Lord through his puppet, the archdruid Fandral Staghelm. That taint had spread to the flora and fauna upon Teldrassil, and only recently had the tree been cleansed.

But as inspiring as the vast tree was to all who saw it, the newcomers almost appeared oblivious to its presence now. The taller of the traveling pair—male, with long, silver hair spilling out from his hood—paused to eye with much interest the adult hippogryphs. The slighter and clearly female figure at his side coughed harshly and teetered against her companion. The male quickly turned his attention from the avian creatures and tightened his hold on her.

"The portal," he murmured. "It will be nearby and quicker. Just hold on . . . we are almost there. Hold on . . . please!"

The female's hood briefly bobbed up and down. "I will . . . do my best . . . my husband. . . ."

Her reply was very weak, and by the stiffening of his form the male showed his grave concern for his mate. Guiding her forward, he searched for what neither had ever seen but should have been readily identifiable.

A Sentinel officer noticed the pair. Her gaze swept over the concealing cloaks. Frowning, her glaive gripped at the ready, she confronted them.

"Welcome, visitors," she said. "May I ask from where you come?"

The male looked at her, his face briefly becoming visible.

The Sentinel's words trailed off, and her face flushed with shock. "You . . ."

Without a word, the male led his mate past the stunned officer. As he did, that which he sought became visible through the buildings and the crowd.

"The portal . . . ," he murmured.

A stone path followed a gentle slope up to Teldrassil. At the base of the tree loomed a tall portal, a huge, shimmering mark in Darnassian script emanating from its side. Yet, even as high as it stood, the magical entry was dwarfed by some of the great roots arcing down from Teldrassil.

The portal was a magical, direct link to the city far, far above. Two Sentinels were the only evident guards, but the male traveler knew that there were others hidden near and, in addition, safety measures built into and around the structure.

Undaunted, he led his mate toward the portal. The Sentinels eyed him suspiciously.

From behind the travelers came the officer's voice. "Let them pass unhindered."

The guards did not question the command. The male traveler did not waste time turning to thank the officer; all that mattered was getting his mate to Darnassus . . . to help.

"Watch your footing," he whispered to her.

She managed a nod. They had succeeded in making it to the portal itself. His hopes rose. *Almost there!*

A fit of coughing overtook her. It became so brutal that he lost his grip on her. She fell to her knees, her hooded face nearly to the stone.

He quickly retrieved her, but as he helped her straighten, the soft patter of liquid caught his ear.

A small pool of blood decorated the area near where her face had hovered.

"Not again . . ."

Her hand, which held his, suddenly squeezed with the incredible strength of the truly fearful. "Husband—"

She collapsed in his arms.

The guards moved to assist, but he had no time for them. They might even suggest that he wait while they check on her condition. But in his harried thoughts, any second meant disaster . . . loss. . . .

His only hope was reaching the high priestess.

Gripping his slumped mate, the male lunged into the portal.

2

INCURSION

Moving against the slight breeze passing through the forest, the long, thick branches from the nearby trees stretched down. The leafy appendages moved with utmost purpose toward the bearded figure they surrounded. He stared up at the oncoming branches and did nothing . . . but smile.

Malfurion Stormrage stood silent as leaves from the first branches caressed his face. Even among those of his calling, he was unique. At first, it appeared that he was adorned with the marks of the great animals whose shapes those most versed in his calling could summon. Only closer inspection revealed that some of these attributes were a *part* of him, the results of his ties to Azeroth and the many years his spirit had spent in the Emerald Dream. While his dreamform had become more and more attuned to that other realm, his sleeping body— still bound to his spirit—had begun to take on elements of these powerful creatures. Thus, the edges of his arms grew into the expansive gray wings of the storm crow. The nightsaber, its bond especially close to those of Malfurion's race, was marked by what were not boots but the archdruid's very feet. They now mimicked the look of the feline's mighty paws. In addition to all this, his kilt bore in front as decoration the curved teeth of the nightsaber, and his hands were clad in gloves ending in the claws of the bear.

One mark that had nothing to do with beasts and perhaps more with Malfurion in particular was the blue bolts of lightning that crossed his torso from shoulder to opposing side of the waist. Smaller, complementing bolts darted from his elbow down his forearm. *Stormrage* was not merely the archdruid's surname; it was also a hint of the tremendous power at his command, power that he sought to use only when all other efforts failed.

The ends of the branches shifted his long green hair, but artfully avoided that which most made the proud-featured night elf stand out from his brethren. Magnificent antlers, more than a good two feet in length, sprouted from his forehead. They were a sign of his deep ties to Azeroth and his shan'do—his *honored teacher*—the demigod Cenarius, and also represented the form of the stag.

Some of the stronger branches shifted under his arms. Then, as gently as a parent lifting an infant, the branches took Malfurion up among the trees.

The archdruid opened his mind and touched the heart of Teldrassil. Malfurion studied its health and saw that there was no apparent taint left from the sinister grafting attached by the mad archdruid Fandral Staghelm. Malfurion gave thanks for that; he had been against the creation of the second World Tree, but it had become an integral part of night elf existence. Yet, that it had become so had been the opposite intention of Fandral, who had first proposed the tree in Malfurion's absence. To the other archdruid, Teldrassil had been only a means to a monstrous end, which, thankfully, had been averted.

Despite the lack of any noticeable taint, Malfurion swore to keep monitoring the tree. There was still a pocket of the Nightmare remaining in the Emerald Dream, and as long as any trace of that darkness existed, renewed corruption threatened Teldrassil and, thus, the night elf race.

Still, satisfied as to the World Tree's present condition, Malfurion took a moment to survey his surroundings. A moonwell—one of the sacred founts of water known for their mystical properties—stood not all that far from the archdruid. He had chosen the Oracle Glade northeast of the city for what his senses indicated was its unique tie to the gargantuan tree in which it was nestled. Here, the archdruid felt he could best meditate and, using his spirit—or dreamform—reach out to the Emerald Dream.

The druids still traveled with their dreamforms to the other realm, but did so with some new precautions. Malfurion had not taken long to return to that place, despite having been trapped there for years by the Nightmare Lord. He did not consider himself courageous for having made the choice; the archdruid hoped to further study the Emerald Dream for any changes he might have missed earlier . . . and also use this particular journey to clear his mind of certain thoughts.

As if to mock his hopes, a sharp twinge suddenly went through him. It was not the first he had felt of late, nor did he think it would be the last.

Mortality was beginning to catch up with him.

The archdruid had witnessed the aging of comrades belonging to other races, but to experience it was admittedly not so simple a thing, even if his race was still much longer-lived than humans or dwarves. Malfurion fought down a brief moment of petulance, of thinking that *he* was not supposed to grow old.

The twinge had disrupted his thoughts. Trying to restore his calm, Malfurion focused deep into Teldrassil's being. He felt his center calming. Seeking Teldrassil's touch to help him reach the point where he could separate his dreamform from his body had proven correct after all. His body now lay nestled in the boughs, protected by the trees that were in their way an extension of the larger one upon which they grew.

Malfurion's dreamform rose above his still body. Ghostly and emerald in shading, it hovered for a moment—

Malfurion!

As if thrust by a terrible wind, the archdruid's dreamform flew back into his mortal shell. He knew who reached out to him, for she had a unique link to him.

Tyrande? the archdruid immediately responded. At an unspoken request by Malfurion, the branches were already lowering him to the ground. *Tyrande! What is it?*

Too much to be said now! Please come!

The urgency in her tone was undeniable. The moment his feet touched the ground, Malfurion hurried on. But after a few steps he found the pace too slow. Concentrating, the archdruid leaned forward.

His bones made crackling sounds as they shifted, and his skin rippled and sprouted fur. The archdruid's face extended, the nose and mouth becoming part of a wide muzzle adorned with long whiskers. Malfurion's teeth grew and his eyes narrowed. His shape transformed, becoming a huge, dark cat akin to one of the saber-toothed felines the night elves used for mounts. Malfurion's pace increased tenfold and more.

The sleek cat darted out of the glade. The short distance to Darnassus passed swiftly. Sentinels who saw him approaching wisely stepped aside, aware of who it was rushing to the city in such a form. The archdruid's cat shape was a recognizable thing to the defenders of the city, who had witnessed its power in battle.

Much of the city was divided into what were called "terraces," where elements of night elf civilization concentrated. The Warrior's Terrace was already behind him, and that of the Craftsmen was already to his right. Malfurion scarcely noticed either, just as he paid little mind to the elegant and artistically formed gardens and lake that were the center of Darnassus. His focus was on the shining edifice to the south, the Temple of the Moon.

But something did suddenly intrude on his concentration, an unsettling gathering of night elves. Malfurion smelled their anxiety, and that stirred his other feline emotions. He bared his great saberlike teeth and dug harder at the ground with his sharp claws as he turned to find out what was the cause.

Even before he came to a halt, the archdruid had resumed his true form. The night elves nearest had already scattered from the cat's path, and now they and others who had noticed Malfurion bowed in respect to the august figure.

However, Malfurion paid them no mind, for he now

knew what had so caught the throng's attention . . . and why from them there had radiated such a high level of anxiety.

The hooded figure stumbled toward the same destination in which the archdruid had been heading, but his efforts were slowed incredibly by the terrible burden in his arms. The shape under the other travel cloak was clearly female and also a night elf.

Malfurion could not make out the male's visage, but the hood had slipped from the female's. The slack mouth was a grim enough sign.

A Sentinel tried to give aid to the female's companion, but the male shook the guard off. The Sentinel retreated with an odd respect in both her expression and stance.

The same Sentinel glanced beyond the stricken figure to Malfurion. With some relief, she started, "Archdruid! Praise Elune—"

"'Archdruid'?" The hooded male gasped out the word, as if it meant all the world to him.

A sudden shock ran through Malfurion. He could not place the voice, but, even though it was clearly changed by stress and other factors, it was one he should have known very well.

Gingerly adjusting his precious burden, the male shifted enough to peer over his shoulder at Malfurion.

The agony that gripped the male had made some distinct changes in the face. However, the archdruid still immediately recognized the night elf before him even though it had been centuries since the latter had last been among their kind. Malfurion could scarcely believe his eyes; he had gradually come to the conclusion that accident or some other violent demise had taken the hooded figure long ago.

The name escaped as a whisper of disbelief. *"Jarod Shadowsong . . ."*

Haldrissa Woodshaper had been a Sentinel since nearly the creation of that army. Although she had been born some centuries before its general, Shandris, Haldrissa had recognized the skills in her leader and eagerly learned. She had thus risen up in the ranks, well earning her position as a commander.

Narrow of face and with a persistently wrinkled brow—as if she were always deep in thought—Haldrissa had just prior to the Cataclysm been promoted to overseeing night elf forces in Ashenvale. Although far from Teldrassil and Darnassus, Ashenvale, located in the northern half of the continent of Kalimdor and stretching across much of its width, was not only sacred to her people but of significance to the preservation of their civilization. The night elves and their allies carefully harvested only select areas of the vast forests, making certain not to disturb nature any more than necessary.

Haldrissa squinted as she peered into the forest ahead of her party. Like the others, she rode astride one of the muscular cats called nightsabers after their long, curved fangs. Both night elves and nightsabers were, as their names suggested, nocturnal creatures, but circumstance more and more demanded that they move about during the day too. Most of the other races with which they dealt were diurnal, day dwellers, which did not preclude *their* being active at night . . . which presented her with the most complicated and potentially deadly aspect of her role here.

There had been no sign of nearby activity by the Horde, but Haldrissa knew better than to trust the orcs and their allies to stay in the eastern side. Bad enough that they had a foothold in Ashenvale at all.

"What do you see, Xanon?" she asked of the male night elf to her left. He was not the most senior of her officers, but he was known for his sharp eyes, even among the Sentinels. "Anything amiss?"

Xanon leaned forward a moment, then replied, "All clear to me, Commander."

No one else indicated otherwise. Haldrissa signaled the party to move on. The commander led a contingent of some fifty night elves on the way to inspect one of the foremost posts. Haldrissa made it a point to do regular inspections herself; nothing kept post commanders on their toes better than the knowledge that she would be checking on them.

The post was only another hour's ride. The reason for the halt had been what thus far appeared to be a lapse on the part of the officer in charge. Haldrissa insisted that guards be set up to face not only the directions from which the Horde could be expected to attack, but also those from which it could not. If Haldrissa could imagine successfully sneaking past a post and either attacking it from behind or moving on to attack locations deeper within night elf territory, then surely the orcs' new warchief could.

A short distance later, Haldrissa turned to Denea, her second-in-command. "I want two scouts to ride to the post, then report back . . . without being seen."

Denea summoned the riders needed, then sent them off. Haldrissa watched the pair first become two blurs, then vanish into the distance. She hid a moment of frustration; her vision was not as sharp as it had been only a few months before. In fact, it seemed to have worsened in the past few days.

"Weapons at the ready," she ordered the others. Denea, who already had her bow out, repeated the order.

They moved on, noticing nothing and growing more suspicious because of that. Haldrissa estimated the time the scouts would need to reach the post and get back to her, and knew that there was still quite a wait.

Thus it was that the growl of a nightsaber racing toward them only minutes later sent her and her fighters into preparations for immediate battle.

The beast was sorely wounded, arrows pin-cushioning its hide. That it had gotten this far was a credit to its stamina. Blood stained its claws and teeth, showing that it had not left the struggle without inflicting pain on its attackers as well.

And astride it, very dead, was one of the scouts.

Xanon let out an epithet and looked all for urging his cat forward. He was not the only one, either. Haldrissa waved the eager ones back, not that she intended to hold off pursuit. Denea already had the dying nightsaber beside hers. She looked over the rider and scowled.

"We will have to leave her here for the time being. We can retrieve her on the way back so that she can receive a proper burial." Haldrissa nodded to her second. Denea and another Sentinel swiftly dismounted and removed the body from the suffering cat. Gently setting their comrade beside the nearest tree, they returned to the nightsaber.

The cat panted heavily. Up close, the intensity of the wounds was more evident. There was blood everywhere. The nightsaber peered up at Denea with eyes filled with pain. One of its sabers was broken.

The wounded mount coughed violently, throwing up more blood. It was clear that nothing could be done to save the beast. Drawing her dagger, Denea leaned down and murmured to the animal. The nightsaber gently licked the hand that held the weapon, then calmly closed its eyes in what was clearly expectation.

Gritting her teeth, Denea expertly slit its throat. The animal died instantly.

"Spread out!" Haldrissa ordered as her second-in-command mounted again. "Xanon . . . you take those up that way. Denea, take your group to the south. The rest, with me."

Moments later the night elves cautiously moved into the area in question. Haldrissa's nightsaber sniffed the air and snarled low. The commander quieted her beast with a touch of her hand to its head, then slowly reached for her bow.

An arrow struck the warrior beside her. The strike was a perfect one, piercing the throat.

It had also come from above.

Quickly nocking an arrow, Haldrissa raised her bow to fire. Before she could, though, two swiftly spinning glaives shot up in the direction from which the arrow had come. The arched, triple-bladed weapons cut a deadly swathe into the foliage.

A pained grunt escaped from the treetop. One of the glaives darted back out of the tree, returning to its wielder.

The other reappeared a second later—buried in the chest of an orc. The enemy archer dropped like a stone to the ground, his slashed body sprawling.

But even before the orc's corpse had the opportunity to settle, from out of the forest ahead charged nearly a dozen of his fellows, many astride powerful black wolves. Axes, spears, and swords raised high, the orcs plunged toward Haldrissa's group.

The night elves wasted no time in meeting the charge. Haldrissa fired once at the first orc approaching, but what should have been a clear shot ended up only piercing the shoulder. The wound was not enough to even slow the brawny orc, who then tried to bury his axe in the skull of her mount.

Another shot from above hit a nearby nightsaber in the neck. The animal stumbled, sending its rider flying forward. An opportunistic orc leapt from his wolf and swung at the fallen night elf. The Sentinel turned, trying to defend herself, but was too slow. The orc's axe bit into her chest near the collarbone.

The wounded nightsaber sought to attack the orc, only to be confronted by the warrior's wolf. The two great beasts tore into one another with fang and claw, each seeking an opening. The nightsaber had some advantage in size, but the wound slowed it.

Steering around the monstrous pair, Haldrissa fired at the orc. Up close, she could not miss. The force of the bolt as it sank into the orc's chest sent the dying attacker flying back several feet.

Another arrow whistled past the commander's ear. Cursing, Haldrissa fired back at where she thought it had originated. Her arrow evidently missed, but it forced the orc in the tree to move more into the open, where a bolt from the south finished him.

Waving her bow, Denea let out a triumphant cry, then led her group in against the orcs. At the same time Xanon's surged in from the north. Steel met steel. Nightsabers clashed with wolves.

Denea had changed her bow for a glaive. She slashed through the throat of a slavering wolf as it seized her by the leg. Her sleek, raven-colored hair, bound in a tail, darted like a whip as she looked this way and that for her next foe.

The orcs fought savagely . . . even more savagely than Haldrissa had expected. They left themselves open at times, seeming to prefer simply to try to get to an enemy no matter what the risk. While by sheer force they kept the larger contingent of night elves momentarily at bay, the odds were clearly too great against them.

Could it be—? the commander started to realize, only to have to forgo completion of the thought as another mounted orc dove in at her. Haldrissa dropped her bow and brought up her glaive, using the nearest of the curved blades to deflect the axe. Her arm shook as the two weapons rang together.

The wolf dodged to the side of her nightsaber's claws in order to give its rider a better opening. The commander's cat twisted to protect Haldrissa, but the orc had already swung.

The foremost blade cracked under the force of the strike. The upper half flew into Haldrissa's face. She felt stinging pain by her left eye, then her sight there vanished. A wetness spread over her left cheek, and she nearly passed out from shock.

A part of her mind screamed, *The orc! Beware the orc!*

One hand clutching her ruined eye, Haldrissa tried to focus on her foe. Through her tears, she made out his general shape. He was nearly upon her, even with the nightsaber now doing its best to fend off the wolf.

Haldrissa twisted the glaive in order to bring one of the remaining blades between her and where she thought the axe was. Her head pounded, and the outline of the orc faded.

She knew she was going to die.

But the killing blow never came. Instead, the nightsaber ceased its violent rocking, as if the battle between it and the wolf had come to a sudden conclusion.

"Commander!" someone shouted in her ear. She recognized Denea's voice.

"The orc—"

"The orc is slain!" A slim hand seized her weapon arm. As Haldrissa blinked away tears from her remaining eye, Denea came into focus. "Be still, Commander! You need aid, quickly!"

"The battle—"

"Is over! The orcs are slain to a warrior, their wolves perishing with them!"

A prisoner would have been good to have, Haldrissa knew, but a capture could not always be accomplished in the midst of frenzied fighting. As another Sentinel came around her blind side and began working on her wound, Haldrissa finally managed to better focus on the situation. One thing immediately came to mind.

"The outpost . . . we must reach the outpost. . . ."

She was forced to wait while they finished with her eye, and even then Xanon suggested that they turn around. Haldrissa began to feel like an old grandparent rather than their commander, and grew angry. The other night elves acquiesced to her orders, and the party finally raced toward the outpost, all expecting the worst.

But as they neared the wooden structure, to their surprise, a pair of sentries stepped out from among the trees. They looked stunned by the party's appearance, especially that of the commander, who now sported a long cloth over the damaged side of her face.

Before they could speak, Haldrissa quickly asked, "The outpost—all is well?"

They glanced at one another in some confusion, one finally replying, "Yes, Commander! It has been very quiet!"

"Were there other sentries posted in the trees behind us?"

"Two . . ."

There had been no sign of either the pair or the other scout Haldrissa had sent. She had no doubts as to their fate.

"A scouting force," Denea declared to her. "They managed to maneuver around the outpost without being caught, but the missing sentries must have run across them." A dark smile crossed her features. "Well, they will not be ferreting out any secrets to pass back to their warchief; we have seen to that and avenged our lost comrades as well!"

Xanon and the others seemed to agree with her, but Haldrissa remained silent. She thought of the fatalistic determination of the orcs as they had thrown themselves against impossible odds. Such an act was not extraordinary where orcs were concerned: they often reveled in showing their willingness to sacrifice themselves.

"But what were they sacrificing themselves for?" she murmured to herself.

"What did you say, Commander?" Denea asked.

The pain from her wound coursed through Haldrissa, forcing her to put a hand to her head. Still, the notion of what had truly happened burned deep. "Send word ahead to the outpost. Have them survey the area carefully—"

"You think there are more orcs?"

"No." She wished she were wrong. That would help matters. They were too late, though. The attackers had done their part, giving their lives for the Horde. "No . . . by now they have slipped back through. . . ."

There had been forays by orcs in the past, but something about this particular one struck her as sinister. The Horde had never sent a party this deep in this region, and certainly not one of such size.

She would have to send word to the general as soon as possible. For months, Shandris and the high priestess had been awaiting some act by the Horde that hinted of a change in the delicate balance between the two factions. Haldrissa now believed she had witnessed that very act.

But what does this incursion augur? the wounded commander wondered anxiously.

She had no answer. Still, whatever form it would take, the one thing Haldrissa did know was that there would be much, much *more* blood than had been spilled this day. *Much* more.

3

JAROD SHADOWSONG

"She is dying . . . my Shalasyr is dying!" the male night elf blurted to the archdruid. Jarod Shadowsong's face was lined like no night elf's that Malfurion had ever seen. While some of those lines had probably been the result of Jarod's life away from his people, others were clearly more recent and likely had to do with the unmoving female so carefully held in his arms.

Jarod's hair and beard had silvered, a stark change from how Malfurion recalled him. Jarod had been younger than Malfurion when they had first met—more than a thousand years, in fact—but the silvering and the lines made him look that much *older* than the archdruid. Malfurion wondered what the night elf before him had lived through since their last meeting.

"Jarod . . ." It felt so strange to Malfurion to say the

name, the two not having seen one another in nearly ten thousand years.

"It has been a long time since we last met," the former commander and still-legendary hero from the War of the Ancients murmured, his eyes hollow. "Forgive me for coming to you like this. . . ."

Malfurion waved aside Jarod's apology. Looking over Shalasyr, he saw how grave her condition was. "I could *try* to heal her, but I think it best if we bring her straight to Tyrande so that we have all options available to us! Quickly, now!"

Jarod looked hesitant to surrender any part of his hold on his companion, but at last he let the archdruid aid him. As the throng watched in absolute silence, the pair carried Shalasyr toward the temple.

The two Sentinels at the entrance moved respectfully aside as the archdruid neared. One gaped at the sight of Jarod; even with the cropped beard and long, loose mane—both utterly silvered now—there was something in his weathered face that remained absolutely recognizable to any who had seen him in the past.

"She will save you," Malfurion heard the onetime captain murmur to the still female. "Tyrande will save you. . . . She will speak with Elune. . . ."

Malfurion hid his frown. Shalasyr felt extremely limp, and from the position by which he held her the archdruid could not tell if she breathed. She was beyond his power at this point, which only left Elune. Yet, how much would even the moon goddess do in such a drastic case?

Through the corridors of stone and living wood they rushed. Some of the priestesses they saw quickly offered assistance, but the archdruid understood that only his beloved would have the power to help Jarod's mate at this point.

Her personal guard came to attention as Malfurion and his companions neared the sanctum she utilized in her role as high priestess. One of the guards wordlessly opened the way. Malfurion noted how every set of eyes focused first on Jarod before taking in Shalasyr. Everyone had long assumed that Jarod Shadowsong had perished at some point during the past millennia, else why would he not have returned to his people during some of their most desperate moments?

They were not even through the entrance before Tyrande met them. Jarod started to speak, but the high priestess shook her head. She directed them to take Shalasyr to a long, sloping couch next to her, then bade the attendants without to close the doors.

Her expression grave, the high priestess went down on one knee next to the other female. Tyrande began murmuring a prayer under her breath, and her hands continuously passed over Shalasyr's body.

The light spread from the high priestess to Shalasyr. Jarod let out a hopeful gasp. The two males watched with anticipation as the soft silver light settled down over the stricken figure.

Without warning, the light faded.

Tyrande pulled back. A sound escaped her, one that Malfurion recognized from times in the past.

"Jarod," Tyrande said in a low voice as she rose and turned. "Jarod . . . I am sorry. . . ."

"No!" He shoved past the archdruid. "I told her she could get help here! I told her you or Malfurion could save her! Why will you not save her?"

Tyrande halted his lunge toward Shalasyr with a simple touch of her hands against his shoulders. Eyes more hollow, tears beginning to stream, the former guard captain from lost Suramar stared into the high priestess's sympathetic gaze.

"She had already slipped away. There was nothing that could be done."

He looked aghast. "No . . . I brought her as soon as I could! I pushed for us to reach here—" His own gaze veered toward Shalasyr. "I did it, then! I pushed her too hard! She would be alive if I had not—"

Tyrande shook her head. "You know that is not true. Her fate was cast. She knows that you did all that anyone could have done. It was simply meant to be—"

"*Shalasyr!*" Jarod dropped down next to his mate. He clutched her face to his shoulder.

Malfurion quietly joined his own mate. They watched in solemn respect as Jarod rocked back and forth and whispered to his lost wife.

Finally, Jarod looked back to his hosts. Tears still slid down his cheeks and into his beard, but his voice sounded stronger now, more resigned to the truth. "We both feared that she would not make it, but we both agreed that it was best. Yet . . . I remember from her tone at times . . . now that I look back on it . . . she knew the truth. She did this more for me than for her own life. She wanted me to come back here to be with others, not be alone when she . . . she passed."

"You called her 'Shalasyr,'" Tyrande replied soothingly. "I thought I recognized her. She was a novice here for a time. We all assumed she had wandered away from the old city and that some accident had subsequently befallen her, even though searchers found no body. No one knew that she and you were together, though the timing of your mutual disappearances should have spoken volumes to us. . . . Yet we never made the connection. . . ."

"We kept our love secret . . . mainly out of concern on my part. I had already considered leaving *everything* . . . long before. I had grown disenchanted with the polarization of our society. Your druids—forgive me, Malfurion—your druids had been becoming more and more remote, spending most of their time away or in the Emerald Dream rather than sharing in the responsibilities of keeping our people safe and secure. . . ."

The archdruid said nothing. He had heard this from others, including Tyrande. The guilt for all those centuries of abandonment still remained with him.

Jarod exhaled. "And though I loved her with all my heart, I hoped that she would see the folly of being with me. I believed that if and when I chose to depart, I would save her from having to answer questions about my choice."

"Jarod . . . ," Malfurion began, but the other male continued as if hearing nothing.

"Instead, she proved determined to follow my path, wherever it might lead. She always tried to do what I wanted, even when I tried my best to see to *her* happiness. . . ." Jarod kissed Shalasyr's forehead. "Little fool . . . first she wastes her life following me into the wilderness . . . and then she sacrifices what strength she has to ensure I return here so that I will not be . . . alone. . . ."

Softly placing a hand on his shoulder, Tyrande said, "You are always welcome among us. She knew that. She also seems to have savored her life with you, or else she would not have stayed with you all these centuries."

"We did have many moments of joy. She loved the wilderness, I admit. In some ways, more than I did, even."

"I shall see to arrangements for her. She will receive proper rites."

He looked up at her, then down at Shalasyr again. "She *is* dead." Still holding his beloved, Jarod rose. He accepted no assistance as, with tender care, he adjusted Shalasyr's position on the couch. To all appearances, she was sleeping. "It barely seems any time since the illness touched her."

The high priestess and the archdruid looked at each other. With the loss of their immortality, the night elves as a race had begun to experience afflictions that they had only witnessed in others. There had been a few other deaths, and Shalasyr's showed that there would be more and more as time went on, deaths that could not be avoided.

"I had heard rumors," Jarod went on, straightening. "It is all true, then. We are mortal, are we not?" After Malfurion nodded, the former guard captain grunted. "Meaning no offense, but I think that a good thing, even with this happening," His hands curled into fists as he looked at Shalasyr. "We were so damned complacent about our great station in the world and our endless, jaded lives, and that is why the Legion nearly slaughtered us all."

A different darkness spread across his weathered face, one that Tyrande and her mate recalled from the far past. Malfurion quickly stepped over to Jarod and deftly guided him from Shalasyr. "You are exhausted. You need food and drink, also—"

"How can I sleep or eat?"

"Shalasyr would want you to take care of yourself,"

Tyrande added from Jarod's other side. "And I promise you that I will spare no effort for her."

"I should stay—"

The archdruid shook his head. "No. Give yourself the time you need to be able to better honor her. I know where to find some healthy fare and perhaps how to bring some calm to your heart. Once you have recuperated, you can return and help oversee the final arrangements."

To his relief, Jarod acquiesced. However, he looked back at his mate one last time. "I would like a moment alone with her, if I may. . . ."

"Of course."

They watched him kneel beside Shalasyr once more. Jarod took her hands in his, leaned close, and whispered. Malfurion and Tyrande stepped out of the chamber. There they took the opportunity to briefly discuss another matter.

"Varian is coming to the summit," Tyrande quietly informed her husband. "So Shandris's contacts say. It worries me, though, that we still have no official confirmation from Stormwind."

"We both know that if Shandris trusts her information, it is generally true. Good. One way or another, the news will filter to the other kingdoms. If Stormwind is attending, the remaining holdouts will rush to join." He frowned. "As to whether he is coming to ensure the success of the summit or to condemn it . . . we will have to wait and see."

"If we do not hear official word from Stormwind before he arrives, it may be the latter."

"Unfortunately, too true." Malfurion's frown deepened. "But you could have told me all this when you initially contacted me."

"There is more." She described Elune's vision and what it had revealed.

He brooded over the revelation for a breath or two, then asked, "You have faith you could not be mistaken?"

"The Mother Moon made it abundantly clear."

"It makes sense in great part, and yet not in other ways." He brooded for a moment. "Leave this matter to me. I will see that somehow things come together . . . if it is indeed Varian Wrynn on whom the Alliance's future most depends."

Tyrande accepted his decision to take control of that situation with a nod. Then, also eyeing Jarod, she continued, "We have another, more personal situation here . . . perhaps two. Jarod left behind some unfinished relationships of significance."

"Those will have to come to their proper conclusions without our efforts. There is so much more at stake. I welcome Jarod back . . . but his life is his own to master, in the long run."

They glanced back into the chamber. At that moment the newly returned Jarod rose again. Malfurion and Tyrande heard him exhale deeply as he gave his Shalasyr one last kiss.

"Let us hope Shandris and his sister see it that way," the high priestess wryly returned under her breath as they moved to attend to their old friend. "Though I doubt they will."

Most night elves of military status utilized the training areas in the Warrior's Terrace to hone their skills. There they had the use of target ranges and dueling grounds.

The night elves were respected by both their allies and enemies as strong and skilled fighters, especially General Shandris Feathermoon's Sentinels.

But Maiev Shadowsong was no Sentinel and considered herself far more skilled and dedicated than any of them, including their commander. Indeed, in her opinion the Sentinels knew nothing about dedication . . . and sacrifice.

Her face was narrower than many night elves', and weathered. Scars marked her face—scars from both battle and torture. She had been warrior, jailor, prisoner, executioner. Her eyes held a fatalistic gleam.

Her armor was more elaborate than that of a Sentinel, with a thick breastplate, heavy shoulderguards, and high metal boots, all of a dark silver-gray bordered by a golden bronze. Wicked gauntlets ending in claws covered both hands, and even the draping forest-green cloak was lined with sharp blades that were not merely for show. A face-obscuring helm lay to the side of where she trained, with it a jagged, round blade known as an umbra crescent.

There had been a title for what she had once been— what she still considered herself—though some no longer saw purpose in it. Those were the same people who did not sufficiently understand the dangers facing the night elf race, dangers against which the Sentinels were poorly equipped both physically and mentally. Fortunately, Maiev had found others who still saw as she did and so had begun recruiting and training the best of those to rebuild the elite force wiped out by Malfurion's brother.

The elite force known as the *Watchers*.

For some ten millennia, Maiev had been a Watcher. Their leader—the warden, in fact. The Watchers, originally volunteers from the ranks of the Sisters of Elune and later also chosen from those outside the temple, had been charged with the daunting task of acting as jailors for the traitor Illidan Stormrage and, later, other monstrous criminals from not just the night elves but other races as well. As leader, Maiev had made Illidan her utmost priority . . . and utmost focus.

No, in Maiev's view, the Watchers had been a far more dedicated force than even the Sentinels.

Maiev practiced her skills, not in the Warrior's Terrace, but out in the forest beyond. There, she could unleash the energy ever pent-up inside her. This day she practiced with smaller blades—daggers—striking out at preselected targets while bounding through the area. One after another, the daggers sank deep into the centers of their targets, no matter at what angle Maiev threw them.

It was not by skill alone that her aim was so perfect, though. Incentive pushed her as much. In her mind, each target bore the visage of a male night elf whose eyes were covered by cloth, as if he were blind. Sometimes the details of the face changed, but it was ever recognizable in her thoughts. She knew that face better than her own, having stared at it so much. In fact, her current exercise was also a futile attempt to eradicate the memory.

But still she tried, slaying him again and again. That she had done so in truth did not matter. Whether as a cunning prisoner in the barrows or a demon seeking power over the world, Illidan Stormrage would forever be burned into Maiev's very soul.

Drawing the last dagger, Maiev lunged under a branch. Alighting onto a lower one, she brought her hand back for throwing, then spun around to face the intruder she had felt coming up behind her. At the same time Maiev tossed the dagger up, catching it by the hilt as it came down.

The tip ended up touching the throat of another female. To her credit, the newcomer flinched only slightly. Maiev nodded her approval; Neva was her best student.

"Forgive this interruption," Neva said calmly, eyes never going to the hand that held the dagger under her chin. "I would not have disobeyed your command if it were not important."

Maiev removed the dagger. "I trust your judgment. You know me better than anyone."

This straightforward comment elicited a brief but odd look from Neva.

Maiev's brow arched. "Why are you here?"

"I was crossing through from the Temple Gardens when I saw the gathering. The archdruid Malfurion Stormrage was there."

"Was he?" Maiev's memories coursed back to much younger days, when she had been a senior priestess of Elune. There again she saw Illidan Stormrage, though as a younger, handsome, but haughty figure, next to his twin brother, the future archdruid.

"Yes . . . the archdruid had evidently arrived just a moment before I had. He stood only a few feet from where I did. He was staring at a male in a travel cloak. The male was carrying another, a female. She looked to be dying. . . ."

"Get to the point."

The other female gave a slight nod. "The archdruid recognized the male. He whispered the name, which I was just barely able to hear." Neva hesitated, then concluded, "It was your brother's name."

Maiev revealed no reaction. She simply stood there as still as a statue. After several seconds, she finally blinked; then, with deft ease, she spun and threw the blade at the final target. The strike was perfect.

"Jarod . . . ," Maiev muttered.

"I am not mistaken, Warden."

"I did not think you were. So my brother has come back."

Neva bowed her head. "I had thought him long dead."

"We were both mistaken, then." Maiev retrieved her helmet. "He will be in or near the temple—probably in it."

"You are going to visit him?"

"Not at the moment. I need to think—" Maiev suddenly paused. Her eyes swept over the trees to the region to her right. Neva followed her gaze but saw nothing.

"Never mind," Maiev ordered her companion as the senior Watcher put the helmet on. "Let us go. I must see my dear long-lost sibling."

"But you said you were not going to visit—"

Jarod's sister looked at her companion with narrowed eyes. "I said I must *see* him."

Neva nodded her understanding.

Without another word, Maiev bounded down through the branches toward Darnassus. The younger night elf leapt after. Despite millennia separating their ages, Neva found herself hard-pressed to keep up with her instructor.

He watched the night elves leap gracefully out of sight, moving with an inborn skill that few other races could match but which made him sniff in contempt. He had not meant to cross their path, but perhaps it had been for the best. While the news of which they had spoken did not outwardly seem of import, anything that in the least concerned Archdruid Malfurion Stormrage would be of interest to his own master. Information was always valuable, especially in these times.

With a slight growl, the figure leapt in the opposite direction. He moved through the foliage with as much skill and grace as the slimmer but taller night elves had. Perhaps more, even.

After all, they did not have long, long claws with which to better grasp a tree branch . . . or rend a foe, when necessary.

4

THE MESSAGE
FROM ASHENVALE

Haldrissa had returned to her headquarters after her inspection of the outposts with more than the loss of her eye causing her frustration. While all of the outposts had proven to be in top condition, some of the activity reports that she had received from the officers in charge did not settle well with her. Where in several places there should have been some nominal orc activity, nearly all had reported nothing whatsoever. And where there had generally been no activity, odd little occurrences—though nothing as drastic as what she and her retinue had encountered—had taken place. Reports of a few footprints here, a broken arrow with Horde markings found there, a vanishing of game in another location . . . by themselves they were hardly anything to think about, but, when all were added together, they hinted at some growing trouble.

The commander sat cross-legged on a woven grass mat in her quarters. To her right, a toppled mug and a small, drying pool of water marked an earlier, failed attempt to adjust to perception problems due to her impaired vision. Haldrissa was doing better now, but still there were moments when her fingers had to hesitate before she was certain she was reaching for a parchment correctly.

She stared at the array of reports from the various outposts, her remaining eye darting from one to the next. However, as Haldrissa looked at one to her farthest left, she suddenly realized that Denea stood waiting there.

Just for a brief moment Haldrissa noted what she knew to be impatience on her second's part. That emotion quickly melted away, leaving only the steady expression of a Sentinel lieutenant.

How long Denea had been waiting, Haldrissa could not say. The commander tried not to think of what would have happened if it had been the middle of combat and, rather than Denea, it had been an orc standing in her blind spot. Haldrissa revealed no frustration with either her lapse or her second's impatience as she rose to meet Denea's eye.

"What is it?"

"You sent for me."

Haldrissa *had*, but it had slipped her mind. Simply nodding, she said, "I have gone over all the reports. I believe it urgent we send warning to Darnassus. The orc incursion near the one outpost was the most intrusive, but by far not the only one."

"They have pushed into the area before. You think this incident that important?"

"Important enough to send a message to General

Shandris immediately. Have a hippogryph rider ready within a quarter hour."

Denea saluted and left. Haldrissa looked over the reports one last time; then, taking quill to parchment, she wrote all she felt pertinent and how in her opinion it tied together. By the time she was done, Denea had returned.

"The rider is ready. I chose Aradria Cloudflyer."

The commander nodded her approval. Aradria was an expert rider, perhaps the best in all Ashenvale.

Sealing the parchment into a small pouch, Haldrissa again rose. With Denea a step behind her, she strode to where the courier already waited upon a huge forest-green animal with the clawed forelegs and crested head of a bird of prey—a head also adorned with long, wicked *antlers*—and a body otherwise like the sleekest of stags. His wings were a brilliant orange, like a setting sun. The hippogryph's eyes radiated fierce intelligence. These creatures were not property or pets but rather allies. Riders did not control so much as work in concert with them.

Aradria leaned down as the commander stepped close. She was even more wiry than Denea. On the other side of the saddle were strapped her glaive and a quiver full of arrows. Her bow was looped over her head and shoulder.

"No one sees this but the general," Haldrissa ordered as she handed the pouch to the courier.

"None shall," Aradria promised. She saluted Haldrissa as she straightened. The courier thrust the pouch into a larger one attached to the curved saddle on which she sat.

"Fly with all haste," the commander continued. "Beware the sea."

"Windstorm is the fastest we have here." Aradria patted the hippogryph on the neck. The winged creature nodded, his eyes gleaming in anticipation. "No one will catch him."

With that promise, she urged the magnificent mount to flight. The others stepped back as Windstorm spread his broad wings and readily rose into the air.

Watching the pair, Haldrissa felt a pang of jealousy. As commander, she rarely had the opportunity to ride such a mount.

"I want to double the patrols, Denea," she said once the courier and the hippogryph had become a blur. "Daytime and night. Especially night."

"The orcs would be better off trying to infiltrate during the day," Denea pointed out, indicating the time when most of the night elves still slept.

"Which is why we need to pay special attention when it is night."

Her second did not contest her judgment. Haldrissa dismissed Denea, then returned to her quarters. They were sparse, little more than the mat and the necessary tools needed for her reports and such. Another woven mat, this one longer and thicker, served as her bed. Unlike some officers, Haldrissa did not pamper herself. She slept as her soldiers slept.

It will not take her long, the senior officer thought. *It will not take Aradria long to reach Darnassus, not by air.* She was glad about that. General Shandris would see her concerns and move to address them.

Still, Haldrissa realized that there was yet need to build up the outposts beyond their current strength. As the weary commander lay down on her sleeping mat, she began calculating how to best rearrange her present level of troops. That further calmed her. Between her missive to the general and her own plans, the Horde was surely in for a dire surprise should it be planning a new attack. The orcs were nothing if not predictable in their overall methods.

Satisfied and eager to let rest ease some of the pain returning to her eye, Haldrissa finally slumbered. Ashenvale would soon be secure again....

The courier grinned as she and the hippogryph soared above the trees. Already deep into night elf territory, they both knew that they could save time skimming above the forest. Aradria had promised Haldrissa that they would get the report to Darnassus as swiftly as possible, and she and Windstorm had every intention of fulfilling that promise. Besides, they had a reputation to keep among the other riders and mounts.

The hippogryph's powerful wings beat hard. The miles vanished behind them. Aradria left it to her companion to judge where and when he would need to rest; experienced riders never assumed that they knew better than the hippogryphs themselves.

The cool wind felt bracing to the night elf, and she knew that it touched Windstorm the same way. Peering at the landscape below, Aradria made a judgment call as to a change in direction that might cut down their time even more. She tapped the hippogryph on the left side of his broad, muscular neck, using a short series of touches to communicate what she thought. Such a method was far better than trying to shout against the wind.

Without warning, the hippogryph rocked violently, his wings flapping in an awkward, jolting manner. As she clutched tight, the night elf glanced at one of the wings.

Two thick bolts had pierced it, right near the muscle. Blood stained the brilliant plumage and also sprinkled the treetops below.

Aradria looked at the other wing. There, a third bolt had likewise punctured the appendage, and more blood streaked across not only the feathers but the sky behind.

The shots were expert, so much so that the wounds kept the hippogryph from maintaining altitude. Windstorm's talons and hooves raked against the trees as he struggled to stay aloft. Torn leaves and bits of branches assailed the courier as the mount's battle against descent faltered more and more with each passing second.

"Ungh!" A stray branch as big as her arm hit the night elf in the chest. Aradria lost her breath, then her balance. She fell back.

Windstorm crashed among the trees. The collision was the final straw for the Sentinel, who tumbled off the saddle.

If not for the thickness of the forest canopy here, Aradria would have been dead. As it was, she slammed through one heavy branch after another, until the accumulation of debris falling with her created a barrier that put an end to her fall. She lay there, stunned, with her head and left arm hanging down.

The wounded hippogryph became tangled in a mass of trees just a short distance ahead. Instinct overwhelming thought, Windstorm twisted and turned in an attempt to free himself. The saddle, caught on some of the branches, held him fast for a moment, until brute fury enabled the mount to rip free of it. The saddle dropped several yards farther down the tree.

Aradria heard the hippogryph's frustration and

caught glimpses of his struggles as she pulled herself up to a sitting position. From her shoulder she removed the bow, broken in the fall. Scratched, bleeding, and with one smaller finger bent at an unlikely angle, the night elf nonetheless thought only about her companion and the pouch. Pausing just to reset the finger in order to better her grip, she moved nimbly toward Windstorm.

She had barely begun when the hippogryph, still turned awkwardly despite having freed himself from the saddle, broke through the stressed limbs holding him. The massive beast let out a squawk as he violently descended through one level of branches after another, finally vanishing from Aradria's sight.

Her desperate gaze fixed on the saddle some distance below. Though she still wanted to help the hippogryph, Aradria knew that her duty was to retrieve the pouch. With one last glance in search of Windstorm, the night elf leapt toward the saddle.

The branches held her, but barely. Even those not directly near where the hippogryph had crashed had been damaged by the falling limbs. Aradria made a swift calculation as to which would best suit her, then jumped to it.

She landed just a few scant yards from the saddle. Only then did she see that the larger pouch was empty. The small one containing the missive now lay somewhere farther below, perhaps even on the ground.

Aradria retrieved her glaive, slinging it on her gauntlet. After a moment's consideration, the Sentinel also took the quiver of arrows along.

From far below came Windstorm's angry cry. The night elf began leaping down from branch to branch. At last she spotted a patch of ground . . . and the pouch.

"Praise Elune!" Aradria murmured. Ignoring the pain in her finger, she grasped another branch and descended farther.

An arrow shot past her ear.

She did not see the archer but estimated his position from the bolt's flight. Aradria whipped the glaive free and threw it.

It cut through the remaining foliage and briefly vanished from sight.

A gruff voice roared in agony. Seconds later the glaive returned to the night elf's waiting hand. The blades were stained with fresh blood.

Taking a deep breath, the courier dropped the last distance. She could still see the pouch. It leaned against the trunk of the very tree from which she had just descended. Aradria reached for it—

From around the trunk burst a tusked orc, his huge axe already raised high to cleave the night elf in two. His thick mane of hair, bound tight, swung wildly as he ran at her, and the grin spread across his wide face revealed that, while he still had tusks, several of his other teeth had been broken in past conflicts. The damage did more to enhance his already fearsome appearance.

The courier brought up the glaive just in time to deflect the strike. Her entire arm vibrated from the force of the muscular orc's blow. Aradria gritted her teeth as she fought not to cede her position near the pouch.

The grinning orc slashed away at her again. Every bone in the already injured night elf's body screamed, yet she held her place. Still, she knew that the impasse could not last: more orcs would surely join the fight.

When her foe raised his axe for his next swing, Aradria

retreated a step. The orc's grin widened as he took this action as evidence that the duel was tilting more in his favor.

Aradria threw the glaive with all her might. The distance was not much, but her determined effort gave the triple-bladed weapon the force it needed.

One curved blade buried itself deep in the orc's chest.

The green-skinned warrior stumbled. Although he was not dead, the wound was a grave one. With his free hand, he tried to pull the glaive free.

The night elf barreled into him, pressing the glaive deeper as her opponent staggered back. At the same time she reached up to the quiver and grabbed one of the shafts.

Aradria shoved the arrow through the orc's throat.

The orc let out a gurgling sound. Despite dying, he clutched the night elf tight. The two fell to the ground.

She struggled to free herself. Not far off, she heard movement that did not sound like a forest creature. Anticipating more orcs, the courier finally managed to shove the body away. Unfortunately, she could not immediately free the glaive.

A rustling of brush made her look over her left shoulder in time to see three more orcs racing toward her from behind the nearby trees. Aradria tugged hard, the glaive finally coming out with a grotesque slurping sound. She whirled to face the trio, already aware that she had little chance against them.

Then . . . two more orcs stepped into the area from the opposite direction, cutting off what little hope she had of still fleeing with the pouch. Aradria surreptitiously glanced at the object. There was still a chance to at least destroy the contents if she could buy herself a few moments.

With a brief murmured oath to Elune, the night elf charged the nearest three. Her audacity served her well: the orcs hesitated, all but certain that she had intended to go against the pair. Aradria threw the glaive as she lunged.

The spinning missile forced the trio to scatter. The glaive soared past the orcs, then arced back, but not to the night elf's previous position. Rather, both it and she converged on the location where the pouch lay.

But she had underestimated the swiftness of at least one of the other two orcs. Even as Aradria caught the glaive, he reached the pouch. Clutching the prize in one hand, the brutish warrior turned to battle her.

The courier swung the glaive at him, then suddenly kicked. Although the orc outweighed her, the force was still enough to shove the air from his lungs. Aradria pressed her attack, hoping to take him down and retrieve the pouch.

Much to her dismay, the other nearby orc came between them. His intrusion enabled his comrade to recover, and both dueled with the tiring night elf.

Aradria knew that the other three had to be closing. She was trapped.

Suddenly a deep squawk shook the combatants. A huge form shot past the night elf. Mighty talons tore through the torso of one orc.

Though bleeding in many places and clearly favoring one front leg, Windstorm was yet a tremendous threat. The orcs could not get past his sharp beak. His body blocked them from reaching Aradria.

The night elf used his timely entrance to beat back her other two adversaries. She then took a quick look at the hippogryph, trying to estimate his condition. Windstorm could not fly—that was clear from his one badly drooping wing—but perhaps he could still carry her from the struggle.

First, though, she needed the pouch.

"Windstorm!" As the hippogryph responded, Aradria gestured at the orc with the stolen prize.

The huge beast might not be able to fly, but he *could* leap very well. Using his talons, he scattered the two orcs near him, then turned and made a tremendous jump over Aradria.

The other orcs backed away at his landing. Windstorm ignored the one without the pouch. The hippogryph snapped at the key warrior, but that orc refused to give up the pouch even in the face of such a threat. At the same time Aradria moved up, hoping to attack the orc while he was distracted by Windstorm.

Windstorm thrust his head forward, his beak opened wide.

A spear caught the hippogryph in the side of the chest. Windstorm let out a startled cry and teetered. In doing so, he collided with his rider, bowling her over.

The world spun as Aradria rolled. A horrific pain shot through her chest. She almost blacked out.

A nerve-wrenching keening cut briefly through the agony. Aradria heard a moist thwacking sound, then Windstorm's shriek. A moment later the ground shook as something heavy and limp crashed next to her.

The pain consumed her . . . until finally there was nothing left.

• • •

One of the orcs with whom Aradria had been battling started to lean over the night elf's still form. Blood seeped from a deep wound near the courier's left lung, where one of the curved blades from her glaive had pierced her during her roll.

"Why bother?" another orc questioned. "The wound's deep. She can't be alive."

"If she is," rumbled a deeper voice, "she deserves a warrior's death for such determination against impossible odds."

A shadow passed the second orc, the shadow of a much brawnier warrior than he. One hand—brown rather than green—gripped an axe more suited for two hands in combat. The sharply curved axe head was massive, well worn, and permanently stained with old blood. One of its most distinctive features was the many small holes in the head near the handle.

Other orcs gathered in the area, their numbers totaling just over a dozen. Three bore injuries that indicated a previous encounter with the hippogryph.

The warrior who had retrieved the pouch presented it to the leader.

"I saw no breathing. She is dead. This was what she fought so hard for, great warchief. . . ."

The leader hooked the huge axe on his back, then took the pouch. Because he was a Mag'har orc, his skin was brown, not green. His jaw was broader than that of most orcs, and from it jutted a pair of thick tusks with points as sharp as daggers. Unlike the others in the party, he was bald. He wore shoulder armor fashioned in part from the skull of a huge predator that he himself had slain, and over each shoulder had also been set a massive, curved tusk. The last was in homage to his father, Grom, for they were those of the pit lord Mannoroth, the great demon his sire had slain. By killing Mannoroth, Grom had freed his people from the fiend's blood-curse, which had made them servants of the monstrous Burning Legion.

Tearing open the small pouch with ease, he read the message. A single, satisfied grunt was his only initial reaction.

"The spirits have guided us. We were where we needed to be to catch this prey." He crammed the parchment into a pouch at his belt. "Destiny is with us. All falls into place. The night elves react exactly as I said they would."

"Garrosh Hellscream knows all!" declared the orc who had handed him the pouch. "He guides his enemies to their doom and laughs at their feeble attempts to keep their necks from his mighty axe, Gorehowl!"

"Gorehowl will taste much night elf blood soon. The Horde's glory is eternal," Garrosh replied, his tone filled with rising anticipation. "This is our land now. . . ." He looked around. "So much timber. So much untouched ore. The Alliance was foolish not to use its bounty. We—we will build a city here to rival even Orgrimmar."

The other orcs gave a lusty though low cheer. Although in the wilderness, they could still not trust that there might not be others who would hear them. None of the orcs feared battle, but this mission was of the greatest import to the plan, or else the warchief himself would not have chosen to lead it. The courier had been an exception: the scout who had spotted her in the distance had suspected from her route and pace that she surely carried something of importance, and had reported the sighting immediately. Garrosh had not hesitated for a moment before ordering his archers to bring down the hippogryph.

"I have seen all I need. We return now. The ships will soon arrive." He grinned, already envisioning the carnage their contents would create. "My gift to the Alliance must be readied. . . ."

The rest of the band let loose with another low cheer. Garrosh pulled free Gorehowl and briefly waved it. The unsettling keening arose once more, then quieted as the warchief lowered his axe. Gripping the weapon in both hands, he then led his followers east.

Behind them, Aradria stirred, let out a brief moan . . . then grew still once more.

5

BITTER REUNIONS

rue to her promise, the high priestess arranged matters for Jarod Shadowsong. Shalasyr lay at rest in the temple in an area reserved for such sad tableaux, her body now garbed in the raiment of the Sisterhood. She had been placed on a marble platform with the sign of the goddess—the crescent moon—etched multiple times into each side. The light of Elune shone down upon her, and her face bore an expression of peace. Those who had known her came to give their respects, each going down on one knee, then murmuring a prayer for her spirit to the Mother Moon.

The temple never closed its doors to the faithful, although most of those coming to honor Shalasyr came during the evening. However, time meant nothing to Jarod, who ever leaned over his beloved, either praying to Elune or silently speaking to his mate. The travel cloak lay bunched up to the side, but otherwise he was clad in the same forest-green and brown garments in which he had arrived. His beard and hair were slightly unkempt; such mundane matters were of no interest to him at this time.

Generally, there were two priestesses in attendance for such occasions, but at the former captain's request Tyrande had removed them. Although grateful for all that had been done for his mate, Jarod desired privacy when no other mourners were present.

Head resting upon his folded hands, he spoke again to Shalasyr, this time reminding her of when they had built their first dwelling together. It had been a simple one, designed to give them shelter while they made plans for something more permanent. The mistakes they had made in its creation had done more to bind them together.

Jarod looked up, well-honed instincts alerting him to the presence of another. He glanced over his shoulder at the entrance.

"My respects for your loss," Shandris quietly said. "The Mother Moon guides her spirit now."

The general of the Sentinels moved as smoothly as a nightsaber and, to Jarod, seemed much unchanged physically from when they had last met. She carried her helmet in the crook of her arm, which allowed him to study close her face. As usual, Shandris's true emotions remained hidden, save for a brief flash of what he read as either anger or uncertainty.

Shandris had been adopted by Tyrande, but they looked enough alike in the face to have passed for true mother and child. However, the high priestess had a softness to her expression that Jarod had seldom seen on Shandris. The general was also clad very true to her nature, her sleek, violet armor covering most of her form.

The armor had been designed as much for swift movement as protection; even the shoulderguards were set so that Shandris could raise a bow or sword at a moment's notice without any hindrance. The helmet—which only covered the upper half of the face—had also been forged with those two thoughts in mind. It could be easily set atop or pulled off of the head without ever catching on the long, tapering ears of a night elf or, in Shandris's case, tangling with her long, dark blue hair.

"Thank you." As she strode toward him, Jarod straightened to better face her. Her somber expression matched well his own.

"I recall her," the general continued, looking at the still figure. "She had much merit."

"She had *life*. She breathed life. The world brightened wherever she went."

Shandris turned more toward the body, in the process her expression becoming hidden from Jarod's view. "You truly loved her."

"Of course."

"Then I envy her."

He gaped. "Shandris—"

The female night elf looked back at him. Her eyes were moist, but the tears were clearly not entirely for the deceased. "I am sorry. I have been rude. You know that you have my deepest sympathies. To lose her so suddenly after so long . . . it is not right."

"Shandris . . ."

"I must go," she muttered, looking even more uncomfortable than Jarod felt.

He tried to gently take her arm, but Shandris evaded his touch without seeming to try. She could not keep him from following her, though, and thus the two walked in silence out of the chamber.

Jarod looked around, saw that no one was near, then quietly said, "I have owed you an apology for a long time—"

"You owe me no such thing. Nothing ever truly happened between us."

He looked back at the chamber, his face radiating guilt. Then: "I do not deny I was enchanted by your attention, especially once you had grown up, but we were heading in opposite directions in life. Those years right after the war were hard on all of us. All I wanted was to try to forget the carnage and the deaths. I never wanted to be a leader . . . a *hero*. . . ." Jarod said the last word with much self-derision. "I felt out of place, something you did not. You had purpose. You had your duty to the temple and the high priestess."

"She has—"

Jarod held up a hand for silence, and, clearly to his surprise, Shandris obeyed. "That you would be devoted to Tyrande not only for saving your life but for becoming the mother you lost is hardly something with which I would find fault. Yet she . . . and through her, our people . . . have been and always will be your foremost focus."

Shandris opened her mouth, then shut it. There was no denial in her eyes. Instead, she leaned up and suddenly kissed him on the cheek. There was not even the mildest attempt at seduction; this was a token of sympathy for his plight.

"I am here if you need to talk," the general said.

With that, she turned and departed. Shandris did not look back, and Jarod did not say farewell. He only watched as she headed in the direction that he knew the high priestess's sanctum lay.

The former officer started back, only to notice another armored figure far off in the opposite direction.

"Mother Moon!" Jarod whispered, thinking that he recognized the other despite the helmet. He waved to her.

Yet, unlike Shandris, the newcomer, once noticed, did not approach. Rather, she turned to leave.

"Maiev!" If she heard him, she did not respond. He stood there for a moment, completely perplexed, then rushed after his sister.

She had gone around a corner before he had managed half the distance. Certain that he would lose her and not sure when they would meet next, Jarod ran. He cut around the corner, only to see his quarry vanish out of the temple.

Following suit, Jarod exited onto the long bridge leading to the gardens. By that time, Maiev—if it was her—was already across the bridge and well into the area. He rushed through the gardens after her; then, beyond them, he twisted east as the ever half-glimpsed figure of his sister moved swiftly through the city and beyond the boundaries of Darnassus into the forest.

Jarod was not far behind, but still too far for his tastes. As he entered among the trees, he wondered if this would all prove a futile chase. Still, he was determined to follow.

Jarod darted among the first trees, trying to estimate the right path. He caught one glimpse of what he thought was an arm just noticeable between the tree trunks to his right and immediately veered toward it. Although he had no knowledge of this forest, Jarod allowed his natural instincts to guide him. He made swift judgments about the most accessible routes and where, from what he could make out of the landscape ahead, Maiev would likely head.

Although he could not see her, he was certain that he was at last closing on her. A sudden rush of intense satisfaction at this vied with his guilt for having left Shalasyr's side. He was not going to let Maiev get the best of—

A muzzle full of long, sharp teeth confronted him.

The image that filled Jarod's view over the next few seconds was one of nightmare. He saw something lupine . . . yet roughly humanoid in shape. It was at least as tall as he was, but nearly twice as wide and far more muscled. Long, deadly claws flashed by his face but did not touch him. The eyes—

The eyes were those of no beast.

A powerful fist thrust against Jarod's chest, shoving the air from his lungs. The night elf bent over as he struggled for breath. In the back of his mind he waited for the killing strike, by either claw or bite.

But the strike did not come, and when Jarod managed to lift his head enough to see before him, it was to discover that he was again alone. The only hint that anything had stood before him was the already slowing shift of branches.

Jarod darted after the unseen creature. He ducked around another tree—

—and then nearly ran into his sister, Maiev, who suddenly stood right in front of him. She had removed her helmet, revealing deep scars across her face that startled Jarod as much as her sudden presence in front of him.

"Never go chasing someone alone in unfamiliar territory. I thought that was one of the first things I taught you."

Jarod looked down to see the point of her umbra crescent touching his chest. He had noted the weapon at her side when he first spotted her, but had never expected to have it wielded against him.

Chuckling at his discomfort, Maiev withdrew the weapon. In one smooth movement she hooked it at her side again.

"I thought that, of all people, I could trust in my sister."

"Perhaps more than a scorned love," she returned. "That *was* General Shandris Feathermoon I saw retreating in defeat in the temple, was it not?"

"Maiev . . ."

"She was quite in a shambles when you vanished so long ago—"

"Enough, Maiev!" His joy at reuniting with his sister quickly became tempered by her comments about Shandris. Still, he tried to regain his initial enthusiasm. After all, it had been so long. . . . "It is so good to see you again! I wondered if we might meet when I returned here. I had hoped so."

"Why?"

Her question put him off balance. "You are my sister! My only flesh and blood! We have not seen each other in millennia!"

"And whose fault is that?" she snapped without warning.

"Maiev—" Suddenly, Jarod faced a person whose expression was filled with anger, with bitterness. This was not the reunion for which he had hoped.

Maiev shook her head at his obvious naïveté. "Did you think I would forget even after all this time? You shamed us! You were one of the leaders of our people! I was quite

proud of you then. My little brother, commander of the
night elf host! I watched you grow during the war, taking over after the death of that aristocratic imbecile, Star-
eye, and proving to everyone that the name *Shadowsong*
should be respected by all!"

"You do not understand—"

"*You* never will, it seems. *You* apparently never understood duty and loyalty—"

She hesitated when she noticed something on his face.
Only then did Jarod feel the moistness running down his
left cheek and the stinging near his eye. He touched his
hand to the moisture, then looked at his fingers.

Blood. Jarod could not recall when it had happened,
but assumed that it must have been during his encounter
with the mysterious creature. Yet, he did not remember
the beast scratching him there.

"That got dangerously close to your eye," his sister
commented, with a surprising hint of softness in her tone.
She put a finger to the stinging area. "Did you fall or slip
on the path? I remember you being better skilled on the
hunt than that."

It only occurred then to Jarod that he had not yet had a
chance to tell her about the startling confrontation. "Maiev! There was something *here* in the forest with us! Something I have never seen before anywhere. I ran into it just
before I caught up with you! It could still be nearby—"

Her mockery died away, and Maiev the warrior took
over. "Did it do that to you? What did it look like?"

"No . . . the scratch I must have gotten from a tree
branch after I collided with the creature. It did not attack me!" Jarod collected his thoughts. "I did not get a
good look. It happened so quickly. Something lupine . . . I

think! All I saw were claws, teeth, and a shape not unlike our own, but wider. . . ."

"Oh." Maiev no longer looked interested. "One of *them*. There is nothing to fear there. They do not dare get on the high priestess's or Archdruid Malfurion's bad side."

He could not believe that what he had seen could be so easily dismissed. "'Them'? There are more like that? Roaming around Darnassus's boundaries?"

"Forget it, Brother. It fled, did it not? That tells you all you need to know. They are cowardly skulkers with no bite! The worgen are undesirables who could not even save their own home."

"What are—" But before Jarod could finish, Maiev had begun to move on. She did not head directly toward Darnassus, but rather took a path that would make her skirt the east side of the capital. Jarod had to rush to keep up.

"Do as I say and forget them," she repeated. "Besides, it is certainly not your duty to police the capital. You gave up any sense of duty millennia ago."

The barb hit true. Jarod grimaced but sought to defend himself. "Maiev, I gave our people centuries of dedication to duty, of devotion to—"

"*Centuries* of dedication?" she laughed in his face. "That is nothing! Jarod, I have remained true to my duties as a protector of the night elf race from the moment I became a priestess of Elune, and afterward as a Watcher, until even now! I *volunteered* to oversee the imprisonment of Illidan Stormrage, even though that meant my fate was locked for millennia with his! I pursued him when other misfortunes enabled his escape! I survived torture as *his* prisoner and finally had the chance to do what should have been done in the very beginning . . . slay the arch-druid's accursed twin!"

"*Maiev!*"

She waved off the hand he reached to her. "Spare me any sympathy! I chose duty where you did not. Sometimes that has meant that I have made decisions that to others were not always evident as the right ones until much later, but I regret none of them."

"I understand. You have ever been determined to do what was best for all, regardless of how it made you look at times. I have always admired that steadfastness in you."

The muscles in his sister's face grew a little less taut. A hint of weariness touched her gaze. "I do what I must do."

This time he would not brook her blocking his hand. He put a hand on her shoulder and wished that the armor would not prevent him from gently squeezing Maiev there. "I have missed you. Of all those I left behind, I missed you the most."

"The general would not enjoy hearing *that*."

"Do not joke with me about that. Not now."

She patted him on the arm. "My mistake. You have had a terrible loss. I recall Shalasyr. Well skilled in the martial arts training of the Sisterhood. She would have made a good Watcher."

He grew uncomfortable. "I need to return. I am sorry, Maiev. Later—"

"Yes. Later we will talk more. Be off with you. My condolences."

Jarod hesitated, then turned. However, a nagging guilt at leaving matters so unfinished made him almost immediately look back.

Maiev was gone.

The former guard officer nearly called out, then hesitated. Brow furrowed, he eyed where his sister had stood, then resumed his journey back to Darnassus and his Shalasyr.

In another part of the forest near Darnassus, others had gathered. They were clad much more elegantly than other night elves and bore about them an inherent air of superiority. Their sleek robes were flamboyant and brilliantly colored.

These were the *Highborne*, the highest caste of old night elf nobility. However, due to their continued use of *arcane* magic, they had been shunned by their brethren following the War of the Ancients. Once, there had been many more of them, but some had fallen serving their arrogant and evil queen, Azshara, while others had been later transformed in other manners, turned into the reptilian, sea-dwelling fiends called naga.

Refugees from *Eldre'Thalas*—better known to most in this age by the more apt title *Dire Maul*—these night elf magi and their fellow survivors remained shunned by many of those in Darnassus. Though the Highborne even now maintained an air of absolute independence, in truth they found themselves in need of others. However, that by no means meant any lacking in arrogance or in their desire to continue their study of the arcane, no matter what the cost.

There were twenty at this gathering, twenty of the strongest. Var'dyn Skyseeker was leader of the twenty and had aspirations to be much more: the eventual successor to the Highborne's speaker, Archmage Mordent

Evenshade. Var'dyn now guided the spell that the twenty cast, a test of their power. The swirling energies gathered within the circle the casters formed. The faces of each male and female in the group glowed from not only the radiance but also his or her deep enthrallment.

Var'dyn gestured, and the energies came together in one powerful yet compact sphere. He gestured again, and tendrils reached out in the four directions of the compass.

We are now ready, he told the others through the link that their spellwork created.

As one, the Highborne drew a sign in the air. The tendrils grew stronger, and more erupted from the sphere. The sphere itself pulsated rapidly—

A horrific wind tore through the region. Highborne cried out in surprise as they were buffeted. The circle broke, but Var'dyn kept the link solid. They had come this far with their efforts; he was not about to let them all fail.

Then, what at first some mistook for thunder roiled through the area. Var'dyn looked up, but there were no clouds. He stared at the treetops, which shook violently . . . more violently than the wind demanded. It was they, in fact, that were the source of the deafening roar.

"Keep to your efforts!" Var'dyn snapped at some of his companions, the clearly unnatural actions of the forest finally unnerving them enough to cause risk to the spell. He led the way, concentrating harder and trying to draw the others back into the effort.

A tremendous wrenching drowned out the roar. One of the nearest trees *bent* down. Its limbs now acted like so many tentacles from some kraken. They reached for those Highborne below them.

More wrenching arose from beyond the boundaries

of the gathering. Everywhere, the closest trees stretched their branches toward the spellcasters.

The link weakened beyond Var'dyn's will to keep it intact. The gathered energies faded, and the tendrils dissipated. The sphere shrank—and then melted away with a pitiful hiss.

As it vanished, many of the exhausted Highborne slumped to the ground. Var'dyn remained standing, although it was secretly an effort to do so. Gritting his teeth, he searched the forest for the cause of the disaster.

"I made matters very clear regarding the practice of your arcane arts!" boomed a voice from every direction. "This goes against everything upon which the archmage and I agreed!"

One of the other spellcasters thrust a finger toward Var'dyn's left. There, the branches and underbrush gave way of their own accord to open a path to a lone figure wielding only a staff.

"Archdruid . . ." Var'dyn did not bow to Malfurion Stormrage, though he did nod his head in respect. "I have petitioned over and over about some mild changes in our agreement, but received no suitable answer. We *need* more leeway in our efforts; our powers will stagnate if we cannot utilize them in a sufficient manner—"

Malfurion strode up to Var'dyn, then raised the staff slightly. Var'dyn wisely quieted. "Your petition is still under consideration by both Mordent and me—as you have been informed more than once—and there has been no answer on it for reasons you have already been told! The reputation of the Highborne will always be stained by their past. As the archmage's thero'shan, you should understand that. You Highborne chose to stay in

Eldre'Thalas, defending and hiding in your special city as the war bloodily played out elsewhere."

"We fought for our home!"

"You stood by while the queen's counselor, Xavius, oversaw the creation of the portal that let the Legion into our world; you stood silent when Queen Azshara chose the demons over her own people; and you continue your practice of arcane magic, even though it is the same magic that drew the Legion to us. Even the millennia have not stripped the people's memories of those final days. It was difficult enough even to gain your kind the right to come to Darnassus. . . ."

"We came here thanks to your promises, Archdruid! We came here with the assurance that we were to be a part of night elf society again, yet also with the understanding that we will maintain our own identity too! However, as you yourself so eagerly point out, we are still ostracized! We must be able to openly practice our arts; otherwise, that alone proves your promises and those of the high priestess amount to *nothing*!"

The archdruid stepped closer, only pausing when he and Var'dyn were within reach of one another. Malfurion's gold eyes gleamed sharply. Some of the Highborne's arrogance faltered.

"There is every intention of the Highborne becoming a part of our society again, but such things cannot and will not happen overnight," Malfurion quietly but sternly replied. "This is a process that will have to play out over time . . . perhaps years. Patience is a virtue we must all nurture, Var'dyn. If we can, we will succeed. Mordent understands that."

Var'dyn did not look convinced, but nodded. Malfurion

turned to the rest of the assembled Highborne. "Go back to the others and tell them what I said. And tell them that the high priestess Tyrande and I keep our promises."

The other spellcasters wasted no time in beginning their retreat. Even the Highborne greatly respected the power of the legendary archdruid.

Only Var'dyn remained behind. "I mean no disrespect, Archdruid. I am simply seeking the best for my own."

"Mordent and I are aware of what you seek." With that, Malfurion returned to the forest, not once looking back or speaking to Var'dyn.

The mage eyed the archdruid's receding form, not stirring until Malfurion was long gone. A scowl spread across Var'dyn's handsome face.

"We *will* be patient . . . to a point," he muttered. "Only to a point."

Still scowling, the Highborne followed after his companions. Caught up in his fury, he ignored his surroundings. To his kind, trees were just trees, the forest merely a gathering of trees. The undergrowth through which he pushed was only overgrown weeds that, if not for his hosts, he would have razed instantly in order to clear a proper path. The Highborne lived for their arcane arts; they were used to having the environment bow to them, not the other way around, as it was with those who had built Darnassus. Like many Highborne, Var'dyn respected only power. The archdruid and the high priestess were powerful; thus, Var'dyn bowed to them. The rest of Darnassus, however . . .

The mage's foot shoved against something that momentarily caused him to stumble. Well used to the disorganized manner of the forest, Var'dyn kicked at the object without looking, then continued on through the underbrush. He had led his band out to this location due to its supposed remoteness, but otherwise had only contempt for it. He looked forward to returning to the relatively civilized settlement the Highborne had set up.

And so the hand that Var'dyn had kicked, the hand of the dead Highborne who had been but recently one of his band, lay, with its owner, for the time undiscovered.

6

STORM AT SEA

The storm struck suddenly, battering the ten great ships mere days from port. It quickly became one of the worst storms the orc captain could ever recall. Thunder crashed and lightning continuously lit up the sky. The rain came down in torrents and the sea rocked. Briln roared orders to the crew, trying to keep the flagship under control. If it looked as if he could not maintain command during the storm, then the entire fleet risked slipping into chaos as other captains turned to their own initiative. With the cargo they were carrying, such a choice would spell even greater disaster.

The ship leapt into the air as another huge wave rolled by. Briln gripped the rail as the vessel came down hard. Those who had never sailed the seas could not appreciate just how much like *stone* water could feel at such times. The entire ship shook, and the hull creaked ominously.

A scream from above made the fleet captain force his gaze into the downpour. He looked just in time to see one of the mariners who had been working on some of the snarled rigging fall into the sea. Briln grunted but did not call for a rescue. In this storm, the hapless mariner was already dead. The orc officer was more interested in getting the rest of his crew and his ship—all the ships—to safety. Briln had sworn an oath to the warchief that he was capable of fulfilling this mission.

A shout from one of the crew made the captain turn. The other orc pointed frantically toward one of the trailing vessels. Briln wiped the rain from his good eye and squinted. There was a glow rising from the ship in question.

Fire.

Such a blaze could have started by lightning. Yet, this fire already appeared too spread out and was confined to the deck for the most part. Generally, lightning caught the sails, rigging, or masts.

Thunder rumbled. Briln, caught up in the distant spectacle, all but ignored it . . . until it ended not by fading but rather by being accented by a ferocious and much-too-near *roar*.

He spun around and ran to the opposing rail. There, crashing through another humongous wave, the second ship in the fleet rocked wildly about in a manner that was contrary to the currents and wind. Something was shaking the ship from within its very hold.

The captain took up a spyglass that he always carried on him when aboard. Holding the copper tube, he focused it on the sister vessel, where oil lamps secured to the masts and other strategic areas gave enough illumination to reveal what was happening.

The captain of the second ship, a gruff mariner personally promoted by Briln, had his crew arming themselves with sea lances. Near the aft, three other orcs were lighting torches using oiled rags. Hardy warriors, they nonetheless looked very, very anxious.

Briln swore. He waved the spyglass in an attempt to get the attention of one of those aboard the other ship. No one noticed. The fire spreading over the more distant ship now made more sense. That crew had been trying to do the same as these mariners and had somehow lost control of the situation.

Thinking of the previous vessel, Briln turned the spyglass toward it.

To his shock, it was no longer in sight. Such a blaze should have still been evident . . . unless the ship had already sunk.

Cursing, Briln looked to his first mate. "A signal lamp! Hurry!"

But as he gave the order, the flagship shook as if it had struck a hard reef. Briln fell to the side. The first mate dropped to his knees. Another mariner dropped over the rail and into the voracious sea.

Another thump rattled the deck. Briln struggled to rise. "The storm's woken *all* of them up! Forget the lamp! Have the sleep powder readied, and spread it both on some food and the points of four spears! I want that thing below quieted or we'll be in as bad a shape as those other vessels!"

As the first mate and the others followed his orders, Briln returned his attention to the sister ship. Matters there were only worse. *Why haven't they quieted the beast?* he wondered.

A quick scan of the deck revealed the answer. Blackened wreckage marked the area where the barrel with the herb powder used to keep the beasts sedated had been kept secure. Rain by itself could not have touched the tarp-covered container tucked under the overhang of the door to the captain's cabin, but *lightning* could have—and had. The entire area had been blasted, and with it the only certain way to keep their savage cargo docile.

The flagship's own thumping slowed. A desperate notion occurred to Briln. He raced over to the hold entrance just as the first mate emerged. The other orc looked exhausted but triumphant.

"He was just wakin'! We caught him in time—"

The captain cut him off. "Who's the best shot?"

The first mate grinned. "That'd be me, Captain! You know that!"

"We've got a good amount of the powder left! Can you shoot a couple of sacks over to her?" Briln gestured at the other ship. "They've lost all their supply!"

"Aye!"

Another roar echoed from the direction of the other ship. Briln brought up the spyglass.

The orcs with the torches were racing toward the hold. There, several mariners with lances prepared to descend.

The deck behind them erupted.

A gasp escaped Briln. He had seen no lightning. What could have—?

As the shattered planks settled, the answer revealed itself. The silhouette of a huge hand briefly rose above the ruined deck, then sank back down. As that happened, the ship rocked back and forth even more violently.

Some of the crew hurried to the hole. As that happened, Briln's second returned.

"Two pouches!" the other orc shouted over the storm. "Where?"

"Somewhere on the deck where they'll see them! Just hurry!"

"Aye!" The first mate bound one tiny sack to an arrow, then readied the latter for firing. Even in such a storm, a skilled orc archer could be certain of hitting his target more often than not.

But before Briln's second could let loose, the other ship rocked even more wildly. Several of the crew, focused on the hole in the deck, suddenly went stumbling toward the rails. Two fell over, and one only saved himself by grabbing hold at the last moment.

The first mate shifted, trying to compensate. With the other orcs being flung this way and that, there was now more of a risk of shooting one of them.

The second ship tilted again, nearly falling sideways due to the additional impetus of another wave. As the vessel righted, the archer finally fired.

Briln let out a lusty roar. The arrow landed true, about a yard from the gaping hole. One of the crew noticed it and ran to retrieve the pouch. It was clear that he had a fairly good idea what the flagship had just sent over.

"Quick! The other!" the captain commanded. One pouch likely had more than enough powder to quiet the beast, but a second would guarantee success.

The first mate raised his bow—

The side of the hull facing the flagship shattered. A fearsome hoofed leg shot out, then pulled back in.

The rough sea turned the damaged ship, bringing the new gap to the water. The sea flooded into the fractured hold.

"Forget the powder!" Briln roared.

He needed to say no more. Abandoning the effort, the

first mate rushed to give the order to heave toward the floundering vessel.

A wave briefly righted the ship, but its cargo, obviously growing more enraged, lashed out once more. Planks splintered as the hoof kicked again. The hole nearly doubled in size.

When the ship listed this time, there was no doubt of its imminent fate. With water rushing in, the Horde vessel quickly sank. Within moments, the deck was at sea level.

Orcs leapt for the churning water, trying to reach the flagship. Several were immediately swept under by the waves and did not resurface.

Wild roars escaped the hold. The gargantuan hands ripped away at what remained of the deck. Yet, for all the creature's brute strength, he could not climb free in time.

The deck sank below the water. The sea shoved the ship farther from the rest of the fleet. One by one, the lanterns were doused, leaving only a silhouette of the ill-fated vessel.

A final frustrated roar cut over the storm. The silhouette changed as something seemed to erupt from the sinking ship's deck.

Briln grasped hold of the rail, the rescue attempt for the moment erased from his thoughts as the fear of a new threat to his own ship occurred to him. He envisioned the titanic creature wending his way closer. . . .

But with one last huge bubble of escaping air, the floundering ship went completely under. The last plunge happened so swiftly that the beast had no opportunity to react.

The flagship drew near two of the survivors. Briln

doubted more than a handful would make it, if even that many. He mourned their brave deaths . . . then considered what the night's events might mean. He had lost a fifth of his precious cargo.

"Eight should do," the captain muttered. "Eight should surely do. . . ."

But that was up to the warchief. That was up to Garrosh.

Briln hoped for no more losses. Surely, if there were no more losses, then Garrosh would forgive him for this failure.

But if the warchief did find fault with him, Briln asked only that the great orc leader let him see the crushing of the Alliance in Ashenvale.

That would make the captain's own death worth it all. . . .

There is a change in us, Malfurion noted as he strode through Darnassus. *And not one for the better. . . .*

The archdruid knew exactly when this undesired shift in the mood of the night elves had happened, and what had caused it. *Shalasyr. They cannot forget Shalasyr. . . .*

Night elves were used to death in battle or by accident. What they were not used to was the loss of a life due to infirmity tied to aging. Tyrande had spoken with Jarod and through him learned the extent of Shalasyr's troubles.

The illness had not been the only trouble, only the final straw. Jarod and his mate had been suffering from a number of minor but increasingly consistent aches and pains that sounded all too familiar to Malfurion, whose shoulder suffered twinges even now.

He eyed those nearest his path as he crossed the gardens. A dour atmosphere pervaded them. Malfurion could imagine their thoughts; each wondered not only if this was the fate awaiting them but also just how imminent it might be.

And he was no better than they were.

There was no escaping the inevitable, but through the use of the Sisterhood, Tyrande was already trying to stem the rising fear. She also looked to the examples of the younger races—the humans, especially—for how to handle the aging and sickness. True, the humans, too, suffered great emotional distress from both, but they also had a resilience that in most cases salvaged them. At the moment, neither the archdruid nor his mate was certain that their own race as a whole would prove as equal to the tests.

Malfurion forced the situation from his thoughts. He had to concentrate on the summit. Preparations had at last been finalized, and the arrivals of the representatives were close at hand. Malfurion now had to concern himself with the specifics of what he hoped would be accomplished.

"Archdruid Malfurion Stormrage . . ."

It was next to impossible to come upon the archdruid without his noticing, but the speaker had done just that. Fortunately, Malfurion was not one of tender nerve. He simply turned and, to no surprise, found himself gazing down slightly at a human.

The man was in the prime of life, strong of jaw, and with narrow eyes. He was clad in loose, simple brown garments. Despite being unarmed, he bore a stance that marked him as a fighter.

Malfurion knew him. "Eadrik."

Eadrik bowed low, his long, brown-black hair falling forward. "My lord Genn Greymane hoped to have a word with you, if you've time this day."

The archdruid's brow furrowed. "As a matter of fact, Eadrik, I should speak with him right now. Where is he?"

The human straightened. "I left him near the Warrior's Terrace, by the path leading to our refuge." Eadrik grimaced. "To be frank, Archdruid, I think he hoped you might do as you suggest. He knows time is short."

"Then lead me."

As Eadrik obeyed, Malfurion saw how the presence of this one human distracted the night elves in the vicinity almost as much as their concern over their aging did . . . despite the fact that humans and other members of the Alliance had had access to Darnassus since its founding. It was clear that Eadrik was recognized as one of Genn's aides and, thus, also recognized for what *else* he was. For his part, the young human kept his gaze straight ahead, almost as if nothing else existed but the path. Malfurion knew that the truth was just the opposite; Eadrik was as uncomfortable as the citizens of Darnassus, if not more so.

Eadrik moved as silently as any night elf, no mean feat for a human. He said nothing as they exited the city, but Malfurion noted that he finally relaxed as they entered the forest. The archdruid found it fascinating that a human would be more relieved to be in the wilderness than in a city.

As ever, the trees welcomed the night elf's presence. Branches gently swayed against the wind, and leaves rattled. To Eadrik, it was not noticeable. To Malfurion, it was a pleasure. He made a gesture that he knew the trees would sense, acknowledging their greetings.

Then the welcome gave way to something else. In the language of the trees, Malfurion heard, *He waits . . . he waits behind Three-Knob Growth. . . .*

All trees had names. Most were incomprehensible to even the archdruid. What the night elf heard was an approximate definition of what those names *meant*. Tree names were almost always physical descriptions of their characteristics, and no two trees to his knowledge had the same one.

Malfurion knew Three-Knob Growth, one of the first to rise in this part of the forest . . . so the tree had proudly informed him upon their first encounter some weeks earlier. He turned toward it just as Genn Greymane stepped out.

"Hail, King of Gilneas," the archdruid solemnly declared.

"Gilneas . . . ," murmured the brawny, dour figure. Genn Greymane resembled a bear, albeit an aging one. No handsome man, he yet had a commanding presence and eyes still sharp and quick for a human of his more mature age. Unlike the night elf, Genn sported a much shorter, clipped beard. He stood taller than Eadrik, which brought him slightly nearer to the night elf in stature.

"Gilneas . . . ," the king repeated. "In name only, Archdruid."

"For now!" Eadrik piped up.

"We shall see." Glancing at the other human, Genn added, "And why is the archdruid *here*? I asked you to see about an audience with him, not drag him to me—"

Malfurion interjected before the misunderstanding

could grow out of proportion. "I told your man to take me to you, Genn. Your request coincided with my need to talk with you. Following Eadrik back saved valuable time."

"It's about the summit, Archdruid."

"Of course. Gilneas is one of the most prominent reasons I sought to bring it to fruition. Your people's admission to the Alliance is—"

"*Re*-admission, you mean," the king growled with much bitterness. "After I was foolish enough to think that Gilneas was best served taking matters into its own hands."

"Genn! The curse was something beyond your control! You could not have—"

"It doesn't matter!" the lord of Gilneas growled, for the moment sounding more like an animal than a man. He leaned into the archdruid, and although Malfurion was still taller, to the night elf it seemed that their gazes met evenly. Genn seemed bigger, wilder. "It doesn't matter! We are and will always be cursed!"

Malfurion fought to take command of the conversation again. "We wanted to speak to one another about the gathering. The first emissaries will be arriving tomorrow."

Genn deflated. "Yes. The summit. They'll all have their chance to judge me for my foolish mistakes."

"I have been in contact with several of them. They understand the necessities of the time. They understand that you regret all that happened. They also can appreciate what you and your people can offer."

"And do they understand it's a double-edged sword they're offered, Archdruid?"

The night elf extended a comforting hand to the human's shoulder. Genn accepted it without question. "You have gained far better control of it than you think. You offer nothing but advantage, Genn. At the very least, they will have to seriously consider that aspect."

"Even Stormwind?"

"I have no answer there," Malfurion admitted. "But I have great hope." The archdruid leaned closer. "He is coming. That was what I especially wanted to tell you."

"Stormwind is coming?" blurted Eadrik. "My lord! That means—"

"Exactly nothing," the king of Gilneas responded at first. Still, his eyes shone with hope of his own. "No . . . perhaps it means much . . . if he and I can set aside our differences. I know that I'm more than willing."

"Varian Wrynn is a wise man," the archdruid pointed out. "Stormwind would not be what it is if he were not."

Genn finally could not help smiling at the news. "As you say. This lightens my heart! There *is* a chance, after all. If he's coming, he must be willing to let bygones be bygones. . . ."

Malfurion pulled back. "I need to return to dealing with the summit. I merely wanted to assure you that there is every reason to believe that Gilneas will be accepted into the Alliance. I want your promise that you will attend as previously stated and be willing to show your humility as well as your strength."

"I'll be doing my part, don't you doubt it, Archdruid." Genn offered his hand, which Malfurion shook. "There's my promise again on all we agreed to. If there's any hope of seeing our home again, it's to get through this summit."

"And I promise again to see that *everyone* understands the import of this . . . even Stormwind."

Genn Greymane signaled to Eadrik, who slipped into the forest. The lord of Gilneas gave Malfurion one last grateful nod. "I know you'll do all you can. It wouldn't have gotten this far without you, Archdruid." Genn gritted his teeth. "But from here on, you know it all lies in one man's hands."

"He will come to see things as they must be for all our sakes."

"I believe that, but let us pray to your Elune just the same. I'll take all the help we can get. . . ." With that, the king slipped into the forest.

The archdruid stood there, momentarily caught up in his thoughts. His gaze fixed on the area into which Genn and Eadrik had departed.

A large, dark shape momentarily arose among the underbrush, then disappeared among the trees again. It was tall enough to be a man . . . but was not.

The sight, though expected, still jarred the night elf slightly. As he turned, he again silently swore to do everything he could to help the refugees from Gilneas, including ensure that they were welcomed back into the Alliance by everyone.

After all, they might never even have been cursed if not for *Malfurion*.

7

INTO THE FOREST

Haldrissa expected no word yet from Darnassus, but that did not mean that she remained idle in the meantime. She did not trust that the orcs were not already on the move. Thus it was that the very next day she had led another party out to investigate an area near the foothills east of the night elven camp Maestra's Post. With her was Xanon, chosen for his sharp eyes. Denea had been left in command back at the fort, not something Haldrissa's second had been happy about.

"As seniormost officer, it would behoove you to remain behind," Denea had even suggested in her most courteous manner. "Just in case of trouble in the wilderness."

Her point had had merit, but at the time Haldrissa had not been able to get past the thought that perhaps Denea had believed herself more capable of facing the rigors of the journey and any encounters during it. Haldrissa had declined the officer's suggestion without hesitation.

However, now, some time into the ride, the twinges Haldrissa felt made her occasionally wonder if she should have listened more.

But all thought of that vanished as Xanon returned with two other Sentinels from scouting the territory up ahead. Haldrissa had purposely chosen an obscure area less likely to be of interest to the Horde for the very reason that the enemy might have played on that reasoning. The commander had survived so long by learning to try to think like the enemy, however repulsive that might be to her at times. She had to do her best to expect the unexpected.

Of course, both Denea and Xanon had looked dubious when first informed where she intended to lead the party.

However, Xanon did not look so dubious now. In fact, his concerned expression made everyone who had been waiting—especially Haldrissa—sit straight and taut.

"What is it?" she asked the moment he was near.

"Best see," he gasped, still exerted from the swift ride back. "This way!"

One brow raised at this curious reply, the commander waved the party to follow Xanon. The trained nightsabers leapt effortlessly and silently through the forest, dodging around trees and across uneven terrain with an agility that Haldrissa still admired after all these millennia. Each cat was in the prime of its life. For the first time the commander considered her previous mounts and the ends of their turbulent lives. While some nightsabers did perish in battle, more than a few had survived their last years crippled from previous injuries. It brought home again her own encroaching mortality.

The night elves kept a wary eye out, though thus far

there was no indication as to what Xanon and the other pair had sighted. The male Sentinel hunched low as he rode, a sign of just how determined he was to get his commander to wherever they needed to be as quickly as possible. That boded ill, in her mind.

Then, deep into a dense part of the forest, amidst a small patch of winding hills, Xanon abruptly signaled for the party to slow to a trot. Haldrissa urged her mount alongside his, then leaned close.

"What . . . ?"

"Listen."

She knew his ears were sharper than most, too, but, even taking that into account, the commander marveled that he heard anything. Even the nightsabers appeared not to notice anything out of the ordinary.

"I do not—" Haldrissa began, then paused. There *was* a very faint sound from far ahead. An odd, unsettling sound. It even had a strange rhythm to it, the same beat over and over and over.

"What is that?" one of the others murmured. "It sounds familiar. . . ."

"I want to see more." Peering back at the party, she ordered, "The rest of you, keep back! Xanon and I will investigate from here on. If you are needed, we will try to signal."

The rest of the Sentinels did not look pleased, but they obeyed. Xanon urged his nightsaber on, but at a much slower, more precise pace. Haldrissa made her mount match speed.

As they neared, Xanon readied his glaive. Haldrissa did the same.

The buzzing now dominated. It was a harsh, painful

noise and was accompanied by a cracking sound. That sound, at least, the commander knew. It was the sound of wood breaking.

She now had a fairly good idea of what was going on, though the specifics of it still eluded her. Ever seeking expansion, the Horde had a voracious appetite for wood. They needed it for building, for their forges, for their growing fleets.

And that was why they most coveted Ashenvale.

"It would be wiser to go on foot from here," Xanon whispered.

Nodding, Haldrissa dismounted, and then she and Xanon loosely tethered their cats. Highly intelligent, these nightsabers would obey the command to stay until called by one of the riders. In an emergency, it better served Haldrissa if the animals could quickly come to their aid.

Xanon once more took the lead, the younger night elf crouching low. The wind shifted toward them. While good in that it kept their scent from the orcs, it also brought a stench that answered some of Haldrissa's other questions.

The smell included a combination of fuel and steam. Those were signs of a goblin machine. *Several* machines, judging by the potent and often suffocating odor. Goblins were almost the antithesis of night elves; they believed in the might of machines over nature and had little, if any, respect for the latter.

"There!" Xanon rasped, thrusting a finger to the northeast.

At first Haldrissa thought some armored giant stalked the forest, a giant intent on carnage. What in some ways resembled a glaive with far, far sharper, curved points spun madly at the end of one arm. The other arm ended in a monstrous claw with four digits that at that moment seized the trunk of a thick oak. The giant then thrust the spinning blades at the tree.

To her horror, the blades cut into the wood as if it were water. Within seconds the mighty oak teetered, its life already gone.

But the giant figure was not satisfied with just that. It shifted position and began slicing the tree into smaller pieces.

Only then did Haldrissa see that atop the head, there was a *seat* . . . and in that seat, a short figure with green skin, long ears, and a sadistic smile manipulated levers.

"A *shredder*," she murmured back to Xanon. "A goblin shredder!" There had been reports of the machines being brought in farther east, but to find one this close was disturbing.

"Wait," Xanon whispered. "Keep listening."

Before she could ask why, the buzzing arose from another location. As the two looked, a second shredder trundled into view. The silver and crimson mechanism paused. The upper half turned to one side as no true creature could without breaking its spine. In the seat and half-shielded by the armored front, another goblin surveyed the nearest trees. Choosing one, he tugged on a lever, and the spinning blades began their diabolical work.

Haldrissa silently swore at such sacrilege. She started to rise—only to have sense make her duck down just as a third and fourth shredder stepped into sight.

"They have a major lumber operation in progress here," the male night elf told her. "I counted two more before. They are ripping apart this area of Ashenvale as if the trees had no feelings, no importance!"

"Six shredders." Haldrissa did some calculations. "We can handle that many—"

And then the scene became an even more horrible nightmare. Another shredder joined the others, followed by another and another and another. . . . More than a score quickly filled their view, and yet the numbers continued to grow.

"By Elune!" gasped Xanon. "This is worse than I imagined!"

"We must leave!" returned Haldrissa, beginning to back away. The two Sentinels, their eyes ever on the horror, retreated, heading for the area where they had left their mounts.

The wind shifted direction again. A thick smell of fuel and steam assailed Haldrissa from their left.

"Beware!" she cried, shoving Xanon away from that direction.

The shredder came crashing through the trees and brush, the metallic claws ripping away branches that blocked the path. High-pitched maniacal laughter cut above the sound of spinning blades. With a death's-head grin, the goblin adjusted the levers.

The blades came at Haldrissa. She was forced to dodge toward her blind side and thus stumbled. The blades just barely grazed her shoulder. However, despite that and the fact that Haldrissa wore plate armor, the shredder was still able to cut through the metal and rip a tiny but painful gash in her flesh.

The wound, though shallow, startled the commander enough that she again made for a tempting target. The upper half of the shredder turned toward her. Another wild laugh escaped the goblin as he maneuvered the whirring blades.

The Sentinels' only good fortune thus far lay in that this goblin had moved far ahead of the rest and, because of the din created by the destruction of the forest, their struggle went unheard. Haldrissa could not hope for that to continue, though. At the very least, she and Xanon had to escape.

A whirling glaive flew by her. It came within a yard of the goblin before the other arm deflected it. Xanon's weapon went skimming wildly through the air, at last sinking deep into a nearby trunk.

The attack had at least served to give Haldrissa breathing space. In that time, she jumped out of reach, then readied her own glaive.

The goblin shifted levers. The shredder marched toward her. The one arm continued to act as shield while the other with the spinning, toothy blades stretched forth.

Haldrissa took the measure of the shredder, then, compensating for her impaired vision, threw. Her toss looked as if it had gone wide at first, but as it passed the grinning goblin, it arced around. The commander kept her expression frozen, afraid of giving warning.

But she had underestimated both the goblin and his device. The squat creature tugged a lever, and the protecting arm twisted over his head in a manner that would have been impossible for a living creature.

With a harsh clang, her glaive rebounded off of the arm and away from the struggle. Haldrissa swore.

"C'mere, purple!" the goblin mocked. "Lemme give you a hug!"

The arms swung toward her from opposite directions, seeking to pen her between them so that the blades could do their work. Haldrissa dropped to the ground, barely avoiding being beheaded.

She fully expected the goblin to immediately compensate, but instead the arms began flailing madly. As the commander pushed herself up, she saw Xanon scrambling up the side of the shredder. He did not have his glaive, but the dagger in his left hand was more than sufficient for dealing with the shredder's operator—if the male night elf could get a little closer.

The goblin was having none of that. The flailing was accompanied by the swiveling of the torso, all in an attempt to knock Xanon free. While it had not succeeded in that respect, it did keep the Sentinel from using his blade.

Aware that trying to signal the others now might also alert all the goblins and whatever other elements of the Horde were nearby of the Alliance presence, Haldrissa tried to think of some way to quickly put an end to their lone foe. She peered around. Her own glaive was too far away, but Xanon's remained stuck in the nearby tree. She darted for the weapon, hoping that her companion could keep the goblin distracted long enough—and without dying in the process.

But though she reached the glaive without difficulty, pulling it free proved a much more troublesome task. The glaive had buried itself deep, and even though Haldrissa tugged as hard as she could—all the while gritting her teeth as her effort made her wound sting much greater— it would not come free.

Buzzing filled her ears. She glanced in the direction of the other shredders, but they were not even in sight . . . and therefore not the source of the increased buzzing.

Haldrissa ducked.

The blades of the lone shredder tore into the tree. Splinters and sawdust rained down upon the night elf.

A screeching sound tore at her eardrums. As she rolled aside, she saw that the shredder's blades had met the glaive. The resultant collision had made both the shredder and the tree shake violently.

Swearing, the goblin adjusted several levers. The other arm came up and braced against the trunk. With amazing strength, the shredder used the leverage to push free.

Haldrissa saw no sign of Xanon and had to assume the worst. With his glaive ruined, she surveyed the area for her own.

The damaged tree creaked ominously. Haldrissa stepped back but saw that the danger was not as imminent as she had thought. The tree shook slightly, then stilled.

The goblin adjusted the levers, then moved in on her again. As he did, Haldrissa finally caught a glimpse of Xanon. He lay sprawled next to another tree. She could not see any sign of injury, but the stillness of the body did not give her much hope.

However, seeing Xanon stirred a desperate plan. The commander hoped that she judged the damage to the tree correctly, or else she was about to throw herself into the jaws of death.

"Xanon!" she roared. "To his left!"

The goblin reacted accordingly. Straining at the levers, he made the torso spin around to confront the threat he believed there.

Had Haldrissa attempted to leap up at him, he would have had more than enough time to notice her and prevent success. Instead, the night elf ran behind the damaged tree.

The goblin saw that the male Sentinel still lay unconscious or was dead. He pulled a lever, and the shredder started to turn back to her.

Bracing herself, Haldrissa threw her body against the back of the tree. The collision shook her to the bone, but she heard the wood give a satisfying snap.

The tree toppled.

Haldrissa made a silent prayer to Elune.

She had judged both the damage and the angle true. The huge tree fell toward the shredder.

The goblin looked up as the shadow covered him. He frantically adjusted the levers, raising both arms in an attempt to stop the tree. However, when it became clear that the arms would not stop the tree in time, the goblin pushed himself out of his seat.

He did not make it.

The tree reduced the shredder and its handler to a squat ruin. The tanks that fueled the mechanism ruptured.

The shredder exploded, sending metal fragments and bits of goblin flying everywhere.

Even before the tree had struck, Haldrissa had headed for Xanon. She did not want to leave her officer if there was even a chance he lived.

"Xanon!" the commander hissed. "Xanon!"

He did not stir, but Haldrissa saw that the male Sentinel did at least breathe. There was a heavy bruise on the side of his head, and blood stained his face and arm.

With no other option, Haldrissa wrapped her arm around the other night elf's upper torso and, ignoring the pain in her arm, dragged him from the site. Peering over her shoulder, she caught a glimpse of one of the other shredders starting to move toward the ruined one. So low to the ground, Haldrissa believed that its operator could not yet see her or her burden, but she nonetheless hurried as best she could. If the pair was spotted, they would never escape.

A glint caught her eye. Grimacing, Haldrissa set down Xanon long enough to retrieve her glaive. It meant the cost of a few valuable seconds, but without the glaive there would be absolutely no chance of defending the two of them.

The sound of encroaching shredders increased. There were no cries of discovery, though. The commander counted on the hope that the goblins would focus on their own, thinking that perhaps the operator had miscalculated while trying to bring down the tree rather than that he had been sadistically hunting down night elf prey. She only needed that false belief to last long enough for her to reach the cats.

Dragging Xanon, Haldrissa finally paused at a spot several yards away and out of sight. She let out a low whistle.

Her heart pounded as she waited. Finally, her mount trotted into view. The nightsaber rubbed its muzzle against her side.

The second cat joined them. It sniffed Xanon and let out a low growl. Haldrissa shushed it, then settled the unmoving officer over the creature's back. When that was done, she mounted her own animal.

Behind her, a commotion arose as the goblins investigated what Haldrissa hoped still passed for an accident. Exhaling deeply, the commander urged the nightsabers forward.

She did not relax in the least until they were far away.

Haldrissa counted the seconds until she reached the rest of the party, all of whom eyed her arrival with trepidation.

"Take care of him!" she ordered two of the others. As they took control of Xanon, Haldrissa faced the rest. "It is worse than we had imagined! More mechanized goblin shredders than I had thought could exist! They are already ripping apart the forest over here. We can assume that they are doing the same elsewhere, I am sorry to say."

"We should charge in and take care of those little vermin!" snarled one Sentinel. "We should be able to handle such scum!"

Some of the others issued their agreement by raising their glaives, but Haldrissa immediately cut off any notion of an attack. "There will be no suicidal attack! We ride back now! This information must be passed on to Darnassus!"

"And then we just wait?" blurted one of the others.

"Of course not! Enough questions!" To the two night elves handling Xanon, she commanded, "Secure him well! We will have to ride hard!" Haldrissa paused as she saw their faces.

"He is dead," the nearest Sentinel informed her and the rest. "For some minutes. The wound to his head was too grave." To emphasize her point, she tilted Xanon's head until the party could see the blackening bruise and increased blood flow, something to which Haldrissa, caught up in the escape, had not been able to pay attention.

The commander scowled. Another death at the Horde's hand. Though her body ached, her pulse pounded.

"They will pay. They will pay for all the deaths . . . including those of the forest."

Haldrissa urged her mount on, the others following in her wake. She glanced behind her. The body of Xanon, secured well, rode with them—the dead rider very likely a harbinger of things to come, she knew.

8

ARRIVALS

Although there would be an official entrance by the various members of the Alliance once the summit had commenced, arrangements had been made for the representatives' personal arrivals beforehand. The night elves had been willing to host everyone in the capital, but by majority vote from the others, it was agreed that the emissaries and a small personal escort would stay in Darnassus while the rest of their people remained aboard the various vessels. The full contingents would march in the procession opening the summit; then, after the ceremony, they would return to the ships until the gathering's end.

The high priestess had finally seen the wisdom of the decision, though not for the reasons her guests had used. The more members of each nation staying in the capital during the delicate proceedings, the greater the chance of tempers flaring and incidents overtaking their goals. With each realm still reeling from the Cataclysm, the risk of that happening was very high already.

Theramore was the first member of the Alliance to reach Teldrassil. Tyrande and Malfurion met the key representative and his escort as they exited the portal into Darnassus.

"Well met, Archmage Tervosh," the high priestess greeted.

The black-haired mage bowed his head to both. "In the name of Lady Jaina Proudmoore, ruler of the isle of Theramore, I thank you for your hospitality during this most significant of functions."

"We are honored to have you here in her stead, though we hope that Lady Jaina is well."

Tervosh smoothed his black and violet robes. As one of Jaina Proudmoore's aides, he also wore a somewhat elaborate gold vest with ornamented shoulders. "With the troubles brewing all around us, she chose to stay in order to continue organizing Alliance forces. You can trust that she would rather be here, High Priestess."

"Her martial knowledge has been invaluable during these dark days," Malfurion put in.

"In that, at least, she takes after her father." Tervosh said nothing more, the subject of Admiral Daelin Proudmoore a delicate one. His obsession with the orcs had led to his untimely death in battle against the half-breed Rexxar during the storming of Theramore's keep. Rexxar, in whose veins ogre blood also flowed, had not wanted the admiral's death, but Daelin had given them no choice. Admiral Proudmoore's daughter still mourned him, even though his actions had forced her to side with the Horde over her own father.

The high priestess hesitated, then asked, "And how is *Pained*?"

Tervosh pursed his lips. "She performs her duties for Lady Jaina as stoically as ever. The great scar from her confrontation with dark magi is nothing compared to the scars left in her mind because of that event." He shrugged. "But she will not accept any help. Her stubbornness has always been both a detriment and a saving grace."

"I will continue to pray for her healing, both without and within." Tyrande shook her head, then smiled once more. "But on to more immediate matters. You will wish to refresh yourselves." She indicated one of her aides. "Please show the archmage and his escort to their quarters."

Tervosh bowed again. "I look forward to the summit."

As the emissary from Theramore departed, the high priestess murmured, "And there goes probably the easiest of those with whom we shall deal. Would that all the others could see matters as straightforward as Theramore."

"They will see sense, Tyrande. They must."

The archmage had barely left them when news came that the dwarven emissaries had arrived on the island. From all *three* clans.

"This can hardly be coincidence," Tyrande declared as she and her mate, joined now by several priestesses, waited before the portal. "Could they have traveled together?"

"The Bronzebeards and the Wildhammers had agreed to, due to Rut'theran's limited dock space, but I had not heard about the Dark Irons. Amazing to think that they managed to sail here with them aboard as well. If they did, I suspect that the clans stayed in separate parts of the ship throughout the entire journey and very likely even disembarked separately."

"I would not have wanted to make that journey," the high priestess returned with a shake of her head.

They waited for the three emissaries to come through the portal, but time went on and still nothing happened. The archdruid and Tyrande exchanged concerned glances.

"Perhaps I should go down—" But Malfurion got no further before the portal flared and the first of the dwarves entered the capital.

"Hail, Thargas Anvilmar!" Tyrande said, immediately recognizing the grizzled dwarf known as a hero among the Bronzebeards. Thargas had acted as representative during previous discussions between his people and Darnassus.

"Hail to ye, me lady," the squat but muscular figure rumbled. Although he stood much shorter than either night elf, he was more than twice Malfurion's width, and all of that muscle. "Fergive the delay! Bit o' an argument over who went up first. . . ."

The dwarven race was in flux, the tensions among the clans of much concern even to Tyrande and her mate. Other than Stormwind, the dwarves as a whole had been one of the most questionable of the possible attendees. The night elves were pleased that they had arrived . . . but if it only meant that the emissaries would come to blows, then all would be for naught.

"How was it settled?" *Not by* axe, Tyrande hoped.

Thargas chuckled. "Wildhammer suggested we roll the bones! Best idea! We did that . . . an' *Bronzebeard* won, o' course!"

The high priestess and Malfurion allowed themselves smiles. Trust dwarves to choose such a basic path to solve their problem.

"We are pleased to see you," the archdruid added. "Thank you for coming."

"Ye've been strong allies. Bronzebeard wouldna turn its back on that. Now, the Dark Irons, maybe . . ."

Tyrande led the emissary and his band forward. "You must be hungry after your travels. These two will guide you to your chambers and to the meal we have arranged for you."

"There be drink too?"

"Both night elven wine and dwarven ale."

Thargas's grin widened. With a nod, he led his group after the two priestesses. Tyrande relaxed a little once the dwarves were out of sight.

"Well done, my love," the archdruid whispered. "Best to get them moving so as not to stir up troubles again, especially if the next ones through are—"

The portal flared, and a small band of dour black-clad dwarves warily stepped through. They were of a pale, almost deathly complexion and, to the archdruid, were almost interchangeable save for the fact that some had dusky brown hair, others a dull black or faded red. Only the lead dwarf seemed to have any true individuality, and that from the cunning the night elf could read in the emissary's burning red eyes.

Although their weapons were not drawn, the Dark Irons' hands hovered near them, just in case. However, upon seeing only Malfurion, Tyrande, and the priestesses waiting to help guide the guests, the group relaxed . . . slightly.

"Hail, emissary of the Dark Iron clan . . ." Tyrande uttered, unfamiliar with any of the party, including the leader.

"I am Drukan. I speak fer Moira Thaurissan," the shadowy figure in the forefront rasped. His red eyes took stock of the two chief figures in front of him, clearly sizing up their potential as threats.

"You are welcome, Drukan, you and your escort. We have your quarters available, not to mention meal and drink."

"We've brought our own." Drukan indicated several heavy sacks and kegs of ale his companions carried. "We'll need nothin'."

"As you like. I will see that they are removed. If you change your mind, please let me know."

Drukan grunted. He and his cohort trailed after the two guides Tyrande provided.

Once the Dark Iron dwarves had stepped out of earshot, Malfurion muttered, "Trusting souls."

"They came here. That says a lot. And from what little you have told me, they seem to be in about as much agreement with us as the Bronzebeards."

"The Dark Iron dwarves cannot afford to become isolated right now. They need to maintain ties with the Alliance in general, if not perhaps their fellow dwarves."

The portal activated again.

"Wildhammer greets its hosts!" the short, rather stout figure in red and gold armor roared cheerfully from the forefront of the latest arrivals. The other dwarves behind him added their own boisterous rumbles of agreement, a few accenting their greetings with waves of their hammers.

Tyrande stepped forward to greet the leader. "Welcome, Kurdran. A pleasure to have you with us."

The dwarf, his long, thick beard an even more fiery red than his armor, smiled. "I thought I'd waited long enough before poppin' up. Those Dark Irons give any problem?"

"Other than refusing our food and drink, they were very polite," the archdruid answered.

"Like as nae they're afraid o' bein' poisoned by someone, as it's nae so uncommon among their ilk. Glad tae hear everythin' went as I'd planned, then."

"'Planned'?"

The Wildhammer dwarf leaned close and in a conspiratorial tone explained, "None o' us wanted the others tae get tae the island first, an' no one wanted tae be dead last. So we all agreed tae arrive at the same time, our honor on that sworn on the hammer." Kurdran snorted. "No one mentioned this portal, though. Got tae it, an' arguin' broke out about who had the right tae go up ahead o' the others!"

"And that was when someone suggested gambling for it?"

"Well . . . I didna exactly say it that way, but, yes, that's what I told 'em."

The high priestess's eyes narrowed knowingly. "*You* were the one who suggested it. . . ."

"That's it! And worked out very well, I think."

Tyrande pressed. "So it is sheer coincidence that the order happened as it did? You seem very cheerful for being third, and the Dark Irons' being second is perhaps the safest situation there."

Kurdran cocked his head. If anything, his grin widened more. "Now, would I be the type to go fixin' a game o' bones?"

"You must be weary after your long journey," she said, as if the question had not been asked. Tyrande, smiling back, gestured to two more priestesses. "They will take you to your quarters. Food and drink have been made ready."

"I thank ye fer all o' us!"

The dwarf gave both his hosts hearty handshakes, then led his party off after the guides. The encounter with Kurdran proved only a slight reprieve. As other representatives arrived, both night elves again became aware of just how much hung on the success of the gathering—and how much also hung on not only Varian Wrynn's arrival but his agreement on the most important matters as well.

There had still been no official word concerning the king of Stormwind's coming, and while both trusted Shandris's report, they could not help but grow concerned. With the arrival of each other faction, the thought that perhaps something had happened grew stronger.

When it seemed clear that no more ships would arrive for some time, the duo gratefully retired. There were no official audiences: Tyrande had wanted the emissaries to relax first, the better for their minds to be calm for the upcoming debates.

"No one spoke of his own realm's troubles," the archdruid noted as they neared the temple. "Perhaps that will not be a situation during the gathering."

"Do you really think so?"

Malfurion shook his head. "No. Not really."

Their conversation ended as both noticed a pair of conspicuous figures waiting outside the temple. Even from a distance, their brilliant garments marked them as Highborne.

"Archmage Mordent," Tyrande greeted politely. The Highborne leader was slightly thinner than his companion, and his face was more lined. "Var'dyn. To what do we owe this unexpected pleasure?"

Neither Highborne gave any indication that there

might have been some hint of sarcasm on her part. They knew the high priestess well enough to know that she treated them respectfully.

"Var'dyn here insisted that we come. I knew you had other pressing matters to attend to, but it seems the only way to assuage his concerns and those of the younger, more impatient ones."

"Is something amiss?"

The younger Highborne cut in. "The perfect question, save that instead of *something*, you might say *someone*!"

"Mind your place!" Mordent insisted to his protégé. "There can be a hundred innocent reasons for Thera'brin's absence!"

Malfurion took command of the conversation. "One of yours is missing, Archmage? When was he last seen?"

"He was one of those with me," Var'dyn answered. "No one noticed that he did not return until much later."

"Everyone was unaffected by the spellwork?"

"Of course! We knew what we were doing!" The younger Highborne looked very offended by any suggestion otherwise.

Mordent shook his head in disappointment. "Behave yourself! You will answer with the proper respect the archdruid and high priestess deserve."

Var'dyn grudgingly nodded. "My apologies, Archdruid. Continue, please."

"Does anyone recall where they last saw him?" Malfurion pressed.

"None remember him returning after the spellwork. I asked all of them."

The archdruid considered what Var'dyn had said, then turned to his mate. "I had best deal with this now."

"I think so. Please be cautious."

He smiled grimly. "I will be."

Var'dyn led Malfurion back to the location of the spell-casting. The mage obviously still distrusted anyone who was not one of the Highborne, but answered all of the archdruid's questions.

"And no one recalls at all where he even stood?"

"There was no need to."

Malfurion could not fault that logic, though it seemed to him that if the Highborne had as much concern for one another as they pretended, someone would at least have remembered *something* concerning the missing spell-caster's whereabouts. The archdruid knelt down near the area where the circle had formed. He waved his hand over the grass and murmured to the blades.

Have you seen? Malfurion asked of them. *Have you seen?*

The grass was eager to speak with him, for no one generally asked any favor, but it could only state that some group of creatures had tread upon it. It was the answer that Malfurion had expected, but despite not having learned anything, he still thanked the grass.

"I cast spells over the area but found no clue," Var'dyn offered.

"Did everyone head in the same general direction after I departed?"

"Why would we go any other? You think we want to wander into those humans you have got settled farther out?" Var'dyn did not hide his contempt.

Malfurion chose to ignore the tone. "And Thera'brin returned alone?"

The mage looked impatient. "You have asked this before."

"And I will ask it again, if I have to. You would be surprised how an answer can suddenly change." The archdruid slowly rose, then, after catching his breath, started off in the direction that he recalled most of the Highborne heading. "Do you remember your own path back?"

"Of course."

"Lead on."

With a shrug, Var'dyn obeyed. He pushed through the underbrush, Malfurion right behind him.

As they walked, the archdruid continued to reach out to the flora, speaking to various trees, bushes, and more . . . but with the same predictable lack of results. This was not a use of his skills for which even Malfurion was prepared.

"Are we done here?" asked Var'dyn at last.

"I see no reason for you to stay. I would like to survey the area a bit more."

"As you like." The Highborne departed without another word.

Sighing, Malfurion looked over the territory. In truth, he could think of little else he could do, but he had not wanted to give up in front of the Highborne. He suspected that Var'dyn had not quite shown him the path that the Highborne had followed. But even if Malfurion had known the precise path, it was doubtful that he would have gleaned anything useful from the plant life. The flora had taken notice of the spellwork but had otherwise paid no mind to the creatures involved in it once it had ceased.

One of the largest trees shifted its branches. In doing so, it spoke to the archdruid.

Someone was watching him from deeper in the forest.

Without even turning, Malfurion set the forest in motion to deal with the spying eyes. The trees in that direction bent down, their branches creating an impenetrable wall around the hidden observer's vicinity. At the same time, the underbrush sprouted, ensuring that it would tangle in his or her footing. Flowers, suddenly blooming, released clouds of pollen.

With easy steps, the archdruid strode toward the area. As he neared, he heard not only futile struggling but also coughing.

The flora gave way to him, creating a passage just wide enough. Malfurion held his staff ready, although in truth he feared little.

A figure became visible as the foremost trees straightened and the underbrush shifted. He continued to cough and also sought to rub his eyes clear. The pollen, while seemingly insignificant, had invaded both his lungs and his eyes with effectiveness.

Malfurion gestured. A selective wind swirled around the other figure. With the direction that only Malfurion could give it, it not only blew the pollen from the other's gaze but also provided fresh air that helped lessen the coughing.

Through bloodshot eyes, Eadrik stared at the night elf.

"A-Archdruid!" The human sneezed. "Praise be! I thought some monstrous creature had me!"

"Merely a precaution. When others are spying on me, I like to know who they are."

Genn's man looked aghast. "*Spying* on you? Hardly

that! I was just on a hunt. I flushed out the prey, but lost it around here. I thought I heard it in that direction"—he pointed where Malfurion had come from—"and a moment later the entire land seemed to fall upon me!"

Malfurion gestured, and the rest of the barrier vanished. He need not have made any motion, but felt it was good to further remind Eadrik of just whom he faced and why it might be wise to speak truthfully. Of course, Malfurion intended no true harm to the human, but keeping Eadrik off balance might provide the night elf with some information.

"You are far from the encampment, Eadrik. It must have been quite the hunt to bring you this far. Now . . . would you like to explain again?"

The Gilnean looked away. Malfurion could all but read him. Eadrik feared betraying his lord in even the slightest manner.

"Your loyalty is commendable, but if you do not tell me now, I must demand the truth from Genn. With the summit imminent, any question I have concerning Gilneas's application to rejoin the Alliance might tilt matters in a direction neither he nor I would prefer."

The human swallowed, then finally nodded. "It's nothing, Archdruid! I wasn't meaning to watch you at all! It's just that you happened to be here—happened to be here with one of them. . . ."

"One of . . . the Highborne? You have been watching the Highborne?"

Swallowing again, Eadrik continued: "My lord knows some of their history from you and others. He distrusts whatever influence they might have."

It was something Malfurion had heard before. Those

previous to state this belief had all been night elves, though.

"No slight was meant to you," the human quickly added. "My lord has the greatest respect for your abilities and word."

"Then he may take my word that the Highborne are of no concern to Gilneas. That should keep him from sending you or anyone else on unnecessary excursions."

Eadrik bowed his head. "Yes, Archdruid."

Malfurion took on a kinder tone. "I know that you are all on edge due to the summit. It *will* go well."

"We understand."

"Please give Genn my best."

The human gave a short bow, then scurried into the forest. Malfurion frowned and turned toward Darnassus. He believed that Eadrik had told the truth when he had said that Genn Greymane distrusted the Highborne. The archdruid also believed that Gilneas had not had anything to do with the one mage's disappearance.

But what Malfurion Stormrage *also* believed was that this incident somehow was tied to the summit . . . and possibly the desired failure of it.

9

A FINAL FAREWELL

The funeral for Shalasyr was a short, relatively modest affair despite Tyrande's desire to see Jarod's bride honored appropriately. That had been due to Jarod's choice: he had felt that Shalasyr would have not wanted much pomp and circumstance. She had preferred simplicity, and he believed that included her final rites. Of course, there was also the nagging guilt that perhaps Jarod had insisted on the shorter ceremony simply so as to lessen his agony a bit.

Attendance was limited to those who had known her best. The high priestess stood behind the funeral bier upon which the body of Shalasyr had been placed. The light of Elune shone down through the temple ceiling, focusing on both Jarod's beloved and Tyrande.

"Darkness covered us in the beginning," she uttered, "and we could not see. We cried for guidance and the moon shone down bright upon us. Her soft light not only illuminated the night for us but also gave comfort. Her light touched us from within, enabling us to see even when the moon was not visible. . . ."

Whether this was entirely fact was not something debated among the night elves. What the high priestess stated concerned as much the souls of her people as it did actual events. What no one could argue with was that the Mother Moon took special care with her favored children, and they were grateful to her for that.

Jarod knelt at the forefront, his gaze never leaving Shalasyr's beautiful, almost ethereal face. She could have been a marble statue, so perfect did she seem to him. His mate looked utterly at peace, even appearing to wear the hint of a smile.

"Now," Tyrande went on, "we ask that the Mother Moon guide our sister Shalasyr on her sacred journey and that her ancestors and loved ones who have gone before her will make her welcome. . . ."

Jarod heard nothing after that. He saw only his life with Shalasyr and all the mistakes that he had made during it. He was grateful that she had put up with him despite all those mistakes when, had she remained behind, she could have been a revered priestess of the Mother Moon.

Tyrande raised her arms, reaching toward the moonlight. Jarod broke out of his reverie for a moment, then lost interest again.

He looked up a moment later as a silver aura suddenly radiated from Shalasyr's body.

No one else seemed to notice . . . or at least no one reacted. Jarod stared at the soft, comforting glow as it rose over his beloved. It took on the vague shape of a figure and slowly separated from the still form.

"*Shalasyr . . . ,*" Jarod murmured.

The shape paused and, to his mind, looked in his direction for the space of a single breath. Suddenly he recalled other tender moments in his time with his mate, in some cases moments he had not remembered in centuries. Jarod relived each as if it had happened only yesterday.

Shalasyr's spirit shrank in upon itself, becoming a tiny, glowing ball. It hovered a moment more, then moved as if drawn by the moonlight.

As the sphere swept into the moonlight, it *dissipated* . . . and Jarod felt Shalasyr's presence vanish at the same time.

Jarod let out a gasp, but, fortunately, no one paid him any mind. At some point Tyrande had lowered her arms, and from her expression it appeared that the ceremony was nearly finished.

Indeed, all that remained was for her and Jarod to lead the bier and a procession of mourners out of the temple, through the gardens, and into an area beyond the city. There a small party of druids, led by Malfurion, greeted them.

Tyrande spoke to all. "As Shalasyr's spirit has departed her mortal vessel, let that vessel now return its strength to the world. . . ."

The druids took up the body. With reverence, they set it into a soft patch of grass and small bushes. Two female druids lovingly adjusted Shalasyr so that she again looked as if she were only dreaming.

"Teldrassil welcomes this child," Malfurion intoned. "The world welcomes this child back."

The archdruid raised his staff. A soft wind swept through the area. The treetops gently swayed.

Around Shalasyr's body, shoots grew, then bloomed

into white and golden flowers. At first they simply outlined Jarod's mate, but then their numbers grew so great that they began to drape over her. More and more flowers blossomed, quickly spilling over her. The effect was a beautiful draping of the female night elf, and Jarod could not help thinking how fitting the sight was.

Her serene face was the last part to be covered by the foliage. The flowers continued to sprout, rising into a tremendous cornucopia of color. A rich, wondrous scent wafted past Jarod's nose, a scent that reminded him so much of Shalasyr.

Those who had come now paid their respects to him, then left. Soon there remained only a handful of observers, including Malfurion and Tyrande.

"This went as well as it could have," the archdruid offered.

"There will be more and more of these ceremonies as mortality catches up with us," Jarod returned, before Tyrande could say so herself. "I am honored that Shalasyr was one of the first. It made her . . . her departure a little easier to take, I admit." He bowed his head to the high priestess. "I must confess I was especially touched when you made it seem as if Shalasyr's spirit had risen up to join the Mother Moon. . . ."

Tyrande looked puzzled. "I planned no such thing. I would have been very afraid of offending you, Jarod." She gazed deep into his eyes. "You *saw* that happen?"

"Yes, but—"

"Elune favors you! I would envy your moment, save that I respect that she made it one between you and Shalasyr only."

"It . . . was not you?"

"No."

Jarod's eyes widened, but he quickly recovered. He glanced at the lingering attendees. "I was hoping Maiev would come."

Tyrande cleared her throat. "You should not take it personally. Your sister has been through much; there was a time when she and I could not face one another—"

The former guard captain frowned. "I know of it, High Priestess. She related part of it to me earlier. The rest I was told by some of those who knew my sister and me when we were young or who were privy to events."

"But only Malfurion and I, or Maiev herself, could tell you about what truly happened. . . ."

"I—I know that she was Illidan's jailor and that at some point she was his prisoner . . . and that he tortured her."

The high priestess looked sad. "I blame myself for so much that happened to Maiev. I should never have left her for so long in charge of Illidan's imprisonment."

"I should have realized more than you, my love," the archdruid countered. "He was my brother. My twin." To Jarod, he explained, "When Illidan was liberated—after so many millennia—it was as if her entire life had been for nothing. Her greatest purpose had become keeping him imprisoned. Maiev was all but shattered."

"Yes, that would be how my sister would react. There was never a greater love for her than her duty."

Tyrande took control of the story once more. "She was determined to hunt him down. It went from duty to obsession. Unfortunately, circumstances were not so simple; events happened that led to disaster for all of us. I tried to stop a threat and nearly lost my life to it. Rather than come to my aid, Maiev chose to pursue Illidan—"

"Just say that she chose to sacrifice you!" Malfurion blurted with revived anger.

"Mal! Remember yourself!" Tyrande's eyes went from her mate to Jarod.

The archdruid bowed his head to Maiev's brother. "Forgive me, Jarod. I should not put your sister in such a light, especially at this time. . . ."

"I care only for the truth . . . however terrible it might be."

"The truth is," the high priestess muttered with much sympathy, "that she convinced others, including Malfurion, that I was dead—swept away in a raging river—and that his brother was to blame. Nothing mattered but that Illidan be caught and finally made to pay for all his crimes."

She nearly succeeded, Jarod learned. But when Malfurion had seen the horror in Illidan's face when he had learned of what had happened to Tyrande, the plan had fallen apart. Through the confession of the mage Kael'thas—who would later become the guiding force behind the creation of the magic-addicted blood elves—they had then learned of Maiev's falsehood. The archdruid had kept Maiev rooted where she was while he and Illidan had gone on to rescue Tyrande. Afterward, Malfurion, feeling that he owed his twin for that, had been instrumental in seeing to Illidan's flight and exile into the otherworldly realm called Outland.

What felt like a chill wind coursed over Maiev's brother, making him briefly shiver. Jarod found it strange that neither the archdruid nor the high priestess noticed the cold. Then he realized the chill had actually come from within, from becoming more aware as to how his sister's sense of duty had relentlessly driven her on.

"I know what happens next. My sister would not give up even then," Jarod remarked dourly. "She followed, and the rest of what I learned came to be. The pursuit through Outland, her capture and torture, and finally her part, alongside others, in the slaying of—pardon, Archdruid—of your brother."

Malfurion shook his head. "You have no reason to apologize. This is all knowledge you should have—if not from us, then from Maiev."

"For a time, we thought her dead . . . as we had thought you, Jarod." The high priestess looked down. "Her Watchers had all but perished due to her obsession. When Maiev did return, there were bitter feelings and mistrust. Her mind had been ravaged, yet she endured. Her resilience is one reason we were able to make amends, Jarod. There is much to admire about your sister and much we owe her despite all that happened." Tyrande put a comforting hand on his arm.

"It is kind of you to say that." Jarod shifted uncomfortably. "If I may, I would like to spend some time here alone."

"Of course. We must return, anyway. More of our guests are arriving."

The former commander nodded. "May all go well with the summit."

"We can only hope."

The high priestess and the archdruid each respectfully bowed to Jarod, then left him by the burial site. He watched them depart, aware that he had not been told everything. However, none of that truly mattered now. All he cared about was this final place of rest for his Shalasyr.

Jarod knelt by the flowers. Their scent touched his soul

and immediately made him think of tender moments with his mate. He imagined her with him.

And at last, with the visual evidence of Shalasyr laid to rest, and with his mind now forced to think beyond the moment, Jarod Shadowsong looked to the flowers and quietly asked, "So what becomes of *me*?"

Malfurion did not speak until they were far from Jarod, and even then he kept his voice low. "You were not honest . . . at least, not fully. You did not tell him everything about the conflict between you and Maiev when she reappeared."

"It was not necessary. Maiev and I understand one another. Her devotion to duty is not something to be taken lightly. She has made amends and that is the end of it."

"I am glad, but then, why did you not tell him more?"

Tyrande smiled softly. "That right belongs to Maiev."

Their attention was caught by a young priestess moving toward them. Her expression was anxious.

"High Priestess," she greeted, bowing. "There are more arrivals below . . . apparently from a submarine."

"A submarine. That means the gnomes have arrived too. Almost everyone is here, then," Malfurion said.

Tyrande nodded. "There is no sign of any ship from Stormwind?"

"No, High Priestess."

"I see." Tyrande exhaled. "Thank you for the news. We shall go directly to the portal. Have attendants ready for our new guests."

"Yes, High Priestess." The other female rushed off to obey.

"He will come," the archdruid offered. "He *has* to."

"That is what Shandris indicated . . . but if Varian Wrynn is coming, he is waiting until the very last moment. We cannot very well hold off the summit until we know with all certainty."

"No . . . but there will be little point to it if he does not come."

"Now, Mal . . ."

They did not discuss the point more. Returning to the portal, the night elves waited for the gnomes. As the pause lengthened, Malfurion and his mate looked at each other in curiosity and not a little concern.

"Could one of their devices have gone off down there?" the archdruid finally asked.

"Someone likely would have come through to report it."

"Assuming anyone *could* . . ."

The portal abruptly shimmered again. With some relief, they watched for the gnomish leader to step through.

But what took shape within at first looked like nothing with which the archdruid, at least, was familiar. It had two long legs bent back like a bird's, a stout, round carriage, and what seemed two pairs of arms, the upper ones much smaller than the lower duo. For its size and girth, it also appeared to have a relatively tiny head.

The figure fully formed, and despite all his concerns, Malfurion could not help chuckling quietly at the newcomer.

The bald gnome had the large-nosed, round face of his ilk and in some manner resembled a short, fat human, although there was no known link between the two races. This particular gnome, despite being elder in status, seemed as animated as a child. He was not so tall—in fact, standing, he was a foot shorter than Kurdran and certainly barely a third of the latter's bulk. Malfurion had to make all these assumptions from past visits, for most of the gnome was hidden by what had first appeared to be his body and was instead some fantastical *walking* device.

The newcomer raised a pair of odd goggles, then peered at the night elves with inquisitive eyes. "High Priestess Tyrande Whisperwind and Archdruid Malfurion Stormrage!" the gnome rattled off at a breathtaking rate of speech. "I am pleased to be here!"

"High Tinker Gelbin Mekkatorque, you are most welcome," Tyrande declared.

Gelbin tugged on his short white beard in thought, then grinned. The machine marched him forward until he was within a yard of his hosts.

The huge right arm of the machine suddenly shot toward Malfurion. Although not frightened, the archdruid chose caution and took a step back. A three-fingered "hand" paused within a couple of inches of his chest.

"Oh, do excuse me! I've been trying these experimental arm attachments for the newest mechanostriders! Still fine-tuning the movements! I only meant to have it shake hands!"

Steeling himself, Malfurion reached to the mechanical hand. The gnome shifted a lever and the hand gripped the night elf's own.

Tyrande let out a slight gasp of concern, but Malfurion simply did as the high tinker suggested, shaking the walker's hand. The moment that was done, the fingers released their hold on the night elf, and the arm retracted.

With clinical interest, Gelbin Mekkatorque leaned

over and asked, "How was the pressure? Any fractures or breaks?"

"No . . . none at all."

"Ah, finally!" Gelbin sat back in triumph.

Behind the walker, other gnomes stepped through the portal. Unlike their leader, they came in on foot, although all wore objects or gear that clearly were devices of their own manufacture. They peered up at the high tinker, then at the night elves.

Tyrande greeted the rest of the party, then said to Gelbin, "We have food and drink prepared . . . and space set aside for your . . . *endeavors*."

"Wonderful! We've still some equipment to bring up! Will we be near where your Sentinels practice their archery? Dwendel here has a new possible weapon that may be able to fire fifty arrows in a minute . . . if it would just stop doing so in every direction each time."

Dwendel, a redheaded gnome clearly much younger than most of his party, looked a bit sheepish.

"I have seen to those arrangements as well, High Tinker. If you will follow these Sisters . . ."

Making some adjustments, Gelbin did as she bade. The walker strode like a large, flightless bird after the priestesses. Gelbin's companions—the huge sacks each carried clanking ominously—tried to keep up as best they could.

Watching the gnomes, Tyrande murmured, "That is nearly everyone but Stormwind."

"Yes. For the sake of the others, we will not be able to hold off."

The high priestess looked disturbed. "Elune would *not* have granted me that vision if it did not have significance to the summit. *Varian Wrynn* must arrive soon."

"We can only—"

A terrible uproar erupted from the direction of where the gnomes had gone. Without hesitation, both night elves rushed to see what was happening.

They found Gelbin and his party confronted by Drukan and several of the Dark Iron dwarves. The dwarves had their axes and blades out and their faces were filled with fury. Gelbin had the arms of his walker extended toward the Dark Iron emissary, but it was clear that the high tinker was not proposing that Drukan shake hands.

Behind Gelbin, the rest of the gnomes had drawn a variety of odd-looking but no less sinister devices. Even Gelbin himself had stashed on his mount a weapon the night elves recognized as Wrenchcalibur—so named in part because it was roughly shaped like the tool. The complex series of cogs, pistons, runes, and levers somehow enabled it to serve as a good mace.

The other weapons were not so recognizable to the archdruid and the high priestess. Some resembled blunderbusses, while a few made absolutely no sense. However, in the hands of gnomes, they could only be dangerous . . . even to their wielders.

"—yer tongue I'll cut out and slice up fer meat between me bread!" growled Drukan, clearly having uttered several threats already. "And that infernal device ye sit on will make a good still fer strong dwarven spirits!"

"I am still very much in the early stages of testing the strength components of this mechanism," Gelbin dryly responded. "It would be fascinating to discover just what force would be required for it to divide you in half!"

Drukan's followers muttered, and two started for the gnomes. Drukan angrily waved the pair back.

"What is the meaning of this?" Malfurion called out in the hopes of quickly distracting the two sides.

The Dark Irons seemed no more pleased to see him than they did the gnomes. A fiery-eyed Drukan waved his axe at Gelbin. "This—this gnome tried tae run me over with his stinkin' toy!"

"And I said that the incident was purely accidental!"

"Cease yer babbling!" Drukan took a step toward the gnome. Both sides leaned in toward the inevitable struggle.

But a brilliant silver glow coming between them startled the two factions. The dwarves and the gnomes pulled back.

Tyrande lowered her hands and the glow dissipated. Striding between Drukan and Gelbin, she calmly said, "Now, I am certain that this is a misunderstanding. The high tinker had already admitted that his creation had some corrections that needed to be made, and perhaps should have taken those into account before moving among others. Also, Master Drukan may be wary of his surroundings, but he should understand that he was invited here, and that means that his safety is guaranteed by me and my husband, as it is for all honored guests. I only ask in turn that he respect that this guarantee applies to the others as well."

"Yes . . . yes . . . I suppose I should be a bit more cautious until the controls are fine-tuned," Gelbin responded. He frowned. "Although I am growing dubious about the worth of these arm attachments. . . ."

Drukan put away his weapon. With a grunt he said, "The fairness o' the high priestess and the archdruid is known even tae us. The journey's been long. I'll leave it at that."

To the gnomes' escort, Tyrande said, "Sisters, I believe you were leading High Tinker Gelbin and his party to their quarters?"

They took the hint and immediately guided the gnomes on before hostilities could boil over again. At the same time Drukan gave the high priestess a cursory bow and led his companions off.

"And so it begins," the archdruid muttered. "The pretense that all is well with each member of the Alliance is starting to unravel. Even the Dark Irons should have been able to understand that Gelbin meant no harm, and the gnomes should have not become so defensive so quickly. Their nerves were clearly already frayed before their arrival."

"No one wishes to show weakness, my love, even if in these extraordinary times it would certainly be reasonable to do so. We already knew how terrible things are in some of the other regions; that they have all come here is a sign that, despite everything, the Alliance holds together."

Malfurion shook his head. "But to what extent?"

She took his arm and led him off to the temple. "That," the high priestess answered soothingly, "we will find out come the morrow. Until then, there is little point in worrying too much."

Malfurion frowned but said nothing. As he and Tyrande headed off, though, he took one last look at the portal.

But the one figure he hoped would materialize did not do so . . . and the archdruid wondered if he truly ever would.

10

THE BANQUET

With all having arrived save Stormwind, it behooved Malfurion to indeed see that the summit began. In order to build the mood to a positive level, he and Tyrande had agreed to host a banquet for all the guests. Accustomed to dealing with diurnal races, the night elves held the dinner banquet at sunset in an open area just beyond the confines of Darnassus. With food and drink of countless varieties set before them and the tranquil forest nearby, the rulers, emissaries, and their staffs gradually relaxed. Even Drukan went out of his way and permitted food not brought by his vessel to be served to the Dark Irons . . . but only after his chosen taster had verified that nothing was poisoned.

Night elf musicians played not only music composed by their own race but also favored works from among the peoples represented by the guests. There was only one common thread between the songs: all of them had been chosen to stir the heart, to suggest promise in the future.

Yet, there were still undertones of trouble brewing. Malfurion had spoken with more than one representative and in the process sought to verify his suspicions concerning the state of each realm. What he had learned at times discouraged him far more than his confident face reflected.

Among the dwarves, food was growing scarce, and old, bitter rivalries threatened to engulf the race. To add to the troubles, many of their underground passages had collapsed during the Cataclysm and still needed to be cleared. Thus far, matters had not come to a head, but they needed only one incident to have that happen.

The human domains also had to rebuild, and some of them were arguing over where current borders existed. Food and shelter were common problems, and Tyrande and Malfurion had already promised what aid the night elves could offer. Sisters of Elune and druids now journeyed through each part of the Alliance, using their abilities to heal both the people and nature.

But, from what Malfurion had heard, it was not enough.

Still, overall, the banquet began to have the effect that he sought. The dwarves did not even argue among themselves, and the gnomes had not set off any disastrous inventions.

Seated by Tyrande, Malfurion looked at the empty places to his right. "Genn indicated he would be arriving soon," the high priestess informed her husband. "Eadrik just came with the message."

"I thought I saw Eadrik, but I was not certain. There should be—" He hesitated as he caught sight of a shape nearing the banquet. "Odd. Who is that approaching now? It looks like—a *draenei!*"

Tyrande squinted—something she was having to do more and more often—in the direction he was staring. "Not just any draenei! That is *Velen*."

Others began to notice the extremely tall figure—he stood nearly a foot taller than Malfurion—in the golden robes. His skin was alabaster white and his legs ended in thick cloven hooves. The Prophet had silver hair that reached past the shoulders and was set in ornate braids. He also had a matching beard that hung nearly to his waist.

Velen's eyes were a brilliant blue and literally *glowed*. But most arresting of all was the luminous sigil just above his head, a sign of the gift he had been granted from the mystical naaru, energy beings from beyond Azeroth, beyond the otherworldly realm of Outland. They were creatures with an affinity to the Holy Light, of which Velen was now the chief prophet of the draenei. Other draenei wielded the power of the gift, but none so much as the figure before the assembly. In fact, the Light not only emanated from the sigil but at certain times almost seemed to faintly *surround* the august arrival . . . though it could have also merely been some trick of the eye.

Velen himself radiated timelessness, with only wrinkles around his ancient eyes. However, up close, one could see minute cracks in his alabaster skin, as if he were a statue hewed aeons ago. Malfurion did not know how old the draenei was. Older than any night elf alive, that much was true.

Even Drukan stood as Velen joined the banquet. Almost as one, the guests dipped their heads or bowed in respect. There was something about the draenei that spoke of an inner peace and knowledge that most could only dream of attaining. Small wonder, since Velen was not only leader of his people but a priest as well.

The draenei raised the crystalline head of a long, purple staff in Malfurion's and Tyrande's direction. Both the large crystal and the smaller one at the bottom of the staff briefly shimmered brighter. "Hail to you, Archdruid and High Priestess! Forgive this intrusion. . . ."

"The presence of the Prophet is never an intrusion," Tyrande returned as solemnly, speaking to the others as well as their new guest, "and Velen himself is ever welcome here as a friend to all. We are all grateful for the aid he and the draenei gave us during the recent conflict with the demons of the Burning Legion."

The priest bowed his head. "It is we the draenei who must thank the Alliance for taking us in, and even more so for standing against the foulness of the Burning Legion! Do not think so little of that! Never had there been a world that could stave off the demons not merely once, but *more!*"

Tyrande once more acknowledged this for all in attendance, but insisted more personally to the Prophet, "The final victory might not have been ours if not for you and your people, Velen. None here will deny that, either."

"I am honored that you think so, but know that we will always be indebted to Azeroth. Thus, I come to promise you now that the draenei will do all we can to help the various lands of the Alliance in whatever capacity we may best."

There was startled rumbling from the attendees, the night elves included. Malfurion leaned forward. "Your people are not returning to Outland? We just assumed . . ."

Velen smiled as if well aware that he would be faced

with this very question. "Some have been sent back to revitalize our civilization there, but the rest of us will remain here on Azeroth for so long as we are needed."

The high priestess looked around at the others. "I think that I speak for all of us when I say that this is a noble gesture for which we can only express again our own gratitude."

Most of the other representatives of the Alliance murmured their agreement. The Dark Irons were the only ones to look not entirely satisfied with this revelation. Velen looked pleased at this overall acceptance.

"Please, join us, revered one," Tyrande added, immediately signaling the servers to add a seat next to Malfurion and her. The two made certain that none of the other representatives would be deprived of space for this unexpected addition.

"I would be happy to join all my friends here. A little water is all I need."

Despite that insistence, Tyrande had some food and wine also brought. Some slight surprise at the announcement aside, the draenei was a welcome guest.

The banquet settled down. The mood lightened. Tyrande exchanged a hopeful look with Malfurion.

From their right, just beyond Velen, Kurdran let out a hearty laugh at something the draenei said, drawing the night elves' attention. The Prophet looked mildly amused at the effect his words had had on the dwarf. Kurdran turned to tell one of his countrymen something in regard to what he had heard from Velen—and paused to warily eye a party approaching. At the same time, the musicians, evidently also noting the newcomers, paused.

Genn Greymane had arrived at last.

The king of Gilneas was flanked by four of his people, three men and one woman. Eadrik was one of the escort, and he at present listened to something that Genn whispered.

As before, the Gilneans looked like any other humans, though Genn's escort obviously consisted of seasoned fighters. If not for his confident stride and bearing, Genn might have simply been one more member of the band; he wore little ornamentation marking his regal status. The most evident sign of his rank was the Gilnean crest embossed on his shirt just over the heart, which Genn absently touched as he entered the gathering. The downfall of his kingdom had very much humbled the once-haughty monarch.

If there was anything to distinguish the Gilneans from most other humans, it was a wariness in their gazes as they neared. It was not a look of distrust but rather of defiance. Yet, defiance not against anyone in particular but at the world in general.

As they reached the center of the banquet, Genn raised his hand shoulder high. The other Gilneans stopped. The king took a half a dozen steps more, then halted in front of the night elves.

"My apologies. The delay was unavoidable." His eyes fixed on Velen. "You must be Prophet Velen. I've heard much of you. I wasn't aware you'd be here. I am Genn Greymane."

The Prophet bowed his head. "Greetings, King of Gilneas. I am also familiar with you."

Tyrande and Malfurion rose, the former declaring, "Welcome, Genn Greymane! Please take your place with us!"

"Before I do, I must say something to all here."

His announcement spurred glances of curiosity and concern among the other leaders and emissaries. Malfurion fought off a frown.

"Please speak, Genn," the archdruid finally encouraged. "We will be glad to listen."

Malfurion's declaration quieted the others, though some, especially the Dark Irons, still watched with wariness and concern.

The king nodded. "I'll make this short. I made some terrible decisions years ago. I abandoned the Alliance for what I thought was the right course for my people. That proved to be a sorry mistake." He cleared his throat. "What I'm saying is that I thank you all for giving us this second chance."

With that, Genn bowed to the other guests, then led his party where they were to be seated. Rather than prolong what had clearly been an awkward moment for the human, Tyrande immediately signaled for the musicians to begin anew. She also made certain that the Gilneans were quickly fed and that the other guests had more drink and food brought to them.

The meal progressed. Personal conversations began to develop and a serious note crept into some aspects of the scene. Kurdran had shifted over to Tervosh to speak about something that caused the archmage to frown but nod. Across from them, Drukan watched with narrowed eyes, then returned to his food. A moment later, though, he rose and, to their surprise, went to speak privately with the high tinker.

"Do you think these conversations are a sign of hope or fragmentation?" Malfurion quietly asked his mate, his serene face belying his concern.

"Each of their lands is trying to recover, as even we are. They are no doubt attempting to see what they might be able to gain from others. In a sense, that might bring them together . . . but only if they do not feel that they have to sacrifice too much in turn."

"Which means that you think these conversations are both."

Tyrande touched his hand. "Yes, my love, unfortunately I do." She smiled slightly. "But at least they are talking, and that is something to work on—"

He noticed her look past him. "What is it?"

"There are two Sentinels seeking our attention."

The archdruid casually turned in that direction. *Seeking* their attention was an understatement; clearly only the fact that so many officials from the Alliance were gathered here prevented the pair from racing toward its leaders. The two had purposely kept where the vast majority of the banquet could not see them. Both gripped their weapons, frequently looking over their shoulders at something behind them.

"Stormwind, perhaps?" he asked.

The high priestess rose. "If so, from their stances, it cannot be good news."

He surveyed their guests, then muttered, "I am coming with you."

She made no move to stop him. Velen looked up at her as she stepped away, nodding as if to show that if they needed his support—whatever the matter—he would give it.

Some of the other guests watched as they departed, but the night elves pretended not to notice. Moving with measured steps, they finally reached the two Sentinels.

And there they discovered that behind the pair stood at least half a dozen more, along with a very dour Maiev.

Tyrande wasted no time: "Speak."

But it was Maiev, not the lead Sentinel, who spoke. Stepping forward, she answered, "High Priestess . . . there is a body."

The archdruid looked grim. "Show us."

Tyrande gave orders to one of her senior priestesses to take care of the guests. That problem dealt with, she and Malfurion followed the others from the vicinity of the banquet.

Maiev and the Sentinels headed directly for the temple.

"My decision," the Watcher informed them. "I thought it best."

"You did right," the high priestess acknowledged.

In one of the lesser-used inner chambers, they at last came across two Sentinels guarding a night elf–size form covered in cloth.

"Who?" Tyrande finally asked, unwilling to wait even long enough for the makeshift shroud to be drawn away.

Maiev removed her helmet and tucked it under her arm. Jarod's sister stared directly at Malfurion. "A Highborne. The one, I am told, you were informed went missing."

One of the Sentinels uncovered the face. As Maiev had said, it was a Highborne. Malfurion knew immediately which one too.

"Thera'brin . . . ," the archdruid rasped. "Where was he discovered?"

"Not all that far from where I and the other Watchers practice," Maiev responded with a scowl.

Tyrande looked grave. "He did not die by accident, did he?"

Maiev reached down and pulled the cloth further. The savage gaps just under the Highborne's chin greeted the shocked duo. "Only if he decided to slit his own throat twice—the second for *pleasure*, I assume"—she straightened—"and made sure that a missive we found with him remained pinned to his body when he fell."

She spoke in a clinical tone, as if describing the general shape and appearance of a stone rather than the murder of one of their own. It did not at all surprise either Malfurion or Tyrande to hear her speak so: Maiev was ever precise, ever to the point, when performing her duties.

"What did this note say?" the archdruid demanded, a new chill running through him.

Maiev was prepared. She handed him a ragged piece of parchment stained in great part with the unfortunate Thera'brin's blood. On it had been scrawled in what also appeared to be the mage's bodily fluids a message written in a long-disused style of night elf script that stirred memories of the days when Zin-Azshari was still the capital and the evil of Queen Azshara was as yet unknown.

Suffer Not Traitors . . .

"We knew that there would be those who would never forgive them," Tyrande said.

"But we thought that they would listen to reason, at least up to the point of not going through with such a heinous act." The archdruid returned his gaze to Maiev. "Found near where you practice?"

"Yes. Either someone thought him a gift or they decided that the Watchers could be blamed."

Her declaration was not without merit. Maiev and her Watchers were among the many uncomfortable with the thought of the Highborne's eventual return to the fold.

"This will not remain a secret," Tyrande said. "And should not."

Malfurion agreed. "More important, we must find the assassins and deal with them before this grows worse. The timing can be no coincidence! This is not just about the Highborne; this is meant to cause chaos during the summit."

"You are right, my love. I will ask Shandris—"

Suddenly kneeling before Tyrande, Maiev bent her head and declared, "Let me uncover the culprits! I know the facts better than any! I have investigated the body for all clues and studied the area in which it was found! There is nothing more anyone else could do. Give this matter to me! I swear I will do all in my power to see that those who would seek to foment unrest among our kind will be dealt with!"

Tyrande looked to Malfurion, who nodded. The high priestess gently put a hand on Maiev's shoulder. The kneeling night elf looked up, gaze intent.

"I can think of few more dedicated to our people and their needs. Take command of this investigation, Maiev, and do it with my blessing."

Some of the Sentinels did not look entirely pleased with this choice but held their peace.

Maiev looked as if Tyrande had granted her the greatest desire of her life. She rose and saluted the pair. "I will see this through, whatever sacrifice it must take!"

"I insist you take care, Maiev."

Jarod's sister grudgingly nodded, but her eyes did not show agreement. Both Tyrande and Malfurion were aware how focused Maiev could be when set upon a mission. In this case they needed that focus, and thus neither said more to discourage the warden from following through as she might need.

"The Highborne will want Thera'brin's body returned," Malfurion commented. "I think it best if I lead that effort. They already believe that the rest of us would rather see them wiped from the face of Azeroth; this will hardly improve their disposition."

"Do as you say." The high priestess touched his cheek. "But take care around them."

"You know that I will."

Maiev bowed her head again. "With your permission, I will begin this hunt immediately."

Tyrande nodded. Replacing her helmet, Maiev silently departed.

"I will send four Sentinels with you when you go to the Highborne," Tyrande informed her husband. "They will act as bearers for the body."

"Let me seek the aid of some of my calling. It might not be wise for the Highborne to be confronted by armed fighters just now."

She saw the wisdom in his choice. "Are you going to leave immediately?"

"Not just yet. I wish Velen's opinion on this and some other matters. I had not expected his arrival, but it may be that it was fortuitous. We will need his steady demeanor to keep temperatures from boiling over once all know of the murder. Every distrust among the various factions will suddenly rise to the forefront."

It was decided that the Sentinels would remain on guard here for as long as needed. Tyrande also summoned another pair of priestesses versed in the preserving arts to do what they could to maintain the freshness of the body.

Aware that they could not let the Highborne wait long before being told of the discovery, the archdruid and the high priestess quickly returned to the banquet. They had feared that their absence might have caused a wariness to settle over the other participants, but, to their relief, everyone still seemed at ease. Part of that likely had to do with Velen, who had departed his seat to speak with the Dark Irons. What matter there was that would bring the draenei and the dwarves together, neither night elf could say, but Velen had somehow managed not only to keep Drukan distracted but also to make him feel cheered.

"The Light truly works in amazing ways," Malfurion murmured to his wife.

"And Velen is clearly schooled in the art of diplomacy." Tyrande hesitated as she saw another Sentinel approaching. "More news . . ."

The Sentinel saluted and immediately said, "High Priestess, Stormwind has arrived."

The news brought both relief and concern to Malfurion and his mate. Tyrande asked, "How long ago?"

"When I left with this news, they had just disembarked. I searched for you here, but could not find you."

The high priestess eyed her husband. "The attendants on duty at the portal have orders to guide the party to their quarters, but I should go and greet Varian. . . ."

To their other side, Genn Greymane's voice suddenly rose above the din. He had an audience that consisted of most of Kurdran's party. Genn, clearly much more relaxed due to not only the acceptance the others had shown but also the dwarven ale he had just finished downing, had begun regaling the others with some of his past battles against the Horde.

"The key was to keep our front united," the king was saying as Malfurion and Tyrande moved on toward Velen. "Split us apart, and we'd all be crow food! Each man knew that to falter would mean his comrades dying for his mistake, and none would have that! We let out the Gilnean battle cry—"

"Consisting of a pleading for mercy so great the orcs no doubt turned from the lot of you in disgust," said a mocking voice.

The effect of the words on Genn Greymane was immediate. He leapt up from the table, in his fury sweeping aside the food and drink before him without care to where or upon whom it landed. A dark cast fell upon his features, and for a moment he seemed to swell and even begin to change.

"Who dares spout such a monstrous slur upon me and Gilneas? Who?"

His outraged gaze swiftly pored over each and every person seated there, seeking the culprit. Most simply stared back, as stunned as he at the savage pronouncement. A few looked about anxiously.

And a few, such as Malfurion and Tyrande, looked from Genn Greymane to the direction from where the speaker actually stood. Malfurion took a step toward the commanding figure, but the high priestess stayed him with a hand.

The king of Gilneas caught their movement. He followed their eyes to his accuser.

"You . . ."

"And having swayed the orcs so eloquently, you no doubt did as all brave Gilneans do so well: skulked away and hid until the battle was over. . . ."

Genn clearly desired to lunge for his counterpart's throat. His hands grasped at the air as if already crushing in the windpipe. Yet, somehow he managed to stay his ground and simply growl.

For his reaction, he received nothing but a look of contempt from the newcomer, who then, with a much more polite manner, turned to the banquet's hosts and bowed.

"High Priestess Tyrande. Archdruid Malfurion. It's a pleasure to see you again," Varian Wrynn calmly remarked.

11

DARKENED HEARTS

"Never—never have I nor any of my warriors acted so basely!" Genn declared, visibly struggling with himself. "The bravery of Gilneas—"

"'Bravery'?" Varian Wrynn cut in. Tall, commanding, his features handsome in a brooding manner, the king of Stormwind was to his own people already a hero out of legend. He had, in point of fact, lived a remarkable and dangerous life that had not only for years separated him from those he most loved, but also left him for a time bereft of his memory. His trials made for rousing tales that bards could sing before swooning ladies. And his two long scars, one running across his cheeks and the bridge of his nose and the other descending down the left side of his face from the forehead to the cheek—both legacies of the several times he had barely escaped death—only added more flavor to those stories . . . stories for which Varian himself had no taste whatsoever. "The definition must be different in Gilneas from what it is in most other lands . . . the very opposite, I'd say."

The insinuation that Genn and his people were utter cowards proved too much for the elder monarch. His expression darkened. Some of those in his retinue growled low and seemed ready to move toward Varian, but Genn staved off their advance with a sharp glance.

Malfurion moved to intervene. "King Varian! We had no news of you and your retinue arriving below. . . ."

"I preferred it that way," the former gladiator answered, acting now as if Genn did not even exist. Varian shoved aside an unruly lock of dark brown hair. The eyes of a hunter surveyed each and every person in sight, Varian Wrynn ever instinctively marking those around him by their potential threat.

The archdruid purposely stood between the pair. "And your son? Is Anduin with you?"

"Naturally." Varian said it with such an absolute tone that Malfurion felt slightly foolish for asking, though many monarchs would have left their only heirs in the supposed safety of home rather than bring them on any sort of journey.

The king briefly tilted his head back. The night elf looked beyond Varian to where four members of the king's personal guard flanked a slightly shorter figure dressed in the regal blue and gold of Stormwind. Prince Anduin, his own blond hair cut short, bowed his head to the archdruid. He wore a high-collared shirt covered by mail that was in turn draped by the golden lion head crest of his kingdom. The prince was not armed save for a dagger at his belt, but with so many guards in Stormwind's party, his safety would have been ensured in almost any place, much less Darnassus.

In contrast to his father, who was every bit the fighter, Anduin was a studious youth. Moreover, there was an aura of selflessness that reminded Malfurion of only one other person present. Without thinking, Malfurion glanced over his shoulder at Velen.

To his surprise, the Prophet's eyes registered the same intense interest in the human boy. Velen sensed exactly what Malfurion did . . . perhaps more.

Genn was taking long, deep breaths that were designed to bring his temper back under control. Varian looked unimpressed by the other king's efforts.

The archdruid continued to try to defuse the tension between them. "King Varian. Forgive us for not being there to greet you! You, your son, and your companions are welcome to join the banquet immediately if you wish! Your seats await you, and food and drink will be shortly coming—"

"I'm not inclined to stay here," the monarch of Stormwind bluntly replied. "I sailed to Darnassus for the sake of the Alliance, not *him*." He indicated Genn. "If it's all the same to you, Archdruid, the journey was a tiring one, so I think I'll retire already. . . ."

Genn moved toward his counterpart again. In a lower tone he said, "Varian . . . let us talk. I did what I thought was best for my people; you must understand that! I never realized the full folly of my arrogance when I chose to build the wall and what it would mean, cutting off Gilneas from the outside. . . ."

Varian's gaze never left the archdruid. He said nothing to Genn.

This only stirred the king of Gilneas to further effort. "I swear an oath that we will be as brothers to all other members of the Alliance, that we will give aid in whatever manner needed! Gilneas will not shirk its duty! There will be no more loyal member, especially to its fellow human realm, Stormwind—"

"Stormwind wants no such brother at its back!" Varian burst out.

"Varian . . ." Malfurion murmured.

The younger king's body shook from fury. He lowered his gaze, staring bitterly at Genn from under his brow. "I didn't ask to wear the mantle of responsibility, to become the bearer of humanity's standard! It was enough to rule Stormwind and protect my son! But I did it because I had no choice! Who else was there? Not *Gilneas*! Stormwind, with Theramore at its side, has had to face the dangers . . . and now you want to come in under our wing and pretend you'll stand with us *this* time?"

"We will stand—"

"You needn't worry yourself, Greymane! Stormwind and I have done without you, without Gilneas . . . and certainly without the worgen . . . and we'll continue to do so! What you truly desire is redemption for your traitorous crimes, which you'll not get from me!"

"Gilneas was a sovereign nation. We seceded during a time of peace, not war, and for good reasons. You know that. As for the coming vote—"

However, Varian turned his back on the other human. "Excuse me, Archdruid and High Priestess. I will see you later. . . ."

Before Malfurion could even respond, Varian whirled back the way he had come and stalked off. In his wake followed his retinue.

Malfurion looked at Tyrande, who had already signaled

a pair of priestesses to hurry after King Varian. As she focused in Malfurion's direction, her eyes widened.

A low, animalistic snarl escaped from where Genn stood. The archdruid immediately returned his attention to the human.

Genn bared his teeth in a feral grin that stretched far beyond where human limits should have allowed. His body swelled. . . .

And then, again, the human regained control of himself.

"F-Forgive me, Archdruid," the sweating figure muttered. "I should've known better. I should've."

"I suggest you return to your seat and—"

"No. No, I can't." Genn gestured to Eadrik and the other Gilneans. With Genn in their lead, the party silently departed for the forest.

The other guests murmured among themselves. Tyrande indicated for the musicians to play again, but it was clear that the banquet would soon be winding down. The confrontation had eradicated the hopeful mood of the participants, a situation that Malfurion would have to work hard to correct.

However, as he turned to discuss this with his mate, he noticed that one member of Stormwind's party had not left: Anduin, who was at this moment quietly speaking with Velen.

As the night elves approached the pair, they heard the draenei saying, ". . . and what you know of the Light is indeed true, but that is only the slightest of its many facets, young Anduin! To fully appreciate the wonder of the Light, you must look at it from the perspective that best lets you see its full place in the universe and how it may become part of our very being! Such requires patience and learning. . . ."

"I can do that, but what I want—"

"Prince Anduin!"

Two of the king's personal guard had returned. Their flushed faces and hurried movements bespoke of the intense reprimand their monarch had no doubt given them upon discovering that his son was not with the party. The two burly soldiers barged past the night elves and came at their prince from opposing sides.

The one who had called to the prince—a hardened veteran with a nose that looked as if it had been broken more than once in battle—reached for Anduin, who did not hide his frustration as he rose to face the guards. "Prince Anduin! Your father was most upset when he discovered that you'd neglected to follow us! The king has commanded that you come immediately!"

Anduin looked as if he were ready to snap something at the unfortunate guards—who all knew were only doing their duty and likely feared being punished—but held back. With a resigned nod, the prince joined his two keepers. He briefly turned to face the night elves and the others, bowing to each group. Only then did he silently gesture to the two anxious men to lead him to his father.

"Young Anduin has a quiet strength," Velen commented once the boy was gone. "A pity his father seeks to cage him as he does himself."

"Varian nearly lost him more than once," the archdruid remarked. "His fear that Anduin might vanish or be taken is not unfounded." Malfurion frowned deeply. "Nor are his harsh words to Genn Greymane, I am sorry to say."

"Genn will make amends for all," Tyrande interjected. "You know that as well as I. We already know how much he sacrificed to get matters to this point."

"But will it be worth it in the end? They nearly attacked one another. Genn came very close to losing control of himself, and with some reason!"

"Perhaps we should discuss this at another time," the high priestess commented. "Velen, if you could—" But to the surprise of both night elves, the Prophet had surreptitiously departed the conversation, almost as if he knew the two were about to enter subjects best discussed purely between them.

"Well, we can trust Velen, that is for certain," Malfurion murmured. Then, sobering, he added, "Tyrande, before you speak, I have to tell you—"

"He is the *one*, Mal."

"I know Elune tells you so and I understand that it should be so, but you saw him! Varian could perhaps be the leader the Alliance needs, yet he also stands a very good chance of becoming the one who further guides it to disaster!"

"Varian is troubled, I agree—"

"More than *troubled*, though with good cause." The archdruid tugged on his beard in contemplation. "And his disdain for Genn strikes me as being as much for himself as it is for the king of Gilneas. There was that in his tone that hinted more of self-reproach. . . ."

"I heard that, also." The high priestess casually glanced to her side. "The others are beginning to leave. The banquet is over."

"The banquet was a *debacle*. The others here have seen Varian proclaim the worgen unfit to be part of the Alliance! We cannot let that notion stand. . . ."

"I will go speak with the others. Perhaps you can do something with Varian."

"Perhaps." Malfurion could not hide his doubt concerning such a hope.

She put her hand on his. "Elune will guide us. Have faith."

He grunted. "I of all people should, should I not?"

"Go. Speak with Varian."

Malfurion knew better than to argue when she used that tone. They kissed, then the archdruid, with a bow to the remaining guests, followed after the king of Stormwind.

To someone who had slept in bug-infested cages and grimy, blood-soaked cells during his days as a slave and gladiator, the woodland quarters offered by his hosts seemed far too soft in comparison. Even Varian's chambers back home were not nearly so calm, so *peaceful*. The king considered departing Darnassus for the relative familiarity of his confining quarters aboard ship, but respected his hosts enough not to insult them . . . or at least not insult them any more than he had with his denunciation of Genn Greymane.

Varian had no regrets there. In fact, he had a rather great satisfaction. He knew that he had behaved badly, but in Greymane he had found an outlet for some of the fire ever raging within him.

There was a knock at the door. The night elves had gone out of their way to make their guests feel at home, and so the chambers set aside for Varian and his retinue were fairly human in design and accommodations.

Unfortunately, they still had that "nature" feel he always associated with those of the archdruid's race. Far better were the oppressive stone walls of the keep.

One of the guards cautiously opened the door. Even in Darnassus, one did not take chances. Varian had already caught wind of something amiss, something that had happened just before his arrival.

Anduin and the two bodyguards sent to retrieve him entered. Varian, his heart lightening, went straight to his son.

"You had me worried!" To the two men, he growled, "Let this not happen again! Should any harm come to my son, I will have—"

"Leave it be, Father."

Anduin spoke quietly, ever calmly, but still he did momentarily what no one else could: silence the king.

Recovering, Varian said, "Anduin, you must understand! You are the prince of Stormwind! Nowhere, not even here, should be considered safe enough for you to go wandering off! You always need at least a guard with you."

"Yes. I'm not very good at defending myself," the prince retorted. "I'm not the great warrior you are. You and Magni have already seen how badly I handle a sword, even in practice."

"I didn't mean—"

The prince sighed. It was a sound Varian heard often and usually because of something he had done out of concern for his son. "No, you don't. You never do, Father. I'm back, safe and sound. As usual."

"Anduin—" Against any foe, the king could stand resolute in his next move. Against his son, he constantly floundered.

"Good night, Father." The prince walked on, following his guards to the room set aside for him.

As unsettling as the conversation no doubt had been to their guards, Anduin had actually kept it from getting worse by cutting it off. Varian knew that—could even appreciate it—but that still did not ease the sting of his son's obvious reprimand.

Now the serenity of the night elven dwelling finally proved too much for him. "Stay here," he commanded the guards, aware as much as they that he was placing them in a similar position as when Anduin had not remained with the party. "I need to walk."

They knew better than to argue. No longer paying them any heed, Varian strode out. However, like in his quarters, the tranquility of the capital did nothing to ease his heart. Instead, he stared at the forest beyond.

His pace quickened. The wilderness beckoned.

"King Varian! I was just coming to see you."

The human hid his disappointment, though for a moment his eyes lingered longingly on the trees beyond the city.

"Archdruid," he responded, finally acknowledging his host. "My thanks for our quarters. They will do just fine."

"Which is why you had to flee them at the first chance," the night elf returned with a slight smile. "Please. I will not stand on ceremony with you. Call me Malfurion."

"Then I'll ask you to call me Varian."

"As you wish. If you do not mind, I hoped to have a word with you."

The lord of Stormwind exhaled. "My sincerest apologies for ruining your banquet."

"The banquet is of no consequence. The gathering is.

You appreciate bluntness, Varian. I am more concerned about your confrontation with Genn."

The mere mention of Greymane's name stirred the embers within. Varian's pulse pounded. "I'd prefer not to speak about that, Malfurion."

The night elf would not be dissuaded. "Varian, I must ask you to consider everything that happens before, during, and after the summit in light of what Azeroth has become due to the Cataclysm. Each choice we make has to be carefully weighed."

"You're referring to the induction."

"Of course. I hope you will see reason—"

The king no longer had any desire to head to the forest. *Is there nowhere I can be free?*

Malfurion was clearly intent on pressing forward with his point. Varian could see only one way to at least end the conversation.

"I'll give Genn and the worgen a fair consideration. You have my word."

Malfurion heard the finality in his voice and wisely accepted the answer as it was. "Thank you, Varian. That is all I can ask—"

Another figure intruded upon them. Varian fought down his impatience with the seemingly never-ending situation. His trained eyes took in the newcomer, who, though a night elf, was dressed in a colorful outfit that the king thought Malfurion surely also found gaudy.

"Archdruid Stormrage," the other greeted solemnly.

"Var'dyn."

Varian's sharp ears caught a slight inflection in the night elf's voice, as if the archdruid not only knew what this other figure wanted . . . but dreaded it for some reason.

Exactly what the other elf was finally registered with Varian. He recalled the reports. *So this is a Highborne.*

The Highborne barely seemed to notice the human. The king recalled the apparent arrogance of Var'dyn's kind. He also remembered that they were magi . . . and reckless ones at that.

The archdruid said, "I thank you for your time and your reply, Varian. I look forward to speaking with you further."

The king took advantage of the situation. "Naturally. Forgive me now; I must be going. Good evening."

He did not even acknowledge the Highborne as he left, thinking that the other elf did not deserve any better than he gave. Varian gratefully departed the pair, silently wishing he had never sailed from Stormwind.

A slight movement in the trees nearby caught the corner of his eye. Varian did not focus on it, aware that by the time he turned the source would be gone from sight. Besides, the king was fairly certain just what had been lurking at the forest's edge.

His scowl deepened. Under his breath, he muttered, "Damned worgen."

Var'dyn did not speak until the human was long gone. Malfurion, aware of the news he had not yet had the opportunity to present to the Highborne, solemnly waited. The archdruid wanted to hear Var'dyn out to see how much the latter knew.

"I am here concerning the disappearance," Var'dyn bluntly stated. "You know that."

Malfurion waited for the Highborne to continue, but

that apparently was all the mage wished to say for the moment. Instead, Var'dyn looked expectantly at the archdruid.

There is no use delaying the inevitable, Malfurion thought. "So, Maiev Shadowsong has informed the Highborne of everything already—"

He got no further: Var'dyn's perplexed expression told him that the mage had no idea whatsoever about anything concerning Maiev—or her discovery.

"What should we know about, Archdruid?"

"Thera'brin is dead. Murdered."

Var'dyn stiffened. "Tell me."

Malfurion did, leaving out no detail. The spellcaster remained stone-faced throughout. The only true sign of his growing fury was his hands, which folded into tight fists and stayed so.

"The body will be returned to us immediately," Var'dyn declared when Malfurion finished. His voice held no emotion. He stared past the other night elf, as if seeing something far, far away. "There will be no further desecration of it by anyone for any reason."

"That was the intention. Maiev—"

"Yes . . . the warden. She can continue with her investigation, but she will not speak with us. If there is anything we learn, we will relate it to you, Archdruid. I leave it to you to let her know what she needs."

It was hardly the most logical system, but the Highborne were not very trusting—and, at the moment, Malfurion could not entirely blame them.

"I will speak to her as soon as I can," he promised Var'dyn.

The mage did not answer, his gaze once again distant.

The edge of his mouth twitched. Malfurion grew disturbed.

"Var'dyn. I swear that Thera'brin's death will be investigated thoroughly and the assassins brought to justice! I only ask that the Highborne have some patience—"

"We cannot afford patience, Archdruid," Var'dyn blurted. He finally looked directly at Malfurion again, and in those eyes the archdruid read a sense of dread. "You see. I did not come to speak with you about Thera'brin. *Another* of my people has gone missing."

12

THE HORDE STRIKES

There was still no word from Darnassus, although Haldrissa hoped for it soon. Nevertheless, she went on with her own plans to organize against this latest Horde incursion. Of necessity, that meant a swift, simple ceremony for poor Xanon.

The commander said appropriate words for her dead officer, then turned over the final moments to Kara'din, one of the two druids assigned to her here in Ashenvale as part of some project of the high priestess and the arch-druid's to bring the night elf race closer together. The other, Parsis, was somewhere in the forest behind them, wandering the Emerald Dream or something—Haldrissa was not quite sure. She was as devoted to the ways of her people as most night elves, but the druids were a lot that sometimes baffled and frustrated her. They often seemed to be half-asleep—or more, even—and spoke about as-pects of the world that had no practical use for a soldier.

As soon as the funeral finished, Haldrissa headed back.

Denea followed close. Although her second obeyed every order she gave without question, Haldrissa could sense a distance growing between them. She was certain that Denea and some of the other officers blamed their commander for not only Xanon's death but the other losses as well. Of course, most of her officers had not been out in the field as long as Haldrissa, so for the moment she forgave their naïveté. If they survived life half as long as she had, they would learn.

But will they get that opportunity? she suddenly asked herself. This latest intrusion by the Horde looked to be on a far greater scale than in the past.

"Denea . . ."

"Yes, Commander?"

"I want four scouts to take their hippogryphs toward the northeast. Not so far as we journeyed. From the air, they should be able to see enough even then."

"Yes, Commander."

"Oh, and how soon will the full mounted contingent be ready?"

"We can ride first thing tomorrow." Although Denea tried to maintain a steadiness in her voice, a hint of anticipation crept into it.

Haldrissa made certain that her own voice remained calm and in command. "If the scouts return with their report by then, we shall. We do not move until then."

"With your permission, then, I will go get the scouts."

Haldrissa's nod was all Denea needed. She rushed off, obviously determined to see to it that the Sentinels did indeed ride off the next day.

I remember being so eager once, the senior officer thought . . . then immediately cursed herself for such maudlin notions. The only difference between Denea and her was that Haldrissa had the millennia of experience to know how to temper eagerness with caution. A commander's trait.

A low rumble stirred her. From the west trundled in a short train of supply wagons guided by an armed Sentinel escort. The captain in charge of the escort anxiously peered around, not a good sign at all.

Haldrissa immediately headed to her.

The captain saluted. "Commander Haldrissa?"

"Yes. Did something happen?" She surveyed the wagons but saw nothing out of the ordinary.

Nothing, that is, save that the last wagon had an extra burden draped out of the back. A large, winged form. The stench of decay, so familiar to the veteran officer, was strong even before Haldrissa reached the wagon.

"We found the hippogryph about a day out," the captain reported as she dismounted. "Been dead for some time."

Wordlessly, Haldrissa rushed to the huge corpse. She wanted to deny it for what—and who—it was, but as she neared, the distinctive markings verified the worst. It was definitely Windstorm.

And that meant only the worst where Aradria and the message for Darnassus were concerned.

"He had many wounds, mostly from arrows, but a great axe is what finally did him in," the captain concluded.

Haldrissa peered into the wagon. Windstorm's corpse was set against a number of barrels. Of Aradria Cloudflyer there was no sign. "The courier! Where is she?"

"We found only the hippogryph, not her, though there

were traces of blood elsewhere that could have been from the courier. We did discover several dead orcs—"

"Never mind the orcs! What of the courier?"

Cowed by Haldrissa's fury, the young officer blurted, "As I said, she was nowhere to be found, but—"

"'Nowhere to be found' . . ." The commander took heart from that. She saw the scene playing out. Windstorm, sorely wounded in the sky, had no doubt brought his rider to the ground so that she could escape on foot with the pouch while he sacrificed himself to keep the orc scouts at bay.

That the orcs had penetrated so very deep bothered her, but Aradria's escape made up for that. There were places en route where an expert courier such as Aradria could gain another mount.

The captain had been saying something, but Haldrissa had not been paying attention. "What was that?"

"I said that we also found this there."

Haldrissa herself could not see it, but her expression must have been terrible to see, for the captain suddenly gaped at her.

The tattered pouches gave testament to the folly of the commander's earlier hopes. Aradria had *not* gotten away. She would have never abandoned the missive. Either the orcs had disposed of her body or some beast had dragged it away.

And Darnassus still had no idea what was happening in Ashenvale.

Denea. Abandoning the confused captain, Haldrissa hurried after her second. Denea already had scouts preparing for the mission. However, rather than sending them ahead as originally planned, this time she would have *all* of them wait until she had had four more copies of the previous message written. Then the scouts would head to Darnassus. Denea would just have to bridle her eagerness to hunt down the orcs for another day or so. Matters could wait *that* long, at least, so Haldrissa believed.

"Denea!" she shouted. Her second stood with the four scouts, evidently just about to send them off. "Denea!"

Her voice did not carry enough. Eager to march off herself, the younger officer signaled permission for the four scouts and their hippogryphs to depart. The group quickly rose into the air.

Denea finally turned in response to Haldrissa's shouting. "Commander?"

"Signal them to return! Aradria never made it! I want all four of them to head to Darnassus instead!" She had considered using owls to carry the messages; however, not only were the hippogryphs much faster, but the riders could also defend the missives.

The other Sentinel rushed to one of the signal horns set aside for summoning the warriors to action. It was their only hope of recalling the hippogryph riders in time. Denea put the curved horn to her mouth and blew as hard as she could.

The blare caused every Sentinel to pause in what she or he was doing. Too late, Haldrissa realized that many of them, already preparing for the deadly march, might think the call to action had come sooner than expected.

But if the horn stirred the post for the wrong reasons, at least she saw that it served its other purpose. The lead scout glanced over her shoulder, saw Denea gesturing, and had the party turn about.

"Praise Elune . . ." Haldrissa moved forward to meet the descending hippogryphs. She had a few instructions to pass on to the scouts before hurrying to write out the new messages to Darnassus.

A cry above made her stumble. Near her, Denea let loose with an oath.

One of the scouts dropped limply from her mount, plunging to the ground as the other night elves stared in horror.

The fletchings of two arrows thrust up over her back as she landed. Haldrissa had fought too many battles not to recognize the Horde markings.

The sky was suddenly filled with arrows. At first the commander thought that the archers had miscalculated the distance, for the bolts flew too high to properly descend upon the Sentinels below.

Only when one of the other scouts and her mount were struck several times did Haldrissa see the terrible logic: it was not the encampment that was the immediate target; it was the scouts.

The Horde was *already* prepared for her plan.

As the arrows brought down the second scout, other shouts arose ahead. Haldrissa saw several warriors pointing to the east.

Smoke rose from two other locations. She did not have to guess its origins. Two of the outposts lay in those directions.

"Sentinels, form ranks!" Denea cried out. "Prepare for imminent attack!"

As Sentinels—including blue-armored huntresses with shields and glaives—raced to obey, Haldrissa stirred in frustration. Those were orders she should have given. She eyed the forest beyond, wondering how the Horde had gotten so near in such numbers. They had clearly made several forays into the area to have such an excellent understanding of their surroundings.

But she also knew the terrain well. "Denea! Twenty to the southeast edge of the post! They will have to come from there! I want a mounted force of huntresses with shields and lances readied!" With the Horde presence in Ashenvale having grown over the past months, General Shandris had decided to include lancers—a seldom-utilized aspect of the night elf armies since the end of the War of the Ancients—in the Sentinels' arsenal of weapons. "Get the other—"

A hippogryph's squawk cut her off. Another of the winged creatures dropped. Her rider, a shaft through her arm, managed to jump off before the creature hit.

The last of the scouts managed to land. However, even the ground proved no sanctuary. More arrows flew, these designed to target those within the encampment and, Haldrissa saw, especially the area where the hippogryphs were kept. Worse, the landing scouts had given the archers a fairly good notion of just where that was.

Someone among the attackers had planned very, very well.

"Get the hippogryphs to cover!" Haldrissa ordered. She drew her glaive. There was still no sign of the invaders themselves, but that would surely change in moments. Haldrissa had to use what little time remained to her advantage.

Her gaze fell upon Kara'din, who ran from wounded fighter to wounded fighter, using his druidic powers to heal them as best he could. The commander chose to leave Kara'din to his own devices for the moment as additional concerns occurred to her.

"Archers, form ranks!" She saw that some had already begun to, but as a whole they were not moving as quickly as Haldrissa would have hoped. "Northeast, east, southeast! Twenty paces from the gate!"

Of necessity, the main post was surrounded by high wooden walls. When it was being built, the trees sacrificed had been honored as if they were fellow warriors. Haldrissa now prayed that the trees had retained their great prowess even in death. She suspected that the Sentinels would need it.

Guards on the wall crouched low as they surveyed the forest beyond. Thus far, they had given no sign of sighting the enemy, although a few moved about as if momentarily believing that they had.

The deadly whistle of another rain of arrows filled Haldrissa's ears. Denea shouted a warning to the gathering huntresses to quickly raise their shields.

Arrows clattered against the shields. Unfortunately, some of the huntresses did not move fast enough. Screams rose as at least three of them fell with shafts sticking in them and others struggled with wounds. Haldrissa looked for her own archers and was grateful to see them ready to return fire.

Arrows nocked, the archers awaited the word. The commander gave it to them without hesitation.

Now the whistling became a sign of hope as night elven arrows soared out over the wall. Haldrissa raced toward it, aware that she would not be there in time to see the bolts descend, but hopeful that there would be evidence of their success.

She heard cries from without as she climbed. More than a few. The orcs might have good archers among them, but they were not Sentinels. Haldrissa was certain that her people would inflict far more damage. She only hoped that it would be enough.

As if in answer to her question, another stream of arrows returned just as the commander reached the top. Although she managed to duck, the Sentinel nearest to her was too slow with the shield she carried. The thick arrow completely piercing her throat, the dead night elf toppled back off the wall.

Haldrissa peered into the forest. For the first time, the Horde began stepping from the protection of the trees. They were spread throughout the edge of the forest in various positions, and while a few had bows, others seemed intent on merely watching.

No . . . not watching. *Counting.* Counting the return fire and the number of Sentinels on the walls.

Squatting down again, Haldrissa turned back to those farther inside. "Cease fire! Cease fire!"

Below, Denea looked as if her superior had gone mad. She hesitated long enough for another rush of arrows to answer those from the Horde. Haldrissa silently cursed as the bolts flew over her. The orcs were expert warriors; by now they could make a good estimate on the Sentinels' strength in terms of the archers.

Sure enough, as she looked outside again, she saw the orcs at the edge begin to creep back. Simultaneously, the forest quieted. No new flight assailed the night elves.

"They have retreated," one younger Sentinel naïvely murmured to a comrade. "They are gone."

"No," the commander replied, startling the pair and others nearby who, in the excitement, had forgotten that she was there. "No, they have only moved back a little for a short time. We remain under attack. The first person to forget that will likely not have to worry about punishment from me. The Horde will have already killed her."

The warriors grew solemn, and several tightened their grips on their weapons. That was how Haldrissa wanted it. If they remained ready for the worst, they had a far better chance of survival.

She quickly descended to Denea. "How are the archers?"

"A few wounded, three dead. Say the word and we will send another greeting to those vermin!"

"Never mind that. The hippogryphs! Were they able to get most of them to cover?"

"Four are uninjured. Two more are wounded but able to fly. Two others have injured wings and cannot be counted. Another is sorely wounded, and I fear he will die."

Six viable hippogryphs. It was better than Haldrissa had hoped, although fewer than she would have liked.

"We do not have much time. See if Kara'din can do anything for the less-injured ones first," Haldrissa ordered. She paused as a dark look passed over Denea's face. "What is it?"

"I meant to tell you next. The druid is dead. In the last flight of arrows, a good number fell his direction. He was focused on our wounded and failed to protect himself sufficiently. I believe he died quickly, pierced so many times."

Haldrissa cursed. "They saw a chance to take out the druid. Where is Parsis?"

"No sign. He may be dead already."

The commander could not waste more time on the subject. The Sentinels had survived without druidic assistance for millennia and would do so now. "We move on, then. Get every archer ready quickly. The Horde will not wait long before beginning their attack in earnest. We do not know how many of the outposts have been hit and how many of those have been overrun already. We need to get word to Darnassus, but this time I want sufficient cover for the hippogryphs and their riders."

"Do they each carry a copy of the message?"

"Damn the message! At this point all they have to tell General Shandris is that Ashenvale is under full assault. Now, go get them ready!"

Denea rushed off with a swiftness that the veteran warrior suddenly envied. Haldrissa already felt as if she had fought an entire battle, not merely the opening skirmish.

The archers reassembled, though initially they kept in a loose enough arrangement that if the orcs fired at where they had initially stood, there would be few casualties. It bothered Haldrissa to even think of success being measured by trying to have losses kept to a minimum, but that was war. The more of her fighters she saved, the better, even if it meant some others might have to sacrifice themselves . . . including her.

The hippogryphs were ready just a few minutes later. In all that time, the orcs had not fired one shot nor even sounded one horn. Haldrissa worried about that. Whoever was in charge of the attack had something insidious in mind, she was certain.

Denea signaled her. Haldrissa silently motioned for the archers to ready themselves. When they had their bows nocked and aimed, she nodded to the brave scouts and hippogryphs, then to her second.

Denea waved off the party. The great winged crea-tures flew into the air, their riders bent low. Each animal took a slightly different direction, but all headed toward the west.

"Fire!" Haldrissa commanded.

The front ranks of the archers let loose. The second held back, though, just as she had ordered.

The stream of arrows soared out toward the forest. As that happened, the hippogryphs beat their wings harder. They rose higher and higher.

Again, Haldrissa gave the order to fire. The latter ranks shot. All the while, those who had first fired readied their bows once more.

There was no return fire yet. Haldrissa almost held her breath, waiting for the Horde to try to shoot down the hippogryphs. Yet, they did nothing.

At last, the winged creatures and their riders were out of bow range. The commander finally breathed a sigh of relief.

"Look there!" someone cried.

Haldrissa looked for the long-awaited flight of Horde arrows, but instead a more stunning view awaited her. High above and closing fast from the east were nearly a dozen blurry specks that coalesced just enough to reveal reptilian forms with batlike wings. *Red* reptilian forms.

"Red dragons . . ." Haldrissa at first gasped before rec-ognizing that these were more bestial in appearance, and more primitive of form. "No . . . red proto-dragons . . ."

She had only heard of them in Northrend, but there had been rumors that the Horde had attempted to bring them to other regions. Savage creatures with stouter, toothy muzzles, they raced along the sky with clear intent. Their wings had sharp points to them, and the proto-dragons roared with monstrous eagerness as they closed.

Too late, Haldrissa realized that she had played exactly into the Horde's hands. With an attack already under way, they had expected her to try to send another warning to Darnassus.

Haldrissa had just sent the riders and their mounts to their doom.

The Horde could not have many proto-dragons. These were likely most if not all. However, these were all they needed. Almost double the number of hippogryphs, the proto-dragons broke off in pairs to pursue the as-yet-unsuspecting riders.

A horn blared, Denea seeking to warn the scouts. Yet, even though some clearly reacted, it was too late. The proto-dragons—and their orc riders—had been waiting in hiding so near that it did not take them much time to overtake their quarry.

Hippogryphs were hardly defenseless, and those working with the Sentinels were especially adept at battle. Unable to gain enough distance on their pursuers, most of the hippogryphs turned to face the proto-dragons. The scouts readied their bows.

One fortunate scout got off a shot that swiftly dealt with the orc astride one proto-dragon. The dead warrior tumbled off the side of his mount and dropped like a rock toward Ashenvale.

Two proto-dragons caught a hippogryph between them. The hippogryph slashed with his talons, raking the snout of the nearest proto-dragon. The orc rider tried to aim his own bow, but the wound made his shot go wide.

The hippogryph's rider fired back with success equal to the previous scout, sending another Horde corpse falling to the ground.

Unfortunately, in focusing on the one proto-dragon, the hippogryph by necessity had to pay little attention to the other. The scout tried to nock another arrow in order to deal with the second, but in the process left herself open to the axe of that proto-dragon's rider.

The orc struck hard, the axe blade crushing through armor, flesh, and bone. With a cry, the scout clutched the bleeding stump of an arm. The night elf was put out of her misery by a second swing of the blade, leaving the hippogryph to fend for himself while still bearing the dead rider.

The brave creature managed another good swipe, this time at the underbelly of the second proto-dragon. The beast let out a pained roar and tilted to the side. The orc tried to cling on, but with one hand still gripping the axe, he could not.

What saved him was the first proto-dragon, which appeared as if by silent command under the dropping orc. Grabbing hold, the orc repositioned himself on his new mount.

Both the badly injured proto-dragon and its comrade closed on the hippogryph. Fangs tore into a wing. Claws ripped at a neck.

The hippogryph made one last lunge at the most wounded of his adversaries. He tore into the throat of the proto-dragon. The proto-dragon planted its nails on one of the hippogryph's wings.

So entangled, both plummeted to their doom.

In an attempt to see their mission to fruition, two

of the hippogryphs attempted to flee west. One did not make it far, and although the scout tried to aid by firing at their pursuers, a proto-dragon managed to cut the creature off. Unlike in the previous struggle, the hippogryph and night elf were unable to put up much of a defense before both were ripped to shreds by the combination of teeth, nails, and axes.

The full aerial combat quickly began to shrink as the trapped defenders fell one after another. Two more proto-dragons perished—as did their orcs—but soon there were only the one scout and hippogryph still seeking to outrace the two mounted proto-dragons slowly but surely closing. The trap had been set well, and Haldrissa felt personally responsible for each death she witnessed.

Worse, there was nothing she could do but watch as the last was trapped. The scout and his hippogryph fought as valiantly as their comrades, even bringing down one of the other proto-dragons and its rider, but in the end, they, too, fell. The entire struggle had taken place over perhaps four minutes, though to Haldrissa it had seemed a horrific eternity.

The Sentinels had not simply stood by as this all happened. Lancers astride nightsabers readied to lead the charge out the gates. Sentinels on foot held their glaives steady. Archers held off their fire, now awaiting the word that the Horde was finally attacking in earnest.

The guards on the walls cautiously peered through carved gaps, waiting for the first rush of orcs.

But nothing happened.

JAROD'S HUNT

Although Velen's arrival had not been expected, there was no question as to his staying as an honored guest, just like the rest of those representing the Alliance. However, the Prophet was not one who desired much in the way of accommodations, and insisted on a simple chamber. Tyrande saw that he received one that still faced him toward the temple proper.

The tranquility of the Temple Gardens appealed to Velen, and so the present moment found him meditating there. The draenei sat with legs crossed, facing the center of the gardens, his concentration on the Light. The two honor guards the high priestess had assigned to him he had requested to stay behind at his quarters, their presence surely not needed in this of all places.

He suddenly sensed the presence of someone else approaching him—someone who also had a tremendous affinity for the Light. It could be only one person. Without looking, Velen quietly said, "Welcome, Anduin Wrynn."

The human did not seem at all surprised that Velen sensed him, a further sign that the Light was very strong with King Varian's son.

"Hello, Prophet. I—I'm sorry if I disturb you."

"Please, the title is one given to me by others. I prefer simply *Velen*." The draenei smoothly rose. "Your father does not know you are here."

"No . . . he thinks I'm asleep. . . ." Anduin could not hide his guilt.

"It is not for me to judge whether you should have stayed in your quarters or not. That is for you to decide."

This statement seemed to put Anduin at ease a bit. "I'm old enough to make my own choices, despite what my father thinks. I love him, but he fears so much to lose me again—or to lose me forever, as he did Mother—that he nearly smothers me. I can never be out of his sight for more than a few minutes."

"One can understand his concern . . . and your difficulty with it, as well."

"Proph—Velen, you know why I've come here."

"You wish to speak more of the Light. I am happy to tell you what I know, if you respect that I will not seek to guide you from your father."

Anduin nodded, at that moment looking to Velen much like the king. "I wouldn't ask it. I only want to learn more." He put a hand to his heart. "I feel the Light here. I feel it more every day. It's as much a part of me as anything else is."

"Yes. It is extremely strong where you are concerned." Velen glanced around the gardens, but there was no one else about. "We can talk for a time, if you like, so long as you promise me you will return to your quarters afterward."

The gratitude with which the youth radiated was almost as strong as the Light within. "I promise."

As they walked, Velen studied the boy closely. *Yes, I must teach him all I know, if that is possible. This one has a destiny with the Light. . . .*

Velen ever remained aware of just who walked with him. Anduin was heir to Stormwind, and the draenei knew how important Stormwind was to this troubled world just now. The Alliance needed Stormwind, perhaps more than even its king realized. Anything that threatened the stability of Stormwind threatened the long-term stability of the Alliance, especially in the face of a resurgent Horde.

Yet, if the Light had other plans for Anduin Wrynn . . .

You must move on, Jarod heard his wife's voice murmur to him. It was not the first time since coming here that he had heard it, and while some might have thought that they were going mad, Jarod accepted it as her simply still watching out for him as she always had in life.

He had already departed his quarters some time ago in the hopes of trying to regain some focus. Even though he would continue to mourn Shalasyr—perhaps for the rest of his life—he knew that she would have expected him to do more than that. As much as Jarod hated the thought, Shalasyr would have wanted him to fit himself back into night elf society, find some other purpose. Yet, what that purpose might be, he did not know and, in truth, did not completely care. Still, Jarod knew that he had to try.

There was no question about returning to the military. In part, that had to do with dealing with Shandris, something he was not prepared to do for the time being . . . if ever. However, it also had to do with Jarod's lingering feelings concerning how he saw night elf society. There were hints that things had changed, that Malfurion and Tyrande had begun bringing the various segments of their people closer again . . . but he needed to see more. The war had left too much of a mark on him.

I apparently am beginning to grow old. Jarod hoped that he would not become as he had seen some of the elder night elves he had witnessed just after the war's end. Their entire world turned upside down by the struggle against the Burning Legion and the destruction of Zin-Azshari, they had been unable to cope with their new, unpredictable future. Several had slipped into fantasy worlds of their own that consisted of safe memories of the past. Many of those had never found their way back to reality.

But for Shalasyr's sake alone, Jarod was determined to live. Forcing himself to leave his quarters and start walking among his own kind were the first steps. He had even made it a point to keep an eye out for anyone he remembered and be sure to greet them. That had caused a few startled expressions, but Jarod had felt that his wife would have been proud of his initial effort.

Still, he was more than happy to finally head back. In fact, the closer he got, the more he picked up his pace, eager to return to what had become his sanctuary.

And thus it was that Jarod nearly fell atop the body in his path.

He saved himself from doing so at the last minute by grabbing hold of one of the last trees within reach. Even still, the former guard captain dropped down on one knee upon the arm of the corpse.

The years since the war melted away as Jarod reacted like a soldier once again. Pressing against the tree, he peered around for the assassin. Seeing no one, Jarod cautiously bent low to investigate the grisly find.

At first, he wondered if perhaps he *was* losing himself in old memories. He had not seen such a figure since the war. That Jarod had not even noticed the brightly colored garment bespoke just how deep he had been in his reverie.

"A Highborne . . ." Belatedly, it returned to him that they had come seeking readmittance to night elf society.

With the exception of his accidental leaning on the arm, Jarod was careful not to touch the body. It was already evident what had likely proven the spellcaster's end—the two jagged slits in his throat indicated a large dagger wielded by an enthusiastic hand. There was also something pinned by a rock to the dead mage's chest.

Questions filled Jarod's head, some of them very disturbing. One that particularly vexed him from the start was why the Highborne should be here in the first place. What business had the spellcaster had so near where Jarod lived?

The answer came to him as he studied the ground nearby. Someone had been careful to remove any footsteps, and he knew why: the Highborne had been slain *elsewhere* and then dragged to this spot. Despite the efforts to cover that fact up, there were still some tiny, telltale spots of what could only be blood. They led toward the east for a few paces before ceasing. From all this, Jarod decided that the reason that the Highborne had been found by him was simply that the assassins had not wanted the victim to be discovered near the place of his demise. Something there would have possibly given searchers a clue to the truth.

It occurred to him suddenly that this was not his task. By rights, he had to report this to the Sentinels or, more to his preference, the archdruid or high priestess. Jarod looked around again, saw no one, and decided to risk leaving the body alone while he searched for someone with authority.

Being a druid, Malfurion was likely somewhere beyond Darnassus, so Jarod headed toward the temple. At the very least, he believed Tyrande would be there, and if it turned out the archdruid also was, so much the better.

"Jarod?"

He stopped at the sound of Shandris's voice. Flanked by four Sentinels, she, too, headed toward the temple.

"Shan—General," he responded, trying to regain his composure.

After her initial outburst of his name, she, too, sought to bring things to a more detached level. "Jarod. You have business with the high priestess?"

It took but a moment's debate before he admitted the truth. "Yes . . . someone has been murdered."

Her guards immediately tensed. Shandris signaled them to calm down, though her eyes burned at the revelation. "Where? Who?"

"I found the body near my quarters." He gave her a more precise location. "It was one of the Highborne. I do not know him. There was some note under him, but I did not touch it."

"A Highborne . . ." Shandris looked at the guard nearest her left. "Send word to Maiev Shadowsong"—she hesitated a moment as she noted Jarod's reaction to his sister's name—"with the details you just heard." To the guard next to that one, she continued, "Take Ildyri and hurry to where he said the body was located. Keep guard over it until Maiev or her people arrive."

The other Sentinels rushed to obey, leaving Shandris with just the one guard. The general bade Jarod join her, the other Sentinel following them.

The guards did not hesitate to let Shandris pass. She strode unerringly through the temple to where they found Tyrande.

The high priestess greeted them with a knowing expression. "There has been a death."

Shandris went down on one knee, the other Sentinel and Jarod doing the same. "Another Highborne."

Tyrande bade them to rise. "You found the body, Jarod?"

He realized that she had read the fact in his urgent manner. "Yes. Not far from my quarters. I judged that the body had been moved from elsewhere after the murder. I assume to hide facts about the true location. . . ."

"That seems logical to me," Shandris added. "I have sent someone to inform Maiev and others to guard the body until she or the Highborne do something with it."

"And we shall do something . . . not only now with Ha'srim's body, but also with these curs who think the Highborne will stand by and be slain without repercussion!"

Malfurion and a Highborne had entered the chamber from another direction. Jarod understood that this was someone high among the magi, though he doubted it was the leader.

That was verified by Tyrande's reply. "Do you speak in the name of Archmage Mordent now, Var'dyn?"

"I presage his words, High Priestess! Patient though he is, the archmage will not let this stand! This lack of progress has been discussed among the Highborne. We would hate to have to make these crimes more public, especially with the emissaries now present for your summit, but we will do so if necessary. Perhaps, then, something will be done about the murders." He glared at all in the room, finally fixing his blazing eyes upon Jarod. "You! You are the one who claims to have found the body, are you not? I am curious how you happened to be near—"

"I do not 'claim' to have found it. I did." A rare fury stirred in the former guard captain. "And if you are considering me as the possible assassin, you will find yourself sorely mistaken."

Malfurion raised his staff between the pair. "I am certain that Var'dyn is not making any unwarranted accusations, Jarod. We are all struggling to come to grips with this foul matter. I am sure Var'dyn joins me in commending you for immediately alerting us to this second murder."

The mage hesitated, then replied, "Yes. Of course. Thank you, Jarod Shadowsong."

It surprised Jarod that Var'dyn knew who he was, especially considering his threatening posture a moment before. He nodded to the mage but said nothing.

"All is being done to find the perpetrators, Var'dyn," the high priestess assured. "Maiev is dedicated to the truth, and nothing will stand in her way."

"She has a coarse way about her, but I have spoken with this one's sister and find her as you say," the Highborne admitted. "However, she is one, where these assassins could be many. . . . Darnassus is surely riddled with those plotting against the return of the Highborne, and we will not stand idly by any longer!"

At that point, Var'dyn gave Tyrande and Malfurion a fleeting bow, then turned on his heel and marched off. Jarod could not tell whether he had been satisfied by the high priestess's promises or he merely knew that he could do nothing without this Archmage Mordent's permission.

"Amazing that anyone should dislike the Highborne," Shandris remarked under her breath. "They are the epitome of respect and congeniality."

Jarod made no response, although he was aware that she had spoken so that he was the only other one who would hear.

Both Malfurion and Tyrande turned their attention to him. Jarod suddenly felt uneasy. He was certain that the pair desired something of him.

"Jarod, I want to again express our appreciation of your handling of the vile discovery," Tyrande said.

"I did as should be done."

"Not everyone would have behaved the same way. Your training and common sense shone through." She glanced at her husband, who nodded back. "Var'dyn is correct in one thing. Maiev will need some assistance. We cannot afford for this to continue, not only for the Highborne's sake, but also for everything we are trying to accomplish with this summit."

"My sister is very competent and very determined. I cannot think of anyone more suited for the task."

Tyrande smiled. "Perhaps, but her brother would certainly be an asset to the search."

Even though he had seen the suggestion coming, Jarod

did not know how to answer. "If the high priestess—if you think this a necessary duty—"

"It is a *request*, Jarod. No command. You can refuse and we will understand perfectly."

He knew that she truly meant that, but hearing her say so proved the impetus to his decision. "I will do my part, though I will bow to Maiev's authority on this."

"Of course." Tyrande looked grateful.

The archdruid also showed his pleasure. "Your support will be invaluable, Jarod. We need everyone right now."

"I will do all I can . . . and the first thing I need to do is find my sister and explain this."

The high priestess shook her head. "I will inform her."

"With all due respect, I would like to tell her myself. It would be . . . more appropriate in this case."

"As you wish, then."

Jarod bowed to both. Shandris did the same and joined him as he departed. The general sent the Sentinel accompanying them on to other duties.

"I am very glad to have you a part of this," she said quietly once the pair was alone. "Your sister is very dedicated, but often her focus is a bit too . . . narrow."

"I know Maiev has faults, but I have as many if not more. We will do all we can to stop these assassinations."

"Let us hope so. I am no admirer of the Highborne, but I can see how they might grow restive as their members are cut down. Darnassus—the night elf race in general—can ill afford a conflict between them and everyone else."

He stopped. "You have dealt with my sister. Where would I most likely find her at this point? Where I left the body?"

Shandris took the unspoken farewell without a beat. She pointed. "No. By this point, she and her Watchers are probably moving it for better study. I would say your best bet is to meet her there instead."

"And where is that?"

"The place where she and her Watchers train. I know that she organized and conducted her investigation of the first murder from there."

"Thank you." He dared not say anything more, though her eyes showed that she waited for him to do so. Steeling himself, Jarod bowed to her and headed in the direction she had indicated. As he journeyed, Jarod drew the dagger sheathed at his side. He probably did not need it . . . but then, two people *had* been slain. That they had been Highborne did not rule out that the perpetrators might not kill someone interfering with their plans.

The sounds of Darnassus muted abruptly as he neared the location Shandris had suggested. The dark mood of his surroundings fit well with how he saw his sister. She had always been the driven one, while he had simply stumbled through life, rising—in his estimation—more by chance than by ability. Still, Jarod hoped that Maiev would see his value in this mission.

The practice area used by his sister and her followers appeared empty. The crudely drawn expressions on the row of wooden practice dummies seemed to mock his failure to find Maiev. False swords raised high and chipped shields ever at the ready, even as savagely hacked as they were, they looked at the moment far more capable than Jarod felt. The male night elf looked around, pondering where to go next if Maiev did not show up soon. He considered the fact that she might have gone to the

Highborne encampment, but ruled that out as reckless, even by his sister's standards.

Frustrated at not finding Maiev here, Jarod turned—

And stared directly into the eyes of what could only be one of his sister's Watchers. She wore armor akin to Maiev's, but of a slightly duller shade. Her helmet hung from a branch just to her left, as if the Watcher had just taken it off. Propped against the trunk of the same tree was her umbra crescent.

"You are he," the younger night elf stated without preamble. "You are her brother." She eyed him critically. "I expected you to be taller and more scarred from all those battles."

Her comment made him wonder just what Maiev had said about him over the millennia. Had he so disappointed her that she had been forced to make him more in the image of what he should have been?

When Jarod did not respond, the Watcher added, "I am Neva." She started walking, her movements as smooth as those of a nightsaber. Jarod felt as if she were sizing up prey. Neva circled him, taking in every aspect of Maiev's brother. "No . . . you are as you should be. Like her."

Not certain how to take that, he asked, "Where is Maiev? I need to speak with her."

"She was here not long ago, but no sooner did they bring the body of that spellcaster than some of his kind showed up to take it away. Maiev was not too pleased. She was not done with it."

Neva might as well have been talking about a chair or some other insignificant object. Jarod sighed. "So she is at their encampment?"

"Very possibly." Neva sauntered to his side, then

leaned uncomfortably close. "You can wait here with me. She will be back very soon; I am certain—"

Jarod suddenly pushed past Neva, but not because of her. Rather, something watched both from beyond the area—something that did not remind him of a night elf.

He heard Neva speak, but her words were lost as he threw himself after the spying figure. Whoever it was moved swiftly and surely between the trees. He remembered what had been mentioned about the *worgen*, whom he had yet to meet. This would not be the first time they had lurked around the area during troubling times.

Jarod tore through the forest, moving automatically. He was certain that he was on the path the figure had gone. All he had to do was keep to the right behind the next tree—

His body was wracked by agonizing pain, and he felt as if a hundred bolts of lightning had struck him simultaneously. Jarod shrieked and felt no disgrace in doing so. No one could suffer such torture and not react as he did.

He tumbled forward—or tried. Falling to the ground in some ways would have seemed at least a little relief. Jarod had the great desire to curl up in a ball and pray that the continuous shock would cease, but some force prevented him. It was as if a web held him in place to ensure that his suffering continued unabated.

Jarod tried to tear his arms free. If it had allowed him to escape, he would have at that moment gladly given up those arms. Anything to escape.

The hope for death began to stir within him, but then Shalasyr's face appeared in his thoughts. She had always enjoyed life, even under the most primitive of circumstances. Jarod, who had never been able to forget the horrors of the War of the Ancients, had learned from her. She had drawn him back to the world in a way nothing else could.

And he knew that she wanted him to live, wanted him to go on, not follow her unless there was no other alternative. Feeling her love again gave Jarod new strength. The torture continued, but now he had something upon which to cling. With Shalasyr, there had always been hope. . . .

The unremitting shock ceased.

Jarod crumpled to the grassy earth at last. He welcomed the collision with the soft soil, the rattling of his bones far less painful than what he had been through. The cool surface felt good against his skin.

A hand gripped his left arm. The touch was initially enough to resurrect some traces of the monstrous pain. Jarod cringed, fearing the full force of it would return; but although the fingers held tight, the pain receded again, becoming nothing but memory.

"Can you understand me?" asked an unfamiliar male voice. "Can you?"

The former guard captain managed a croaking sound that the other apparently took as an affirmative. The figure moved Jarod to the side, finally resting him against a tree.

"I'm sorry," his rescuer whispered. "I didn't know that would happen. I didn't realize that it was there."

Jarod managed another croak. His vision was still clouded by tears. His companion could have been invisible for all he was able to make out of him.

He felt the hands stiffen as an unidentifiable sound in the distance reached them. Jarod's rescuer suddenly released him. The night elf did not hear the other depart, but felt certain somehow that such was the case.

Jarod's breathing returned to near normal. His vision remained teary, but shapes began to coalesce. Vaguely, Jarod finally registered that he had been caught in some insidious trap. So close to where Maiev and her Watchers met, he thought it was possible that it had been set by the assassins to catch one of them. After all, his sister *was* in charge of the investigation.

Barely a minute had passed when light footsteps alerted him to someone's approach. Jarod did not think it his rescuer, and when he heard the intake of breath—a sign of the newcomer's apparent astonishment at discovering him—he knew it to be female. The former captain could only assume it was Neva, who had finally managed to follow his trail.

"You live . . . ," he heard the Watcher say.

"Of course he does," responded another, stronger female voice that made Jarod look up. He saw a vague shape standing over him. "He is my brother, after all."

14

THE WORGEN

More resembling a ghostly fleet worthy of the undead Forsaken, the eight remaining Horde ships at last reached Bilgewater Harbor, located off of Azshara, which lay east of greater Ashenvale. Captain Briln wasted no time disembarking once the goblins who ran the port had set everything in place. He had delivered what he could of his cargo and now was happy to be rid of it . . . even if that also meant that he would have to face the warchief over his failure.

Since his last visit here, the port had been built up considerably, and now covered the entire small island. The main keep rose high above the other structures and a thriving population—mostly goblins—scurried about as they dealt with not only the docking ships but also countless other Horde-related activities. At one of the other docks, a crane ending in a large hook lowered supplies into a warship.

A goblin operating a foul-smelling mechanism used for

unloading cargo trundled by in the distance. As deadly as the shredders could be when turned on a foe, they paled in comparison to the natural fury of Briln's cargo.

The first of the huge hold doors opened, and the crews began unloading the covered cages. None of those who had been part of the journey looked like the orcs that they had once been. Everyone was drawn, anxious.

From the docks there came some sniggering from a pair of goblins watching the activities. Growling, Briln turned on the short, wiry figures, towering over them.

"The warchief's pets're hungry after this journey! They could use a snack—or two. . . ." As the goblins fell silent, he added, "Now, you can either help your lot take over control of the cages, or you can be part o' what I feed them. . . ."

With great swallows and suddenly polite demeanors, the two goblins saluted the captain and hurried to obey.

Briln allowed himself a short chuckle before the seriousness of his own situation again arose to the forefront. He was more likely than the goblins to become food for the cargo.

He suddenly noticed a flurry of movement from the mainland. A fair-size party was approaching by boat, one that included at least half a dozen capable guards who could only be part of the warchief's famed Kor'kron.

"Garrosh," he whispered. Not for a moment did Briln think of seeking to avoid the encounter. His honor meant more than his life, and he would not be branded a coward in the last moments of it.

The crews and the dockworkers already had all but two of the cages settled in an open area reserved just for their arrival. Briln was proud of those who had served under him during the epic journey. He would commend them all before his execution.

Dust and bits of leaves decorated Garrosh and his retinue, a sign that they themselves had also but recently arrived in Azshara. The warchief had an expectant look on his face, but whether that boded good or ill for the captain, Briln could not say, and thus he did not raise his hopes.

Orcs and goblins slapped their right fists to the left sides of their chests as the Horde leader passed. Garrosh did not demand such signs of fealty, but was the type of commander who simply received them due to the immense respect and fear his followers had in him.

Briln did as the others and in addition kept his head low. Garrosh, should he desire it, could have that head immediately.

"Briln," rumbled the warchief. "A long journey you've had."

"A short one, when in service to the Horde and you," the captain returned, daring to peer up under his thick brow. "And surely less dangerous than the trek from which my warchief's obviously just come!"

"We do what we do for the greater cause." Garrosh stared past him at the cages. "Eight. There were supposed to be more."

"There were . . . troubles."

"Storms?"

"Yes, and the unrest of the cargo. Much of the concoction meant to keep the beasts docile was lost, and so we could do only what we could do." Even as he spoke, Briln felt his shame growing. His replies sounded so weak, he thought it a wonder Garrosh did not cut out his tongue to make him stop.

"Eight," the warchief repeated. "Show them to me."

Briln was now certain of his fate. Garrosh would not take his head; he would let one of the beasts rip the captain to shreds. Briln could not blame the warchief. It was a reasonable punishment for one who had so badly failed.

He led Garrosh and the others to the first of the cages. Inside, the beast, smelling the nearness of so many orcs, stirred. The sides of the cage shook.

"Pull back the tarp!" the captain ordered.

Four of the crew used the attached ropes to pull back the tarp over the cage door. As they did, the shaking increased and a growl rose. From the other cages there came answering sounds. Briln felt a moment of déjà vu and half expected one or more of the creatures to break free. Guards with spears quickly moved in just in case they had to defend the warchief.

The captain took no comfort in the awed expressions of several of those with Garrosh. They had every reason to be amazed and not a little wary of the prizes that their leader had ordered shipped from Northrend. However, none of them had been assigned the task. They were safe. Briln was not.

Garrosh stepped closer . . . too close for the captain's taste. The beast, apparently of the same opinion, leapt forward and tried to fit an arm through the bars. Unlike the one monster, this creature failed. He sought then to bend the bars in order to make a better attempt, but although they creaked ominously, they did not give . . . for now.

The warchief appeared unimpressed by the ferocity of the caged horror. Looking to the Kor'kron, he said, "They'll have to be reminded of their purpose . . . and what will happen if they don't follow through."

It was the first time in ages that Briln was reminded that, despite everything, the beasts were nearly as intelligent as their captors. Much more primitive, certainly, but *nearly* as intelligent.

One of Garrosh's guards gestured to another Kor'kron standing by the entrance to a metal longhouse just north of the area. Something had been planned for just this occasion, and the captain had an idea what it was.

The grim guard disappeared into the longhouse. All the while, the beast before Garrosh raged, now joined with savage gusto by the other seven. Everywhere, orcs and goblins tensed, awaiting disaster. Only the warchief and the Kor'kron remained absolutely calm, even expectant.

Several startled grunts suddenly arose from the longhouse. They were like nothing Briln had ever heard.

No . . . they *did* resemble something. Although higher in pitch and sounding more curious than frightened, they were very much akin to the deeper voices of the cargo.

And the creatures in the cargo knew it also. Almost as one, the eight cages grew silent.

Garrosh nodded to the one before him. The warchief did not look happy with what had just taken place, but seemed resigned to it. "You understand. They are well, as *I* have promised. You will all thus keep *your* promise."

There was a grunt from the cage. Garrosh signaled for the tarp to be let down again. Only when it had completely covered up the cargo did Briln breathe easier.

The guard who had entered the longhouse exited again, this time to report to the warchief. He looked a bit anxious as he neared. Garrosh indicated that the party—including the captain—should step farther away from the cages.

"I did as you commanded," the Kor'kron muttered, speaking so that only those with Garrosh could hear. "I gave some of the younglings a share of that sweetened meat their kind likes so much. They raised a real ruckus. Was it enough?"

Garrosh nodded approval. "The adult beasts heard them. They should stay docile now. They just had to be reminded about our deal."

At that moment Briln found he did not envy Garrosh; the complexities of command in such times surely tore at Garrosh's sense of honor constantly as he sought to do what was best for his followers in the long run.

He must have stared too long at the warchief, for Garrosh abruptly looked back at him. The legendary warrior's brow furrowed. "How many died to bring even these eight here?"

Briln made an estimate that included not only those lost when their ships went down but also those lost in getting the beasts to the port in Northrend. Having tried continuously to avoid thinking of those who had given their lives while he had survived, the captain was dismayed by the number he told the warchief.

Garrosh was equally dismayed and did not entirely hide that fact. "As many as that? A great price . . . but it'll be worth their sacrifices and more when Ashenvale falls to us!" The Horde leader straightened, now looking every bit the dedicated, confident commander. "They who've died to bring these beasts here will stand beside us in spirit as we crush our foes! When the last outpost falls, this victory will belong as much to them as to those of us who are there to see it happen!"

His vow brought cheers from those surrounding him,

even Briln. If he was to be executed, he hoped that at least he would be remembered along with all the other dead involved in this mission. It was more than he could ask.

"Captain Briln."

The mariner swallowed. He immediately slapped his fist against his chest again, then bent his head so as to offer his neck. "My warchief, I can't give any excuse for my failure! You command that we bring you ten, and I deliver only eight! Many of those who perished did so as part of the fleet that I oversaw!" Briln waited for Gorehowl to fall, but when the fabled axe did not cut off his head, he went on. "My warchief, I confess all these failures, all these stains to my honor, and await my fate!"

There was silence, then he heard Garrosh say, "Your honor is your life."

"Yes, my warchief."

"And your life you offer to me."

Again Briln agreed. At the same time he thought to himself, *My disgrace is great! Garrosh rightly makes me suffer for my failures before granting me a proper death to atone for them!*

"So, if your life is mine, then your honor is mine . . . and as it is my honor at stake, I would have it redeemed in battle!"

The captain could not help gaping as he looked up. "I don't understand, Warchief. . . ."

"You will join us as we march through Ashenvale and see your work crush the Alliance! You will stand at the forefront, and if you die, your name will be spoken with pride by our people for generations!"

Garrosh himself offered Briln a hand up. The captain stared wide-eyed.

"Your first mate will now be captain. You'll now command soldiers in combat, and you will serve directly under me."

Briln's chest swelled with pride. "I will slay a hundred night elves before they bring me down! I will destroy Silverwing Outpost myself!"

The warchief chuckled. "Fight well. That's what I ask."

"I will!"

There was a rumble from the closest cage, but a tentative one that did not threaten. The creatures were subdued.

"We leave at sunrise tomorrow," Garrosh announced with confidence, ignoring the fact that he had clearly just arrived himself after what must have been a strenuous ride. "The first stage of my plan's at work on the night elves in Ashenvale already! Their communications with Darnassus are cut off and they will be making many assumptions as to what comes next based on past wars!" He gestured at the cages. "They'll die discovering just what great fools they've been made. . . ."

The nearest beast rumbled again, this time seeming to echo the warchief's triumphant tone. Briln's grin widened. He would live to see his work unleashed upon the night elves. He would live to know that he had served the Horde well.

And he would live to see the beginning of a new world—one forged by the hand of the Horde, not the Alliance. . . .

Tyrande and Malfurion had chosen to have the summit outside, in an area often used for grand events. They could have used the temple, where they had held their wedding, but part of the choice had to do with the Gilneans. It had been agreed by both that the introduction of Genn's people to the Alliance would be better served outside, where some of those who might be discomforted by their presence would be able to avoid feeling *trapped*.

Now, with seating arranged in more circular fashion save for an entrance to the east, the highest-ranking night elves seated themselves and then awaited the entrances of their guests. All had now arrived save the magi of Dalaran, whose ruling council, the Kirin Tor, had declined to send a representative due to Dalaran's desire to remain a bridge between the two warring sides. In Dalaran, magi of the Horde were as welcome as those serving the Alliance.

Tyrande and Malfurion had the seats of honor at the opposing end from the entrance. Sentinels in their full uniforms stood as honor guard near not only the high priestess and archdruid but also the entrance, where they would flank each of the visiting contingents.

But this was more than merely the official introduction of the summit. The entrances would be climaxed by the Ceremony of Induction, when new members of the Alliance would be added by call of vote. If a new member was accepted, it made sense that its representatives would then seat themselves and become part of the discussion to follow. To wait until a gathering was nearly at the end was ludicrous.

And if a supplicant was rejected . . . it also made sense for that party to depart as quickly as possible so as to keep its shame to a minimum.

On the surface, there was no sign of the turmoil

going on in Darnassus. News had reached the pair that something—exactly what it was had not been made clear—had happened to Maiev's brother in the course of the investigation. Malfurion and Tyrande only knew that Jarod was bedridden from injury. The high priestess had sent healers, and so there was apparently no fear of permanent injury, but both leaders desired to speak with Maiev's brother as soon as matters permitted.

Archmage Mordent had also promised that the Highborne would remain quiet about the investigation during the events, though Var'dyn had voiced some opposition to that. The spellcasters had no active role in the summit, their situation strictly a night elf matter and of no business to the Alliance as a whole.

When all were seated save for those making their entrance, Tyrande signaled the trumpeters.

The horns blared, and the procession of Alliance members commenced.

So that there would be no quarrels, the positions were chosen by lots. Thus it was that by sheer chance the first to enter were the gnomes, led by Gelbin Mekkatorque in his mechanostrider. The gnomes were followed by the representatives of Theramore, and so on.

Each contingent sought to display to the best of their abilities their prowess. Wondrous and unnerving mechanisms traveled with the gnomes. The dwarves performed martial feats with their hammers as they marched, revealing the swiftness and dexterity their stout forms belied.

Each time one faction stepped through the entrance, the anthem of its land played. At the sound of the first note, the night elves rose in respect to their guests and remained so as one group followed another.

Around the place of gathering, the banners of each delegation fluttered proud and strong, even though those in attendance did not feel any breeze themselves. The well-focused wind was the archdruid's doing.

Each procession halted before the high priestess and archdruid. There, the ruler or lead representative was greeted by a nod from the two night elves. It was yet another manner by which the pair thanked all those who attended—and also hopefully helped put their guests in a good mood for the discussions to come.

Stormwind was one of the last to enter but was among the most impressive. Varian led a crack contingent of his finest soldiers, and he himself was clad in armor that shone like the sun, so polished it was. Across his breastplate was emblazoned a regal lion's head. At his side was sheathed his legendary blade. Next to him strode Anduin, the prince dressed in a blue and gold suit designed for the royal court, as opposed to war.

Upon reaching Tyrande and Malfurion, Varian gave a sweeping bow. The theatrical flourish was not in keeping with his stolid demeanor, but before Malfurion or the high priestess could decipher what it might mean, the king of Stormwind had moved on.

The last of the members of the Alliance seated themselves. Tyrande looked about, saw that all awaited what was next to come. Sharing a hopeful look with the archdruid, she rose.

"Sisters and brothers of the Alliance, comrades and friends, I call for a vote to open this gathering!"

In the same order that they had entered, the representatives cast their vote as she requested. The motion was a formality and passed without any dissension.

"My friends," Tyrande went on. "It is with gratitude that the archdruid and I greet all of you! That you have chosen to join together at this summit is a true sign of hope in a troubled time."

There were murmurs of agreement from some of the members and their parties.

"We have many grave matters to discuss," the high priestess continued. "Many of you have suffered dearly since the madness of Deathwing tore Azeroth asunder, and are rightfully concerned that the Alliance might demand more from your people before the lands can heal themselves. I cannot promise that this will not happen."

Now there were wary glances. Yet, all respected Tyrande and her husband so much that no one saw fit to voice their concerns on that very subject . . . for the moment.

Malfurion's hand touched hers. Tyrande looked at the entrance. She saw no one, but the archdruid had clearly noted some signal.

"But before we can begin those discussions in earnest, we must ensure that we do so with every possible valued member present! And today we have those who would seek to become one of us, who would seek to share in our efforts to strengthen the Alliance. . . ."

A horn sounded . . . and immediately after, the anthem of Gilneas played.

Heads turned with anticipation toward the entrance. Tyrande and Malfurion glanced at King Varian, but his expression still revealed nothing.

A stillness fell over the audience as the first figure stepped into sight. Genn Greymane. He himself bore the banner of Gilneas—a red design consisting of a circle with three vertical lines akin to lances and another line bisecting the circle itself, all set in a field of gray—into the assembly, carrying it with a pride and strength worthy of a warrior much younger. In contrast to the splendor displayed by many in the audience, Genn wore the same simple, loose garments that he had during the banquet, and when the first of his people followed him into the assembly, they were seen to be dressed similarly.

Where there had only been a small band at the banquet, with Genn now marched a number that not coincidently matched the strength of Stormwind's contingent. Genn obviously desired to show the others that he could offer the Alliance a powerful ally.

Yet, although the men and women of Gilneas looked to be sturdy of build and clearly willing fighters, they were noticeably unarmed. Even the pole upon which their banner fluttered had no point at the top, meaning that it could not represent any sort of weapon. It was as if the Gilneans sought to prove to their counterparts that they had no use for such.

Genn paused before the night elf leaders, acknowledging them as those before had. Then, in a change from the entrance of the other kingdoms, he took the pole and thrust the bottom hard into the ground.

"Gilneas stands before you!" the king called to all around him and his followers. "Gilneas stands before you to atone for its sins by offering its might to any and all of the Alliance who need it! No truer brother will there be to any in their time of distress!"

He stepped back to join Eadrik and the others. The Gilneans formed an arc facing every direction except the entrance, pointedly making certain that no matter where one sat in the assembly, he or she would be viewing some member of Genn's band more or less in full.

"And lest anyone think us of weak use in battle, of being unable to defend our brothers beside us, we now hope to dispel that misconception. . . ."

With that, Genn and his people *transformed*.

Their bodies swelled, growing a third again in girth and height. Although originally loose-fitting, the Gilneans' clothing still proved too tight for this shift, and shirts and jerkins ripped loudly. Hair sprouted over the Gilneans' arms, legs, chests, and faces, spreading so thick that it became fur. Beneath the fur came the sounds of cracking and popping, of bones shifting and tendons stretching into positions of which they should not have been accustomed. Their arms and legs twisted as their forms contorted, the legs turning sleeker, more akin to those of a swift predator. Each figure became hunched, but in that manner of a powerfully built beast.

As the audience watched, rapt, the Gilneans' hands stretched and the nails grew into long, savage claws. Yet, that paled in comparison to the astounding metamorphosis of their faces. It was not just that the ears narrowed and stretched but that the mouth and nose pushed forward, *melded* together, and created a muzzle filled with sharp teeth capable of rending through flesh without trouble.

The *worgen* stood before the Alliance.

The lupine figures held their ground, although there was in them the evident urge to run, to hunt. They did not turn from the gazes of the crowd, instead staring confidently back.

Genn Greymane, his chest heaving from adrenaline, eyed Malfurion and Tyrande. They nodded in turn.

There was no greater way to emphasize the worth of the Gilneans to the Alliance than for the refugees to reveal their full strength.

The Gilneans had not always been among the worgen, though, and not all of their people were affected. Many were, however . . . and it was, to Malfurion's shame, he himself who was in great part to blame.

It had begun with other druids, those experimenting with the pack form. They had called upon the power to shift into large wolves, only to discover too late that in these forms they lost control of themselves. Blood had been shed.

Malfurion was one of those nearly lost, the aid of the demigod Cenarius all that saved him. Finally aware of the threat, Malfurion had banned the form's use. However, unbeknownst to him, a group of druids had gathered in secret to continue its efforts. Using the legendary artifact called the Scythe of Elune, they had sought to tame the wolf form . . . only to have the scythe transform them into the first of the *worgen*.

Bringing the savage creatures under control, Malfurion dismissed the advice of others who demanded their destruction and cast the worgen into a pocket dimension within the Emerald Dream, where they lay in a taming sleep under the tree Daral'nir.

That was supposed to have been the end of the tragic matter—and it would have been, if not for the human archmage Arugal. Under the orders of a desperate Genn seeking aid against the Scourge outside Gilneas's great wall, the mage had pulled the worgen to the kingdom . . . and once the curse of the worgen had entered, it spread through the populace swiftly.

Yet, the Gilneans had discovered the means to control their feral nature and turn what had been evil into—at least to a point—a force to benefit themselves in regards to not only the Alliance but also the eventual liberation of their homeland.

"We are Gilneas," Genn Greymane rumbled, his voice still distinctly his own, albeit now with a guttural addition to it. "We are the worgen. . . ."

The king howled.

The sound was not meant to disturb or frighten, only to again point out the power of him and his people. In that, it served well, for even the dour Dark Irons looked with great respect and interest at the might of the worgen.

As Genn's howl reached its crescendo, the others with him added their voices. Yet, even that paled when from beyond the summit, from deep within the forest, other worgen voices answered the call.

Their combined howl lasted but a scant few seconds, yet that was long enough for the moment to burn into the memories of most there. As Genn ceased—and his people near and far immediately did the same—the king of Gilneas concluded, "We humbly submit ourselves before our brethren for full membership in the Alliance. . . ."

No one responded at first, so unsettling was the sight. Rising, Malfurion pointed at the worgen. "A few of you know the old tales of the worgen and their ferocity! You know the stories of their unthinking evil! To both you and those unfamiliar with the stories, what stands before you has little link to either legends or the past! These fighters of Gilneas have tamed the curse! That which was once a deadly threat is now forevermore a force for good, a force for the Alliance!"

The archdruid's words rang throughout the assembly. Genn and the worgen waited as the emissaries digested both what Malfurion had said and, more importantly, what they had just witnessed.

Murmuring rose among the representatives, and they quickly became more animated.

Kurdran suddenly rose. "Wildhammer welcomes the strength o' the worgen . . . and o' Gilneas!"

Tervosh immediately followed. "Theramore seconds that welcome!"

At these pronouncements, applause burst from many sections of the gathering, applause for *Gilneas*. Several of the emissaries and members of their parties saluted Genn's people in one manner or another.

Tyrande, touching her husband's hand, took command of events again. "You have witnessed the might of Gilneas and heard its request to enter back into the Alliance!" the high priestess called, echoing Malfurion's sentiments. "I say that, after seeing this display and if there are no objections, we shall begin a vote for approval *immediately!*"

The high priestess let her gaze sweep over the assembly, focusing no longer on Stormwind than she did any other faction. There was no objection, and even Varian seemed in a reasonable mood.

"I call for a vote by acclamation!" the archdruid next proclaimed, following the course of action that they had discussed previous to the gathering. "A single voice to acknowledge the welcome of the worgen into the Alliance! All those in favor—"

The chorus of ayes began to resound, their enthusiasm matching that of the worgen's earlier howl. Malfurion and Tyrande glanced down at Genn, who gave them a grateful look in turn.

And then, from where the contingent of Stormwind sat, King Varian silently stood.

The effect was immediate. The shouting died. The two night elves and Genn stared at Varian, whose face revealed nothing of his intentions.

"Members of the Alliance, my good night elf hosts, I'd like to speak."

Even Prince Anduin appeared uncertain as to what his father planned, although he did not seem worried, only curious.

Tyrande signaled for attention, then said, "Stormwind has asked to speak. Please go on, King Varian."

The ex-gladiator and slave brooded for a moment. Finally he said, "Everyone knows that there's no love lost between Stormwind and Gilneas. Everyone knows why."

Utter quiet fell upon the assembly. Genn's expression was unreadable as he waited for Varian to go on, but his ears lay flat in concern.

A Sentinel suddenly stood behind the high priestess. Tyrande touched Malfurion's hand again, and he nodded to indicate that he would keep the proceedings going. The archdruid understood that whatever it was that would make someone interrupt the high priestess at such a delicate time had to be as significant as the murders of the two Highborne.

A third? he wondered. Praying that it was not so, the archdruid leaned forward so as to indicate to Varian that while Tyrande might have to leave, it was no slight to Stormwind.

Varian cocked his head as if to say he took no insult

from the high priestess's departure. The lord of Storm-wind then continued, "The benefit that an ally such as Gilneas offers us is obvious. While our skills in combat more than match those of the orcs and their allies, there's always been a hunger that the Horde has thrived upon that we—so civilized—no longer seem to have. The worgen offer us that righteous hunger to overcome all obstacles in battle, to keep the Alliance from splintering or merely sitting back as the orcs take one land after another. . . ."

Genn's eyes widened, and even Malfurion could not help but feel his hope stir at such a speech.

"I considered damned long and hard on this, I promise you," Varian told all. "Such an ally can help us easily hold the Horde's ambitions at bay, maybe even push them back!" The king indicated Genn and the Gilneans. "An ally of such honor, of such courage, I'd be more than pleased to fight beside!"

His words brought cheer. Even the worgen could no longer restrain themselves, several of the younger ones giving out short howls.

Varian now turned his attention to Malfurion. "Arch-druid! You called before for a vote by acclamation, a vote I interrupted! My apologies for letting that happen! I'd meant to ask to speak sooner. . . ."

Smiling, Malfurion answered, "I would be happy to call for it again, King Varian—"

"That won't be necessary." The human monarch's expression went through a stunning transformation. A dark cast spread over it as Varian eyed Genn Greymane.

Varian spat in the Gilnean's direction.

"Calling for it again would be a waste of time," the lord

of Stormwind snarled at his counterpart below, "for I'd never give consent to allow these mongrels into the Alliance!"

Shouts of consternation erupted, especially among the worgen. The one that was Eadrik took a step toward Varian, but Genn grabbed the young warrior's shoulder and pulled him back. The two worgen bared their teeth at one another, Eadrik quickly becoming cowed.

"Honor and trust! These are what the Alliance needs, not these beasts that even when they paraded as men were lacking in both! What happens if they choose to cut themselves off once more? Will they even bother to give us warning? Can we trust them even to do *that*?" Varian snapped his fingers, and his retinue joined him on their feet, Anduin the last and most hesitant. "As I've already said to many, I find nothing worthy, nothing honorable, in this pack of hounds . . . and so I will never vote aye to their admission back into the fold!"

And with that, Varian led Stormwind out of the summit as chaos erupted among the other representatives and Malfurion Stormrage watched all his hopes crumble before his eyes.

15

CHOICES

"**E**veryone! Remain seated, please!"

The crowd, though, did not hear the archdruid. Everywhere, the various factions of the Alliance argued with one another as to what had just happened and what it meant to the summit as a whole. The voice of one night elf was easily drowned out by such a din.

But Malfurion Stormrage was more than merely a night elf and more than merely a druid.

Deafening thunder shook the assembly, and a single brilliant bolt of lightning right before the archdruid's position guaranteed that all attention returned to him.

"You know my feelings on this situation," he said to them. "And I can assure all of you that this is not over."

No one argued, although in many eyes he read disagreement. Malfurion looked to Genn Greymane to reassure him, only to find that the worgen had slipped out as swiftly and silently as the wolves they resembled.

Concealing his own dismay, the archdruid pressed:

"I will attend to this matter. For the moment, I call for a vote to end the summit for today and invite all representatives and their retinues to partake of the splendor of Darnassus."

"Sounds like a good notion tae me! Me throat's parched from all this politickin'," Kurdran bellowed. "If it means gettin' some ale an' food faster, it's got me vote!"

The dwarf's lusty response eased the situation, and the vote to end for the day passed without further question as to whether there *would* be a second day.

As the assembly dispersed, Malfurion summoned one of the Sentinels flanking his and Tyrande's seats. "Did the high priestess inform you as to why she had to leave?"

"No, Archdruid."

"Do you know where she went?"

"The temple, I believe."

Malfurion thought for a moment. "Please take a message to her. Tell her that I will be there as soon as I can, but that I must go speak with the king of Stormwind. Tell her that he voted against Gilneas, but I believe there is still hope. Do you have that?"

"Yes, Archdruid!"

"Go now, then!"

The Sentinel saluted sharply, then rushed off. Malfurion took a breath, using the moment to organize his thoughts.

The vision insists that Varian is the one, the archdruid thought with much frustration. *Perhaps he is, but the vision does not have to deal with his obstinacy! He must be convinced . . . or, despite visions, the Alliance must find someone else!*

A determined look crossed his features. Varian Wrynn *would* listen.

He went in pursuit of Stormwind's bitter king.

Malfurion likely felt betrayed, and Varian could not blame him, but the night elf had been presumptuous to think that he could convince the lord of Stormwind to change his mind. The king of Gilneas had much blood on his hands—human blood. Where had he been when Lordaeron had beseeched others for aid during the Third War? True, Stormwind had not directly participated in the war, but it had been a strong supporter of the Alliance. Stormwind had also been going through much more turmoil at that time . . . and Varian had been at the heart of most of that turmoil. Already a king at eighteen due to his father's assassination, he had been trying to oversee the kingdom's reconstruction when he had been politically outmaneuvered after his wife's death by the foul sorcery of Lady Katrana Prestor . . . who, in truth, had been the black dragon Onyxia. And when Varian had sailed at Lady Jaina's suggestion to Theramore for a summit, he had been kidnapped and subsequently lost his memory.

No, Varian felt that he could not be blamed for Stormwind's inability to do more for the Alliance. Genn had been his own man and fully in charge when he had refused to answer the call more than once. He had built his damnable wall to seal off Gilneas; then, during the Third War, he had not deigned to contribute so much as a token force. That last affront had been too great even for some of his own people, who had taken up the challenge themselves and formed the valiant Gilneas Brigade.

Varian felt no satisfaction for what he had said, but neither did he have any remorse. Genn Greymane had only
gotten what he had much too long deserved.

"Tomorrow we sail home," he informed the others as
they neared their quarters.

"Father—"

"Not now, Anduin."

In what was an uncustomary anger, the prince waved
off the rest of the party. Those assigned to guard the royal
family's quarters hesitated, but Anduin stared them down
until they, too, left. They all knew that look. They had
seen it often in the father but never in the son, until now.

Ignoring what Anduin was doing, Varian entered their
quarters. He seized the bottle of night elven wine he had
started just before the summit and drank from it.

"Where're you, Broll?" Varian muttered. The one
thing that he had hoped would come of this fiasco of a
gathering was a short reunion with the brawny druid
who had fought beside him as a gladiator. Broll, though,
was on some mission for Malfurion, yet another reason
for the king to be annoyed with his hosts.

"Father . . ."

"I said not now, Anduin—"

"Yes. Now."

For a boy barely in his teens, Anduin's tone was measured and strong . . . and full of disappointment. Putting
down the bottle, Varian faced him.

"I did what needed to be done. You'll understand that
when you're king."

"I understand that you're still living in the past, Father. That you can't ever seem to escape it. People change.
People can redeem themselves. You've not given Genn

Greymane any chance, and in doing that, you've also condemned the rest of his kingdom—"

"They're fools enough to follow his lead despite the bloodshed and horror his choices have caused; they can follow him through this."

"You don't mean that. Don't you see—"

"Enough!" The outburst surprised Varian as much as it did his son. Anduin deflated. Varian read the immense sadness filling his son.

The prince headed toward his room.

"Anduin—"

"Good night, Father. I pray you'll understand some day."

Not quite certain as to what his son meant by that, Varian returned to the wine. Then, thinking better of it, he stepped back outside. There he found his guards anxiously awaiting.

"Safe to go in," he jested. "I'll stay out here for a moment."

They did not argue. Varian felt some sympathy for the men, who wanted to do their duty but were constantly being dismissed by their charges. He would reward them when the party returned to Stormwind.

"Varian."

"*Oh, by all that's holy, am I allowed no peace?*" The king turned to face Malfurion. "I said my lot back at the induction! There's nothing left to discuss!"

The night elf's brow rose at this unexpected outburst. "There is much left to discuss, if I may be so bold. I am aware of why you said what you did and the right you had to say it. The summit, though, must continue, and I—"

"Your summit's failed. You should know that. Failed

like so much . . ." Varian looked off as he spoke, his thoughts turning to distant memory, not the evening's events.

The shift did not go unnoticed by the archdruid. In a calm, quiet tone, he replied, "Failure is not always the end of things. It can be a method of learning to better succeed in other ways. Cenarius knows I have met with failure enough myself, if I may use my brother—and perhaps the worgen themselves—as examples. I can also appreciate the troubles you have struggled with, and I know the blame you still lay upon yourself for them. You still think that you could have saved Tiffin from the riot or somehow prevented Deathwing's own daughter, Onyxia, from stealing your kingdom while in the guise of Lady Prestor! Neither of those events could have been prevented by you—"

"Couldn't they? Easy to talk so, after the fact and so far removed, Archdruid, but you weren't involved in those troubles! My wife was killed by a brickbat! A good man, Reginald Windsor, was burned alive by the damned dragon's breath! I let agents of the Defias capture me, and in my absence, my son, my only son, was left defenseless and abandoned! I will not let that happen again! *Ever!*"

"You were not—"

Varian thrust a condemning finger in the night elf's face. "You've no right to speak of any of this, anyway! What do you even understand of the kind of horrors I've seen and suffered? Two wars came and passed while you cheerfully meditated and wandered that accursed Emerald Dream! Two wars in which countless lives were lost! You never saw the sacrifices Stormwind had to face, much less the rest of Azeroth, while Greymane sat back and did absolutely nothing! Nothing! You druids preach of the harmony of the world and the creatures on it, but harmony is easy to ask for when you don't have to struggle to survive like the rest of us!"

"I understand more than you think," the archdruid started. "I have faced war and strife too. When the Burning Legion first invaded—"

"You must reach back ten thousand years for your example?" Varian interrupted. "And what about something a bit more recent . . . or relevant?"

The pair stood in silence, their unblinking gazes fixed upon one another. Malfurion radiated calmness, which only served to increase Varian's frustration.

The night elf considered, then tried a different tack. "Much of what you say is true; I will not deny that. I have made many mistakes, but I have sought to learn from them, learned to accept my shortcomings, and strived to do better for those around me. That is something a druid, gladiator, or ruler should always do."

It was not by accident that the night elf mentioned Varian's past role. Without saying anything direct, he reminded the king that, while Malfurion had been elsewhere during the most recent troubles, so had Varian. Stormwind had suffered for many years without its rightful monarch to guide it, first for a decade when Onyxia had used her magic to influence Varian following Tiffin's death, and then after his kidnapping. While Varian had not had any choice in either incident, the fact that the king often yearned for a return to the days when he only had to deal with his own immediate future was something that the night elf would not let be forgotten at the moment.

"Has Genn done anything so terrible other than seek

to do what he thought best for his people?" the archdruid went on. "Gilneas has suffered deeply and more than once because of those choices. Genn regrets that and has offered to do everything he can to make amends. Do not judge him as you judge yourself, Varian. He will never stand a chance of redeeming himself, if that is the case."

Varian grunted. "If that's all you can say to try to convince me to change my vote, you've wasted your breath, Archdruid! Stormwind leaves tomorrow. Whatever the rest of you want to do after that is your own choice."

"Varian . . ."

"For a place surrounded by forest, it's damned hard for a man to even get a breath of air! I've said all I intend! If you *will* excuse me . . ." The king all but shoved past the archdruid and headed toward the edge of Darnassus. He had not gone far when he heard footsteps behind him. The sound served to agitate him further.

"Are you so desperate, night elf?" he snapped as he turned. "The great archdruid—"

Yet, it was not Malfurion but rather Anduin who had followed his father.

"Anduin . . . I thought you'd gone to bed—"

"No . . . I was up. . . ." There was something secretive in the prince's voice. "I heard voices . . . I heard everything."

"With the archdruid? You heard nothing that matters. We still leave tomorrow—"

"I'm not going with you."

The statement sounded so fantastic, so ridiculous, that at first Varian had to think whether he had actually heard his son speak it. Incredulous, he said, "Go get some sleep. We leave early."

Anduin gave him a look that Varian usually reserved

for himself when dealing with fool-headed courtiers. "You never listen to me. Please listen now, Father. *I am not going with you.*"

"You're tired! You—"

Anduin looked exasperated. "I should've done what I had planned, but I started to have second thoughts until I heard you and Archdruid Stormrage arguing! He couldn't make you see sense any more than I ever could, and he's lived more than ten thousand years!"

"Age doesn't mean wisdom," Varian retorted, annoyed that the night elf should have more of his son's respect than he.

"I'm afraid I know that, Father." The moment Anduin said it, he looked as if he regretted it. "I've not come to renew our argument. I went to my quarters and started to write you a letter explaining everything."

"Son . . . what—"

The prince held up a hand for silence, again very much mimicking his father's stance. "I'm no warrior. We both know that. I've said it more than once. I'll never be you. My path lies elsewhere. . . ."

"You're heir to the throne!" Varian insisted, using whatever course he could to convince his only child that he was being absurd.

"I'm not abandoning Stormwind, but I need to leave to complete what I've begun." Despite being only thirteen summers, at the moment Anduin sounded like a much older person. "I started it with High Priest Rohan in Ironforge. You *know* what he said about me. Even you agreed with him about my potential."

"The Light can help you when you come to rule Stormwind, but it's only a tool, like—"

"The Light is no tool. The Light *is*." Anduin smiled softly. "Someday, I'll make you understand that too. Father, I never felt more alive than during my training in Ironforge! Just think of it! As a priest of the Light, I could do so much more for our people—"

"As king, you have the ultimate ability!" Varian's heart pounded. Of all that was happening, this was the one thing with which he could not cope. His son *would* come home with him. There would be an end to this talk about the Light, clearly a misguided influence. Varian would see to it that Anduin would overcome his lack of sufficient battle skills and train to become a proper ruler!

"Father?" Anduin's smile faded. "You aren't listening. Fine. I tried."

The boy turned to leave. Something snapped in Varian. He saw his beloved Tiffin again with their infant son snuggled in her arms. Tiffin faded away, leaving only the child . . . and then the child began to fade away.

Varian could not let that happen. Without thinking, he lunged forward, snaring Anduin's arm.

The prince let out a cry. Some of the overwhelming fear faded, and Varian realized that he was crushing Anduin's arm.

"I—I—" The king released his grip. Anduin, his face filled with shock, grasped at his injured arm. He knew as well as his father that Varian not only could strangle a foe with one hand, but *had* several times. Few men there were who could match the strength of the legendary Lo'Gosh.

And now, in a fit of utter madness, he had used that same might, however briefly, against his defiant son. . . .

"I—Anduin—" Varian could not summon words. The

person most precious to him in all the world stood horrified at the sight of him. "I never meant—"

Their guards suddenly came running. Varian could only guess that they had heard Anduin's cry and feared for the prince's life.

"Your Majesty!" called the captain. "Did someone attack the two of you?"

"It's all right," Anduin interjected, rubbing his arm. "There's no danger . . . is there, Father?"

"No . . ."

Anduin turned to leave again. Varian started to reach for him, but stopped the moment it appeared that the guards would follow his example and try to keep the prince from wandering away.

"Where are you going, Anduin?"

The prince paused and looked over his shoulder at his father. "To Velen. I'm going with him and the draenei when they depart."

It did not startle the king, but did sting him. The Prophet could probably speak far easier with his son than he could. "Did you—have you discussed this with him?"

"I talked to him about resuming my studies of the Light."

"You can do that back in Stormwind with Archbishop Benedictus!" Varian did not care how he looked to the guards. This was his son and he was losing him.

Anduin's brow furrowed at mention of the archbishop. "Benedictus . . . is not right for this. . . . I can't explain that. I just know. For what I need to learn, I need to go elsewhere. Rohan even once told me that."

The king had not been aware of that little fact. He silently cursed the dwarf, silently cursed Velen . . . and then finally himself.

"They can take my things to the ship, Father."

"Velen may not take you with him to the draenei capital."

Anduin paused to consider this, and Varian's hopes stirred. Then: "If he won't take me with him, he'll know that I have to go elsewhere to achieve what I must. Good-bye, Father."

"Don't—" The former gladiator bit off what he was going to say, for the guards, more aware of what was happening, looked as if all they waited for was the smallest signal. Even a hint by their king that they should step in and surround the prince would have served enough as a direct order.

His decision not to let them act brought the sad smile back to Anduin's face. "Thank you."

"I—I swear by your mother that I'll never hurt you again, Anduin. Not in any way!" He started toward his son with the intention of hugging him.

The prince's eyes widened. He stepped out of reach, then replied, "I know."

Anduin walked off in what Varian could only imagine was the direction of the Prophet's quarters. The king watched until his son was no longer visible to him, aware all the while that the last thing he had seen in Anduin's eyes was a shadow of fear that Varian might, after all, hurt him.

"Your Majesty . . . ," the captain hesitantly began. "Are you certain we shouldn't—"

"You're dismissed," he responded curtly. "All of you."

Aware of his mood, the guards obeyed swiftly and without question. Varian was at last left alone.

And only then did he realize just how much he was afraid he would be that way for the rest of his life.

• • •

Some of the certainty with which he had left his father began to evaporate the farther from the king Anduin got. Yet, something continued to urge him on his course.

He knew somehow that he would find Velen in the Temple Gardens again. The draenei had just begun to meditate and so was not disturbed by the youth's sudden appearance.

But that did not mean that Velen had no inkling as to why Anduin had come.

"You spoke with your father," the Prophet murmured. "I sense the troubles between you."

Anduin saw no reason not to be blunt. "Velen, I know my path now. I want to go with you."

The draenei looked perturbed. "How did you find out?"

"What do you mean?"

"Matters have arisen that take me elsewhere. I planned to choose another priest to act as representative of the draenei and leave in the morning after giving my farewells to our hosts."

His revelation cemented Anduin's course. "I knew nothing. I knew only that I can learn best if I come with you."

"Your father . . ."

"I've told him."

The Prophet frowned. "Perhaps you should reconsider. The path of the Light is not a simple one, and you are young. Gifted, yes, and I say that honestly. Come to me in three years, perhaps—"

"If you try to leave me behind, I'll follow. I know that I've chosen right. I feel it."

"So young . . . and yet so old," the draenei remarked with a sigh. He noticed the youth rub his arm. "You have an injury. Let me help you." The Prophet placed an open hand on the area in question.

The Light emanated from the draenei's palm, a wondrous glow no larger than an apple yet radiating so much majesty. It spread to the injured region. The pain in Anduin's arm quickly receded, becoming little more than a memory in but the blink of an eye.

And as that happened, Anduin felt a stirring in his heart. Emotions arose, feelings of love and forgiveness.

Along with those feelings, an image formed, one not of memory, but rather imagination. Anduin only knew his mother from pictures, and so the vision he had of her was one formed throughout his young life. In that vision, she was glorious, comforting. . . .

"You love her very much, your mother," Velen murmured. He did not bother to explain how he knew what Anduin was thinking. Velen was the Prophet, after all.

"She died when I was a baby, but all I've seen and heard from my father and others of the court makes me feel I know her . . . and love her."

The draenei nodded. "And you love your father much also."

Anduin swallowed, recalling the pain and the constant frustration with the king . . . but also all that Varian had sought to do for him. "Of course. Whatever our disagreements . . ."

Velen lowered his palm. The Light faded from both his hand and the prince. The emotions faded, too, though they never completely vanished.

"And that is in great part why the Light touches you so deep." The Prophet smiled slightly. "Very well, Anduin. We leave come sunlight."

16

A MESSENGER'S RESOLVE

Malfurion rushed back to the temple, his sense of failure with Varian compounded by the knowledge that the Sentinel who had spoken with Tyrande at the summit—subsequently drawing the high priestess away—no doubt had news of some other disaster. He suspected that it might concern the Highborne, but prepared himself for anything at this point.

To his surprise, it was not one of the priestesses who greeted him but rather one of his own. The anxious druid bowed low as Malfurion approached.

"Parsis!" The other druid was skilled, capable of shifting to storm crow form, and, given a bit more seasoning, could someday become an archdruid of high standing. Naturally, Malfurion never quite mentioned this future he saw to the younger druid himself. "You were assigned to Ashenvale! Why are you here?"

"It is not for me to answer that, Shan'do," Parsis respectfully responded, the younger druid clearly exhausted. "There is another who has more than earned that right."

Malfurion did not question him further. Parsis led him to the area where but recently Shalasyr's body had lain shortly after Jarod had brought it to Darnassus.

He heard voices within, the voices of priestesses at prayer. The archdruid glanced at Parsis and saw the younger night elf look disturbed. Something had changed for the worse since he had left this place.

As they stepped inside, Tyrande turned from where she had been leading four other senior priestesses in the prayer. The light of Elune shone down upon not only her and the priestesses but also a figure lying on the platform between them.

It was a Sentinel. Malfurion did not recognize her. Her violet skin had paled considerably, not a good sign.

In silence, he joined his mate. Tyrande leaned close and whispered, "Her name is Aradria Cloudflyer. She is a courier from Ashenvale."

"A wounded courier?" Malfurion did not like the direction this was taking.

The high priestess started to continue, but the Sentinel suddenly moaned. Her eyes fluttered open and she gazed up at the pair, eventually fixing on Malfurion.

"Arch—Archdruid . . . you know, then . . ."

She fought to shift so she could face him better, and in doing so revealed a long, wicked scar running across her upper torso. Based on what Malfurion could see of it, it was a wonder that she was still alive. Other, smaller scars decorated what he could see of her body, but the huge one was clearly what had done the worst to her.

"The irony is, her own glaive did it," Parsis muttered in his other ear. "She fell upon it during a struggle with several orcs. She had slain at least two before that happened."

"What was she doing in orc territory? And why bring her here?"

"She was not in orc territory. She was well on her way here with an urgent missive from Commander Haldrissa."

The archdruid looked to Tyrande for verification of the dread news. She sadly nodded.

"They—they snuck behind the lines . . . ," Aradria rasped, evidently hearing well despite her condition.

"You must rest," the high priestess advised her. "Your will and strength will aid in your recovery as much as the blessing of the Mother Moon."

Aradria coughed harshly. Blood spattered Tyrande's gown but she made no attempt to either move out of the way or wipe it clean. There was only concern for the messenger.

"I p-prayed to her . . . as I lay there, fading," the Sentinel managed. "I prayed th-that if she let me survive long enough to do my d-duty, then I—I would be g-glad to give my life after. She granted that—that p-prayer."

"I found her while communing with the forest some distance west of our outpost," Parsis explained. "The trees were unsettled about some event that had taken place nearby. I searched around . . . and then I came upon her."

The druid quickly described finding the bodies. Parsis had found at least four dead orcs, two of them ripped apart in a fashion that could only mean that they had been the victims of the hippogryph.

"P-poor Windstorm," Aradria murmured. "He was such a loyal friend." She coughed again. Tyrande took a cloth and wiped the Sentinel's lips clean.

"I did what I could for her, but she had been bleeding for so long." The druid looked ashamed.

Tyrande shook her head. "No one could have done more, Parsis, not even one of the Sisterhood."

"He—he also brought me here . . ." the Sentinel said.

"I healed her as best I could, then shifted into storm crow form," Parsis explained. "It was a very strenuous flight, but I knew not to stop."

"They t-took the message," Aradria continued, gulping in air as she spoke. "But I knew—knew what the commander wanted to s-say. . . ."

"Save your strength," Tyrande insisted. "Let me tell them what you said to me."

Aradria nodded, then shut her eyes. The high priestess quickly related Commander Haldrissa's observations and concerns. The depth of the Horde's incursions into western Ashenvale startled Malfurion and even Parsis, who had no doubt heard it before. All the while the priestesses quietly prayed for the courier who had risked so much to bring this news while it was still fresh.

"I am inclined to take everything that the commander mentioned—and Aradria swore by—as at least a very expert guess and likely very much the truth," the high priestess finished.

"Does Shandris know Aradria is here?"

"I have sent someone to tell her." Tyrande returned her attention to the stricken Sentinel. "We cannot begin to thank you enough for all you—"

The courier's chest no longer rose and fell.

Bending near, Tyrande let her hand pass over Aradria. "She is . . . no more. She must have died at least a minute or two ago."

"She almost looks as if she is smiling slightly," Parsis said, choking a little at the end. "I wanted to give her a little more time to rest, but she insisted. . . ."

The high priestess straightened. "She asked something of Elune, and the Mother Moon saw how worthy she was. To be frank, I was also very surprised that she made it to us, much less lived long enough to tell us everything."

"Then it behooves us to see to it that her sacrifice was not in vain," Shandris called from the entrance. The sternness in her voice was due to Aradria's loss. Shandris considered her Sentinels part of her.

"I did my best, General," Parsis blurted, somewhat cowed by the famous warrior.

"I know you did, druid. I personally accepted your assignment to Ashenvale." She strode up to the body. "And I remember her. A skilled rider . . . almost as good as I. Haldrissa chose the right person to carry the news." To Tyrande and Malfurion, Shandris added, "We will of course have to send a force as soon as possible."

"What about the summit?" Tyrande asked her husband.

"We turn it in another direction. We brought everyone together to try to strengthen the Alliance; this is exactly why."

Shandris respectfully touched the dead Aradria on the shoulder. "With your permission, I have four of my best waiting outside to take her body. We will give her a proper send-off."

The high priestess nodded. "Go ahead. Her name will be sung in the temple."

"I appreciate that." Shandris whistled two short notes and the other Sentinels entered. The high priestess and Malfurion stepped to the side. The priestesses looked as one to their leader, who gave them permission to depart.

Parsis bowed to the archdruid and his wife. "If I may, I think I should go with General Shandris. I have more recent knowledge of the land there and I suspect she will want to hear it."

"My very thought," the general commented. "Come along."

Before they could depart, Malfurion asked, "Parsis, there was another druid assigned along with you—"

"Kara'din, Archdruid."

"Did you contact him at any point?"

The younger druid looked more anxious. "Not immediately, I am sorry to say. I was—caught up in the matter of the courier. I did try to during the flight, but for some reason could not touch his mind! Forgive me! I wanted to tell you that, but—"

Malfurion could certainly not fault Parsis, who looked as if he were about to collapse despite his insistence that he go with Shandris. "Fret not. Tell the general everything you know, then get some rest. Do you understand?"

"Yes . . . yes, Archdruid."

"I will not hold him any longer than necessary," Shandris promised.

The Sentinels reverently lifted Aradria's body onto a wooden stretcher, then carried her away. Shandris and the druid took up positions behind them.

Tyrande murmured a short prayer for the valiant courier as the Sentinels disappeared with the body. Then, frowning deeper, she said to Malfurion, "I was told what

Varian did. I was stunned. What happened after he left?
Did you go after him?"

"I went to talk with him. . . . It did not go any better
than the voting did. We cannot depend on him to become
the leader we have been seeking, Tyrande. There is no
time now."

"It is more important than ever, my love! Do you not
understand? Elune foresaw this! Varian *must* guide us in
this darkest hour!"

The archdruid grimaced. "He cannot even guide himself where his son is concerned. I heard them having an
argument before I dared approach their quarters. That
boy has had to grow up a lot. He may be young in human
years, but he is much older in human spirit. Varian is going to have more trouble with him, I think."

"Elune is not wrong, my love!"

He mulled things over, then sighed. "There may be
one hope. There may be a way to make him come to
terms with all that he has been through and by that learn
to forgive others, especially Genn, for the mistakes they
in turn have made."

"What are you going to do?"

Malfurion took her in his arms and hugged her tight.
"First, continue to have faith in you. Second . . . I think I
need to take Varian on a hunt. . . ."

"Are you better?"

Jarod stirred. His body felt stiff and his shoulders
ached when he moved his arms, but otherwise the only
reminder of the horrific torture that he had suffered was
the memory of it. That was more than enough for him.

"I am well enough," he responded cautiously. "Where am I?"

"My quarters," Maiev answered. She squatted down next to her brother, who lay on a reed mat that he expected served as her bed. She handed him a mug filled with wine.

"Thank you." Jarod's eyes quickly scanned the chamber. As he expected, Maiev's home was all but devoid of personal effects save for a morbidly fascinating array of weaponry set upon the wall opposite him. Jarod recalled his sister's interest in blades even before she had joined the Sisterhood and noted that, in addition to an exceptional collection of night elven ones, she had several that had obviously been obtained from other races. "What happened to me?"

"You ran into a trap. One intended for a Highborne, no doubt. Some people would have died from what you went through."

"I thought I did."

She found the comment amusing. "You barely got a scratch."

There was pride in her tone, Jarod realized, pride in his stamina.

"Neva informs me that you were coming to see me," Maiev prompted.

He told her his part in the grisly discovery and the request by Tyrande and Malfurion that he assist his sibling in her investigation. Maiev grunted her agreement with the suggestion.

"Looked over the body you stumbled upon," she responded, her tone turning briefly to amusement again when saying the last. "Just like the first. Someone is very dedicated. Cannot say I blame them. Who would want the Highborne a part of us again? You?"

"The high priestess and archdruid want it to happen."

Maiev chuckled. "And you? Have you found forgiveness for the Highborne? Truthfully?"

He could not lie to her. "I think that they have much for which to make amends, but I argued for tolerance at the end of the War of the Ancients and I still do now. I will trust in Tyrande and Malfurion on this. They have our best interests at heart."

"Naturally." Maiev rose, then extended a hand. "Done with that?"

Jarod had not noticed that he had finished his drink. He handed the mug to her, then tried to push himself to his feet.

"Take it easy, Brother."

That only served to make him more determined to stand. Taking a deep breath, the former officer straightened.

"Very good," his sister remarked. "If you are so recovered, I guess we will get back to the task, hmm?"

He thought of the body. "Did you inspect the victim?"

"For what little time they let me. That one Highborne, Var'dyn—you know him?—he had his people spirit their dead comrade away even quicker than they did the last. I suppose that they were not happy with some of the inspecting we did of that corpse."

"Maiev . . ."

"Ha! We did not cut it up any more than the assassin did, so do not fret! I think they were afraid I might find some sorcerous trinket of theirs and keep it." She sneered. "As if I would want anything to do with *their* powers.

No, we are going back to the scene of your little incident. Come on. . . ."

He did not argue with her logic. The trek brought them back through the training area, where Neva again happened to be. She immediately joined them, taking up a place on Jarod's other side and occasionally brushing up against him in a manner that made him nervous.

"You were chasing something, so Neva said. Did you see it?"

"No. Whoever it was proved too quick at every turn."

"Whoever? A person? Definitely not an animal by accident?"

Jarod hesitated for a moment, then answered, "No. A person. He talked to me, even helped me."

The two females halted. Maiev leaned close. "Tell me."

Jarod described the interaction and how very apologetic his quarry had been throughout it all.

"So he saves you, then rushes off. Probably realized that you were not his desired prey, one of the Highborne."

"He said he had not known that the trap was there. . . . And why was it? What would a Highborne be doing near this spot?" Jarod indicated the area just before them, which they had finally reached.

Neva immediately knelt by the spot he assumed was where he had been lying. She inspected the nearest tree trunk. "Here is something we did not notice before. Bits of fur."

"Interesting." Maiev examined them. "Well . . . it is fur. And you were helped here by someone . . . someone *furred*?"

He could easily see where she was heading with her comment. "You think it was a worgen?"

"Very likely. The worgen have been snooping around the edges of the city quite a bit," his sister offered. "They have been given permission to enter and they do, now and then, but they seem to have developed an interest in skulking around too."

The former guard captain bluntly asked, "Do you think that they are the ones who killed the Highborne?"

"I do not know what reason they could have—not yet—but they could also be acting as the dupes of some other party. I am eliminating no one. The notes were written in the same archaic style."

"Then it must be a night elf at the heart of this," he decided. "Someone who lost a loved one during the war."

"Well, that narrows it down," his sibling cut in sarcastically.

"I would like to talk with that worgen again." Jarod tried to recall any detail he could, the voice his most significant clue. "Find out why he was lurking around here in the first place. It might not have anything to do with the Highborne, though—"

Maiev grunted. "Oh, it must! There is no other reasonable explanation."

He could find none, either. "Where do the worgen live? I heard something, but I am still not quite sure. . . ."

"Oh, we know where they are. What do you say, Neva?"

The other Watcher managed to slip her arm around Jarod's. Leaning her head close to his, she replied, "Now is a good time as any."

Jarod was puzzled. "For what?"

Maiev laughed. "To investigate the wolves, of course."

"'Wolves' . . ." He finally understood. "Is that all right?"

"The high priestess and archdruid have given me the authority to follow through this case wherever it might lead. The worgen will just have to behave themselves."

She led them off. Neva pulled Jarod along until, in order to avoid further discomfort around the other Watcher, he lengthened his stride and hurried after his sister.

At first, their trek was simple, almost seeming so much like a carefree walk that Jarod wondered if his sister was playing a game with him and did not truly want his assistance. However, once Maiev reached a crooked oak, she suddenly grew serious again. Neva put a finger to her lips, not that Jarod needed the warning. He could already hear something far ahead . . . and was instantly aware that if he could hear them, then they might be able to hear the three intruders.

"The main encampment is still some distance," Maiev whispered. "But recently a number of the wolves have been coming to this region. Guess they like the hunting here."

She led the other two across a small creek and toward a rise. Not for the first time did Jarod marvel at the landscape. It was very easy to forget that this entire place was all atop a gargantuan *tree*.

"Keep low," Maiev ordered. "We are very close now."

He looked at her. "Are they hostile? I thought we would just announce—"

"Be quiet." His sister moved a step ahead.

It suddenly occurred to Jarod that neither he nor his companions had taken any weapons with them. Why he had not thought of that beforehand he could only chalk up to residual fogginess due to his near death. However, that in no way reassured him. If the worgen were, after all, that dangerous . . .

"We need to turn around," he muttered. "This is not the way to go about this—"

Neva suddenly stiffened. At the same time Maiev whirled to her right.

A savage, panting form lunged from behind a tree there. Another leapt out from the opposing direction. Both landed on all fours just a few feet from the night elves, then stood. They were immediately joined by others as the worgen surrounded the trio. For the first time Jarod had a good look at the long fangs and the sharp claws and the fact that, even while hunched over, all the worgen stood taller than the night elves. The worgen were also at least half again as broad and likely outweighed even him by several pounds, all of it taut muscle.

Jarod remained still, silently and swiftly analyzing the movements of the worgen in order to judge whether they intended to attack. Maiev and Neva, on the other hand, fell into battle stances and all but dared the worgen to come at them. Jarod frowned at the two females' reactions but said nothing.

Nearly a dozen worgen now surrounded them. Their intensity amazed Jarod.

A male worgen stalked up to him. Nostrils flaring, the male sniffed Jarod carefully. The deep brown eyes—the most "human" feature of the otherwise bestial figure—narrowed slightly.

The male moved on to Neva. Her face was a mask. He sniffed at her, albeit in a more perfunctory manner. He turned from Neva. Jarod felt as if the worgen already recognized her scent.

When the apparent leader stopped at Maiev, there was a noticeable pause. As with Neva, the worgen seemed to recognize something in Jarod's sister, as if they had met previously. The lips of the creature pulled back, revealing better the sharp teeth.

Fearing for Maiev, Jarod stepped forward. That brought the leader's attention back to him. Jarod then noticed that, despite looking as they did, the worgen still wore clothes. Most of them were loose-fitting or open and in general kept in good condition. The garments made for a contrast to the raw force the worgen radiated.

"Come to spy on us again . . . ," the male growled, his voice otherwise surprisingly normal. "Do we amuse you?"

It took Jarod a moment to understand that the question was focused at Maiev. She smiled defiantly at the leader. "We are here in the performance of our duty to the high priestess. You know that."

"You found nothing to learn here last time."

"Things change."

The leader's ears twitched in annoyance. "The king will speak with your high priestess and the archdruid."

"Feel free."

The worgen as a whole growled. They sounded more frustrated than angry, however. This argument had evidently taken place once before.

"You say things change," the leader rasped. "What?"

"My brother here was nearly killed by a trap set for the Highborne." Maiev did not explain the Highborne to the worgen, confirming what she had said earlier about their being aware of the spellcasters' existence. "He was chasing a worgen at the time."

The male did not look at Jarod. "Proof?"

"We found fur caught in the bark of the tree where my brother was lying."

This garnered a derisive laugh from the entire pack. "Many animals in the forest." He displayed his claws. "The hunting is good."

"So long as you are only hunting deer and the like, not certain other prey," countered Maiev.

The leader turned to Jarod again. The long muzzle came within an inch of the night elf's nose. Jarod could smell the carnivore's thick breath, but did not show any distaste for the odor.

"Tell me," the worgen demanded. "You saw this one of ours?"

"No . . . I was in too much pain."

"Hmmph. You would be feeling no pain at all anymore if he had attacked you as you claim."

Jarod met the gaze steadily. "I never said he attacked me. He pulled me free of the trap. I do not know how, but he did. He was even sorry that I got caught in it."

The ears of his questioner twitched in thought. The worgen leader remained in front of Jarod, but glanced at Maiev. "A different story from what you hinted. So a worgen on the hunt happens nearby. Out of respect to the high priestess and archdruid, he retreats when discovering night elves so close. When a fool follows, he even rescues the fool, and for that we're judged monsters. . . ."

There were accompanying growls from the others. Jarod tensed, expecting to have to try to fight his way free even despite the impossible odds.

"We are only investigating every possible situation," Maiev countered. "If you have nothing to hide, you have nothing to fear, right?"

The worgen leader bared his teeth again. "You wish to question us, you come to us. It's dangerous to sneak about here. Worse things than traps for magi. Younger worgen can get caught up in the hunt; they might leap before they realize that it's not a deer." His ears straightened. "By then . . . it could be too late."

He made a dismissive gesture with one clawed hand. The other worgen moved back from the night elves. Jarod kept a wary eye on the worgen until they had moved a sufficient distance from the night elves, then joined Maiev and Neva.

The leader of the worgen party snarled. As one, the lupine creatures slipped back among the trees, moving as silently as any skilled night elf.

Jarod exhaled. "That was too close."

"We were never in any real danger," his sister countered confidently. "For all their bluster, they are just a bunch of humans."

He grew angry. "Humans with claws and very sharp teeth—and you knew that they would come for us!"

"Easier than following after them. Think of it as a test. I wanted to see their reaction when I mentioned what happened to you. I saw enough. They know something. More than they realize."

"I would have liked to have known what you planned."

"You might have changed your mind in coming. I wanted you here. Besides"—she slipped her hand behind her; when Maiev brought it forward again, her brother saw that she was now armed—"we were not so helpless as you thought."

Neva imitated Maiev, revealing that *both* females were armed.

Jarod snorted. This was the sister he remembered. Maiev would do anything to see her duty through to the end. It was something to remember while he helped discover the ones behind the assassinations of the Highborne.

"It is likely a night elf behind this," he said with continued irritation. "Our people have a much better reason than the worgen to want the Highborne dead."

Maiev began to head back toward Darnassus. "Oh, you are probably right on that. This will lead back to night elves. But the worgen . . . they need watching, too, do you not think?"

Neva gave Jarod a coy smile as she followed Maiev. After a moment the former guard captain trailed after. He was still angry with his sibling for her recklessness, although in retrospect he could see from her colored history how such a trait could have developed over the millennia. In some ways he suspected that her recklessness had been the difference between life and death for Maiev.

But I will not stand by while you do that again, Jarod swore. If they were to work together, Maiev would have to understand that her brother would be no one's fool, not even hers. Their success—and possibly the stable existence of their people—depended on her understanding him.

It suddenly struck him that his anger at his sister made him feel more alive than any other moment after Shalasyr's death. Aware of Jarod's relationship with Maiev, Shalasyr would have found that amusing.

Ahead of him, Maiev muttered something to Neva, then chuckled. That stirred up another subject, one that he doubted Maiev would have found so funny. Jarod had learned something of interest during the encounter with the worgen—something his sister would have liked to know.

He had gradually recognized the voice of the leader of the group. It had been that of his rescuer. Jarod had not immediately made the connection due to the fact that when this worgen had rescued him, he had done so in his human form, using fingers rather than claws to grasp the injured night elf. He had also whispered then, as opposed to the gruffer, more commanding tone used during this encounter.

But even more important, there had been a look in the worgen's human eyes that had indicated that he, in turn, had understood that Jarod recognized him. Even despite that, the worgen had ordered them released.

Jarod intended to find out why . . . and when he did, it would be without the impediment of his sister. Maiev would just have to wait until her brother returned from the worgen encampment.

Of course, that was assuming that they would let him leave alive a *second* time.

17

INTO THE FOREST

T he next day came, and still the outpost was not attacked. Haldrissa would have taken heart save for
the fact that by now she knew better. The Horde
was merely implementing the next stage of whatever plan
its commander in Ashenvale had in mind. She already knew
that whoever was in charge was high among the leadership,
certainly picked by the new warchief, Garrosh Hellscream.

An hour after dawn, the gates swung wide open and
a force of mounted Sentinels supported by archers and
warriors on foot rushed out to confront whoever might
be there. Haldrissa led the charge herself, her nightsaber
roaring eagerly as the scent of the orcs reached it.

But although they found traces of the archers, there
were no actual sightings of the Horde. It was as if they
had melted back into shadow once their foul task had
been accomplished.

Denea was blunt in her assessment. "We should have
charged out during the night. I knew we should have."

Haldrissa ignored the slight to her decision. The commander considered her options again. Of all the outposts, the two most significant were her own—in great part due to its central proximity to the rest of those lining Alliance-held lands—and *Silverwing*. Silverwing was unique. It was a bastion of defense in, of all places, hostile territory, the Horde's outpost of Splintertree not all that far to the northeast. Even when the orcs had pushed forward elsewhere, Silverwing had prevailed. It maintained itself through the bravery of its fighters and a thin patch of ground connecting it to the rest of the Alliance territory.

There had been no contact with Silverwing, but that did not mean that it had fallen. The smoke that they had seen from their position had been more to the north. Silverwing was slightly more south and across the Falfarren River. Haldrissa suspected that the smoke came from one of the lesser outposts, likely Forest Song. She hoped that the defenders there had managed to hold, especially since she could do nothing for them at the moment.

The fact that there had been no hint of Silverwing's downfall encouraged the commander, but she knew that she had to act fast. If they could link up with Silverwing, they would present the Horde with a more solidified front.

There was no need to wait for word from Darnassus. It was clear that Aradria had perished even if her body had not been discovered by the supply wagons. There would be no help until communication could be reestablished and that would take some time. She already had three nightsaber riders heading west, but suspected that whatever the Horde commander had in mind would be unleashed before the capital could send help.

"Silverwing . . . Denea, I need our force divided in two, one to defend here, another to march with us to Silverwing. This moment."

"We ride there today?"

"That depends on you." Haldrissa did not care if Denea took any offense at her words or tone. The commander had no more patience, and her second had to be reminded who was still in charge.

Perhaps in order to prove that Haldrissa had underestimated her, Denea had the outpost's contingent divided up within the hour. Even still, it felt like much too long. The commander kept waiting for the Horde to suddenly attack again. They did not, but whether that was a good sign, she could not yet say.

She considered leaving Denea in charge, but chose instead to appoint one of the other officers. Haldrissa would need her most efficient officers at the front, and Denea was certainly the best of those, ambitions aside.

The column moved out cautiously, with scouts riding ahead and reporting back on a regular basis. The only traces of the Horde were footprints, and those tended to be so mixed in direction it was difficult to follow any trail from them.

Haldrissa did not like the unpredictability of the Horde strategy of late. This was not the type of war that she was used to fighting. Whoever coordinated the enemy's efforts constantly left her guessing. She could only hope that her own decisions would counter whatever they planned.

Though the world has changed so much, at least war should remain a comfortable constant, Haldrissa mused darkly. She wished that they had already reached Silverwing.

Knowing that they could then make a proper stand against whatever the orcs wanted to throw at them would go a great way toward easing her mind. Give her a clean, straightforward battle with all the accompanying traditions, not perplexing tricks such as the Horde was suddenly using.

Give her war as it was meant to be.

There was war . . . and Varian could not have cared less.

His son had left him. Anduin had left him.

How his opponents in the arenas would have mocked the onetime gladiator for his mournful state . . . had any of them survived. The great Lo'Gosh teary-eyed for his child.

A messenger had delivered the news of war to Varian and his people at the same time that the other members of the Alliance had been notified. The high priestess had some notion of rushing a force to Ashenvale and had asked the others for whatever assistance they could muster on short notice. Naturally Stormwind would help, but that did not matter in the least to Varian. Azeroth meant nothing to him. Anduin had left him . . . and he knew that it was his fault that the boy had.

This was just the latest failure on his part, the latest proof that he would have been better off having remained bereft of his memory and fighting day after day for his life against the other dregs of the world. Better yet, he should have died when his father had; then Tiffin would have never married him and been condemned as another victim of his cursed life. Anduin would have been safe, too, for he—

He would have never existed.

Swearing at himself, Varian downed the last of the wine. He yearned for some good Stormwind whiskey or something not so sweet as night elven wine. Still, enough of it would drown out his thoughts for a time.

That essential mission in mind, Varian ordered his frustrated guards to find him more wine or dwarven ale. He, in turn, sat in a chair facing the quarters where Anduin had recently slept, and buried himself deep in his self-recriminations.

True to his word, the prince had left with the draenei. Varian's own departure had been temporarily delayed. He did not want to return to Stormwind without his son . . . not yet.

I've lost him, Tiffin. . . . I lost you and now I've lost him. . . .

There was a knock at the door. His eyes still fixed on Anduin's quarters, the king frowned. His servants had orders to bring whatever alcohol they found right to him. That meant ignoring protocol about entering the presence of their ruler. The sooner he could drink himself deeper into oblivion, the better.

"Come in, damn you!" he roared when they still did not enter. "And bring what drink you've found quickly!"

The door opened at last, but the voice that followed was one of the last Varian wanted to hear. "I have brought no spirits, but thought there might be a way to raise yours."

The king still did not turn away from his son's quarters. "You'll forgive me if I'm in no mood for company, not even yours."

Malfurion walked around Varian, blocking his view. "Anduin would not want you like this, especially because of some argument with him. Neither would your wife."

The king frowned. "Please leave, Archdruid."

Undaunted, Malfurion said, "If it is not a talk you desire, perhaps you would like to find a way to more directly vent your frustrations."

Despite himself, Varian was interested. "If you've something to keep me from thinking for a while, name it."

"Something much better than all this drinking. A hunt."

"A hunt?" He sat up. "You, a druid, want to take me on a hunt? Doesn't that go against your beliefs?"

"The hunt is an essential part of nature. It keeps the balance. We do not condemn the bear—or the wolf—for its part in it, and if men, night elves, and others take but what they need and respect where that bounty comes from, there is no contradiction. Azeroth nourishes us and, in return, those of my calling aid it in whatever little fashion we can."

"'Whatever little fashion' . . . I know the extent of your power, Archdruid."

Malfurion shrugged. "I have been blessed with gifts, but they come with responsibility."

Varian nodded. "The price of true leadership is to understand that all the advantages come with heavy responsibility. I know that too well."

"Enough of this talk, though. I only came to offer you respite through a hunt. If you are not interested . . ."

The king rose. "Oh, I'm interested."

"Good! We can gather your men—"

This earned the archdruid a snort of derision. "I'm not like some of those overfed monarchs who play at hunting by having a hundred beaters frighten some poor beast out of the bush so that he and his pathetic courtiers can surround it and either hack it to death or fill it with enough arrows to make it look like a pincushion! That's not hunting; that's true barbarism that even the orcs wouldn't accept! No . . . I prefer to hunt alone, with just my bow and my stealth. If that's enough, I bring home food. If not, the beast proves himself my better."

"A reasonable point." The night elf gestured to the door. "Then it will be just you and me."

"You're going to hunt too? You can call the beasts right to you! What sort of hunting is that?"

The archdruid simply smiled. "You do not know me if you think I would abuse my power in that manner. Come, we will see who fares best."

Eager to do whatever he could to forget Anduin's flight, Varian did not hesitate any longer. He seized his bow and quiver from where they were stored and, with the night elf leading, gratefully abandoned his quarters.

As they departed, two of his servants returned. Both had been successful in their efforts to procure wine or ale.

"Leave those inside," the king decided, just in case the night elf's offer proved insufficient to fix what was ailing him. "The archdruid and I are going for a walk. Alone."

The guards eyed the bow but, as usual, did not protest. Varian forgot them as he kept pace with the night elf. Already, doubts were creeping into him. Alone, he might find the hunt to his liking, but if he had to have the night elf at his side at all times, he could not pursue his quarry as he needed. That would only serve to stifle Varian.

He was ready to turn around and head back to the wine and ale when at last they reached a segment of the forest far from any visible night elven structure. Malfurion let his guest view the area in silence.

"Looks like good hunting territory," Varian admitted. He eyed the archdruid, who was only armed with a staff. "You plan on using that thing?"

In answer, Malfurion set it against a tree. "No, I prefer to hunt as the animals hunt . . . and as one."

Now at last the human understood what the night elf intended. "You're going to become a cat!"

"Is that fair enough a hunt?"

Varian chuckled, surprising himself. "It still won't be enough, if you mean will you be more successful than me. Do we hunt together?"

"I thought we would meet back here. I will hunt this direction," and he pointed slightly to the north. "And you can go that direction. I promise you will have plenty to pursue there."

"Suits me."

"Then the best of luck! May you find what you seek!" With that, the archdruid transformed. He slumped forward, falling upon all fours. His hands became padded paws with sharp claws and his garments melted into the ether, to be replaced by sleek, dark fur. His face widened and his nose and mouth became a blunt muzzle.

A powerful nightsaber stood next to the king.

"You'll still need a lot of luck to do better," Varian challenged, now completely caught up in the affair.

The cat rumbled in what could only be called an amused tone, then lunged off among the trees.

"Ha!" Varian did not let his opponent get very much of a leap ahead. The king darted into his area of the forest, his senses coming alive as he moved. Already he had the bow strung and an arrow nocked. The only other weapon was the knife he wore at his waist. That would only be needed if something happened to his bow or the prey survived his shot and he had to end its pain quickly.

His ears picked up movement. Varian smelled deer. It was impossible for him to describe to others how he became during a hunt save that the king transformed into something more . . . free.

Free.

The deer was close. Varian tightened his grip on the string. He rarely needed more than one shot to down his prey. He felt obligated to do his best to honor the kill, just as the night elf had indicated he did.

Much of Varian's anger at Malfurion faded. The archdruid had found the one method by which to give the king some relief. He would thank Malfurion later—

The deer suddenly bolted into view. It ran toward him, not the direction Varian had anticipated. The animal, a young stag, charged into him, forcing the king to leap out of the way.

And as he did, he came face to face with another hunter.

A worgen.

The furred hunter looked more startled than Varian. The two faced off against one another as the stag fled to freedom.

"You . . . ," rasped the worgen. "You're—"

"Varian Wrynn!" snarled a hated voice.

A second worgen burst into the area. His fur was frost white save for the head and mane, which retained some charcoal black. The newcomer's glittering blue eyes were filled with such bitterness that Varian instinctively held his bow ready. Behind the second worgen followed nearly a dozen others, all moving with a clear subservience to this later arrival.

"You've got a lot of gall coming here!" As the second worgen spoke, he changed. He shrank slightly and his fur seemed to just dissipate.

Genn Greymane gestured at the bow. "Fire away! You've already more or less struck me through the heart! My people will suffer for your choice—"

Varian lowered the bow. "I'll not waste an arrow on you. Bad enough you've ruined my hunt! Did you hope to convince me to change my mind by coming here?"

"You talk madness! We always hunt here! You're not far from our encampment and you know it!"

"I don't—" The former gladiator realized that he had been outmaneuvered and he knew by whom. He looked around, no longer as furious with the Gilneans as he was with another. "Where are you, Archdruid? You think this funny?"

"'Archdruid'?" Genn looked baffled.

"I do not find anything humorous about the last few days' events," Malfurion Stormrage replied from behind Varian. "As for Genn and the other worgen hunting here, the knowledge had completely slipped my mind."

The archdruid was the image of innocence. Despite all the evidence to the contrary, Varian found he could not bring himself to accuse the night elf outright. Glancing at Genn, he saw that the other king felt likewise.

"This area is too crowded for hunting, Archdruid," the lord of Stormwind finally remarked. "And I've lost my taste for it, anyway."

"Good," interjected Genn with a hint of disdain. "You'd probably end up blundering into us over and over as you go stomping through the forest, scaring off all the game. . . ."

"There'll never be a day when I can't outhunt you or any of your dogs, Greymane," Varian retorted, advancing on Genn.

"Ha!" The other king also advanced. "One of our younglings could catch a buck faster than you! As for me, I could take down a dozen before you managed to nick even one with those puny little bolts!"

"Always big with the boasts, but never able to follow through with them—"

"If I might intercede." Malfurion came between the two monarchs. "There is little point in such words unless you have the wherewithal to prove your own case."

"That's always been the trouble with Greymane—"

"Spoken like the self-righteous—"

A thunderclap echoed through the vicinity. Ears flattening, the other worgen were cowed.

Seemingly oblivious to his own display of power, the archdruid went on, "As I said, there is little point in braying at one another without being able to justify those words. Perhaps it is time to show what, if any, strength lies behind them."

"What're you talking about?" Varian snapped. Genn nodded toward his rival, indicating the question was foremost on his mind as well.

"You could both go your separate ways and continue this endless argument . . . or you could put some conclusion to your disagreements by seeing who does have the better skill."

"You think to throw us together," Genn snarled, "and make us see each other in a different light! Ha! I know this one well enough—too well, after his damning words. . . ."

"Damning in their truth," Varian retorted. "But I'll

agree with Genn on your intentions, Archdruid . . . and also agree that it won't work."

"Then, the two of you have nothing to fear."

"It has nothing to do with fear," the Gilnean king grumbled. "Damnation! Even if I deigned to hunt with this one around, he'd be stumbling over everything. . . ." Without warning, Genn transformed again. "Now forgive me, Malfurion, but we've lost enough time. We don't hunt for sport. We *hunt*."

Genn darted into the brush. The other worgen turned and followed without a sound.

"Fool Gilneans," Varian muttered, more to himself than to the archdruid.

"My apologies for any offense I have caused," Malfurion respectfully said.

Varian paid him no mind. "Give him furs, claws, even wings, Greymane's no hunter. Still all bluster, even after all the ruin he's caused himself and his kingdom. . . ."

The archdruid gestured in a direction leading away from the worgen. "If you still want to hunt, you will find good game that way, Varian."

The king continued to glare at where his rival had last been visible.

"Varian?"

Without a word, the king darted after the worgen.

18

THE CHASE

T he high priestess exhaled sharply as the last of the Alliance representatives departed. She had spent every moment discussing Ashenvale's needs with the others and had at last managed to gain as much as she had hoped from them. In return, Tyrande had promised what she could of increasing Darnassus's support for various requirements of the allies' homelands. She had also worked to manipulate various deals between the different factions, achieving more in a few desperate hours than in months of negotiation.

But will it be enough to save Ashenvale? she wondered as she paused to drink some water.

One of her attendants entered. "General Shandris seeks an audience."

The fact that Shandris had not simply walked in meant that she understood how hard the high priestess had been working on matters. The general was obviously concerned that her adopted mother might not be up to dealing with one more situation.

She had underestimated Tyrande. "Send her in, of course."

Shandris bowed her head as she entered. "Forgive me if this is a bad time—"

"This is an appropriate time. You come with a status report?"

"Yes. I think that we can get a fleet off by tomorrow midday. Our swift-response force makes that possible."

"A force you put together for just such an occasion," Tyrande said with pride. Months prior to the Cataclysm, Shandris had proposed the prepared and prearranged force in view of elements of the Horde already battling with the night elves in Warsong Gulch. Six ships capable of carrying a full contingent of Sentinels, mounts, and supplies were put on constant call, with everything cycled on a monthly basis to keep all fresh and ready.

And now they were needed.

"I but followed your lead," Shandris pointed out. "You mentioned previously that, after past events, we needed to be ready rather than reactive."

"What about additional strength?" the high priestess asked, not wishing to take any credit for what she fully believed was Shandris's accomplishment.

"Four more ships can sail within a week."

"That is good news. I hope I have some for you. I have been able to secure assistance from the rest of the Alliance in one form or another. Most will offer military might; others supplies."

Shandris smiled savagely. "The Horde will rue their ambition."

"Perhaps . . ."

"Something you know? A vision from Elune?"

The high priestess shook her head. "No. No more visions. Merely a . . . *feeling* . . . on my part."

"And not a good one. What is it?"

"The Horde knows full well that we can muster strong reinforcements. They must be following a strategy unlike any previous."

Shandris was not impressed. "Whatever they have in mind, I will be ready for it."

Tyrande put a motherly hand on Shandris's shoulder. "You know my faith in you is absolute. But I have come to a decision. I will be joining you. I will be leading this expedition."

The other night elf did not show any disappointment, only understanding. "You also had to make promises to some of our allies, promises that require you to go to Ashenvale to see them through."

"Your 'eyes' are as good as ever. I only agreed to most of that a little bit ago."

"It makes sense, especially if we need to keep them from arguing among themselves." Shandris held up a parchment that she had brought with her. "As I thought anyway that it would be the case, I have got all you need jotted down here. Might be good if we go over it."

The high priestess smiled proudly. "Thank you, Shandris."

"Thank me if we survive this." The younger night elf moved to the table and spread the parchment open. It proved much larger than it had first appeared, and there was hardly an empty space upon it. Shandris had made the most use of the parchment, and with necessity. The reinforcing of Ashenvale required great consideration . . . and all of it quickly.

And as Tyrande bent over the parchment and started to listen to her adopted daughter, she prayed to the Mother Moon that there would be time *enough*.

Varian caught wind of the worgen long before he saw the first. He knew that they could not smell his scent yet, for the wind blew toward him. The king also knew that they did not hear him, either, despite their acute senses. The curse might have given the Gilneans heightened senses, but they had not had the years to hone them as he had. They were still basically who they had been, while he had a lifetime of experience.

Those who accompanied Genn included other surviving members of the nobility, male and female. However, in addition, favored officers and Genn's own personal staff and guards would also be included in the "royal" hunt. Aside from Genn, the guards would be the ones that Varian would have to watch out for most. Although the Gilnean monarch was their first priority, in what was considered a safe land the soldiers would also probably have some leeway in pursuing the prey. That meant that Varian would actually be competing against several rivals . . . which suited him just fine.

Varian had only one real reason for following. Malfurion's plot had had the opposite effect. Varian had decided to take the archdruid's suggestion and use it to embarrass Genn in front of his own people. The Gilneans would see that their vaunted leader was still a failure who would only bring them to further ruin.

The idea that, by shaming Genn, Varian wanted to assuage his own sense of failure had crept into the lord of Stormwind's mind, but he had quickly and soundly buried that thought deep. All that mattered was putting the king of Gilneas in his place.

A sleek form darted among the trees to his left. One of the younger worgen. Varian used the momentary observation to judge the creatures. The worgen moved more fluidly than he had first estimated, but the king saw flaws of which he could take advantage.

The worgen glanced back at him. Initial surprise gave way to a reaction Varian found odd. The long ears of the other hunter straightened and Varian had the sense that not only was the worgen studying him, he was also seeing something that was not readily apparent to the king. The worgen briefly ducked his head low as he ran, a sign that Varian had recognized among Genn's followers as one of respect for a pack member of higher status.

The young worgen vanished among the trees, but not because he outpaced the lord of Stormwind. Varian ran as quickly and with as much litheness as his momentary companion. He bared his teeth as he imagined the nearby pack pursuing its prey, and increased his pace in order to better his chances of joining the chase before it was too late. He knew that the pack would not hunt too far apart from one another. Their lupine tendencies would make the worgen follow certain traits that Varian understood very well.

Genn Greymane would rue his audacity, the younger monarch decided with much satisfaction. *Better if he had stayed in hiding, something he's good at.*

The brush ahead shook. Varian immediately froze.

A doe rushed past him. She was small, barely adult. Varian could smell her surprise and fear. He almost fired, then held off. He had no time for his own hunt, no matter how much the urge to give chase swelled within him. What Varian wanted was to follow Genn's prey and show that he could take it even when his rival knew that he was there.

Varian slipped behind a tree just as another worgen burst through in pursuit of the doe. The king recognized the worgen's markings: Eadrik. Genn's servant moved with more assurance than the other male Varian had seen, not a surprise. Genn would have the best around him, as any monarch would.

Eadrik paused. The worgen sniffed the air. Varian watched as the other hunter turned his direction.

A slight movement in the opposite direction caught Eadrik's attention. The doe, acting only on her instincts and unable to meld those with common sense, had chosen an inopportune time to begin running again.

The worgen lunged after her. Varian waited for a moment, then stepped from the tree. If Eadrik was here, the lord of Stormwind considered, then his master could not be far.

The bow once again ready, Varian moved in the direction from which Eadrik had come. The worgen hunted as a pack to a point. Being also men, those like Genn would seek their individual kills.

Varian retraced Eadrik's path, moving through the brush as readily as the worgen. His eyes constantly surveyed the vicinity and his ears and nose sought signs of *his* prey.

And at last he saw a worgen who could only be the Gilnean king. Genn flung himself after a massive boar with tusks so sharp and strong that, if the animal turned to face the worgen, Genn would truly risk death. At the moment, though, the boar thought only of flight.

Genn, however, was fast gaining. He ran sometimes on only his legs, but other times used his hands too. With a litheness that Varian had not even seen from the much younger Eadrik, the veteran ruler closed on the boar.

Having measured the situation, Varian entered the fray. Although without the "benefit" of the curse, he moved with all the skill and pace of one who had survived more critical struggles than surely all the worgen combined. Yet, it was more than merely the reflexes of a former gladiator that served Varian now. Another force guided him, drove him in among the worgen as if he were one of their own and not simply a man. Others in the past had called him Lo'Gosh . . . and, at that moment, that name was more true of him than the one with which he had been born.

Growls greeted him as he moved out into the open. Two raven-black worgen—one a female with a narrower snout—leapt toward him from the trees beyond Genn. Their appearance did not surprise Varian. He had already marked them as guards.

Ahead, Genn's ears pricked up as he heard the warning growls. He glanced to his side and saw Varian with the bow.

Varian purposely ignored his rival, instead following the boar's trail. Out of the corner of his eye, he noted Genn's sudden understanding of just what the lord of Stormwind intended.

With a challenging growl, Genn pulled up. Only then did Varian also stop.

"So . . . ," snarled the worgen. "You've come to prove yourself my better after all?"

"I'll always be your better, Genn."

"Rubbish! You can only imagine the powers that the curse has given us, powers beyond mere humans, powers—"

"Powers to outbrag anything," interjected Varian. "At least, that's all I've seen thus far!"

The other two worgen neared. Genn angrily waved them off. "Don't know why I ever sought your approval for our people! If the rest of the Alliance chooses to follow you down your doomed path, then so be it!"

Varian ignored the insults. "My quarry's running hard. You can stay and blather all day if you like, but I'm moving on. I've a meal to catch."

"*Your* quarry? You jest!" Genn sniffed at his opponent. "You think you can take him from me? Listen to me, Varian Wrynn! The curse more than heightened our senses. We see things that no normal human can. Some call you Lo'Gosh, though that they use a Taur-ahe title for you I find ironic. Still, it is but another name for *Goldrinn*, as we have come to know our patron spirit since our transformation. I saw the aura of that spirit around you the first moment you arrived at the banquet, and even though you gave every indication of crushing our hopes then, I still held out for our chances because I could see his touch upon you as if it were your own skin. . . ."

Although he showed no sign of it, Varian was briefly unnerved by Genn's revelation. He had gratefully accepted the name when given to him, but had always thought it just an honor. Now Genn claimed that the wolf spirit's essence or something touched Varian.

Ignorant of the effect of his words, the king of Gilneas went on, "But even if Goldrinn has blessed you, you're still Varian Wrynn . . . and that's why you stand as much a chance of taking my prey as you do lifting the Greymane Wall with your bare hands. . . ."

And with that, Genn Greymane rushed off after the boar.

Varian followed without hesitation. He saw that Genn had some advantage in speed, but if the king of Gilneas indeed thought his rival less adept at the hunt than the worgen, it was because he had not seen Varian in pursuit of prey. Instincts that no ordinary man possessed overtook the lord of Stormwind again. He smelled not only the scents of the worgen but, even through those many smells, that of the boar. Sharp hearing differentiated between the sleek, subtle sounds of the worgen moving through the forest and the more rushed charge of the huge animal they chased. Varian eyed the landscape before him, instantly understanding the lay of it. He altered his path from that of his rival and rushed toward the south, then turned again.

As he had estimated, the land rose up against Genn, slowing him a few precious seconds. Barely breathing hard, Varian scurried down the other side. He knew from so many past hunts that the boar would be in need of a pause, and he had a very good notion of roughly where.

An exhilaration filled Varian as he pursued the hunt, an exhilaration that had nothing to do with besting Genn. He felt more alive than he had in months. The pain of Anduin's abrupt departure still remained, but the constant exertion, the need to keep his attention focused so hard on the quarry, enabled Varian to better tolerate the terrible loss.

He spotted a shape far ahead that was no worgen. The huge boar stood frozen, either hoping that its stillness would keep it hidden from the hunters, or simply finding itself unable to choose what to do next.

The boar suddenly moved.

Varian swore under his breath. The boar was racing up toward where Genn would likely appear. Somehow, Varian had spooked the creature even from so far away. It was not typical of his hunts, and to the younger king, now was the worst possible time for him to make such a mistake.

But Varian did not give in to defeat. He still had the chance to outwit his rival. More important, the bow gave him an advantage in distance, assuming that he utilized his skill to its utmost.

Varian rushed up behind the boar. Twice he almost had his shot. The second time, the boar turned in a direction that the veteran hunter had not expected. It forced the animal to scramble over unsteady ground, providing both pursuers a better chance of catching up.

Sure enough, a worgen materialized a moment later . . . but not on the path from which Varian expected Genn. It was one of the younger ones, a dark brown male with the tip of one ear missing. Evidently his own hunt had led him back this direction and now he stalked after prey that he did not know had been chosen by his master . . . and Varian.

The boar twisted as it struggled up a hill. The young worgen closed on the animal. Of Genn there was yet no sign, but Varian had to assume that he would be there at any moment.

He aimed. A good shot—a *very* good shot—would down the boar before the young worgen could catch it.

At that moment the boar turned on the worgen. Caught by surprise, the Gilnean did not move out of the way in time. The gargantuan boar used its tusks and snout to toss its one pursuer to the side. The worgen crashed against a tree, stunned by the collision.

The animal's decision gave Varian the shot he desired. He aimed . . . and then held back. The boar chose then to turn and continue its flight.

"And this is how you hunt?" mocked Genn's voice.

Varian turned to find the other king racing up to him. Behind Genn came several others, including Eadrik. The gathered worgen sniffed the air in the direction of the fleeing boar.

"Sometimes you need to let the prey run," Varian replied.

"That makes no sense!"

The lord of Stormwind had no interest in explanations. "Shall we continue?"

Before Genn could answer, Varian ran again. He heard a growl from his rival, then the soft sound of the pack following. Varian was not concerned that the other worgen had joined in. He knew that they would leave the hunt to their lord. This was still a contest between the two rulers.

Varian picked up the boar's trail. He admired the beast's stamina and strength. In some fashion, he related to its struggle. Varian intended to honor his quarry and make certain that the carcass would not go to waste. That would be a true insult to an admirable adversary.

The boar rushed toward thick brush that possibly promised escape. Certainly it would be harder for either Varian or Genn to chase the animal into it without being slowed. The boar was better designed to push through.

Then from another direction came a new worgen. Belatedly, Varian recognized him as the young one with the missing ear tip.

The boar let out an unsettling snort. It fought to stop in its tracks. Caught by surprise, the young worgen landed in front of rather than atop his intended prey.

The boar charged back the way it had come, seemingly ignorant of the fact that it raced toward more of its pursuers. Another startled worgen leapt aside just as sharp tusks would have gored his leg. The light brown hunter landed on all fours and readied himself for another lunge.

Out of the thick brush behind him burst a bear.

The huge black beast stood on its hind legs and roared, revealing a maw wide enough to envelope a man's head and sharp, yellowed teeth more than capable of ripping that head free. The bear loomed over the startled worgen, its long, thick claws more than a match for those of the Gilnean.

The wind was the reason that no one had picked up the other predator's scent. It had been blowing toward the bear, which, perhaps because of its tremendous size, had not been deterred by the worgen's presence. For the young, impetuous Gilnean, that meant that the hunter had now become the prey.

Instinct commanded Varian, who immediately fired. However, the bear turned as he did and the arrow struck the shoulder.

The wound more outraged the ursine beast than slowed it. It continued to focus on the nearest enemy. The young worgen moved too slowly to dodge the heavy paw. The blow sent the Gilnean tumbling, although unfortunately not far enough to keep him safe from the bear.

Another arrow already nocked, Varian fired. The second shot also struck, this time in the upper chest. However, the bear's thick hide and strong muscle were enough to keep the creature from being badly wounded.

As the second bolt hit, another worgen suddenly leapt into the struggle. He threw himself in front of the fallen one, then howled a challenge to the bear. The looming beast roared back at the worgen. Huge teeth snapped at the brave Gilnean.

Despite the threat, Genn Greymane stood his ground.

Behind him, two others seized the stunned hunter and dragged him off. This seemed to further infuriate the wounded bear, which reached for the lone defender with both huge paws.

The worgen jumped above the paws, either of which would have landed a killing blow. Using the bear's own foreleg as a boost, the lupine hunter dove for his adversary's thick throat.

Claws raked at the area just below the bear's jaw. Blood splattered the worgen.

The bear roared in pain now. Yet, that pain also fueled its incredible strength. One foreleg caught the worgen as he sought to leap back. The bear fell upon its attacker.

Varian had come to a decision, albeit one most men would call mad. Alone against the bear, he would have eventually downed the beast with a shot to the throat or the eye. However, the confrontation with the worgen had made his shots more difficult since he did not want to cause any harm to them. Therefore, the bow was of no use.

Letting the bow simply drop free, the lord of Stormwind drew his knife and, with a howl worthy of a worgen, threw himself forward. Bloodlust drowning out attention to anything else, the bear saw only Genn, just as Varian had hoped.

The human landed atop the hulking animal. Without hesitation, Varian jammed the knife into the muscular flesh.

The struggle caused his aim to be off. Instead of the neck, he caught the shoulder blade. The tip of the knife snapped off, leaving an angled edge.

Worse for him, he had now become the center of the ursine behemoth's attention. The bear straightened, nearly dislodging Varian. The huge beast twisted, trying to free itself of the annoyance clinging to its back.

It was all Varian could do to hold on. Even the rippling of the bear's muscles shook him like an earthquake. The king also gripped the broken knife, the end of which still had some use as a weapon—if Varian did not fall.

A snarl that was not the bear's filled Varian's ears. Genn Greymane again jumped up, his claws seeking the furious animal's throat. As the bear sought to shake both of them off, the two monarchs' eyes met and Varian realized that Greymane was trying to distract the beast enough for the lord of Stormwind to strike again.

The thick forelegs wrapped around Genn. Roaring, the bear sought to bite the worgen's face off.

Varian saw his chance.

The broken edge forced him to use every bit of his strength to shove the knife into the bear's neck. Many men would have failed to drive the weapon deep enough, but not only did Varian have the might, he also had the knowledge—from too many gladiatorial bouts—of just where the softest part of the neck was.

The bear's jaws were inches away from closing on Genn's face.

Varian drove the knife deep, nearly shoving it in to the hilt.

The bear roared louder than ever, but this time there was a strained note to it. Agony did what the beast could not accomplish before: both rulers were tossed off as if nothing.

The stricken animal turned around. Varian, sprawled on the ground, stared up at the gigantic creature. The bear could still kill him.

But instead, the animal tried to reach with its paws for the knife. Claws that could shred a man could not even properly grasp the hilt. The bear slapped at the source of its pain several times, its breathing getting more ragged by the moment.

Exhaustion and blood loss sent the bear crashing down on all fours. It rocked back and forth, still trying to twist its head around enough to bite out the knife.

A figure moved in from the other side. Varian heard the familiar sound of tearing flesh.

The bear let out a moan and fell on its left side, its throat now torn out.

A worgen stood above the dead animal, blood and bits of meat still dangling from the end of his claws. The worgen looked at Varian.

Varian nodded to Genn. The other king had done the correct thing. Neither of them bore any malice toward the bear. The creature had only been following its instincts and it had been its misfortune to come across the hunters. That it could have easily killed not only the two of them but also the unfortunate young worgen was simply part of the risk when hunting.

Genn offered a gore-soaked hand to Varian. Varian had heard long ago that the king of Gilneas had been raised not to accept the hand of anyone, to always stand on his own, and at first the lord of Stormwind thought to decline the offer. Then he remembered all his counterpart had promised and was doing to rejoin the Alliance.

Varian took the hand. Genn helped him up . . . and then the two men held their grips a moment longer, two hunters acknowledging one another's skills.

Turning to the bear, Varian studied his counterpart's strike.

"A quick killing blow," he complimented Genn.

"I simply finished your work," the Gilnean ruler returned. "The kill is yours. The hunt is yours."

Varian shook his head. "Hardly. I was hunting a boar."

"A man who hunts a rabbit and brings down a deer is applauded. A man who hunts a boar and brings down a bear should be acclaimed."

And with that, Genn looked to the sky and unleashed a powerful howl, a howl that honored both the kill and the one who made it. His call was taken up by the other worgen, all saluting the skills of the king of Stormwind.

Genn finally finished, the howls of his followers ending with his. He faced his counterpart again.

Only . . . Varian was no longer there.

19

SILVERWING

Silverwing Outpost had had no news in two days from the nearest other outposts, and that worried Su'ura Swiftarrow. She had come from Silverwing Grove at the behest of the outpost's commander, only to find that the other officer had been slain in an ambush shortly before Su'ura's arrival. The ambush had also taken out the second-in-command. Su'ura had not intended to stay, but the only other Sentinel officer was too inexperienced.

She had dispatched two hippogryph riders, one to the next nearest outpost and the other to Commander Haldrissa. From one of the two there should have been some word. Either that, or the riders should have returned with warning of some catastrophe.

But the riders had not returned and Su'ura suspected that they would not. Silverwing Outpost was on its own in the battle against the Horde.

She strode along the edge of the outpost, eyeing the

mist that was fast rising. It could not be blamed on Fallen Sky Lake to the south, not when it was coming from Horde-held lands.

A low rumble of warning rose up from behind her. She did not show any surprise, aware of what kept pace with her.

"Easy," Su'ura said to the huge black nightsaber with her. The beast wore golden brown armor with purple gems over its head and sides. The night elf herself was also fully armored, as were all those on duty, though her shoulder areas were more decorated with fine gold bands over the silver. Those who thought the armor more orna- mental than useful had discovered, if they were orcs or other foes, that it protected her quite well while she was gutting them.

The hoot of an owl seized her attention as the growl of the nightsaber had not. The outpost commander looked up to the roof of the main structure, where a soot-colored owl perched. The bird peered into the forest ahead, then abruptly abandoned its position. It descended to a waiting Su'ura, who stretched out her arm so that it had a place to alight.

"What is it, Hutihu?" she asked grimly. "Where?"

In response, the owl hooted once, then swiveled its head slightly toward a particular part of the forest. Su'ura followed its gaze expectantly.

The sentries at the outpost's edge stiffened as a figure slipped out of the brush. They only calmed when it was clear it was one of their own . . . so to speak.

The figure who returned to Silverwing belonged to a group that was not exactly favored by most Sentinels, but it had its uses, and in Su'ura's eyes some members had more than proven their loyalty. In fact, the one approaching now was so trusted by Su'ura that she had risen up to a level of command, now serving as supply officer.

Of course, her role as a scout—for lack of a better word—along with related *unofficial* duties, was still the most important aspect of her use.

"Illiyana Moonblaze," Su'ura solemnly greeted her. "You are back sooner than I expected . . . and hoped."

The other night elf was a distinct contrast to Su'ura, not to mention most of the others there. It was not just that she wore a dark corseted outfit that reminded Su'ura more of a human buccaneer, but that Illiyana radiated a presence in some manner akin to that of a wild pirate. As tradition went, those of Illiyana's "calling" were not respected much more than pirates even though they had been a part of night elf life for years, but the changing times had more and more found places for such as her among the trusted fighters of the Alliance.

Illiyana sheathed a pair of longswords she utilized in place of a glaive. With a wry smile, she asked, "You did not miss me?"

"Enough jesting. What did you see?"

"More to the point, what did I *not* see? And what did I hear?"

The commander looked at her with some exasperation. Hutihu made a sound that echoed her annoyance.

The wry grin faded a bit. "All right. First, it is so thick out there, you cannot see more than a few feet in front. We do not go charging into it, it should be to our advantage."

"So we stand our ground."

"Unfortunately, it is moving toward us."

Su'ura had already thought so, but hearing that fact verified still struck her now. "You could have said that right away. How fast?"

"Fast enough that it is good you have got everyone in position already."

As bad as that, the commander thought. "You said you heard something?"

"Buzzing. Like a great mass of wasps. There is another thing: the more you go into the mist, the more it stinks of oil, as if someone lit a bunch of lamps and left them burning."

Su'ura knew what that, combined with the buzzing, meant. "Goblins. There are goblins out there."

Illiyana appeared unimpressed. "The night we cannot handle a bunch of goblins is the night Ashenvale *should* fall."

"Be careful what you say," snapped the commander, although she was not overly concerned about the goblins, either. What much more bothered her was what would be marching with them.

She peered upward at the tall trees ahead. The mist was not quite thick enough to obscure the tops. Su'ura had sent scouts high above to see if they could spot anything, but the forest below had been as if under a thick blanket through which the crowns popped like islands.

"Where are the others?" Illiyana suddenly asked her.

It was a question for which Su'ura had been waiting but had not wanted to answer. "You are the only one who returned."

For once, Illiyana looked a little unsettled. "'The only one'?"

There had been three others who had fanned out into

the mist with Illiyana. Based on their destinations, Su'ura had expected them back earlier. The fact that they had not returned yet meant that they were not returning at all.

It also meant that the enemy was even closer than originally anticipated.

"You encountered no one, Illiyana?"

"I found some tracks that went deeper into the eastern mist, but they looked conspicuously visible and so I chose not to follow them."

"Very likely a wise thing." Illiyana was a seasoned tracker, more so than even the other three. They had probably decided to follow similar trails . . . just as the Horde's own commanders had intended.

"Someone has gone through a lot of trouble," Su'ura muttered, stroking Hutihu's feathers.

The owl hooted agreement.

"Should I go and look for them?"

"No, I think that would be—"

She heard a slight buzzing from the forest. Illiyana, Hutihu, and the nightsaber all reacted with the same tensing of their bodies.

"*That* is what I heard," Illiyana said.

"What is it?"

The dark-clad night elf sniffed the air. "Whatever it is, that oily stench comes with it."

Everyone could smell the odor now. The nightsaber crouched, its nostrils flaring in disgust.

"Can goblins build nothing that does not stink?" the commander finally muttered. "Or that does not have evil purpose?"

"Fortunately, half the time, those contraptions either do not work or explode."

"And the other half of the time, they wreak havoc on us."

Illiyana could not argue with her there. Su'ura sent Hutihu to the trees, then stepped forward. "Archers to the ready! Lancers should mount! First lines form!"

In response to the last, Sentinels on foot took up positions just in front of the archers. Armed with glaives, they went down on one knee. Given the word, they would throw the deadly weapons simultaneously, cutting a deadly swath across anything in the glaives' path.

Other Sentinels, some of them arming powerful ballistae called glaive throwers, stood ready behind the archers. In addition to the glaive on their gauntlets, several warriors also wore a second one slung on their backs. They were there to reinforce the front lines as needed.

A pack of armored nightsabers now stood awaiting the cue from their riders, whose senior officer watched Su'ura for the signal. Faces grim beneath their heavy helmets, the riders kept their long lances pointed skyward.

The buzzing grew stronger, more piercing. It was now accompanied by a grinding sound, one that Su'ura thought she now recognized. It said something for the stress of the situation that she had not made the connection earlier. After all, the goblins *had* been known to be cutting wood nearby. . . .

Then silence reigned again. The Sentinels stood uncertain. Officers looked to Su'ura, who watched and listened for the slightest hint of what was happening.

An odd, unsettling groan echoed through the forest. The night elves looked at one another, even Illiyana clearly perplexed concerning the source of the long, mournful sound. To Su'ura, it was almost as if the forest itself were groaning, for it seemed to come from several places at once.

The commander swallowed. She suddenly realized what that groan meant.

Looking to the eastern sky, she tried to see through the offending mist . . . some smokescreen created by the insidious devices of the goblins. Su'ura sought for one particular sight—and then spotted it in more than one place. It was so unbelievable that she could not help but stare at it for a moment, even despite the disaster it presaged.

"The trees . . . they are moving. . . ."

"Hmm?" Illiyana looked up in the hopes of trying to make sense of the other night elf's odd words.

Through the mist, gargantuan stalks plunged toward the outpost, stalks topped by great crowns.

"Retreat!" Su'ura cried. "Watch out—"

Other Sentinels finally registered what was happening. Archers, lancers, foot soldiers . . . seasoned warriors everywhere now broke off and tried their best to rush as quickly to the rear as they were able.

The groan became deafening.

The first of the gigantic trees fell upon Silverwing.

Even as she fought to keep some semblance of organization in the outpost, Su'ura could not help but bitterly admire the tactic. The Horde had clearly scouted the area thoroughly, picking and choosing the right trees for their assault. They had chosen great leviathans whose path would be hardly impeded at all by the smaller ones nearest them.

The crash of the first tree shook the ground like an earthquake. It also crushed part of the main structure of the outpost and two nightsabers and their unfortunate riders. Worse, the gargantuan trunk did not stay where it landed but rather rolled south. In the process, it swept over three other Sentinels, crushing them like insects.

Even as the first tree did its foul work, a second hit. Another terrible convulsion rocked the night elves. Sentinels were thrown about. Nightsabers howled like newborn cubs as they sought escape that was not there.

A third tree came crashing. Somewhat to their fortune, the crown landed in that of the main tree in Silverwing, preventing the severed trunk from doing as much damage. The hapless defenders were still bombarded by falling foliage and cracked branches as big as one of their feline mounts.

Su'ura bent to help a stunned Sentinel. She had no idea where Illiyana had gone and could not blame the other night elf if she had fled. They could not fight *trees*. How did one fend off such a weapon?

Another incredible thud rocked Silverwing. The crash of timber warned that more of the outpost had been ruined. Worse, the shrieks of the badly injured multiplied.

She had counted four trees toppling toward the outpost, and four had fallen. Su'ura prayed that she had not miscounted, though she was hard-pressed to imagine where the Horde could have found a fifth to add to the onslaught. They had needed the gaps in the forest to ensure that their makeshift hammers would strike the target precisely.

Dust and wreckage from the crowns filled the air. Amidst it, Su'ura smelled a great increase in the oily stench created by the goblins. She also heard heavy thumps, as if some giant lumbered through the forest just beyond Silverwing.

"Re-form lines!" she shouted, wondering if anyone would not only hear but also bother to obey. "They are attacking!"

The thumping grew louder, accompanied by loud buzzing. The commander turned to the forest.

Two-legged goblin mechanisms entered Silverwing. They moved like drunk night elves, and one arm of each ended in a toothed, spinning blade.

Barely had the first of the shredders entered than a flight of arrows assailed them. Two goblins fell dead. One of the driverless machines spun around and crashed into a third.

Su'ura looked to see that some of the Sentinels had rallied to her cry. Behind the single row of archers, foot soldiers and lancers also attempted to regroup.

The drivers of the other shredders raised the second arm to shield themselves. Su'ura immediately took advantage of their tactical mistake.

"Huntresses! Charge!"

She had no idea how many there were, but the pack that coursed past her more than met her expectations. Her heart grew lighter. The Horde thought that they had dealt Silverwing a mortal blow, but they had obviously forgotten with whom they were dealing. The contingent here had learned to adapt at a moment's notice.

More than a dozen heavily muscled cats raced at the shredders. The huntresses readied their shields and lowered their lances, the points straight ahead.

The pack charged into the shredders.

Distracted by the flight of arrows, most of the goblins saw the charge too late. A couple managed to get their whirling blades up. A nightsaber howled as a blade cut into its jaw.

But overall, the charge held. The lances, aimed with precision, pierced the shredders at the underarm—where they were most vulnerable—or simply managed to tip them backward. Loud crashes accompanied the shredders' falls.

As per their training, the huntresses immediately retreated. However, as they did, a flight of arrows launched from the east struck.

Four nightsabers immediately dropped, followed by that many more within the first few breaths. Their shields being of less effect when held behind them, the huntresses suffered even more. In seconds, the pack and their riders were decimated.

A battle horn blew. A lusty roar resounded from the forest.

Orcs flowed through the woods into Silverwing. The first line fell nearly to a warrior, shot down by the expert aim of the outpost's remaining archers. Unfortunately, the orcs kept coming and now they were accompanied by arrows flying overhead. Those arrows sought out the night elf archers, slaying several and shattering the line.

Drawing her glaive, Su'ura leapt atop her mount. She shouted toward the remaining lancers, who rallied to her.

"Drive them back!" Su'ura ordered. "Give the archers and the others time to regroup again!"

With her in the lead, the riders turned again on the oncoming orcs. Su'ura threw the glaive at the first of the attackers and watched with grim satisfaction as the flying blades cut through the chest of the tusked warrior. Blood spilling from the red crevice, the orc tumbled forward, inadvertently tripping two of those directly behind him. Catching the glaive, Su'ura took advantage of the confusion by striking down one of the pair before they could untangle themselves.

The orc line faltered. The riders pushed them back.

A new flight of arrows assailed the orcs. It was accompanied by a number of spinning glaives that further annihilated their front ranks.

Su'ura let out a triumphant yell. The Horde was again learning the folly of attacking Silverwing. Despite the astounding ploy by its commander, the defenders would gain the day—

Another horn blew.

The orc lines dropped.

A fresh flight of arrows concentrated on the riders. Su'ura, at point, saw some of the Horde's archers just as they were firing, and shouted a warning.

She planted herself against the nightsaber's neck and prayed the others did the same. However, the many cries she heard in her wake did not give her much hope.

Worse, her mount stumbled, then collapsed. In the process, the animal threw Su'ura.

The night elf fell among the dead, an orc's gaping face barely an inch from hers. She tried to rise, but something held her leg down. Su'ura twisted around and saw that the nightsaber, more than a dozen heavy bolts piercing its body, had fallen on the limb, trapping it. The unfortunate cat was already dead, which meant that she could not even get the animal to move.

She managed to seize an axe from the dead orc. With the carnage going on around her, she was momentarily forgotten. Doubtful that it would remain that way long, the night elf tried to use the axe head to prop up the carcass enough to slip her leg free.

A nerve-shaking wail rose over the vicinity, causing her to lose her grip on the axe. Despite her predicament, she had to see the cause.

Two Sentinels blocked her view, but not for very long. Although expertly wielding their glaives for hand-to-hand combat, first one, then the other, fell. One did so minus her head; the other with his torso cut all the way down the middle. The doom of each was accompanied by the same awful wail.

And as the night elves fell, they revealed the lone foe who had so easily dealt with them. The brown-skinned orc grinned as he looked for another enemy to smite. In his hands he gripped a dreadful axe that had an intricate series of grooves in the head.

Su'ura had never seen him before, but knew instantly from the tales that she stared at Garrosh Hellscream himself.

As if sensing her, his baleful gaze turned in her direction.

The Sentinel seized the axe again and shoved the weapon's head toward the corpse of her mount. Twisting the handle, she used the head to push up the nightsaber just enough to finally pull her leg free.

"Good," declared an ominous, deep voice. "I want a fair battle."

She stared up at the warchief, who made no move yet. Su'ura realized that he was waiting for her to stand. Once she did that, he would move in to finish her. While the night elf did not fear him, she knew from the way her body ached that she was injured inside. More important, this was *Garrosh Hellscream*, whose prowess in combat had already become legendary.

Another nightsaber suddenly came between them. Unafraid, the orc turned to face this new foe. The cat swatted at Garrosh but did not close with the hulking warrior.

"Run!" called the rider. Only then did Su'ura realize that it was Illiyana.

But her would-be rescuer had underestimated Garrosh Hellscream. The orc lunged under the nightsaber's claws. He took the axe and jammed it upward, beneath the great cat's jaw.

Illiyana's mount yowled and pulled back sharply. Blood seeping from the wound above its throat, the animal writhed in agony.

The scout was tossed toward the corpse of the other cat. Illiyana struck the heavy body hard, then rolled over.

Su'ura had not waited all this time. She had risen to a crouching position, trying to determine not where to flee but how to help Illiyana battle Garrosh. Now she instead had to rescue her rescuer.

Although badly wounded by the warchief's daring attack, the trained nightsaber returned to the struggle. Su'ura used the animal's bravery to help Illiyana up.

"That . . . did not work . . . as I planned," the other night elf gasped.

"How are you?"

Illiyana grimaced. "I think my left arm is either broken or perhaps just pulled."

"Then we had better hurry away from here."

"I can fight—"

"No argument! We are behind the line now! We have got to get back to the rest!"

The horrific wail of Garrosh's axe cut through the air

again. It was followed by an angry and pained roar from the nightsaber. Su'ura did not look back. She regretted the cat's sacrifice but had no choice. To stay would be suicide for both fighters.

Several yards to the west, she saw some of the defenders again regrouping, but farther to the east the situation grew more and more desperate. There, individual Sentinels, cut off from hope, fought against one or more foes, odds too often quickly fatal. Su'ura watched in horror as an orc lopped off the head of one of her officers. The body of the Sentinel staggered a few steps before finally collapsing. Elsewhere, severed limbs marked the dooms of other night elves. Now and then, a glaive would go spinning past, but those signs of resistance grew less and less with each passing second.

Su'ura and Illiyana had managed to get within a few yards of a small party of archers when Su'ura sensed that they were not alone. With regret, she shoved Illiyana toward the other defenders, hoping that the other night elf's reflexes were still sharp enough to compensate for the sudden loss of the commander's help.

Su'ura barely got her weapon up in time to prevent an older orc with an eye patch and covered in maritime tattoos from cleaving her in two with his heavy axe. He was no Garrosh, but his experience and sheer determination put her on the defensive from the first moment.

"I'll make this quick," he rasped. "You wouldn't want to be around when he unleashes them, anyway. . . ."

She had no idea what he was talking about and did not care. What concerned Su'ura more was that the leg that had been trapped under the dead nightsaber was now tingling. It had been injured, after all, and now that injury was causing problems with her balance.

The night elf followed Garrosh's trick, suddenly lunging into her opponent when he would have expected otherwise. The startled orc backed away. Su'ura slashed with the axe, but managed only a thin red line across his arm.

An arrow from behind her struck the ground between them. Another bounced off the orc's shoulder armor.

The green-skinned warrior snarled, then withdrew as two more arrows harassed him.

Two Sentinels seized Su'ura and pulled her back to the archers. As they did, the commander heard the buzzing of a shredder. Some of the goblins had managed to get their foul mechanisms on their feet again and were tearing apart what the falling trees had not already destroyed.

Su'ura smelled fire. The main building was ablaze, whether by the goblins or some other source, she did not know. She considered taking a chance and rushing into it to retrieve some of the valuable charts stored there, but knew that it was too late to do anything.

The terrible wail echoed in her ears again. Garrosh, his weapon dripping with blood, yelled an unintelligible command to his warriors. Even the goblins moved in response, the shredders forming a line, then stopping.

"They—they are within range!" Illiyana was incredulous. "Are they committing suicide?"

"It does not matter! Archers, fire at will! I want every glaive flying too!"

More and more of Silverwing's survivors gathered. Su'ura saw that the Sentinels still had a fairly decent line of defense. True, they looked to be outnumbered, but that would not be the first time.

Yet, as the first archers readied their shots, again a horn sounded. The archers hesitated.

"Do not wait!" cursed Su'ura.

A monstrous roar burst from the goblin-induced mist.

Something came flying out of the forest. A huge projectile. A rock several times Su'ura's height in diameter.

It was followed by five more.

She faced what seemed a variation of the same nightmare that had initially struck the outpost. With much the same accuracy of aim, the huge rocks fell upon Silverwing.

There was no choice but to scatter. The final stand of the Silverwing Sentinels collapsed under threat of a force that they could not stop.

The first huge rock struck the ground just before where the archers had stood. As with the massive trunks, the area shook as if the Cataclysm had come anew. However, the rocks—more focused missiles—raised up huge bits of dirt and stone that bombarded the night elves. A Sentinel near Illiyana dropped dead, her skull caved in by one sharp fragment. Two archers were brought down by a rain of earth.

Silverwing filled with thunder as the rest of the boulders hit. Sentinels went flying through the air. Two other boulders completely obliterated the glaive throwers and their operators. Nightsabers, driven wild by the catastrophe, ignored their riders' orders.

The Horde wasted no time in taking advantage. Garrosh let out a cry of victory, waved the wailing axe, and led the charge himself. A few Sentinels, bowled over by the latest barrage, struggled to rise quick enough to at least put up a defense against the oncoming enemy. They gave a good accounting for themselves, managing to bring more than a few orcs down with their glaives and swords, but none survived long against such overwhelming odds.

Illiyana was the first to state the terribly obvious. "We cannot stay any longer! We must abandon our position!"

Although she wanted to deny what her companion said, Su'ura could not. The Sentinels' numbers were fast dwindling. Several of those still alive were wounded, and against the growing ranks of orcs entering the battle, it would have been murder to order them to stay.

"Fall back!" Su'ura called. "We make our way beyond the river to Commander Haldrissa!"

Clearly reluctant, the Sentinels nevertheless obeyed. They gathered those more injured and, under the protective cover of the healthiest archers and warriors, did what none would have ever thought could happen. They *abandoned* Silverwing Outpost.

The orcs gave chase. To Su'ura's relief, there were no orcs mounted on wolves among them. Furthermore, the few nightsabers still manageable helped carry the wounded Sentinels while the rest kept pace as best as possible. Night elves were better built for speed, and finally the pursuers fell behind. Even then, though, Silverwing's remnants pushed on as hard as they could. The others had to be warned.

Su'ura knew that something was not quite right about their escape, but was too exhausted and too busy trying to keep the rest of the survivors together to consider the matter. Her injuries were taking their toll and only with Illiyana's aid could she keep moving. Su'ura glanced at her companion and saw that the other night elf also seemed troubled. While certainly not easy, the defenders' flight should have been much, much harder.

However, there was nothing they could do but keep moving and hope that they had, indeed, managed to evade their pursuers. The survivors *had* to reach Commander Haldrissa.

She peered over her shoulder. Smoke rose from the outpost. The goblins' mist had finally faded to nothing this far west and so she had a good view of the black plumes rising over the trees.

The impossible has happened! Silverwing has fallen. The dread words repeated themselves over and over in her head. *Silverwing has fallen. . . .*

Su'ura feared that Ashenvale itself would be next.

His warriors were chafing to hunt down Silverwing's remaining defenders, but Garrosh wanted the night elves to escape. It was all part of his grand strategy.

Briln and the other officers joined him. The former mariner had proven himself worthy in combat and the warchief gave him a nod. Briln grinned.

"Silverwing is ours," Garrosh declared with immense satisfaction.

The others around him cheered. Warriors beyond them took up the cry. The cheer became a single word, or rather, name. Over and over, the warriors shouted out *"Garrosh! Garrosh!"*

"The survivors'll tell 'em what happened," Briln mentioned when the cheering had finally died down. "The Alliance will have many more fighters when they come to avenge Silverwing. They'll be ready for blood."

Garrosh grinned. "Good. Let them send a thousand fighters—ten thousand." He waved Gorehowl over his head, the axe keening. The other orcs looked with admiration upon the fabled weapon.

"Let them send all the warriors the Alliance has." The warchief eyed the carnage he had wrought. "It will just mean more of them will *die*."

20

DEPARTURES

"Welcome, Shandris," Tyrande greeted as the general entered the chamber where the high priestess and the archdruid had been in grave discussion concerning the events in Ashenvale. "I understand that the readiness of the first expedition is imminent."

The general bowed her head. "The Mother Moon makes my network look slow and inefficient. All is as you say. We will be able to leave shortly."

Malfurion did not look pleased with this news. "I should have never agreed that you take command of the expedition, Tyrande. I am the one who will go."

"No. Elune has decreed that this is my path. It pains me that we will be apart, but in the vision I saw myself there and you here, and knew it the right thing."

He grimaced. "The path of the druid sounds easier and easier when I listen to things such as this."

Two attendants entered the chamber from another

room behind Tyrande. They carried her armor. "I would certainly beg to differ, Mal. If I never have anything to do with the Emerald Dream again, I will be very pleased about that."

"All is in readiness, mistress," one of the attendants informed the high priestess. "We are about to take your belongings aboard and wondered if you would be wearing this for the journey."

"No. Elune promises us a safe voyage. It is in Ashenvale where she cannot reveal what awaits."

With a grunt, Shandris saluted her. "Judging by the pace of your packing, my news was even more out-of-date than I thought. I suspect it would be good for me to get my own gear aboard. We will be sailing *very* soon, will we not?"

The high priestess smiled. "Yes. But only if that meets with your approval."

"The sooner we get to Ashenvale, the sooner we send the Horde running." With that, Shandris saluted Tyrande and Malfurion, then marched off.

Tyrande's smile turned into a fearful frown. She quickly dismissed the attendants and, when finally alone with her husband, said, "I truly cannot see what is happening in Ashenvale, Mal. I do not like that . . . but I still know that I have got to be there and you need to be here. I cannot explain why."

"No need. I will just grind my teeth and do as you say."

Tyrande kissed the archdruid. "Thank you for understanding."

"Hmmph! You know I do not."

"Then thank you for pretending." With tremendous reluctance, she broke from him. "I must go."

"I will not see you off. I promise." Tyrande had earlier

asked him not to be there when the ships sailed. Despite her assurance that Elune knew what had to be done, it was still at least as much a struggle for Tyrande to separate from him as it was Malfurion from her. They had already lost so many centuries in the past. And now, with mortality peering over their shoulders, it was harder than ever to contemplate being in two different lands, especially considering that they did not know what danger might await Tyrande—danger in which Malfurion would be unable to intervene.

"Oh! What news of the assassins?" she asked as she departed.

"Maiev has a theory involving the worgen. I doubt its value, but at this point, it would not surprise me to learn anything."

That caused her to stop. "The worgen?"

"I will follow through on it with Maiev. As I said, it is very likely nothing, but we will see. Go now! I will keep Darnassus in one piece while you are away, even if I am not you."

"Thank you." She left before either could find another excuse to delay the separation.

Malfurion immediately tried to focus on something other than his wife. The murders were the most logical, not to mention urgent, choice. He had not revealed that Jarod had also indicated there was a need to speak to the worgen, but Maiev's brother wanted to do it without his sister present. While the former guard captain had not said as much, his style of investigation was quite different from his sister's. Both were very determined and known for getting the task done. Jarod, though, preferred a less brash, more subtle approach, which was also more to Malfurion's tastes.

And with all the chaos going on at the moment, whatever little calm could be maintained was more than for what the archdruid could hope.

He should have waited for Malfurion, but Jarod could not contain his impatience any longer. Nor did he think that he could keep his intentions hidden from Maiev. That was why Jarod was already on his way to the area where he knew that he would find the group of worgen whom he had previously encountered. More important, he would find that one particular worgen.

Maiev had some other avenue of investigation that she wanted to pursue and had taken Neva with her, so Jarod was able to slip away fairly easily. His sister still did not entirely think him necessary to her work, but so long as he did nothing to interfere, anything he might accidentally discover she would accept.

Someday, perhaps we will understand one another better, Jarod thought as he neared the territory where he had last confronted the worgen.

He sensed the faint smell that he associated with the worgen. A musky sweat. The scent was faint, but that did not mean that the worgen were not nearby.

"Night elf . . ."

Even closer than I thought. . . . Jarod turned to face the worgen who had spoken. He did not recognize the markings, at least not as those of the one he sought.

"What do you do here, again?" the worgen growled.

So this is at least one of those from before. That pleased Jarod, for it saved time in having to explain just who he was. There were enough other things that he might have to explain.

"I would like to talk with one of you. The one who was in charge the last time I was here."

The worgen cocked his head. He sniffed the air, and Jarod realized that the Gilnean was taking in the intruder's scent, perhaps even marking whether there was the sweat one associated with lying or fear.

"I know of whom you speak. He'll not want to talk with you."

"I would just like to have the chance. Let him say so and I will leave."

The worgen's ears flattened and his brow furrowed. Finally, reluctantly, he gestured the direction Jarod had been heading. "That way. Not far."

When the lupine figure did not move, the night elf turned and started walking as indicated. Although he did not hear the worgen behind him, he knew that the creature was following.

They climbed a short hill, then descended the other side. Jarod could not help but feel that more eyes now watched him from beyond the surrounding trees.

Without warning, another worgen leapt into sight in front of them. Having expected something, Jarod did not even flinch as the newcomer first landed on all fours, then sleekly rose to face the night elf.

It was the worgen for whom he had been searching. The fur was unmistakable. What was also unmistakable was the worgen's displeasure at Jarod's arrival.

"You . . . you shouldn't have ever come back here. . . ." To the worgen who had led the night elf to this place, he growled, "And you should know better!"

The other Gilnean's ears flattened and a slight whining sound escaped him. The second worgen dismissed him with a curt wave that displayed for Jarod the long, so very sharp claws.

The chief worgen then turned his gaze toward the trees. Ears pricking up, he let out a slight snarl.

Jarod heard nothing, but a few seconds later the worgen relaxed slightly.

"We're alone now," the worgen announced with confidence.

The night elf did not ask how the other could be certain. He trusted in the worgen's senses. "I appreciate your talking with me—"

"I've not said I would! You should've known the last time you were here that you weren't wanted!"

As he spoke, the worgen's muzzle neared Jarod's face. One snap from the savage jaws could have easily ended the conversation—provided the Gilnean could have accomplished that before Jarod's sword impaled him. That the night elf kept the blade at his side and not in his hand in no manner gave the worgen advantage; Jarod's reflexes had not slowed that much over the millennia.

As if sensing that he could not cow the night elf, the worgen pulled his muzzle back slightly. The two eyed each other for a moment.

"I am sorry," Jarod finally replied calmly. "I came alone so as to not disturb matters any more than necessary. If I can speak with you for a moment, you will not hear from me again."

The worgen snarled but finally nodded. "Ask what you want quickly!"

"My name is Jarod Shadowsong—"

"I care nothing for your name! Ask your damned questions!"

The former guard captain nodded. "You did not say anything about being the one to rescue me from that trap."

"Which should have been enough to tell you I wanted nothing more to do with it. It was a moment of weakness. . . ." But in the worgen's tone there was the first hint of sympathy. "I couldn't leave you there, though."

"For which I will always owe you. But tell me, why were you there in the first place?"

The Gilnean looked away. "We know of the spellcasters' murders. We know that we are believed by some to be the culprits! My lord ordered otherwise, but some of us decided to seek answers ourselves."

"And did you find anything?"

The worgen glared at the heavens. "Yes. We found we die quite easily, too, when snared by traps like the one that caught you!"

Jarod started. "One of yours perished?"

"The trap was not exactly the same. As with yours, it was all but invisible, only the telltale sign of withered foliage where the trap was set revealing its presence. That was how I discovered the one that caught you. This trait we learned, unfortunately, in retrospect from the loss we suffered."

"I am sorry."

His companion nodded in acceptance of Jarod's sympathy. "We could not free her in time. Like yours, it first tortured, yes, but then it made certain that if one managed to escape, a second element would seize the heart from within." He bared his teeth in remembrance of the foul deed. "We found later that her heart had literally exploded."

"By Elune!"

"You see now why I did what I could to release you."

"Where did this happen?"

The worgen again bared his teeth. "Not all that far from where you met your disaster. That was why I was near: I wanted to study the place where she died to see if there was any clue that would help us avenge her."

"And was there?"

"The only clue was the trap that nearly did you in, night elf." The Gilnean's ears flattened. "There's no more I can tell you."

The finality in the Gilnean's tone made it clear that Jarod should not try to push. The night elf understood. "I appreciate what you have told me. It should help."

"I doubt it. Your sister seems set on blaming us."

"Maiev will see that what needs to be done will be done," Jarod replied somewhat defensively. "She has always upheld her duty to our people."

"But we are not your people." With that, the worgen stepped back to depart.

Jarod started to do the same, but paused. "If you think of anything more, you know my name."

The worgen snorted . . . then hesitated. "And mine's Eadrik. I trust you with that on the assumption that you'll keep it to yourself."

"Of course."

The Gilnean vanished among the trees. Jarod stood there for a moment, wondering whether he had accomplished anything. The worgen's words milled around in his head as he tried to make sense of it all.

Tried to make sense of it all . . . and prayed that no other Highborne would be assassinated before he could.

21

A LINE DRAWN

The scouts came rushing back to Haldrissa, who suddenly discovered that she had dozed off in the saddle. Fortunately, neither Denea nor any of the other officers noticed, as they were more caught up in the startled looks of the returning Sentinels.

Haldrissa made a quick count and came up two short. Yet, although the scouts rode with much urgency, they did not move as if the Horde were on their heels.

Unfortunately, the news they brought might as well have been such.

Silverwing had fallen.

The scouts had only sketchy information. It was not until a few moments later that those who could much better attest to the disaster arrived.

The once-proud Silverwing Sentinels had been reduced to perhaps a quarter of their strength, and many of those were wounded. Among their survivors was the acting commander, Su'ura, who related the terrifying tale of the outpost's fall.

Haldrissa grimly listened to the news, all the while thinking that the end of the world as she knew it had finally come. Even the Cataclysm had not touched her this way. Silverwing was gone.

The Horde was sweeping over Ashenvale . . . with Garrosh Hellscream himself leading the way.

"We should ride to meet them now!" snapped Denea. "They will never expect us to be so close already! We will catch them by surprise!"

Several of the other younger Sentinels voiced their support. Haldrissa noticed that Su'ura—no coward—was not among them. Nor was the "scout" who stood near her, and the senior commander would have expected such a one to be the first to demand they turn and fight.

"No," Haldrissa quietly announced. "We will not."

Denea gaped. "But the whole purpose of our march was to meet up with Silverwing in order to better secure a line of defense against the Horde—"

"There was more to it than that, but the point is . . . Silverwing is no more. That changes everything. We cannot properly set up a good line of defense in this region, and attacking the Horde right now would play into their hands. You heard her report and you know what we ourselves experienced. The Horde has new strategies, and if Garrosh Hellscream is at the forefront, they will have more to throw at us than what we have seen thus far."

"You are not suggesting we turn back?"

Denea's arguing was bordering on insubordination, but under the circumstances Haldrissa forgave her.

"Only as far as just west of the river. We cross and

then take up a position not far from it. Let them struggle across. We will better bring them down as they try."

It was clear that Denea and some of the others still looked more interested in supposedly surprising the Horde by moving forward and attacking, but they obeyed orders. Su'ura and Illiyana organized the survivors. Those too weak were given mounts.

They turned about and headed back. Haldrissa had Denea take command of a squad that would protect the rear of the column. While outspoken, Haldrissa's second would make certain that she followed through with her instructions and kept everyone safe from possible Horde scouts seeking to pick off stragglers.

They made good time, in part because, having just come from that direction, they knew the path very well. Recalling the incursions into Alliance territory by the orcs, the senior commander still sent scouts ahead, just in case.

They faced no threat at the river and crossed easily. Haldrissa chose a location that would give them an open area in front of them that would make any army charging toward their position easy targets for the archers. She then set about dividing her fighters along the region.

Day passed into night and into day again. Having fought the Horde at all hours during the course of her career, Haldrissa had become quite used to the daytime despite being of a nocturnal race. She sent messengers to the nearest other outposts and was rewarded with answers from both. The contact enabled the Alliance to build a better line along the western side of the river. During all that time, there were no active signs of the Horde, and although Denea pressed for Haldrissa to let her take a scouting party to the enemy's location, the senior commander refused.

Yet, they all wondered why the Horde had not followed up its victory at Silverwing by pushing forward and meeting the Sentinels head-on. Su'ura could offer no details from the attack that shed any light, and none of her staff's suggestions satisfied Haldrissa. Garrosh Hellscream was waiting for something—likely some opportunity—and the defenders would not know what it was until he finally moved.

Another day passed, then two. Haldrissa finally gave in to her second's constant request and let her take a band to cautiously seek the Horde's lines.

It was not until night that Denea returned. To Haldrissa's relief, her party remained intact. However, the younger Sentinel's puzzled look did not sit well with the commanding officer.

"They are gathered as if ready to march," Denea said. "I have never seen such an army! Legions of restive orc warriors—some on foot, others riding great wolves—row upon row of tauren armed with axes or spears and chanting to their guiding spirits, goblin shredders in numbers never seen, howling trolls who adorn their armor with skulls . . . and more and more!" She took a deep breath and finally explained the cause of her confusion. "But even though many of their warriors are clearly eager for bloodshed, their commanders are holding them back."

"You saw their strength?"

"They have put together a powerful force," the other reluctantly answered. "Enough to crush us."

"And they are waiting? Did you see anything else?"

"I saw the goblins working on their infernal

mechanisms, including some wagons that look to be the source of that foul-smelling mist. Other than that, nothing out of the ordinary."

Haldrissa recalled more of Su'ura's report. "Catapults?"

"A few. The same type we have seen in the past. Not very accurate things."

That dismissive description did not sit well with the veteran officer, who well remembered Su'ura's words concerning the near perfection with which the boulders had been lobbed into Silverwing. If these were indeed the same catapults, then the orcs had trained their crews well . . . in fact, better than ever.

The catapults somewhat explained the reason the Horde might not yet have attacked, such heavy equipment always slower to bring to the front. Yet, that still did not satisfy Haldrissa. Either Garrosh had the expectation of more troops arriving to strengthen his force or he waited for the Sentinels to do something.

But what could that be? she asked herself again.

The growing numbers on the Horde's side forced Haldrissa to make a decision that she had not wanted. Sending messengers back, she called in every available Sentinel to be brought up to the lines. The Alliance had to hold here. If they allowed the orcs to make any deeper headway into western Ashenvale, they risked losing the entire region.

To her surprise, it was not the reinforcements she had summoned who first arrived. Rather, it was a *herald*, riding like the wind. At first, Haldrissa feared that somehow Garrosh had gotten around her line and had attacked the outposts behind, but the rider looked anything but horrified as he jumped off his panting nightsaber.

"Help has arrived!" he called to her, heedless of the fact that others heard his triumphant shout. "The Horde will pay for Silverwing!"

"What are you saying?" Haldrissa demanded as Denea and others gathered. "Are the reinforcements from the western outposts on their way already?"

"They and many more, Commander! They and many more! Our ships landed this morning! The others have already disembarked and pushed victoriously through the Horde stronghold of Zoram'gar Outpost, where they met with little resistance!"

"'Disembarked'? What do you mean? Who? Where are these reinforcements from?"

"Darnassus! Your messenger made it to Darnassus!"

"Aradria?" Denea blurted. "She lives?"

Some of the rider's joy momentarily faded. "Only long enough to tell all she knew. Then her spirit rose to join the Mother Moon."

"Brave," Haldrissa remarked. "She will be honored."

"I will make certain ten orcs pay for her life," growled Denea.

The commander had no time for bravado. Battle had a way of reducing a warrior's desire to simply surviving. To the rider she asked, "And does General Shandris lead them?"

"Nay, though she has come too." The male night elf could not keep from grinning. "It is the high priestess herself who heads the expedition!"

"The high priestess?" All around them, Sentinels looked stunned, awed. Haldrissa could scarcely believe what she heard. "Tyrande Whisperwind is in Ashenvale?"

"Yes . . . and soon, she will be among us. So she promises!"

The startling news could not help but lighten the Sentinels' hearts. The high priestess, the voice of Elune on Azeroth, not only had heard the peril of her servants but had come to personally lead them to victory over the Horde.

"The orcs were fools to wait," Denea said with relish. "You were right to have us hold, Commander! Now they *will* pay for Silverwing . . . pay a hundredfold!"

Haldrissa, too, felt her confidence rising. Garrosh Hellscream was a foe with whom to be reckoned, but against Tyrande Whisperwind, who had some ten millennia more experience in war, the orc surely had no chance. Final victory, Haldrissa told herself, would be the Alliance's.

And yet . . . she could not help glancing toward the direction of the enemy and wondering.

She should be in Ashenvale by now, Malfurion thought sourly. *She is in Ashenvale while I go around hunting shadows. . . .*

That was not exactly the truth. Maiev and her brother were doing much of the investigating, while Malfurion spent most of his time trying to get the Highborne to see reason.

The Highborne were becoming angrier and angrier at the lack of success. They had begun to do some investigations of their own, especially Var'dyn. Unfortunately, that had put them at odds with many of the people of Darnassus. Malfurion had already had to step in once to stop bloodshed.

Even Mordent no longer had much patience. He and Malfurion stood at the edge of the Highborne encampment, separating after three fruitless hours of debate on the best course of action.

"I have tried to restrain the younger ones, like Var'dyn, enough, Archdruid. I find I no longer care to stop them."

Malfurion remembered all too well how close Var'dyn had come to unleashing his magic on the night elves angrily surrounding him. They had not taken kindly to his imperious questioning and not-so-subtle threats when he had been asking after the two murders. "We are doing the best anyone can. Maiev—"

"Had better show results. I understand her reputation. I fail to see anything that supports it. She has badgered us over and over on a variety of leads, some of which infer that perhaps the assassins are among our own. If this is the best she can do for this matter—"

"She has been questioning everyone, Mordent. No one could be more thorough." Malfurion sighed. "I will talk with her and see if there is anything else."

"At least her brother has some tact, not that he has been any more efficient. Still, he shows proper respect."

The archdruid refrained from commenting. Jarod did indeed have more tact. "We *will* solve this."

"As you say," the Highborne concluded, his tone doubtful. "Fare you well."

Malfurion nodded, then headed toward Darnassus. However, he had not gotten far when he sensed that he was again not alone. He glanced over his shoulder but saw nothing. Malfurion turned his attention back to his trek.

The armored figure that now stood in the path ahead had her cloak drawn around her, turning her into a dark, ominous image that surely even Illidan had found daunting at times.

"Archdruid Malfurion," Maiev greeted him.

He glanced over his shoulder at where he had left the Highborne. Malfurion and Maiev were uncomfortably close. "What reason brings you out here?"

"A question or two concerning the assassinations that I need Var'dyn or his master to answer. I think it might clear something up in my mind."

"You have found something?"

She exhaled. "I would rather not say until I know how it turns out."

Malfurion accepted that, but was still uncertain as to the wisdom of her current intentions. "You *must* speak with them?"

Maiev chuckled. "Have I been annoying them?"

"This is no laughing matter."

Jarod's sister sobered. "No. Not where the Highborne are concerned. You are right."

"Is this questioning necessary?"

"I do nothing without reason. And you need not fear that I will upset them so much that they will go running into Darnassus. I heard about Var'dyn. That one is going to be a problem."

"He will be fine if this all gets settled."

She frowned, but answered, "Yes, I suppose he will."

"Be cautious, Maiev."

"I will be."

With a slight bow, Jarod's sister moved on. Malfurion watched her for a few seconds. Maiev did not look back.

He shook his head. *Driven by duty, even if it means walking into danger.*

Malfurion was suddenly struck by immense guilt. It was in great part due to him that she had become so obsessive with her tasks. *She* had watched over *his* brother for millennia because Malfurion had shown Illidan mercy. The archdruid felt tremendous responsibility for Maiev; he did not want to see her suffer more than she already had in her life.

And if she baited the Highborne too much while questioning them, there was a very good chance that she would suffer *greatly*.

Alone again, Malfurion welcomed the tranquility of the forest. The urge to simply settle down somewhere and meditate—even go to the Emerald Dream for a time—grew stronger.

But not strong enough. The Cataclysm had created many situations requiring the druids' efforts and Malfurion was needed to guide those efforts. More important, however, was the fact that Tyrande even now moved to lead the night elves and their allies against the Horde. If there was even the slightest chance that she might need his help, Malfurion was willing to sacrifice himself, if necessary.

The local trees greeted him. They were grateful for his appearance, in great part due to the Highborne living so nearby. The spellcasters made the forest wary; the trees especially could sense the inherent danger in their magic.

The archdruid calmed the trees as best he could. However, there was little he could tell them other than that the Highborne would not be casting great spells around them. Malfurion had promised to treat Mordent's people with respect, and part of that meant allowing them to practice their craft on occasion . . . but only in a limited way and only in a designated area closer to their encampment, where the druids had set safeguards in place. The archmage kept most of his people under control, but, as Malfurion knew, some of the more ambitious, like Var'dyn, had to be watched more. Even here, Malfurion could sense the residue of some arcane spell. Once the murders were solved, the archdruid would have to have a word with Mordent about Var'dyn's grasp on where the line was drawn.

Malfurion continued walking as he communed with the trees and other forest life. He had to return to the temple to see to some of the more mundane aspects of leadership. There were those seeking an audience, requisitions to confirm . . . things that as an ordinary druid he would never have had to deal. It made him feel all the more guilty to think of the millennia that Tyrande had dutifully worked to see to the best for their people while he had been . . . away.

Someone else approached. Frowning, Malfurion sighted two grim Sentinels.

"Hail to you, Archdruid Malfurion," the senior of the two greeted.

"What is it?"

"We have report of another assassination."

The news struck Malfurion dumb for a moment. He stood there, waiting to be told they were in error, but realizing quickly that it was something that he had been expecting.

"Where?"

"In the deep woods farther north from here. The one called Neva sent the news to us, then went to find Maiev."

Maiev. It only stood to reason that she should also be informed . . . and yet, the archdruid hesitated to go after her. He had promised the Highborne that these dread crimes would be solved. Another death would only cause things to boil over beyond even his control.

Neva will eventually inform Maiev. I need to make a study of the scene as soon as possible. . . . Having satisfied himself in regards to the notifying of Jarod's sister, Malfurion indicated to the pair to lead the way.

The Sentinels turned. At first, out of respect for the archdruid, they kept a slower, more even pace. Only when Malfurion purposely took a step or two ahead of them did they finally seem to realize that he preferred speed over propriety.

Although he had a vague notion as to where they journeyed, he was glad that his guides knew the exact location. Malfurion had to assume either that the Highborne had been lured out here or that, like the one Jarod had discovered, the victim had been moved after death.

Even still, his impatience swelled. Eyeing yet another hill to climb, he finally asked, "How much longer?"

"According to what we were told, it should be just over this rise, Archdruid."

"Good." He picked up his pace again, moving ahead of the Sentinels.

The trees around him suddenly shook with warning. The archdruid glanced up at them, reading their fear. However, it was not fear for themselves . . . but rather *him*.

He raised a hand, already casting. At the same time Malfurion shouted, "Get back! There is a—"

He felt as if flames had burst all around him, although he could see nothing. Behind him, Malfurion heard the Sentinels scream. A horrific crackling sound assailed his ears and he suddenly felt not only as if his body were on fire but also as if his skin were being flayed.

Somehow, Malfurion managed to take a step forward. The agony increased, but for some reason the archdruid knew that his best hope was to keep pushing on. In the back of his mind he sensed that the trees were urging him.

The cries of his escorts had faded away. The archdruid could do nothing for them. First he had to save himself. If there was any chance of healing the pair, he could then try. Otherwise they were all surely dead.

He managed another step. The pain lessened ever so slightly.

Through the struggle, Malfurion heard an angry voice. So in pain was he that even had it been someone with whom he was familiar, he could not have identified it. The archdruid only knew that the speaker was very near.

Then, for just a brief moment, the voice became very clear . . . and even closer.

"Why do you not just die already?"

Something struck Malfurion on the head.

22

RITUAL

Genn watched his people continue their preparations to depart. It was with a heavy heart that he had decided to take this course of action, but there was no more reason to stay near Darnassus, and doing so only deepened the shame of the worgen's rejection, at least in his eyes.

Varian's disappearance after the hunt had come as a great blow to the Gilnean king. After the obvious bond that had developed, the other monarch's abrupt behavior had eradicated Genn's last hope that the worgen would be accepted by the Alliance. With that hope gone, Genn's choice had been clear.

Eadrik was nowhere to be found, but otherwise the rest of his aides had the situation well in hand. Another day or two and there would be nothing left to mark the encampment's former occupants.

The hair on the back of his neck suddenly stood on end. Someone was behind him.

As with many worgen, Genn more often than not remained in his lupine form. He felt stronger, younger that way. When human, the king felt the aches of age.

But being worgen now meant that the one behind him had failed if his attempt had been to sneak up on Genn. Moving with the swiftness and grace of the worgen shape, he turned to meet the potential threat with claws and teeth.

But instead of doing battle, Genn found himself standing in utter bewilderment.

"Varian Wrynn?"

Varian could not blame his counterpart for being so stunned. The lord of Stormwind himself felt like an absolute fool, or at least someone who certainly did not know his own mind.

Although on the one hand the hunt had served to do as Malfurion had surely desired, it had also revealed to Varian the utter inconsistencies of many of his own beliefs and prejudices. Suddenly overwhelmed, Varian had chosen the one recourse he felt open to him at that moment: he had retreated in the face of the worgen's honor of him—an honor he felt he did not deserve—and had plunged deeper into the forest, his destination not even known to him.

With Anduin gone, Varian had felt no desire to return to Darnassus. His quarters, while built with the night elves' love of nature in mind, had still been part of a city, part of his life as a king, not as a man. The vibrancy of the forest, with its abundance of life, of freedom, had given him some respite, but had not eased his confused mind as much as he had hoped. Instead, Varian had discovered too late that the quiet and calm around him only better served to bring into focus all his misjudgments and prejudices.

He had lost all track of time, night coming and day returning without his caring. With day had come the knowledge that Varian could not simply abandon everything for the purity of the forest. For his love for his son, for his people, and for his hopes for redemption, Varian had come to a decision. It had to do much with the realization that there were others who had struggled hard with the darker side of their nature, perhaps even in a way that he never had.

The worgen.

And so, after returning to his quarters to quell the growing anxieties of his retinue—and finding that Malfurion had already assured them that their ruler was merely "indisposed"—he had sought out Genn Greymane once more.

"You left," the Gilnean monarch said with some condemnation in his tone. "We honored you and you simply left. I sought word of you from Darnassus, but the archdruid only said not to worry, that you needed time to yourself."

The wisdom of the night elf continued to amaze Varian. "He was right. I had much to consider . . . and when I was done considering all of it, I knew that I had to find you and your people again."

"You want something of us? What? We've nothing. No land, no gold. You have everything. Everything."

"Not everything. I need your help, Genn."

The other king stared without understanding.

Considering their previous encounters, Varian could not blame him.

"How can I possibly help *you*?" the worgen muttered.

"I know something about the worgen curse and the—ferocity—of it . . . but you and yours control that *urge*, not give in to it."

"Ah!" Genn not only nodded in understanding but even showed some sympathy rather than disdain. "I always wondered how anyone could survive what you did and stay intact inside. . . ."

"I didn't." Varian felt uncomfortable even speaking of it. "Tell me what you did."

"It's not as simple as that, my friend. You have to be willing to look deep within yourself, find your balance. . . ."

"I'll fight a hundred orcs barehanded, if that's what's needed—"

The worgen laughed sadly. "Trust me from experience. That might be simpler. We lost several before we were shown the correct ritual by the night elf Belysra Starbreeze. They were consumed by the curse, became beasts without hearts, without souls." Genn looked off into his memories. "We had to put them down. The ritual is still fraught with danger. Now and then, there are those who do not survive it."

Varian was not dissuaded. "Better I die trying than to keep on like I am, Genn. I've lost my wife and now my son. Anduin may be gone forever and it's because of me. . . ."

"I lost a son as well," the king of Gilneas murmured. "Although Liam is gone forever, killed saving my life from a poisoned arrow fired by the leader of the Forsaken, the Banshee Queen, Sylvanas, when we sought to retake Gilneas City." Genn shook his head. "I don't downplay what's happened between you and your boy. 'Tis a terrible, terrible thing, whether by death or the separation of miles, if permanent. I know your loss there, Varian. . . ." The worgen leader peered over his shoulder at his people, some of whom had paused at sight of the recognizable newcomer in their midst. His brow furrowed in deep thought. "We can guide you into the *ritual*, but how you come through it depends much upon you. To conquer yourself—your own worst foe—requires tranquility, balance, and, last and by no means easy, ultimate mastery of your fury. Three struggles, not one."

"Three or a hundred, I'll face what needs to be faced. Show me, Genn."

The worgen nodded. "May your ability be as great as your determination."

Genn did not lead him among the other Gilneans, but rather skirted to the south and then east. However, as they walked, several other worgen left their tasks and began following.

"Why are they following?"

"The ritual needs to be overseen by more than just one."

The lord of Stormwind frowned. "How do they know what we're planning? You gave no sign."

Genn's lupine features showed some slight wry amusement. "None that you saw."

A few more worgen, both male and female, joined in the group trailing behind the pair. They moved in silence, seeming like bearers at a funeral. Varian's hand instinctively shifted nearer to his knife but did not actually touch it.

Genn led him to a small clearing surrounded by trees whose branches reminded Varian of grasping fingers.

The Gilnean ruler guided his charge to the center of the clearing.

"This is where we've made do since our arrival," Genn explained.

The clearing itself appeared unremarkable save for three simple wells sunk on the opposite side from where they had entered. The fact that those wells were here signified to Varian that they had some importance to what was to take place.

That was verified a moment later by the sudden emergence from the woods behind the wells of three *druids*.

At first, Varian expected Malfurion to step out as well, but only the trio—two males and a female—moved toward the wells and the worgen. He did not recognize any of them other than as night elves. They wore solemn expressions and eyed the worgen as if looking for something.

"Who is it to be?" the middle one—his blue hair bound in two long braids trailing nearly to his waist and a smaller one thrusting upward from the back of his head—asked of Genn.

The Gilnean ruler indicated his counterpart. "This one, Lyros Swiftwind. I give you Varian Wrynn."

The druids looked startled. Lyros muttered, "But he is no worgen."

"Yet, still he suffers as we did before attaining balance," Genn explained. "The fury within him is no less than that of any of us, possibly even more."

"Please step forward," the female requested.

Varian obeyed. The three druids each placed a hand on the king's shoulders, then closed their eyes. They studied the lord of Stormwind so for a moment before opening their eyes and withdrawing their hands.

Lyros looked at his companions, who nodded to the monarchs.

"We see it now," he said to Varian. "Welcome, Varian Wrynn. We are honored with your presence and, as keepers of these wells, will do what we can for you . . . though I think it best that Genn Greymane be your guide for this."

"I'd prefer that," Varian replied.

"I'll be glad to," Genn added.

The other male druid—his short, narrow beard and closer-cut hair both green—extended his palm. In it Varian saw a single long, silvery leaf that tapered at the point.

"Take this. Eat it. It is a moonleaf, a symbol of both nature and the Mother Moon. It will help prepare your mind for the ritual."

Varian took it without question. He expected the leaf to be bitter, but instead it had a soft, soothing texture and proved easy to swallow once chewed.

"Now you must drink from each of the wells."

With Genn beside him, Varian followed the druids to the first of the three wells. Here, the second of the two males took over once more.

"I am Talran of the Wild and this is the Well of Tranquility," the druid said, handing Varian a small mug filled with what simply looked like water. "What you drink now will help you rekindle the peace and joy lost so early in your life."

Varian took the mug and calmly swallowed the contents. When he returned the mug, the druid bowed his head.

Lyros gestured toward the second well. Genn looked a little surprised. "He's to drink from all three at once?"

"For his journey, yes. We believe it must be so."

At the second well the female druid, her green hair flowing behind her, served Varian. "I am Vassandra Stormclaw and this is the Well of Balance. What you drink will keep your mind and body as one, thus enabling you to stand with both parts unified for the struggle you take on."

The contents tasted much the same to Varian, who thus far felt no different from either mug of water. As he handed back the mug, the lead druid indicated the third and final well.

"I am Lyros Swiftwind," the night elf said. "And this is the Well of Fury." The druid handed Varian the last mug. "What you drink will enhance the first two mugs you took and also build within you the strength you need to confront and, hopefully, command that which most risks this ritual ending in failure."

Lyros did not explain further. The king of Stormwind downed the contents, then waited expectantly.

The lead druid nodded to the worgen leader. "Genn Greymane, you know what must be done from here on."

"I do. Follow me, Varian."

As they stepped from the druids, Varian suddenly felt as if all his senses had begun to heighten. In doing so, they enabled him to notice some unsettling details he had missed concerning the area. Many of the tree trunks had scars that looked suspiciously as if some beast had madly slashed at them again and again. There were also areas where the ground had been churned up, though not so recently that there was not grass growing atop most of those places. He also smelled the scent of dried blood.

"Back in Gilneas, where my people were the first

worgen to go through the ritual, there were those who required more effort to come to grips with themselves than others," Genn explained, as if aware of what Varian was noticing. "We learned hard from that, very hard, sometimes. When our journey brought us to Darnassus, we planned this place accordingly and it's served us thus far."

The worgen leader gestured to the others. They spread around the clearing, forming a loose circle. Varian estimated how many steps it would take for one of them to close with him. Enough that he could draw his knife, but not much longer than that.

"We shall sit here." Genn smoothly positioned himself with legs crossed, then waited while Varian did the same.

"Now what? I close my eyes? That simple?"

Genn's ears flattened. "If you try, then it's that simple. If you give up already . . . not simple at all."

Frowning deeper, Varian shut his eyes. Immediately, his other trained senses heightened. He heard not only his own breathing, but Genn's. The worgen's musky smell wafted under his nostrils. A light wind grazed Varian's skin and slightly tousled his hair.

"Your senses are very acute. You could be worgen," he heard Genn say with some astonishment. Then, more neutral, the other king began. "Focus. The water from the three wells will aid, but you are the one who must find where to begin. For that, you must look into your memories."

"For what?"

When Genn answered, it was as if he spoke from much farther away. "For those points most relevant to your life . . . and the choices you made because of them for good or ill. Start with the oldest you recall and do more than just remember them. Relive them. Be aware why you did what you did and what that means to you."

Eyes still shut, Varian shifted uneasily. "There's no point in going back and doing that—"

"Then there's no point in continuing," Genn returned, seeming even farther away. His voice also took on a whispery quality, as if the wind carried it.

Varian grunted. "All right. I'll do it."

Gritting his teeth, the former gladiator focused on his past, trying to summon those memories that had for so long remained undesired. He looked far back, thinking of when he was the son and his father the king.

Suddenly he was once again a small boy. A sense of peace draped over him. Varian felt such comfort that for a moment he simply dwelled in it.

Then, the figure of his father dominated the scene. Varian held Llane's hand as the king assisted him in learning to ride his first horse—more a pony, to be truthful. But the riding lasted only moments before the scene shifted to Llane overseeing one of Varian's first fighting lessons. Varian realized then that he had handled a blade barely better than his own son, but Llane's encouragement had helped Varian better learn from his instructors.

The tranquility of those days softened Varian's heart. Still the young boy, he looked up at his father.

That was when the assassin struck.

Llane fell, dead. His slayer, the female half-orc called Garona, loomed like a sinister giant over Varian, who was now suddenly some thirteen years old.

Screaming, tears pouring down his face, young Varian lunged at the killer. Events had not played out this way— in real life, he had not entered the room until the half-orc had already murdered his father—but now they mixed with Varian's turbulent emotions of that time.

But Garona disappeared. Llane's face, contorted in death, filled Varian's thoughts. The teenage version wanted to cry out for his father, but no sound came from his straining mouth.

Then the tragic memory became mixed with others. With Llane dead, the capital was vulnerable. The orcs, who had already invaded the kingdom four years previous, now overran the great city. The capital fell as brutal axes slew hundreds.

Everything wonderful about his childhood vanished. No peace. No tranquility.

But unlike in times past, Varian now realized that the good memories had always remained with him. Even though violence had taken his childhood, it could not erase what he had lived prior . . . not unless Varian allowed it to do so.

And that was what he had always done.

But not now. Despite what had happened to his father and Stormwind, Varian at last embraced what had been before. His father had never ceased loving him and had proven that time and again. Varian had only shoved that knowledge aside.

And now, aware of that, he felt the peace remain within him. Whatever trials had come after the assassination and Stormwind's fall, Varian would always have his childhood. The past could not be changed, but that meant for the good as well as the ill.

Tranquility . . .

Although he managed to keep his eyes shut, the voice startled him, for it sounded like his as a child mixed with that of his father.

Yet, though Varian accepted what had happened, he no longer wished to dwell on it. Instead, his mind sought some other memory to counter what had happened to his father and kingdom . . . and Tiffin naturally occurred to him.

Varian was no longer a child, but an insecure youth caught between the changes both within himself and the world around him. There was much that he had already learned to hide from those closest to him, such as Prince Arthas of Lordaeron and that boy's father, King Terenas— who had also, in some ways, become a second father to Varian. Overall, to others, the young lord of Stormwind had appeared a diplomatic, intelligent, and upbeat ruler wiser than his years. However, the scars within could not always be kept hidden, and servants especially would become familiar with his occasional bouts of despair.

That had all changed with Tiffin. He saw her again as she had been when first they met. A calm and wondrous golden spirit contrasting sharply with his wild, dark self. Varian loved her for the first time again as she strode toward him, even though the first thing he did when she spoke with him was to brush her off in such an arrogant manner that any other person would have rightly fled.

But Tiffin did not. Again she danced with him, laughed with him, and brought out the good in Varian to balance the unchecked. In some ways, even more than his father, Tiffin helped Varian become the king the people loved.

And yet . . .

Varian struggled to keep the memory away, but could not.

And yet . . . the people were the very ones who killed her.

She lay dead at his feet, slain during a riot. An innocent victim of a time when everything had gone mad. Reliving it, Varian nearly slipped back into his darkness . . . but that would have been the ultimate disdain for his beloved. Tiffin had made of him a better man, a worthy leader. Varian finally saw that he had constantly insulted her memory with his later actions. Tiffin would have never acted as he had. She had always forgiven, always sought to do her best for those she loved.

If Varian hoped to redeem himself to her memory, he would have to do the same.

Varian steeled himself against the images of her death, doing instead what he knew she would have hoped of him. He was right to grieve, but he also had to move on . . . and learn. Most of all, he could continue to learn from her life, use it as the example of how he should confront all of the issues he continued to face as a father, man, and monarch. . . .

Balance . . .

Again the voice startled him, this time because he heard not only his own voice, but also that of Tiffin. Varian imagined her again, only this time with the culmination of their love held in her arms.

Anduin . . .

Anduin was all that he had left of family, the most precious member of all, for in the boy was his mother. For the years that they had been together before Varian's vanishing, he had tried to be the father Llane had been. Without Tiffin it had been difficult, but Varian recalled times when he and Anduin had laughed together.

He also recalled the fear that he had felt so often when something had threatened his only child. Indeed, fear for

Anduin had driven much of Varian's later life. He now stood as himself, watching his son, then but three, fall from a pony and almost break an arm. Varian again did battle with an assassin who had snuck into the keep and, in what had too much even then reminded the king of his own father's death, nearly stabbed young Anduin.

Fear . . . Varian refused to give in to it anymore. Fear would only make him helpless against those things that threatened his son and his kingdom. Merely thinking of all those who might harm Anduin was enough to throw Varian into a rage, just as it had so many times prior. However, even as his anger rose, he again saw himself grabbing Anduin's arm . . . and was suddenly reminded how that rage and the fear fueling it had sent Anduin *from* him.

With that realization, Varian turned on his own rage. Where it had in the past always commanded him, now he sought to seize control of it. His rage could be a powerful, devastating force, and Varian saw that simply giving in to it did him little good overall and usually more harm in the long run. True, it aided him greatly during battle—the only time when he could truly unleash it—but beyond that, it was a double-edged weapon.

But although the rage no longer commanded him, it also did not abate. Varian felt the struggle within himself. If he allowed the rage to grow, he accomplished nothing, he realized. He would be the same man that Anduin had left.

And so, Varian held tight to the rage as if it were a horse needing to be broken, and worked to master it. It would no longer aid in further ruining his life; it would have *purpose*. Varian knew only one purpose too. If battle was the single place where his rage did him any good, then it would be where he would channel that force. He would let it fuel his strength against the dragon Deathwing and the orcs and their allies. . . .

The rage surrendered to his will. He had broken its hold over him and now it would *serve* Varian, not the other way around.

Tranquility . . . balance . . . fury . . . came the voice that was his . . . and now also that of someone whom he did not recognize even though he felt he should.

The beast must be conquered so that the man may rise. . . . The rage must be the servant for the man to be . . . complete. . . .

Varian felt his fury growing, but now it did so at his direction. It was now bound to his strength, not his despair. Once again, he felt Tiffin, Anduin, his father, and others who had played loved or vital roles in his life surround him. *They* had never stopped believing in him, not even his son. He saw that Anduin had done what he had for not only his own sake, but in the hopes that it would enable his father to come to terms with himself.

The rage filled him. However, because it had been transformed into a weapon instead of remaining simply a manic force, he welcomed it. With it at his command, no foe could stand against him.

From somewhere, a proud howl echoed. Varian responded to it. He finally knew who called out to him. Goldrinn. *Lo'Gosh.* The wolf Ancient. Lo'Gosh summoned him to battle. Images again coursed before him of those who would seek to harm the ones under his care, especially Anduin. In this new vision, Deathwing laughed as he landed on Stormwind, the mad leviathan savoring the destruction of both Varian's home and countless lands as his power over the very earth caused Azeroth to churn. The world still sought to recover from that evil . . . but it was a battle that Varian understood would take time and careful planning to win. For now, there was another, more immediate threat. He knew the face, knew the name, even before this other foe took the place of the dragon in the king's mind.

Garrosh Hellscream.

Thinking of the Horde leader, Varian summoned his rage to the forefront and tested it. It grew as it never could have as merely a destructive force. Now tempered, now shaped, it was greater than it had ever been.

Lo'Gosh howled again.

Varian leapt to his feet, awake without having noticed that he had been asleep.

Genn Greymane no longer sat directly before him, and perhaps that was a good thing, for it allowed the Gilnean monarch, originally standing a few feet away, to jump back as Varian surged forward. Even though Genn retained his worgen form, he still appeared to move as if in a dream to the king of Stormwind. The entire tableau seemed to have slowed down. Varian surveyed the other worgen, and though they were swift to recover from their shock, their movement yet struck him as slightly slower than his own.

"Goldrinn . . . ," Genn muttered, staring. "Lo'Gosh . . . his aura . . . it surrounds you so completely. . . ."

Around them, the ears of the other worgen flattened, but in awe, not fear.

"Goldrinn truly touches your heart, your soul . . . ," Genn murmured. "The wolf honors you, and so—so do we. . . ."

Varian said nothing, but he, too, was at last able to sense what Genn had known from the beginning. The ghost of the great wolf had made him its chosen, its champion.

And through Goldrinn—Lo'Gosh—and himself, Varian knew what had to be done next.

"I've been reckless, driven by not only bitterness from losing so many things—so many people—of importance to me, but also the fear of losing what little I still cherish, like my son," Varian said to Genn and the other worgen. "But now I understand. Azeroth needs us. All of you—and me—we are what we've become in order to help it. And help it we must. . . ."

Silence reigned around him. Finally, Genn asked, "What would you have us do?"

Varian knew of only one thing. "We follow our destiny together . . . and we follow it to Ashenvale."

23

PURIFICATION

Malfurion stirred. He could not say how long he had been unconscious, only that it had been quite some time. At least a day, possibly more.

As he slowly became aware of his surroundings, he noticed a more troubling thing. He could barely feel his body. It was as if his dreamform had separated from it, yet the archdruid knew that he remained on the mortal plane, not the Emerald Dream.

His head suddenly pounded. Malfurion tried to relax, and the pounding eased. That verified what he feared. He was someone's prisoner, someone who knew something about a druid's abilities.

Malfurion cautiously tried to open his eyes. He began with slits first and when that offered no greater pounding, he pushed for more.

What he saw was that he floated several feet above the ground. Malfurion tried to turn his head, but the pounding returned, this time accompanied by a terrible pain reminiscent of what he had suffered before someone had struck him on the head.

The archdruid was forced to shut his eyes and relax again. Once things settled, he contented himself with looking ahead and trying to guess more from what his peripheral vision offered.

His feet were barely visible and spread some distance apart. From that he judged that he was bound between two trunks. Someone had gone to great trouble to secure him, which seemed odd, considering that they could have just slain him and been done with it. The fact that they had not concerned the archdruid.

He was not far from where he had been caught in the trap. There was no sign of the Sentinels, but Malfurion was of the opinion that they had not survived. Only his power had enabled him to keep from death. Malfurion grew furious at the casual loss of two lives. The Sentinels had perished simply because the pair had been caught at the same time as the archdruid.

The nearby trees had sought to warn him, but too late. The trap had clearly been a subtle one. Malfurion almost would have sworn that it had been set just for him, or else why would it have been in his path? He regretted now not sending word to Maiev.

Something moved at the edge of his vision. A moment later it shifted enough in front of him to be none other than Jarod's sister. Helmet in the crook of her arm, she peered around suspiciously, no doubt seeking Malfurion's captors.

He tried to speak, but the pounding returned. Evidently he made some sort of sound, for she looked up at him.

"So, finally awake."

And with those words, the horrifying truth flashed before the archdruid. Maiev smiled slyly in response to some sign of recognition in his expression.

"The great and powerful archdruid Malfurion Stormrage," she announced with deep sarcasm. "The savior of the kaldorei race. . . ." Maiev spit at the ground below him. "More like the destroyer of all that it stands for. . . ."

Despite the agony that it caused, Malfurion managed a throaty, *"Why?"*

Her brow cocked. "Now that is, I will admit, impressive. You should have been killed by the trap we set, and here you manage to speak coherently. You are stronger than even I had calculated."

Maiev looked to the side. Neva and two other Watchers entered Malfurion's view. They saluted Jarod's sister, not at all a surprise to the prisoner.

"All is in readiness," Neva reported. She glanced Malfurion's way. "We should deal with him before it takes place, mistress."

"No . . . he is good here. No one from Darnassus will come to this area. Our prey will only do so because they think they are beyond threat even now!" She eyed the archdruid. "No . . . he lives for now. I have decided he deserves a special execution."

"Your brother—"

Maiev suddenly glared at Neva. "You know his role. You do not touch him. He will speak for us out of belief in me. Keep him ignorant and forgo your desires for now."

Neva silently nodded, for the moment cowed.

"The fools will be on their way shortly. You lot better get with the rest." She looked around. "Where is Ja'ara?"

"Removing that bit of evidence, as you ordered."

Maiev snickered. "Good. With those Sentinels dead and gone, there is no one left who knows we sent for the archdruid here." She glanced Malfurion's way again. "Get on with it. I am just going to make sure the people's hero enjoys his agony a bit more."

Neva sneered at Malfurion, then led the other Watchers away. Maiev moved just out of the archdruid's sight.

Renewed agony coursed through him. Malfurion tried to scream, but now his mouth would not work at all.

As the agony lessened, Jarod's sister returned to his view. She now studied him with utter contempt.

"That is better. Silence is golden. Especially from you. I am so very glad you are awake, Archdruid. Neva wanted you dead and out of the way, but I have always felt you really deserve far more than a short, sweet death. You have committed so many crimes against our people. . . ."

Although he could not speak, Malfurion tried to relay his thoughts with his eyes. He must have managed, for Maiev shrugged, then answered, "No, I suppose you are blind to everything. Always so caught up in the belief you know best. But if you did, you and Tyrande would not have let those disgusting murderers back among us! There is only one future for the Highborne and it is one you will share!"

Maiev drew a dagger from her belt. She eyed it fondly. "You see this? This is special. I saved it for your brother, but never got the chance to use it. It was taken from me before I was tossed into the Warden's Cage in Outland, and I was not able to retrieve it until after his defeat at the Black Temple. I wanted his death to be very slow, so that he would have time to understand why he had to be punished. You and he are twins, all right! Not just by birth, but by arrogance!"

She threw the dagger. Malfurion watched it fly toward him and expected his end. Yet, at the very last moment, the dagger veered of its own accord and flew past his head.

"Illidan re-creates the Well of Eternity after all the damnation it caused us! Why? Because he *claimed* it was for the good of our people! Then he joined the demons, becoming one of them in nature as well as form! Why? Because he *again claimed* that it was best for our survival to become our enemies and use their own evil against them!" she scoffed. "We know how well that turned out . . . and how false his words always were. . . ."

Maiev held her hand to the side. The dagger landed in it, handle first. She studied it again, seeming to find it very fascinating. "We could have been saved so much trouble where your brother was concerned, but you worried about him more than the rest of our race. You set him on us, Archdruid, as sure as if you had unlocked his prison yourself . . . and that is only one of your crimes. . . ."

There was no doubt in Malfurion's mind that Maiev was mad and had probably been mad for a long time. Adept throughout her life at surviving, she had been clever enough to hide that fact, acting as she knew Tyrande and he expected of her.

"I learned a number of tricks over the millennia, you know. I could not have survived your brother's tender mercies if I had not." Her eyes grew hollow for a moment as she dwelled in dark memories. "Picked up a few gifts like this dagger and learned some abilities necessary to trap demons . . . and Highborne. I have sacrificed so much, but it will all be worth it. I realized that this was the day I was working for, cleansing our people of the Highborne's taint once and for all and removing your foul influence at the same time. . . ."

She replaced the dagger, then simply stared at her prisoner for several seconds. To Malfurion, it was almost as if Maiev no longer saw him, no longer believed he existed.

Jarod's sister started talking again, only now her tone was more friendly. "I have to leave you now, Malfurion. I have guests I must attend to. Archmage Mordent and his associates are dying to know why I have asked them to come, and I do not want to disappoint them. . . ."

Malfurion tried to keep her attention, if only for the sake of the Highborne. He knew that her intentions for the spellcasters were of the lethal kind.

"Do not fret," she jested. "When I am done with them, I will give you my personal attention. I promise, you will not feel slighted. I have chosen a special place where you will be jailed for your crimes just as your brother was." Maiev's tone grew even more contemptuous. "A cozy place where, since you saw so fit to make us mortal, you can gradually rot to death. . . ."

That said, Maiev performed a mock bow, then departed. Malfurion waited, but she did not reappear in his line of sight. He was definitely alone.

Throughout the entire time, the archdruid had been trying to find some weakness of which he could make use, but Maiev's trap was thorough. Yet, he kept trying. He had no choice. It was very clear that Maiev fully intended to slaughter Mordent and several others. The other assassinations had been but tests and taunts. Now she had the confidence that she would be able to take on the leadership of the Highborne.

The pain and throbbing returned as he struggled, but Malfurion tried to ignore everything but his escape attempt. Maiev might be utterly mad, but the archdruid knew her determination, knew her adaptability. She would not seek to slay the spellcasters unless she felt certain she could succeed. If she felt so, then nothing—absolutely nothing—would stand in her way.

After all, in her mind, she was only doing her *duty* for the sake of her people.

Jarod stopped by the Temple of Elune in search of Malfurion, but the archdruid was not there. With Tyrande surely in Ashenvale by now, the former guard captain had expected to find her mate in the vicinity of the Sisters of Elune, who were most likely to be able to tell the archdruid something of the high priestess's current circumstances.

Questioning the attendants on duty availed him nothing. They had not seen Malfurion since the day before. One suggested that Jarod seek him in the Cenarion Enclave, and with nowhere else to turn, the night elf had gone there. However, the druids he met there were equally unhelpful. Their leader often stepped off on his own to commune with the forest. Without any concrete reason to have them search for Malfurion, Jarod had to be satisfied with their assurances that the moment they heard from the archdruid they would alert him to the former officer's desire to meet.

Jarod knew that he should just be patient and wait for Malfurion to return from wherever he was, but the same instincts that had saved him during the war and that had recently stirred again now made him suspicious of this timely absence. It was possible that someone had distracted the archdruid when he might most be needed. However, with no proof, it was up to him alone to find out if that was true.

Jarod decided to seek Eadrik in the hopes that the Gilnean would either know where Malfurion was or even help the former guard captain locate the archdruid. Eadrik shared Jarod's concerns on matters such as the murders, and that was why the night elf thought that the worgen might assist him.

Wary of running afoul of another trap left by the assassins, Jarod veered far more south. He knew the territory well enough by now to know that there was a fair path along there that would lead him to the Gilneans. In addition, Jarod hoped to run into one of those who dealt with Darnassus in the name of their king. Such an encounter might lead to a much quicker answer and save him an unnecessary trek.

But even well on his way to their encampment, the former guard captain saw no sign of any of the cursed humans. That was a bit unusual, according to what he had learned from others. Generally, there should have at least been one or two of the worgen traveling to and from the capital on official duty.

As he neared the encampment, Jarod noticed one other odd fact. True, the worgen were silent in the forest, but he should have heard some sound of activity. It was as if they were all asleep . . . or gone.

But no sooner had he thought that than Jarod sensed he was no longer alone. Impatient with matters, he simply stopped and waited.

As the night elf hoped, a worgen slipped out from among the trees. In fact, it was the very worgen for whom he had been looking.

"Eadrik. Good! I wanted to talk with—"

The worgen signaled him to silence. Jarod obeyed instantly.

From farther back along Jarod's path, there came a muffled gasp, followed by a grunt. Eadrik leapt past the night elf, who turned to join him.

Someone had been tracking Jarod. The night elf realized that he had not even noticed. Whoever it was had been very well trained in moving stealthily.

His mind went to the assassins. If they could murder Highborne, how easy it must have been to simply follow a fool like Jarod. His skill had evidently rusted greatly, after all.

Barely had he begun trailing Eadrik than he almost collided with the worgen, who stood stiffly, staring at something a little farther down the trail.

It was another worgen . . . minus his head. Even in death, he still retained his lupine form, something that Jarod had not expected.

The killer was someone of high skill, indeed. Jarod could see how cleanly the head had been severed. What made that more astounding was that the evidence he saw indicated that the worgen had been *facing* his slayer.

"I *warned* Samuel not to take this lightly! I warned him that they were dangerous even to us!"

"Who?"

Eadrik did not answer. With a growl, the worgen lunged ahead, on the path of whoever had killed his companion. Utterly baffled at this turn, Jarod had no other recourse but to keep up. That immediately proved diffi-cult, for the worgen dropped down on all fours, increas-ing his speed dramatically.

The worgen sniffed the air as he ran, following the scent. The pair quickly left the vicinity of the encamp-ment and, shortly after that, even the most remote part of Darnassus. The deep forest beckoned ominously, but neither slowed even though Jarod had a bad feeling about where things were heading.

Eadrik came to a halt, the worgen rising and lifting his snout to the sky. He inhaled deeply, then bared his teeth and growled low. Jarod, who could see nothing around them but the trees, wondered what the Gilnean was up to now.

"Can't have lost them," Eadrik muttered. "The scent was there. . . ."

Jarod smelled something. A flowery scent. It should have been nothing out of the ordinary, but to him it somehow seemed out of place.

Eadrik did not note it so. His mind was on other mat-ters. "I shouldn't even be here. . . . I should've left this to you night elves! The king wanted all of us able fighters to go with him except for a handful to stay with the young and ill! I was to go with, but I begged him to let me stay! Why did I do it? It's your problem, not ours . . . but the archdruid's tried to do so much for us; I couldn't leave it. . . ."

"What are you talking about?" Jarod asked, distracted by the worgen's mutterings.

His companion stared at him. The eyes seemed too gentle for the otherwise bestial appearance . . . gentle, but not weak. Eadrik was still a human beneath the surface.

"Never mind that! These assassinations! They happened too near us for my tastes! My lord ordered all of us to leave the matter be, but I couldn't. I investigated. I found out the truth, but I didn't think anyone would believe me! That's why I stayed! I couldn't leave it—"

He got no further. Suddenly there came the cracking of a tree branch from deeper in the forest.

Something flew their direction.

"Get down!" Jarod shouted, bowling into the worgen. Eadrik let out a startled growl and fell with him.

The glaive cut through the branches just behind where the worgen had stood, then arced. With sinister grace, it darted back the way it had come.

Eadrik shoved Jarod aside. "Stay down, night elf! This hunt is mine!"

Jarod tried to call him back, but the Gilnean was confident in his abilities. The worgen jumped among the trees even as another glaive soared past him.

The former guard captain seized a heavy rock and threw. The rock struck the glaive squarely, sending it off angle. The deadly weapon flew into a tree, cutting a deep gash. The glaive then bounded off the trunk and fell to the ground a short distance away.

Scrambling forward, Jarod recovered the weapon. He was not very proficient with the glaive, preferring a sword. The night elf cursed himself not only for lacking that training, but also for leaving his favored blade behind.

Gripping the glaive as best he could, Jarod crouched low, then followed after Eadrik. He did not see the worgen immediately but knew roughly where the Gilnean would have gone.

Jarod's body ached as he pushed through the thick brush, but he fought to ignore it. There was always time for aches later, providing that he survived.

He burst through a wall of greenery—and only barely managed to grab a branch before he would have hurtled to his death. The ground dropped nearly a hundred feet. As he pulled himself back to safety, Jarod momentarily pondered the amazing landscape that existed atop the World Tree and how much effort the druids and others must have put in to create a realm that mimicked mainland Azeroth.

Sounds of a struggle brought him back to the moment. He heard Eadrik's growl and a grunt from someone else. There was a crash.

Glaive held ready, Jarod followed the noise. The struggle had to be very close—

A curved blade barely missed his throat. Only a last-minute glint noticed out of the corner of his eye enabled Jarod to get his own stolen weapon up in time.

However, unlike the previous blade, the one that came at him now had not been tossed. Rather, it was wielded in the expert hand of whom at first Jarod thought a Sentinel—until he saw the face.

Neva grinned as she slashed again with her umbra crescent. There was madness in her eyes, but a madness with much cunning. She pressed him against a tree and forced his blades back.

"Is this not romantic?" she mocked, steering the crescent closer to his neck. "Just you and me. . . ."

"Where is . . . Eadrik?"

"The mutt? I have left him for skinning later! Make a nice cloak. . . ."

Anger filled him upon hearing of the brave worgen's death. He had been afraid that the Gilnean had, despite his own warnings to his countryman, underestimated those shadowing Jarod.

The last was something that still puzzled Jarod too. Why had he been followed in the first place? Had Neva been concerned that he might know something and was about to warn Maiev?

Maiev . . .

Jarod cursed as it all made sense to him. Neva's grin grew wider, more mocking.

"Figured it out, did you? You are not just pretty but smart too! Your sister is going to cleanse our people of all their taint! No Highborne, no mutts, no humans . . . no Alliance! We need nothing from them, and all they do is bring their foul ways to us!"

She was insane if she believed what she said, and if she did indeed serve Maiev in this "cleansing," then Jarod's sister was even madder. He could see how it might have come about. Her entire existence had consisted of preserving the night elf race in one way or another. The Highborne's return must have been the breaking point. It was as if Zin-Azshari had once more claimed dominion over their people.

The crescent edged nearer to his throat. Neva was strong, and although she might not be as much as Jarod, she also had leverage on her side.

"Why . . . does she want . . . me dead?" he rasped.

"Maiev does not! She thinks you are useful as a puppet! But I have been watching! You are more dangerous than she thinks! She will appreciate why I killed you. She knows that I believe!"

Jarod saw no point in trying to talk her out of her murderous ways. Neva was a fanatic who saw him only as an impediment.

From behind Neva there erupted a dark form. Daring to look beyond his attacker, Jarod saw Eadrik, his coat matted with both his own blood and surely that of others, fall upon Maiev's second.

But Neva was very skilled herself. She pulled her crescent from Jarod and twisted it around just in time to gut the oncoming worgen.

Unfortunately for Neva, that left her open to Jarod. Too late to save his rescuer, he managed to avenge him. The stolen glaive cut deep into the back of her neck.

Neva spun, then fell to her side. Her foot missed the ground and she started over the edge. Even then, though, her obsession remained with her and she grabbed Jarod by the arm, intending to bring him with her.

A set of claws ripped through the wrist of the hand clutching Jarod. Hacking and coughing, Eadrik shoved into Neva as she lost her grip.

Tangled, the pair fell to the ground far below.

The thud shook Jarod to the heart. The night elf peered down. The two bodies lay separate now, Eadrik on his stomach and almost looking asleep rather than dead, and Neva—

Neva moved. *Barely*. There was no chance that she could recover, not this far from any priestess or druid, but the assassin was not yet dead.

Jarod suddenly prayed that she would hold on. Struggling with his own injuries, he scrambled down to the two as quickly as he could. He who had seen so much death on the battlefield had no trouble assuring himself that the worgen was dead.

Neva moaned. Jarod knelt down beside her just as she managed to open one eye.

"C-come to kiss me good-bye?" she whispered, smirking.

"No. I have come to watch you die slowly, painfully. I have seen injuries like yours. You will survive for several hours, maybe a day or two. I will be gone before then. You will die alone, unless some animal comes to gnaw on you while you are still fresh."

The smirk vanished. Neva looked uncertain, off balance. "Kill me. Y-you know . . . you know you want . . . to."

"I have no reason to grant you any peace. You killed my friend and his friend. . . ."

Neva laughed, which sent blood out of the side of her mouth. "The worgen . . . better than I thought. Must have killed Tas'ira after . . . after we both thought we killed him."

Hearing that there had been another enemy nearby, Jarod quickly looked around, but saw nothing.

This made Neva's grin widen . . . and look even more deathly. "N-never fear. Had . . . had she been around, you . . . you would not be alive! She was with me. . . ." The Watcher suddenly shook. "Ungh! By Elune . . . kill me!"

Jarod did not move. "Tell me where my sister is and I will end your suffering."

"You . . . you will never reach her in . . . in time!" Neva said the last with some pleasure despite her pain.

"I will if you answer me quickly. In return, I swear that I will do what I can for you."

She glared at him. "I will not . . . tell you."

He reached to his belt, where a knife hung. Jarod slowly removed the short but sharp blade. "I will end the suffering. It will only get worse. I know. I saw it on the fields so many times. Good, strong warriors—stronger than you or me—screaming from the pain of their wounds and their shattered insides. The worst ones were those I could not reach because of the Burning Legion so near. They lived for days." He looked off, remembering. "I cannot think of how many I had to send off because there was not any chance of a healer of any sort even easing their conditions."

Neva managed to look away, although she groaned with each forced movement. Her neck was not broken, but Jarod knew that was little comfort to her. The rest of her body was mangled.

He reluctantly sheathed the knife, then rose. That caught her attention.

"You cannot—"

"I am wasting my time here. I will find Maiev one way or another—"

"Wait!" The injured assassin gritted her teeth, then gasped, "Maiev is—Maiev is going to kill the Highborne. First . . . first their leaders . . . then the rest."

The news did not entirely shock him, not from what he had already witnessed. "That I know. Farewell, Neva. . . ."

"Wait!" She coughed and more blood came up. "W-wait. Your sister . . . your sister has another surprise. I . . . I will not let you save the damned spellcasters . . . but I . . . I will give you the archdruid. . . ."

He could not hide the effect *this* revelation had upon him. Jarod returned to Neva's side. "Malfurion? What has happened to him? Where is he?"

She glared. "First . . . your . . . your word. I know you, Shadowsong. Maiev says . . . says you always kept your word . . . just like a good boy. Tell me . . . tell me you will kill me and I will give you the archdruid. . . ." Another cough. More blood. "Will not matter as much . . . if the Highborne die. He will be disgraced. . . ."

Maiev has Malfurion. . . . The awful thought kept racing through Jarod's mind. He could not trust that his sister might not be ready to kill the archdruid at any moment. Time was of the essence. "You have my word. I will take the pain away."

She looked relieved, and extremely pale. As best she could, she told him the path he should take. Jarod, as a soldier well-versed in communicating with the dying, could tell that she did not lie. There were some gaps in her description, but he knew enough, he thought.

"You . . . you promised," she pressed after she was done.

"I know," Jarod answered, drawing the blade.

Neva studied the knife, then turned her gaze skyward.

"You will . . . be too late to stop her," Neva rasped. "Too late . . ."

He said nothing, using the knife expertly to keep his oath.

The deed done, Jarod Shadowsong stood. Even though Neva had been an enemy, he regretted that he had let her suffer for as long as he had. That was not his way. However, Jarod had needed to know what his sister intended and where it would take place. And while Neva had not given him everything, she had offered one item that, frankly, was much more important to him than the lives of all the Highborne combined . . . Malfurion's whereabouts. Nothing mattered more than rescuing the archdruid.

Jarod leaned over Eadrik. With his finger, he drew a crescent moon in the air over the worgen's body. The sign of Elune. He prayed that the Mother Moon would take Eadrik's spirit to wherever the worgen's kind should go after death. Eadrik had proven himself as good a comrade as any Jarod had fought beside in the war. The members of the Alliance were fools if they did not see what having such beings on their side could mean. It might even be able to swing the advantage away from the Horde, who thus far seemed better suited to the wild world Azeroth had become.

The night elf headed off at as great a pace as he could. However, only then did he recall that he had forgotten to make certain from Neva that there were no more traps between Malfurion and him. It would take only one misstep to end the archdruid's rescue before it began.

And this time, there would be no one to save Jarod, either.

24

ASHENVALE AT WAR

As Jarod had begun his day in search of Malfurion, events quickened in Ashenvale. With Elune's guidance, Tyrande had worked miracles in the form of moon-affected currents to see to it that the ships reached Ashenvale even more quickly than estimated. Shandris had immediately sent heralds to the outposts to alert them of their coming and, in turn, learn where matters stood. As this went on, the newly arrived force wasted no time in moving out and marching. During the march, Tyrande explained to those priestesses who had accompanied her as to what their roles would be and what risks they would have to take.

Thus it was that Haldrissa and her Sentinels had the great pleasure—and relief—of watching the reinforcements arrive the next day, and they instantly began melding with the defenders already at the river. With Denea and the rest of her staff at her side, Haldrissa quickly rode up to meet the arrival of the high priestess and general.

Tyrande Whisperwind was an arresting sight. She did not wear the soft, shimmering robes of the temple now but rather the armor of a warrior of the moon goddess. Her formfitting armor, which covered her from neck to foot, had been crafted with layered plates that allowed her ease of movement. A gossamer cloak the color of moonlight and attached at the shoulders fluttered in the breeze. The high priestess also wore a winged helmet that covered the top half of her head.

"Hail, Commander Haldrissa," Tyrande said without preamble. "I give thanks to the Mother Moon that we find you holding here."

"The Horde has made no sign of movement since Silverwing fell. . . ."

Their expressions turned more dour at her answer. Tyrande and Shandris had been informed of the outpost's destruction the moment that they had arrived, but it was still a bitter pill to swallow. For a long time Silverwing had been admired as an example of night elf determination in the face of extreme adversity.

"The damned orcs will pay," Shandris remarked with relish. "Whatever tricks they have been using are not going to help them anymore!"

"Let us temper our desire to avenge the brave defenders of Silverwing and elsewhere in Ashenvale with the knowledge that Garrosh Hellscream commands the Horde now, not Thrall," said Tyrande. "This is a different Horde in many respects, Shandris. We must move with thought and caution."

"Oh, we will. We will move with the thought of crushing the orcs and the caution of not getting their blood in our eyes when we cut them down."

The high priestess's brow arched. Haldrissa said nothing, but Denea and most of the other Sentinels present nodded hearty agreement with the general.

"We need to know all that has transpired," Tyrande told the commander, "and where you think your weakest points in the line might be."

Haldrissa wasted no time in explaining all as best she could. A daring Denea tossed in her own suggestions when there seemed a point of hesitation on the senior officer's part, including the belief that a thrust forward now would enable them to push the Horde back even to Silverwing. Haldrissa did not silence her second, a part of her wondering if Denea had a sharper grasp than her at the moment. Not once did the younger Sentinel pause in uncertainty as she did, and all that Denea suggested sounded reasonable to her.

Shandris and the high priestess took in everything, but voiced no opinion until the pair was done. At that point Tyrande Whisperwind looked to her general. "What say you?"

"It sounds as if the line is well set up. The thrust forward might be wise; one should never keep on the defensive with the Horde. I will have scouts set out immediately while we distribute our own forces along the perimeter Commander Haldrissa has established. The river is a good point of defense in case we have to pull back for one reason or another. We will leave a row of archers to give cover fire in case of that."

"The goblin mist," Haldrissa reminded her.

"No mist, natural or otherwise, will obscure our sight this time," the high priestess promised. "Elune will see to that."

The commander visibly exhaled. Suddenly, she felt very exhausted.

Tyrande looked upon her with sympathy, focusing for one moment on the eye patch. "You have served me well over the millennia, Haldrissa . . . and sacrificed much too. Now serve me by getting some well-deserved rest."

"I know how the commander has laid out everything," Denea offered before Haldrissa could turn down the gracious suggestion. "She can rest easy knowing all will be well."

"It is settled, then." The high priestess's gaze met the commander's. In those eyes, Haldrissa saw nothing but respect and compassion. Tyrande truly believed Haldrissa needed sleep, and who was she to argue with the co-ruler of all night elves?

"As you wish."

Tyrande corrected her. "As you must, Haldrissa. We will need your experience badly. You know Ashenvale better than most."

"Thank you, High Priestess." From many others, the veteran warrior might have taken the comments as simple assuaging of any hurt feelings on Haldrissa's part, but from Tyrande the commander knew that they were honest. That made her feel better as she excused herself and headed toward where she had made her camp.

As she retired, she kept her glaive nearby. It was very relieving to have the high priestess and the general in control of things, but Haldrissa had indeed been stationed in Ashenvale much longer than nearly anyone else here. She was more at home in the forests of this land than she would have been back in Darnassus. She felt attuned to

Ashenvale, and when it suffered, it was as if a part of her did also.

And as she shut her eye, she could not help feeling that, despite the presence of the high priestess, much more terrible suffering was meant for Haldrissa's beloved Ashenvale. . . .

Tyrande missed Haldrissa's presence almost immediately, but gave no hint. Other than Shandris, the rest of the officers were much, much younger than her. Several had grown up only knowing the War of the Ancients as some epic tale of their parents. They could appreciate the obvious repercussions it had created and understood such matters as why most people hated the Highborne, but they still did not understand just how much the high priestess felt as if she were suffering from déjà vu. Here she was again, having to defend a world turned upside down by the evil of a creature who thought itself the ultimate judge. Back then it had been Queen Azshara. Now, it was Deathwing the Destroyer. And because of both of them, the night elves were faced with daunting obstacles to their continued survival.

But although instead of demons she faced the Horde, Tyrande found no solace in that. Blood was blood; death was death.

I am growing old, she mused, then quickly buried the thought. Instead she looked into herself and reached for Elune's comforting blessing. Although she herself did not notice it, the shaft of soft, pale light that often shone down on her when she looked to the Mother Moon for guidance reappeared. Only when several Sentinels went down on one knee did she realize it.

"Rise, please." Tyrande did not like her mere presence as Elune's vessel to cause one disruption after another. While in general she had been successful at lessening the kneeling, moments like this frustrated her. Neither she nor the lunar goddess sought adulation . . . although, admittedly, even she happily revered Elune. Tyrande just did not believe that she also deserved reverence; she was only the Mother Moon's servant.

Shandris was off organizing the troops with the assistance of the ambitious young Denea and several other officers both from Ashenvale and Darnassus. The Sentinel lines had already been shored up.

One welcome addition to the army gathering in defense of Ashenvale was a ship of mixed forces that had unexpectedly been offered to Tyrande just before departure. With Theramore's suggestion, members of the escort of each representative had been offered the chance to volunteer to help. So many had joined that the ship had been packed tight. In addition to Jaina Proudmoore's people, all three dwarven clans—including the Wildhammers *and* a number of their gryphons—the gnomes, the draenei, and other humans stood ready to fight alongside the night elves.

She peered beyond the river, beyond the forest edge on the other side. In the distance, mist gathered over the area. It had begun coalescing almost exactly the moment that the force under her overall command had arrived, as if the Horde had been awaiting *her* arrival.

Elune, guide us, she prayed. The high priestess surveyed the warriors making up the front. They all had that earnest, wary look she recalled too well from the many wars in which she had fought.

A warning horn sounded.

Tyrande searched for the source, but instead found Shandris riding toward her, Ash'alah, the high priestess's own cat, racing alongside.

"Mount!" Shandris called as she pulled up. "Mount quickly!"

"What is it?"

Shandris pointed to the east. As if a silent but raging river, the goblin mist surged forward. Gigantic trees vanished as the thick fog enveloped them. Within the short moment that Tyrande had watched it, the mist had nearly reached the river.

She leapt aboard her nightsaber just as another horn blew from the southeast. It did not surprise either of them to see that the mist now rushed forth there also.

A shout from ahead signaled the mist's advance there, also. Tyrande marveled at the mechanisms the goblins must have put together to create this fog. As the wind shifted briefly, she also smelled the stench that Ashenvale's defenders had reported. The fog was more of a huge patch of smoke, as if the forest were on fire somewhere.

"You would do better farther back," Shandris suggested.

"I did not come here to hide behind everyone else. I am here because I am needed, Shandris . . . especially at this moment."

Tyrande raised her hands toward the sky. Even though the moon was not evident now, the beam of silver light shone down brighter upon her.

Tyrande focused her mind entirely on her prayer. She asked much of Elune but believed that the deity expected what she intended and would grant it.

Shandris gasped, then recovered. Other Sentinels looked her way, but the general angrily waved them back to their watch.

A beam of moonlight shone down upon Tyrande. The high priestess glowed brighter than the day. The glow grew, first spreading before her, then expanding to her left and right.

The light of Elune draped across the Alliance lines, confronting the encroaching goblin mist wherever it was. The foul-smelling fog moved above the river first, reaching the midway point. But then the moonlight met it.

Tyrande stared straight ahead. As the power of Elune neared the mist, she felt the other priestesses who had come with the expedition finally join her efforts. Strengthened by their prayers, Tyrande's plan thrust ahead.

As she had done against the evil of the Nightmare Lord, the high priestess let the light of the Mother Moon burn away the goblins' creation. Compared to the Nightmare's monstrous fog and its frightening shadows, the Horde's mist proved a weak foe. The moonlight ate away at it with no difficulty and within seconds had already cleansed the air above the river.

The defenders cheered. Those cheers grew even stronger as Elune revealed anew the forest beyond. The goblin mist faded as if nothing.

That did not mean that its creators did not try to fight back. Ahead of the light, the fog abruptly thickened. Yet, even then it proved no match for the Mother Moon's gentle illumination. The light pushed on, moving even after there was no visible sign of the mist left to the Sentinels and their allies.

Although she could not see what happened so far away, Tyrande sensed a sudden ceasing of the goblins' fog. Why waste such effort when it was to no avail? She should have felt confidence with this first, very obvious victory, but the high priestess could not shake the feeling that there was something amiss.

Next to her, Shandris screamed something unintelligible. The next moment the world around Tyrande exploded. What sounded like a roar accompanied the eruption, and her first thought was, *Deathwing! Deathwing comes to fight for the Horde!*

Even as she tumbled, a part of her knew that the thought was a foolish one. The huge dragon would not have bothered with such a petty spectacle. Deathwing, who abhorred all "lesser" life, would have preferred razing the entire area, combatants and all.

Her concentration broken, the prayer ended, and with it the light. She felt pain in her left arm and leg. When Tyrande tried to see what was happening, at first all she saw was more fog.

No . . . not fog. Dust. The air was filled with dust and even large fragments of rock and earth that rained down on not just her, but everyone else in the area. Tyrande made out at least three Sentinels nearby who lay either dead or unconscious.

A large, moist nose sniffed her. Tyrande's nightsaber licked her leg, where for the first time the high priestess saw that a shard of rock stuck out near the thigh. Wincing, she seized the shard and tugged it free, then quickly prayed over the wound. The gap healed, leaving only bloodstains to mark it.

Touching her arm, Tyrande only found some blood. No longer concerned for herself, she looked for Shandris.

The first sign of the other night elf was one that made Tyrande shiver with anguish. Shandris's nightsaber lay sprawled, its skull crushed in by a very large piece of rock.

"Shandris!" All else forgotten, Tyrande stepped past her mount and climbed over the dead cat. "Shandris!"

There were two individuals in her life who meant more to her than anything. Malfurion and the orphan who had become her daughter. Tyrande had never let Shandris know just how much she worried about the younger night elf's duties as head of their forces. So many of the high priestess's personal prayers had concerned Shandris's continued safety.

And now . . .

There was no sign of Shandris on the other side. Tyrande looked farther on, fearing that her daughter had been thrown far away. Tyrande spotted another body—a Sentinel, surely dead, from the awkward angle in which she lay—but it was not Shandris. Even though she felt some shame in doing so, the high priestess gave thanks to Elune for even this momentary respite.

Then a groan from the direction of the dead nightsaber made her turn. Tyrande rushed to the area by the tail, a place to which she had paid little mind. There, a good portion of the cat was buried under the rubble of whatever had struck.

Shandris's arm, the covering dust making it blend into the ground around it, lay just under one of the feline's hind legs. It moved as Tyrande neared, and again she gave thanks to Elune for this personal blessing.

No sooner had she knelt to see what she could do than several other Sentinels rushed up to help. They had evidently seen what had happened but could not get to the two any sooner. With careful swiftness they hefted the dead nightsaber off of the general.

Tyrande put a hand to Shandris's back and prayed. She did not know what injuries Shandris had suffered and did not care. She only hoped that Elune would heal whatever had happened to her daughter.

Shandris groaned again, but this time with more life. She glowed with the light of Elune as Tyrande finished her prayer. Only when the high priestess pulled her hand away did the glow fade. To Tyrande's relief, Shandris's breathing was strong and regular.

As the high priestess pulled back, it was as if the world had suddenly returned in all its chaotic fury. There were shouts coming from everywhere and the familiar hiss of arrows on their way to deliver death. She hoped the last sound had come from the bows of the Sentinels and not the Horde, but knew that it was likely a combination of both. Sentinels rushed past her, some mounted, and all of them with anxious looks on their faces.

A roar that reminded her of Deathwing thundered across the area. Belatedly, Tyrande recognized that it was not *one* roar but a multitude of voices shouting in unison.

She looked toward the river . . . and saw that beyond it, the forest was filled with orcs, tauren with massive totems, trolls—including more than one witch doctor— and more. The floodgates had opened and through them rushed the Horde.

"They . . . they were seeking you," Shandris gasped as a pair of the Sentinels helped her rise. "They knew you were here and they used the damned mist to make you act!"

Tyrande peered at the area around them. Virtually all of the huge boulders that had dropped among them had been concentrated on the center, where, indeed, she had been situated. The high priestess suspected that she could thank luck as much as her patron for the fact that she had survived.

Actually, she could thank one more. "You threw yourself at me."

"With all due respect, you are more important to our people than I am," Shandris responded, straightening. "I did not know that I would land just where my mount would fall after the next strike!"

The horns sounded again. Another flight of arrows from the Alliance side flew over the river. The Horde forces held up their shields, creating a wall. Most of the arrows either bounced off the shields or stuck in them, but several still caught their intended targets. A number of warriors fell or pulled back with bolts sticking out of them.

"They have not managed to ford the river yet," Tyrande noticed.

"It is deep and the current is strong, but that should still not be such a problem for them. They are testing us out; I know it!"

Denea rode up. "General, they did much the same when they attacked our main outpost! The commander thought that they were counting our archers!"

"Likely enough! It will do them no good. We have got

far more than we are using. The others will be a nice surprise when they think they have got our numbers down!"

As the Alliance archers continued to fire—and the orcs on occasion fired back—more mounted Sentinels readied along various points of the line. Tyrande and Shandris had come to Ashenvale with a battle plan already in mind that did not need to wait for whatever the Horde intended to throw at them.

Four contingents of huntresses armed with lances now kept their mounts ready for the signal. With them stood double their number of Sentinels on foot, both those with glaives and others with swords. Accompanying them were dwarves of the Dark Iron and Bronzebeard clans, while farther back, Wildhammer dwarves waited for word to urge their gryphons skyward. Humans, draenei, and gnomes—the last armed with some especially vicious devices—intermingled with the first two dwarven clans. A few magi, mostly from Theramore, were also in attendance, their focus on their dark counterparts.

Tyrande's priestesses had separated into two groups. One went about healing the wounded, while the second watched Tyrande expectantly. They were to assist in her own attack.

Another unit consisting of defenders from Ashenvale formed a new center. Denea had volunteered to take command of them in place of Haldrissa, and Shandris had agreed to that. The general gave the younger Sentinel some last-minute instructions, then sent her off to her soldiers.

Shandris turned to Tyrande. "Are you ready? Can you take over?"

The devastation around the high priestess still fresh

in her mind—and especially the deaths of those who had paid for being in the vicinity of her—Tyrande flatly replied, "Be ready."

With a crooked grin, Shandris secured another mount from one of the other Sentinels, then rode off. Tyrande of necessity led her own cat farther to the rear. Although she ached to join Shandris in battle, for this, she had to be in a safer position. Only when her task was accomplished could she enter the fray herself.

The apparent impasse held. Making certain that the assigned priestesses were ready, Tyrande waited for the right moment.

A horn blew from where Shandris commanded.

The Alliance archers ceased firing.

The orcs forming the first ranks roared, then charged toward the river. Tauren and trolls followed them, while in the back, the undead warlocks of the Forsaken and witch doctors from the trolls began casting spells that Tyrande hoped her own side would be able to counter with minimal losses. Arrows flew toward the Alliance's own front ranks, where huntresses, lances ready, were forced to crouch behind shields and barriers.

In concert with the other priestesses, Tyrande prayed to Elune.

Moonlight touched her and her followers. It then reached forth beyond the defenders' lines, stretching across the river. However, where before it had simply glowed everywhere in order to dissolve the false mist, now its light focused as if through a diamond.

And even moonlight in the eyes can blind.

The front ranks of the Horde were caught in their tracks. The hulking warriors stumbled. Whether orc, tauren, or some other powerful fighter, there was nothing they could do. The light caught them by surprise. It dazzled their gazes. Several orcs ran into one another, their positions made worse by the fact that they were half in the water.

Now, Shandris! Tyrande silently called. *Now!*

The blare of a new horn heartened her, as did the battle cry of the rushing Sentinels and the deadly hiss of the protecting archers. Into the river raced the lancers, their nightsabers undaunted by the water or the enemy ahead. Shandris had utilized the knowledge of Ashenvale's defenders to know where the shallowest areas were, aiding the momentum of the charge.

From the other side, there came the bleat of a horn. Still blinded, the Horde fighters shuffled back as best they could.

They will be slaughtered, Tyrande thought with some guilt. She knew that she did the right thing, but still she also prayed that perhaps the enemy would see fit to either keep running or wisely surrender.

The first of the lancers reached the other side, the crumbling lines of the orcs and their allies only a few yards ahead now. The expert aim of Sentinel archers downed several brutish warriors who refused to retreat with the rest. Orcs, by far the bulk of Garrosh's expedition, lay strewn everywhere, their fearsome tusked faces often still seeming angry in death. Some had more than half a dozen bolts sticking out of their thick hides and even more stuck in their armor and shields. The orcs had done their best to protect themselves, but against so many arrows, even the best of armor proved inadequate.

Yet, even despite the deadly downpour, several

orcs—arrows deep in legs, arms, and torso—survived to keep some order as they dragged more severely wounded comrades back from danger. Two grabbed banners from fallen comrades, waving the Horde flags in defiance as the Sentinels moved in after them.

Despite the surviving orcs' bravado, it appeared that the destruction of Silverwing would soon be avenged. However, of even greater import was the growing hope that the liberation of all Ashenvale seemed possible . . . *if* Garrosh's ambition could be crushed here and now.

Again, the enemy horn sounded . . . yet, this time in a more fearsome, defiant manner. Tyrande had to assume that Garrosh intended a stand on safer ground. The only trouble was, the moonlight followed the Horde, continuing to blind them even as the lancers drew within striking range. The warlocks and other casters could not even give proper cover, as they were also unable to face the moonlight. That, in turn, gave more advantage to the Alliance spellcasters, who worked in earnest to put an end to the Horde's magical threat. Fearsome blasts bombarded the warlocks nearest to the front.

The Horde horn blared once more, its signal not at all seeming to call for retreat. Rather, it encouraged attack in its tone, promised victory.

But instead of turning to face their foes again, the orcs and other fighters remaining from the front lines did a strange thing. They scattered to the trees as if trying to get out of the way. How they hoped to escape the nightsabers by fleeing, she could not say. Night elves were more forest creatures than orcs, tauren, or even trolls. Their cats were just as wily and quick in such areas, and the riders knew well how to handle their lances even among the trees.

Shandris must have suspected something, for a horn sounded on the Alliance side, one that signaled for a regrouping rather than a continued hunt through forest. With so many of the enemy now turned from the direction of the battle, the high priestess finally chose to cease the prayer.

Even as the moonlight faded, she urged her mount forward. If there was danger to her people—and to her Shandris—Tyrande needed to be nearby.

The first wave of foot soldiers had made it to the other side behind the lancers. Some threw their glaives at retreating targets, but most already began regrouping. Watching them, Tyrande breathed with relief. Garrosh would find the advance line able to hold against his warriors.

A monstrous roar rumbled through the region.

A massive rock appeared in the sky, then dropped down hard on a band of lancers just about to join their compatriots. The hapless riders never even realized their doom. The rock crushed some, and the fragments from its shattering slew the others.

More rocks came flying through the air. Ashenvale's defenders had warned about hidden catapults, but Tyrande had never witnessed anything like this. There was something different. She was reminded of her own near death and how that assault, too, had seemed not quite what it appeared.

The first rock had done the most harm. Now warned, the Alliance army better avoided the areas where the missiles dropped.

Trees began shaking farther into the forest ahead. Another roar thundered across the landscape . . . and this time was answered by several more, all from the same direction.

What seemed initially a series of rhythmic explosions accented the roars. Tyrande frowned. Not explosions. It was as if they were hoofbeats—but for such, the animals would have to be gigantic. . . .

The tree line flew away, entire oaks tossed as if nothing. A humongous shape, with some resemblance in outline to a *centaur* but much bulkier, burst out among the stunned defenders.

"Elune, preserve us!" the high priestess blurted.

The giant creature seized a lancer and mount with one hand and tossed both casually over his shoulder. Night elf and cat went screaming to their deaths. The behemoth stomped at the closest Sentinels on foot, crushing one beneath his sturdy, elephantine feet.

Indeed, the lower half of the body had much similarity to such a creature—or rather, to its larger, more deadly cousin from Northrend, the mammoth. Yet, where the head and shoulders should have begun, the upper torso of another fantastic creature roughly akin to a human began. The towering monster, two long tusks arching down from the sides of his mouth, eagerly searched the ground before him for more victims.

And as the one behemoth stomped among the scattering defenders, another broke through the forest elsewhere, sending trees down on the fighters and seizing other victims in his thick, four-fingered hands. As the second monster crushed the life out of his prey, the rest of the trees exploded and identical fiends fell upon the would-be victors. The battle had turned into a catastrophe of proportions as terrible as the legendary creatures loose among the tiny night elves.

They have set magnataur upon us! the high priestess marveled grimly. *They have dared set magnataur loose in Ashenvale!*

The danger to the Horde itself surely should have been obvious to Garrosh, but he had taken the risk and thus far had chosen well. To bring the savage giants of the wastes of Northrend to Ashenvale had surely been a mighty test in itself. Tyrande could not imagine how even the Horde could have managed to bring them without some sacrifice already on its part.

With heavy thumps, the magnataur wreaked havoc merely by moving. Tyrande counted eight in all—every one of them *bulls*—and though a small number, it was astonishing to see them together. So violent were magnataur that males such as these lived isolated from one another, or else they constantly came to blows.

The beasts crushed and tossed about their victims as if the mighty Alliance army was little more than ants. A nightsaber lacking its rider attempted to bite at the heavy, cylindrical leg of one of the magnataur. For its bravery, the cat was taken up in one hand, then torn apart with both. The magnataur then threw the mangled pieces into the river, which already ran red with blood.

Somewhere out there, Tyrande knew Shandris was trying her best to save her troops. The high priestess yearned to continue her own charge, but knew that she had to try to stop the magnataur first.

Reining her cat to a halt, she called upon Elune's aid in that regard. As it always did, the light of the Mother Moon shone down upon her. Tyrande prayed for guidance—

Yet another huge boulder soared above her. Too late, Tyrande realized that the magnataur were the "catapults," and for them Garrosh evidently had one particular target in mind. The glow of Elune had actually pointed her out to them. The magnataur, for all their savagery, were intelligent enough to understand what was needed. Garrosh wanted the glowing target destroyed. If it was another priestess, that would be one fewer to aid Tyrande.

And if they slew the high priestess . . . they knew that they would deal the night elves and the Alliance a devastating blow.

The shadow of the boulder passed in front of her. The high priestess pulled hard, turning her mount away from the oncoming crash and the deadly spray that would follow.

As she did, though, a sharp pain caught her near the shoulder blade. Another did near the lower part of her back.

Two arrows had struck the high priestess.

Tyrande knew that she had been tricked. Whether by the magnataur or one or two daring archers, Garrosh wanted the night elf ruler dead. In this case, the boulder had been the decoy the archers had needed.

And as the monsters from Northrend tore through her people, Tyrande dropped limply to the ground.

25

VALOR

Var'dyn looked impatiently at Archmage Mordent as they neared the grove where they were supposed to finally have answers to the horrendous crimes against the Highborne. Mordent moved with the confidence of one who had made the right decision, a decision of which the younger, ambitious spellcaster did not approve in the least.

"What does it matter if we are handed the culprits' heads? Darnassus is complicit in this: you know that! This went on much too long and with too many excuses! The archdruid is—"

"Someone who has given us the chance to survive," Mordent replied calmly as he walked.

"Pfah! We do not need him to survive! The Highborne—"

The senior mage turned abruptly, causing not only Var'dyn, but the rest of the party to stumble to a halt. Mordent studied the other magi—all younger than him—before finally settling his gaze upon Var'dyn once more.

"Azeroth has changed . . . changed in a manner unseen since Zin-Azshari fell. Nothing is as it was before. What we have done to maintain our ways for all these millennia no longer applies! How many are there of us now? How are our ranks replenishing? How many children born to our people over the last generation?"

Although no one answered—not even Var'dyn—it was not because they did not know the answers. Rather, it was just the opposite: they knew too well the truth.

"When we were immortal," the senior archmage went on, "such things did not matter much. Death was a minor occurrence generally due to carelessness. Now, as with our brethren in Darnassus, we face mortality. But unlike our brethren, the Highborne will not be mourned if we cease to exist, unless we prove we can change. We must abide by the rules of the high priestess and the archdruid until we are accepted back into night elf society. . . ."

"We fought beside them—" Var'dyn started.

"A moment of necessity more than remorse. As soon as we could, we reverted to our ways, played with our magic—and did nothing else! We learned nothing from Zin-Azshari's fall!"

"These murders cannot be forgiven!"

Mordent thumped the bottom of his staff on the ground. Sparks flew and the dirt and grass beneath burnt black. "And they will not! If the assassins are captured, they *will* be turned over to us! Darnassus justice demands that as much as our own! Now, will that satisfy you for the moment?"

Var'dyn sullenly nodded.

"I will not betray Malfurion and his mate, Var'dyn. They honor their word; I honor mine. That is the key to our future. We respect each other."

Archmage Mordent turned back to the path ahead and resumed walking. The other Highborne followed, Var'dyn a step after. However, he quickly repositioned himself next to their leader, and no one argued. Var'dyn had the power and skill to maintain his position unless Mordent decreed otherwise and, despite their current differences, the senior archmage still favored the younger spellcaster.

A figure suddenly stepped out onto the path. They recognized one of those who served Maiev Shadowsong. "I have come to lead you." She glanced around at the party. "Best to keep close together. You will need to on the path ahead."

Var'dyn sneered, but Mordent politely responded, "Lead on. We are anxious to have this concluded."

"So are we. This has gone on long enough."

Some of the Highborne nodded satisfaction at this comment. Darnassus after all understood that these heinous crimes had to be punished.

They followed the slim female along the winding route, which wound even more than Mordent or Var'dyn recalled from the directions given to them earlier. Still, all that mattered was that soon they would be at their destination.

"Where is Maiev?" Mordent asked. "Has she the villains ready for us?"

"Justice will be meted out when you arrive there. She promises that."

Even Var'dyn radiated some satisfaction upon hearing that. The Highborne grew more eager to reach their destination, which their guide assured them was very close now.

They entered a clearing. The Watcher strode on.

"Is this not it?" queried Var'dyn impatiently.

Their guide continued walking, not even bothering to look back.

"Insolent whelp." Var'dyn raised a hand toward her.

Mordent used his staff to bring the hand down before the other mage could cast. "Wait. There is something wrong. . . ."

Jagged lines of crimson energy thrust up from the ground. They ensnared the Highborne before any among them could cast a spell. The energy then ran through each of the magi, who doubled over from sharp pain.

"As arrogant as ever," someone commented with contempt. "More than ten thousand years and you still think the world bends to your slightest desire. . . ."

Mordent, Var'dyn, and some of the others managed to look up at their captor. Maiev Shadowsong smirked as she stepped in front of her prisoners. "The archdruid was more of a challenge than all of you put together!"

"What is the meaning of this?" Archmage Mordent demanded through gritted teeth. "Release us!"

She chuckled. "You *are* a dense lot. I am just finishing what I started, only this time to end the game once and for all!"

"You!" Var'dyn snarled. "*You* are the assassin! I was right! Darnassus betrays us!"

"Darnassus betrayed *me*, you mean." Maiev glared. "I served loyally for thousands of years! I protected the sanctity of our life! Then, in one fell swoop, the 'great' archdruid returns to the high priestess, marries her, and is proclaimed co-ruler! He declares us undeserving of regaining our immortality and then, worst of all, he brought your evil back among us!"

"Where *is* the archdruid?" Mordent demanded. "What have you done—?"

"Never mind him!" Var'dyn interrupted. "The assassin stands in front of us!" Grinning darkly, he started to glow with power.

"You have two ways to die," their captor calmly said. "One is to accept the punishments for your crimes. For that, you will die relatively painlessly."

"A little pain means nothing to a Highborne," Var'dyn mocked, the glow about him growing stronger. "Let us see how much pain *you* can stand. . . ."

Despite the magical bonds that surrounded them, Var'dyn clenched his fist and cast. His body flared bright from so much gathered energy.

He screamed—or rather, tried to scream. His mouth gaped, but no sound escaped.

Var'dyn's spell faded. Instead, a black aura enveloped him. Those Highborne nearest to him did their best to pull away for fear that somehow they would be caught up in whatever was happening.

Var'dyn continued his voiceless scream. His skin seared and began to peel away in burnt fragments. His eyes turned black. He shriveled. The burning Highborne struggled to move, but the bonds of energy held him in place as the spell of the black aura slowly consumed him.

His elegant garments became cinders. His flesh

crumbled away, followed by the muscle and sinew beneath. Only when those were almost gone did the life extinguish from him. Moments later, even his bones had been reduced to ash that itself vanished.

The black aura faded.

"*That* is the second choice of death you have," Maiev blandly remarked.

The imprisoned spellcasters looked aghast. Recovering, Mordent said, "There is no need for this. Some agreement should surely be possible—"

She turned from them, but not before giving Mordent a crooked, mocking smile. "Oh, we have. We have agreed on your choice of death. Next, we are sure to agree on the crimes you are guilty of that make you deserve it."

Mordent looked at her openmouthed, aware that he talked to someone who was utterly mad . . . and who held their lives in her hands.

The moment the sounds of war rang out, Haldrissa had abandoned her rest. Long used to sleeping in her armor— a survival trait of any sensible Sentinel—the commander had only had to put on her helmet. Seizing up her glaive, she had rushed to her nightsaber and ridden in search of her troops.

She had spotted them too late. Denea already had them crossing the river with the other groups. Haldrissa had felt an emptiness at watching her warriors go into battle without her.

But then she had witnessed the charge of the magnataur.

Like so many others, the veteran commander stared

at the horrors looming over their comrades. She watched helplessly as one gigantic creature seized part of a cracked tree trunk and used it to bat away scattering Sentinels. Another took sadistic pleasure in snatching one fighter after another and throwing them toward the defenders still on the other side of the river.

Amidst all the carnage that the magnataur created, Haldrissa spotted a more subtle threat. The Horde moved in again behind the behemoths, and among the first were archers. With the Sentinels in disarray, the archers quickly moved across open areas in the river and onto a part of the bank where one of the magnataur's thrown boulders had sent the defenders elsewhere for the moment.

The archers did not move as if simply going into battle, and for most purposes they would have been better suited remaining on the opposing shore. These had some other, more nefarious purpose in mind, although she could not say what.

Then some of the magnataur began tossing boulders again, this time specifically behind the center of the Alliance lines. Haldrissa had to make her cat veer away from that area in order to avoid being struck by sharp flying fragments. As the nightsaber turned, the high priestess briefly came into her view—as did the fact that Tyrande Whisperwind was directly in the path of the hurtling missiles.

There was nothing Haldrissa could do for the high priestess, who she realized was the particular target of the Horde. She gave thanks to Elune when Tyrande evaded the deadly rain, then realized too late why the archers risked themselves so.

By that time two arrows had downed the ruler of the night elves.

Priestesses and Sentinels rushed to the still figure. In Haldrissa's mind, they wasted their energy. She was also furious with herself for not preventing what had happened, even if in truth there was little she could have done.

The Horde became the focus of her collapsing world. They had destroyed Silverwing, slain scores of brave night elves, and now assassinated the high priestess. Haldrissa thought that Azeroth was surely falling into doom, but she swore there and then that the Horde would pay dearly.

The commander turned her mount back to the mayhem. She searched everywhere for some way to avenge her people on the orcs.

And there he stood.

Haldrissa first recognized Garrosh by his stance. He was absolute master of the battlefield. He waved his foul weapon over his head, and even from where she was, Haldrissa imagined she could hear the axe's wail. Beside him were several orcs who were likely guards, one of whom also carried with him a curled horn.

Without at first understanding what she did, the bitter commander charged toward the river. As she rode, reflexes took over, and out came the glaive. When an orc stood in her path, his eyes showing his eagerness for her blood, she rewarded him with a toss of the triple-bladed weapon that shot forth with the speed of an arrow and cut a swath through his barrel chest. Haldrissa had already caught the bloody glaive and ridden past before the orc's corpse could even fall face first into the water.

On the other side, someone shouted her name. The commander stirred from her obsession just enough to see Denea staring wide-eyed at her. Two other mounted Sentinels from her outpost also paused to watch.

Haldrissa paid them no more mind. Only Garrosh Hellscream mattered. Despite a magnataur noticing her, the veteran warrior urged her nightsaber on.

A huge hand grabbed at the commander, but Haldrissa managed to evade the grasping fingers. She rode under the behemoth, avoiding a moving leg. Ahead, an orc mounted on a huge wolf saw her fast approaching and moved to intercept.

She could not throw the glaive here, but was more than practiced at using it hand-to-hand. Haldrissa blocked the axe that came at her chest, then slashed with the curved edge of one blade. The glaive tore through the orc's throat, nearly beheading him. He tumbled back, dead.

But other orcs now saw her and seemed aware that she could be so close for only one reason. They moved to surround the night elf, who vaguely registered that she was going to die here, only yards from her goal.

However, no sooner did the first of the reinforcements join her original foe than he was attacked by another mounted Sentinel. Haldrissa saw that it was Denea. The younger officer fought with a zeal that showed that she understood what her commander hoped to do regardless of the consequences.

Denea was not alone, either. Suddenly several survivors of Haldrissa's command closed with the orcs. With them were some of Silverwing's warriors, including both Su'ura and the rogue. The enemy was now temporarily outnumbered. Two orcs fell swiftly. Haldrissa's makeshift attack force pushed deeper. At last she could see Garrosh himself. The first of his guards faced her. Around

Haldrissa, Denea and the others who had joined the commander fought valiantly to create an opening.

But time was running out. Haldrissa knew that. The longer she remained unable to reach the warchief, the more likely that she never would.

A night elf perished with an axe buried in her chest. Another simply vanished in the melee, her riderless mount battling that of an orc. Haldrissa's comrades were forced to bunch together as more orcs and even tauren moved in from other positions.

Garrosh, seemingly oblivious to the struggle so near him, continued toward the river. Haldrissa swore. There were too many foes between her and the warchief. She had lost her chance . . . and soon she would lose her life.

For nothing.

The trumpeter blew the note to press the attack. The Horde ranks began crossing the river again, the magnataur leaving them an open path occasionally littered by the ghastly remains of their victims.

Haldrissa eyed the trumpeter, then urged her cat on. Caught up in the Horde's impending triumph, the orc did not notice her approach.

The commander threw the glaive.

The orc turned just as the spinning weapon reached him. The movement upset some of Haldrissa's accuracy, and though the blade all but sheared his neck in half—leaving no doubt to the trumpeter's death—the glaive dropped to the ground a short distance farther instead of returning.

"Damn!" Dismounting, Haldrissa ignored the lost weapon and rushed to the body. She found the horn still clutched tightly in one hand. Too tightly, in fact: it took all her strength to force open the fingers enough to pull the horn free.

No one was looking. Thanking Elune for this last chance, the veteran warrior put the horn to her lips and blew.

She knew from past experience some of the general calls used by the Horde. Advance and retreat were the most obvious. Haldrissa now blew the latter as best as she could recall and prayed that in the heat of battle most of those who would heed such a call would not recognize any mistake.

At first it seemed that nothing was happening. Haldrissa blew again. As she finished, she saw the first rows, already almost across, falter. Even the magnataur hesitated.

With all her breath, the night elf blew a third time.

The Horde lines began to return. Their faces were filled with confusion, a contrast to their expressions during their confident rush forward. That confusion grew and the retreating enemy now ran faster.

Managing to inhale enough air, Haldrissa sounded the call one more time.

Even the magnataur began to turn back. One tauren tried to wave the leader back to the front, only to be crushed under one heavy foot as the behemoth, entirely ignorant of his victim, thundered back into the forest from which he and the others had emerged.

"Give me that!" rumbled an orc voice.

She lunged away from the speaker in the direction of her glaive, all the while clutching the horn. In the distance Haldrissa heard the other trumpeters now repeating the call to retreat. They were taking their cue from what they believed to be the master trumpeter with Garrosh. If her adversary succeeded in taking the horn and then blowing the attack once more, all her work would be for nothing.

Her hand came down by the glaive just as an axe tried to cut the appendage off. Haldrissa bit her lip as the edge of the axe left a long, bleeding line across the back of her hand and part of her wrist. Despite the pain, she managed to seize the glaive and turn in time to deflect a second strike.

He has one eye, just like me, Haldrissa could not help thinking upon first seeing her adversary. He was also an older representative of his race, as she was. However, orcs had never had immortality and thus, compared chronologically to her, he was an infant. In terms of suffering, though, they were akin to one another.

"Give me the horn, night elf. . . . I'll not let you steal my last glory! I brought them all the way from Northrend for this!"

Without a moment's hesitation the commander slammed the horn against the ground. When that proved insufficient to break it, she quickly brought her glaive down on it.

A harsh pain erupted from her heart. Acting almost as swiftly, the orc had tried to keep her from destroying the horn. He had succeeded in killing Haldrissa—she knew the wound was fatal—but from his disgusted expression, he understood very well that her death still meant her victory.

Someone far away called Haldrissa's name. She had a vague image of Denea and the others—far less in number than had followed their aging commander—being forced to retreat. The commander's own mount lay dead, several heavy gashes inflicted by either her opponent or some unseen enemy having done in the brave animal.

Her vision grew blurred. A murky figure stepped right in front of her. Haldrissa tried to raise her glaive, but there was too much pain from her chest. No longer caring about war, Haldrissa tried to grab the pain and remove it, but all she did was grasp futilely at the gaping wound.

"You fought bravely," she heard the older orc grumble. "You fought cleverly. You don't deserve such slow, painful dying, night elf."

Somehow she nodded. What he said made perfect sense. She had fought long and hard for her people. It was time to rest. If only the pain would go away, she could rest.

The axe caught her along the throat, cutting deep and at last rewarding Haldrissa's valor with rest.

26

MAIEV

Jarod sensed something close ahead. Although armed only with his knife, he pushed on.

A minute later he saw one of Maiev's Watchers. From her bored stance, she looked as if she had been posted on guard duty for some time. It only took a glimpse past her for Jarod to verify that she was guarding the one he sought.

Malfurion Stormrage hovered above the ground, his arms and legs splayed to the sides as much as physically possible. Magical energy surrounded him, and it was clear that he was in some pain. At the moment the archdruid appeared oblivious to his surroundings, although it was possible, not to mention quite probable, that Malfurion secretly worked to somehow free himself.

The Watcher removed her helmet and wiped her forehead. She looked up at the archdruid, her expression growing from boredom to disdain.

Aware that the moment might quickly pass, Jarod had

no recourse. As the guard glanced at her charge, he threw the dagger.

She fell with barely a sound, the blade through the back of her neck. The helmet tumbled away. Jarod slipped forward, feeling as if he were back in the war against the Burning Legion, so callous about life were his sister and her cohorts.

But how else would she become, considering what she has been through? the former guard captain could not help asking himself, managing yet to find some excuse for his sister, his only remaining flesh and blood. She had done so much for the sake of their race that he felt some guilt at having to fight her . . . and yet, she intended to bring ruin to Darnassus.

Seizing up the knife, he wiped it off and looked up at Malfurion. Not at all to his surprise, the archdruid gazed down at him.

Jarod waited for Malfurion to speak, but when the archdruid only looked down to his side, Maiev's brother assumed that the trap kept him from doing so. He followed the other night elf's eyes but did not see anything.

But there has to be some way to free the archdruid, Jarod thought. He headed toward the area upon which Malfurion focused, all the while thinking about Maiev. Jarod still knew her better than almost anyone, despite the long passage of time. There were traits, ways of thinking, that he was fairly certain remained consistent.

Maiev was no major spellcaster. She knew how to adapt things to her needs, though, and over the millennia—and especially with regard to Illidan Stormrage—she had probably picked up several tricks. This had to be one of them.

Jarod remembered the trap that had almost killed him. Eadrik had freed him rather quickly. Maiev had needed traps that were strong but easily removed. She had used them to capture and subdue her victims, then no doubt had taken a more personal satisfaction in cutting their throats as they lay helpless.

For a moment Jarod hesitated and glanced up again at Malfurion, who could not see him from the current angle. *This is your twin's fault*, the former guard captain could not help thinking somewhat angrily. *She was never like this! You should have had him executed! He deserved that. . . .*

He shook off the dark notions. Maiev had made her own choices in the end. She knew well enough what she did and found life valueless enough to kill as she desired.

Mouth set grim, Jarod inspected the tree and ground around it. That there had been a sentry made him certain that the spellwork itself had little in the way of other defenses. He just had to find the key, hard enough to do—

Something very tiny glittered in the bark near the roots. He gingerly brushed off some loose dirt.

He found a small stone the color of a pearl wedged into a gap in the bark. Jarod waved his hand over it, but nothing happened.

Thinking again of his sister's need for expediency, Jarod simply plucked the stone out.

"Ungh!" Malfurion, his one side released, swung toward the tree on the opposing side from the one from which Jarod had removed the stone. Jarod feared that the archdruid would be injured by the collision, but Malfurion managed to put his free hand between him and the trunk.

The archdruid ceased swinging. As Jarod watched in wonder, the tree to which the spell still held him stretched its branches down to its roots. With precision, two smaller branches removed another stone from near the roots, then crushed it between them. Malfurion gently dropped feet first to the ground.

Jarod, eyeing the stone in his palm, marveled at both the act and the strength, but wondered why the tree had not done so sooner. Malfurion seemed to expect such curiosity and quickly said, "The trees do not see the world as we do or think exactly as we do. They wanted to help, but were not certain what they could do that would not harm me, since I could not communicate with them because of the trap."

"My sister is nothing if not thorough."

The archdruid stared at the dead sentry. "Maiev and her Watchers. I still cannot believe it." He peered around. "We had best watch out for Neva. Of all Maiev's Watchers, she is the most fanatical and dangerous."

"Neva is dead." In answer to Malfurion's curious gaze, Jarod shrugged, adding, "I killed her after she and others slew Genn's man Eadrik and another worgen."

"Why them?" Malfurion asked in some shock.

"Eadrik suspected her but doubted anyone would believe it. He and the other died protecting me. Maiev wanted me alive as a dupe; Neva trusted me better dead."

"And the Highborne will be next if we do not find her." The archdruid raised his hands to the trees. Although he seemed to simply stand there afterward, Jarod had to assume Malfurion now communed freely with the forest.

A breeze came out of nowhere. Above them, the crowns of the nearest trees gently shook.

Lowering his hands, the archdruid confidently said, "I know the path! Come!"

They rushed through the forest toward their destination, Jarod at first fearing that another trap set by Maiev might do them in before they could reach her. However, he soon noticed that Malfurion constantly looked up as much as ahead. It slowly dawned on the other night elf that the archdruid was now in constant communication with the trees and other flora.

It seemed to take forever, but at last Malfurion bade him halt. The archdruid's eyes narrowed as he studied the path ahead.

"Two of Maiev's Watchers ahead."

Jarod could see no one but took his companion's word. Malfurion crept forward a few steps, then gestured.

There was a slight rustle of leaves, followed by a soft grunt.

"Hurry!" Malfurion whispered.

Curious, Jarod followed. He kept watch for the two sentries, but even when he and Malfurion reached the area where Jarod assumed they should be, he saw nothing.

Aware of the other night elf's confusion, the archdruid muttered, "Look up."

The veteran soldier did and saw the figures in question dangling high above. Branches wrapped them as if burial shrouds. They hung very still, and Jarod knew immediately that they were dead.

"They left me no choice," Malfurion murmured as the two moved on.

Jarod nodded his understanding. Even though a veteran soldier, he would have preferred no more bloodshed, but did not shirk from the necessity. Maiev and her Watchers would not show them any mercy.

Barely had they gone a few yards farther when Jarod heard a voice ahead. He knew his sister instantly. She seemed to be proclaiming something, but the words did not carry well. Maiev had chosen a location where even if she spoke loudly, no one very far away would hear.

Malfurion guided him more to the east. His expression grew more concerned as they went.

"What is wrong?" Jarod finally asked.

"We need to move faster, but if we do, she will notice us sooner."

As he spoke, there came a low sound that Jarod finally determined was someone else protesting. Although he could still not understand a word, there was a hint of desperation in the tone.

Desperation from a Highborne? Jarod grimaced. He could only imagine what Maiev might have done to bring one of the spellcasters to such a strait.

Ahead of him, Malfurion uttered a low, angry oath. The archdruid picked up his pace.

They came near enough to at last not only better hear but catch a glimpse of what was going on. Even then, Jarod was slightly confused at what his sister had set into motion.

"Now," Maiev almost cheerfully called, her helmet propped in her arm. "Who is next to be judged? You, I think."

Neither night elf could see to whom she spoke, but once more there was a protest. "I beseech you again to stop this insanity, Maiev Shadowsong! If you think we must be judged, then bring us before the people of Darnassus—"

"'The people of Darnassus'? They will do anything the high priestess or the archdruid tells them! I am the only honest arbiter for this! I am the only one who can mete out true justice for your damnable crimes!"

"This way," Malfurion whispered. "I want you to go by that tree, then wait—"

Jarod shook his head. "No. You will need a distraction. I will draw Maiev's attention." He paused, then added, "I would like to take her alive, but . . . do what you must. . . ."

The archdruid nodded. "As you must, I am sorry to say. Be wary, Jarod. At this point Maiev may consider you nothing more than another enemy to be slain. She let me live only because she wanted me not only to know I had failed to save the Highborne but also so that she could later tuck me into some foul prison and slowly torture me."

The former guard captain's expression grew cold. "Maiev *will* try to kill me. I know that." Jarod's eyes narrowed to slits. "For her sake, she had better hope she succeeds. . . ."

Without another word, he left Malfurion and headed toward his sister. Jarod straightened as he stepped out of the woods, one hand clutching the knife.

"Maiev . . . ," he quietly called.

Without even looking, she replied, "Jarod. Have to say I am proud of you for finding me." She peered over her shoulder at her brother. "Of course, that does not mean I will not make you regret it."

Her hand moved with a speed that surprised even him. A knife shot not toward him—but rather where Malfurion hid.

A branch shifted seemingly of its own accord. The

knife struck deep—and something hidden on the handle flew free.

The forest in that direction exploded into flames.

Jarod gaped. The inferno spread so quickly, he could not see how Malfurion could have protected himself in time.

Even as she tossed the knife, Maiev used her other hand to throw something else at her brother. However, Jarod had already moved by then, lunging toward his sister and not away as she had evidently expected.

Behind him he heard a crackling sound. Ignoring the distraction, he threw his own knife at his sibling.

Maiev, her crooked smile taunting Jarod and her hand reaching for her crescent, *vanished*. Her helmet, released as she went for the weapon, fell to the ground.

But Jarod, aware that as warden she had the ability to teleport herself short distances, and having made a calculation of her viable directions—not to mention her insidious thinking—turned his lunge into a roll.

Maiev reappeared only a short distance away and at an angle that would have given her a clean strike at her brother. However, she had only a moment to finish drawing her weapon when Jarod bowled her over.

The two sprawled together. Maiev lost her grip on her crescent. The blades in his sister's cloak cut Jarod in several places but caused only superficial wounds. Jarod tried to stop his momentum. Unfortunately, he sensed that Maiev had recovered first. Again she vanished, reappearing a few yards from him.

"You are getting sneakier!" she jested madly. "That is more like it! That is how you survive when those above send you on one hellish journey after another! That is how you live when demons torture you or the people you are fighting for spit on everything you swore to uphold!"

As she spoke, another pair of Watchers trotted into sight. They were not armed with umbra crescents, as he would have expected, but rather glaives. Their murderous gazes fixed on Jarod. One then looked to Maiev.

"Oh, by all means, kill my brother," she commanded. "He came here to save them, which makes him as guilty!"

"Maiev—" But before he could try to reach whatever sanity might remain within his older sibling, her two followers threw their weapons. He saw why they had glaives now; the crescents were deadly but could not be tossed. Skilled as they were, the Watchers could adapt to whatever weapons worked best for the moment.

Jarod managed to completely dodge the first, but the second cut into his right calf. Although he still proved sufficiently dexterous to avoid more than a glancing cut, the pain was enough to throw him off balance.

"I had actually hoped you would see the truth of things, Jarod," Maiev said with mock sadness as she turned back to the imprisoned Highborne. "You sacrificed so much in the beginning. But I guess the same thing that made you decide you could just leave behind your duty and go off merrily with some trollop from the temple makes it impossible for you to appreciate what I have been doing."

She eyed the magi. Jarod, trying to find some sort of shield as the glaives returned to his two pursuers, saw that in addition to Archmage Mordent and the other Highborne, there was a corpse of another mage a short distance away. His body was absolutely white, as if covered in frost.

Jarod had no time to wonder at the cause of the

Highborne's demise. He knew that Maiev was responsible, and that was all that mattered. Worse, from the way she studied the other captives, it was clear that she intended to speed up the executions.

Another glaive went flying at Jarod. He judged its speed and dropped to the ground. At the same time he brought his foot up and kicked the soaring glaive from underneath.

He only barely missed having his boot and the toes inside sheared off. Still, Jarod accomplished what he desired: the glaive wobbled, then crashed to the ground fairly close to him.

But getting the weapon was another question. As he moved toward it, the second glaive came at him. He also saw that the owner of the first weapon now had a long dagger drawn and was heading in his direction.

Jarod rolled to the side as the second glaive passed. The spinning blades flew back toward their wielder. He used the moment to reach his objective.

However, instead of using it to defend himself, he threw the first glaive in the direction of his sister.

One of the other Watchers called out the alarm. Maiev vanished, reappearing next to her umbra crescent. She need not have been concerned with his attack, though, for she had not been his true target. That distinction went to a small golden cone that she had been bending down toward—a cone with four stones the color of pearl.

The glaive struck head-on. The cone shattered and the stones flew off in different directions.

Jarod had hoped that by destroying the artifact he would free the Highborne, but such was not the case. They remained prisoners, although he saw that there was relief on the face of more than one. At the very least, Jarod appeared to have either stopped the executions or somewhat delayed them.

His sister answered that question. "So clever, my little brother. I will fix it soon enough, though."

He had no chance to worry about that, for the Watcher with the dagger then attacked. She slashed back and forth at Jarod, in between each slash kicking at either his midsection or his legs. He managed to stumble out of her way each time, although the gash in his calf grew increasingly painful with each movement. Out of the corner of his eye, Jarod saw his second foe calculating the aim of her glaive.

Aware that the second Watcher did not know that he saw her, Jarod pressed his defense against the first. Yet, he kept the other ever on the edge of his gaze.

His immediate foe kicked again. Risking getting sliced through the throat by her dagger, the former guard captain bent forward and seized her ankle.

Although taken aback and off balance, she nevertheless used the dagger as best as she could, cutting at the hand that gripped her. Jarod grunted with pain as the dagger's tip scraped along his wrist to his hand. Despite the danger, he pulled as hard as he could, bringing her to him.

At the last, Jarod spun her around. The Watcher twisted.

But it was not the oncoming glaive that struck. The glaive flew past the pair, then rose up as it began its return to its wielder. Rather, what cut his foe through the back, regardless of her armor and severing the spine in the process, was his sister's umbra crescent. Maiev, her helmet on and using the glaive as a distraction, had teleported up to her brother in order to catch him from behind.

A permanent glare across her lifeless face, the Watcher collapsed in his arms. Maiev disappeared.

The other Watcher reached for the approaching glaive. Scooping up the dagger, Jarod threw it. As the second Watcher started to rise, the blade hit her in the chest. The small weapon did not penetrate the armor but did distract the Watcher.

The glaive spun past her hand and tore through the less protected area at the neck . . . then took the Watcher's head immediately after.

Jarod paused for a badly needed breath—and felt a terrible pain in his left arm. He looked down to see what seemed a long, sharp pin sticking out. Lifting his gaze, he met Maiev's eyes.

It was clear from the dark intent in them that she had not meant to merely wound him. Only fortune had kept her from killing him. His steady gaze on his sister, he plucked out the pin and, with clear indifference, tossed the bloody missile aside. "Another failure. You made a mistake when you did not kill me after the trap caught me, Maiev."

"A mistake quickly remedied," she remarked as she drew something from a pouch. "Just as I have already dealt with our friends. . . ."

Jarod peered at the magi. They were writhing in pain, yet no sound escaped them. A dark aura was slowly surrounding them.

"I would let you admire my work, but you might see fit to try to interfere again. . . ."

Maiev threw whatever she had gathered from her pouch at Jarod.

But instead of flying at the former guard captain, the

small black particles were blown to the side by an unexpected wind. As the particles hit the various trees and other flora, they created a terrible hiss. Jarod saw smoke rise in each spot.

Instinct made him look to Malfurion, who now stood on the other side of the Highborne. The archdruid met his gaze. The millennia faded away as they again became comrades in battle against a dangerous foe. Jarod read the archdruid's intentions and nodded. He moved just as the archdruid bent down in front of another, identical artifact and began concentrating. In doing so, Malfurion presented his back to the insane warden.

Maiev swore and reached for her pouch again. Jarod ran for his dagger.

Ignoring her brother, Maiev honed in on the archdruid. She raised the hand high.

Not caring about accuracy, Jarod tossed the dagger. It collided flat against the helmet just next to the eye slit, momentarily startling Maiev. The contents of her palm—whatever they were—spilled harmlessly to the ground.

Drawing her crescent again, Maiev focused on Jarod.

"You seem to be running out of tricks, Brother! Getting tired—and old? You can blame the grand and glorious archdruid for that too! Everyone cheers him for his part in getting Teldrassil cleansed and purified of the Nightmare's taint, but they forget that he also fought against getting the World Tree properly blessed! Said that it was time the night elves actually *lived* in their world. Death was welcome! You might say that *he* killed your precious Shalasyr, Jarod! She would be just fine, forever immortal, if he had not decided he knew best for all of us!"

"Shalasyr died because it was her time," Jarod responded to his sister. "As we all should."

Maiev smiled again. "Then you will not mind dying now."

She teleported, reappearing at his right side and swinging her umbra crescent. With a desperate twist, Jarod saved himself from death but not injury. The tips of the blades cut through his side, just deep enough to make him scream. He clutched at the wound as he stumbled forward.

Although the wound did not cut into an organ, it was still a harsh one. Jarod had to keep his hand pressed to the six-inch slash as he sought the glaive that had slain the second Watcher.

No longer considering her brother of consequence, Maiev immediately spun back to the archdruid. Malfurion was caught up in trying not only to free the Highborne but also to keep them from dying before that happened. He could not afford to take even the slightest concentration away from Mordent and his companions, which left him entirely open to Maiev.

Pain and loss of blood threatening to overwhelm him, Jarod reached the glaive. Using the one hand available to him, he did his best to grip the weapon. It was almost impossible for him to stand straight, and he knew that if he did, the blood flow would increase. Nevertheless, Jarod forced himself to do exactly that. He had to stand straight to throw the glaive. Worse, he had to do it without his dominant hand.

He had been a guard captain, a military commander, a leader, and then someone simply trying to make certain that he and his wife survived the wilderness. In many ways, even more than his career, his life with Shalasyr had meant that he had been forced to adapt to doing things as necessary, not as convenient.

Jarod threw.

The glaive flew at Maiev. She heard the sinister whisper of it as it moved exactly as Jarod had calculated. His sister brought up her crescent to deflect the oncoming weapon, her casual movements showing her disdain for his "desperate" act.

But Jarod had not tossed the glaive horizontally, as was normal. He had thrown it almost vertically, and in order to block what she thought was coming, Maiev held her weapon nearly the same way.

Thus, unimpeded, the flying glaive tore into her forearm close to the wrist. The blades cut through the armor and into the flesh.

Maiev cried out and dropped her crescent.

Jarod's toss was not perfect. The glaive returned but landed in front of him, not in his grip again. He had to quickly bend for it, which brought about renewed agony and caused him to falter for a moment.

As he stood up, he saw that Maiev was no longer where she had stood. Jarod glanced fearfully in Malfurion's direction, but the archdruid was untouched and well at work. Whatever he was doing had at least caused an end to the Highborne's suffering, though they remained imprisoned.

Jarod found Maiev heading toward the far perimeter of the clearing. The hand near the wound hung limply. She held the wound tight with the other hand.

A few more steps or a single blink and she would be in the forest, making good her escape. Jarod had to stop her.

"Maiev!"

She paused and looked back. Through the slits of her helmet, her eyes were still defiant, still mocking.

He held the glaive ready. "Surrender, Maiev. You have no choice. I do not want to kill you."

She laughed. "And you will not. As I indicated, that is the difference between us, Jarod. I do what has to be done, no matter what."

Jarod started to throw. From behind him he heard movement and voices. By the sound of them, they were obviously not more of Maiev's followers but rather searchers from Darnassus.

Maiev's eyes flashed in triumph. "You are a fool. I will see our people restored to their greatness. . . . You have only delayed the inevitable."

She teleported just as Jarod finally threw. The glaive struck where her lower legs would have been. The blades cut harmlessly into the brush, and the weapon then bounced off to the side.

"Elune, forgive me . . . ," he muttered.

There were weak moans from the direction of the Highborne. Hand pressed against his side, Jarod stumbled toward the archdruid, who had finally found the way to release the magi. Many of the Highborne lay sprawled, unconscious.

Malfurion looked up from assisting Mordent. Jarod felt his shame rising.

"I failed. I am sorry."

"You did not fail," the archdruid pointedly replied. "They are alive."

Jarod weaved back and forth, the adrenaline that had kept him going now fading. He shook his head. "I mean Maiev. I could have stopped her. I could have killed her. She would have killed me."

"I know that." Malfurion turned his head to observe several Sentinels and two druids burst into the area. "They will find her. They will take her alive, if possible." He looked to Jarod again. "You did not fail, Jarod. You remained what a night elf should be. Maiev did not."

"I—" Jarod felt the world starting to turn on its head. His hand slipped away from the wound, enabling Malfurion to see just how bad it actually was. "I—"

"Cenarius! Jarod! You should have told me!"

"She is my sister—"

The archdruid jumped up to grab him as he collapsed.

27

THE HORDE ASCENDANT

The Alliance lines struggled to re-form. Shandris knew that they had little time; if she were Garrosh—as repugnant a thought as she could imagine—she would get the Horde and, especially, the magnataur to turn around and resume the attack. Even if he did not know about the success of his archers in bringing down Tyrande, he would not want to waste the chaos he had already sown.

Tyrande . . . Shandris fought back a shiver. The archers had come closer to killing the high priestess than they even knew. Of course, none of them had survived to tell their master; Shandris had spotted them too late for her mother, but not too late to have her own archers shoot them.

The Sisters of Elune prayed feverishly over Tyrande, who was better but not yet whole. There had been something on the arrow heads that persisted in her body. She would recover, but it would take time.

And time they did not have, for even as Shandris got something of a semblance of order set up near the river, she heard horns in the forest beyond sounding over and over. There was no doubt in her mind that the defenders were mere moments from a new attack, and this time there would be no fortuitous and epic charge such as Denea and the handful of survivors had informed her Commander Haldrissa had bravely led. Haldrissa's choice to convert a failed attempt to kill Garrosh into a trick that had turned defeat into reprieve would be sung by night elves for generations to come . . . assuming that there *were* generations to come.

Shandris eyed the forest to the north; the land rose higher there, low hills that, given other circumstances, might have proved valuable in a counterattack. She wished that they had been able to set up an outpost there back when the entire land had been theirs, but now it was impossible.

The general surveyed the rest of the region and had to admit that Haldrissa had arranged matters as well as anyone could. Shandris had noticed that some of the younger officers, including Denea, had laid hints that perhaps their commander should be permanently shunted aside, but they had renounced any such thoughts after her bravery. Older Haldrissa might have gotten, but she had *gotten* older because she was good.

And a lot of other night elves will not be getting any older after this day is over. . . .

"Take over!" she ordered one of her aides. Turning her nightsaber, she headed back to where the other priestesses had Tyrande. One of attendants looked up as she approached, but the general had no interest in anyone but her mother. Fortunately, to Shandris's great pleasure, Tyrande's eyes were open.

"My daughter," she greeted the general.

Not caring how it might appear, Shandris dismounted and went to hug the high priestess. Tyrande returned the hug with equal vigor.

"You are well?" Shandris asked.

"I still have some trouble focusing, but, yes . . . I am fairly well." She stared deep into the general's eyes. "They are coming."

Tyrande was not asking, but rather informing. Shandris was not surprised. "I expect that they will be at the edge of the forest in two minutes at most."

The high priestess pushed herself up onto her elbows, then had to shut her eyes a moment. "Whatever Garrosh had the archers use, it was very potent . . . not that my wounds were anything small. The Horde has expert shots."

"And we had better ones. The Horde paid." A new horn sounded. This time, it was an Alliance horn.

"Bring me Ash'alah," demanded the high priestess.

"You are not well enough—" Shandris began, only to stop when Tyrande gave her a look. Rather than argue when orcs were about to rush down on them, the general gave Tyrande a hand up.

One of the priestesses brought forth Ash'alah for Tyrande. She mounted and, after Shandris had done the same, the pair raced off to the front.

Horns began to blow in earnest across the Alliance lines. They seemed to echo those coming from the forest. Still none of the enemy was visible to either Shandris or

Tyrande, but something had surely caught the attention of the sentries.

What it was became evident as they rode up. The treetops were *shaking*.

The magnataur were on the move.

"Fire arrows," Shandris decided. "We send enough fire arrows, we burn down the forest and send the magnataur running for their damned lives. . . ."

"'Burn down the forest'?" Tyrande took a breath and straightened. Then, "Perhaps you are right. . . ."

"I do not know if I am. . . . The fire might just make them meaner. . . . I do not know what else to do." The general looked at Tyrande. "Unless Elune—"

"The Mother Moon does not exist to answer our every demand like a servant," the high priestess replied. "But I have been praying to her constantly since I awoke."

"And?"

"And all I know is that we must fight and accept either death or survival."

Shandris grunted. "I just love Elune." She checked that her glaive was secure, then readied her bow. "She ought to consider how lonely it might be for her without us."

"Shandris—"

The general chuckled darkly. "I am only jesting."

The treetops nearest to the river began shaking. The general sent out the order for fire arrows to her messengers, who rushed to tell the archer commanders. As the riders vanished on their missions, a familiar but still horrifying roar burst from the forest ahead. It was answered by five equally monstrous calls.

"Keep praying, Mother," Shandris said as she rode forward. "Keep praying. . . ."

"I have never stopped," Tyrande replied, the high priestess following her daughter into war . . . and probably doom.

It did not matter that the magnataur had already ripped paths to the Alliance lines. Weak things such as trees were easily shoved aside. The titanic creatures from Northrend tore asunder the forest as they reached the river. It was not as if their masters cared. The Horde wanted Ashenvale most of all for its timber, and the destruction of the forest by the angry behemoths would only make the harvesting that much quicker once the enemy was dead.

The orcs and their allies followed behind, although not too close behind. Several had died in the retreat of the magnataur, the creatures not discriminating between trees in their path or soft, crushable bodies. Both the magnataur and the fighters following were more than eager for blood after the trickery they had faced earlier. Slaves to Garrosh the behemoths might be, but they did not like being made the fools any more than an orc or tauren or even a goblin.

And there was more than enough Alliance blood to satiate them.

The moment the lead magnataur bull broke through to the river, flaming arrows assailed him. Several struck the nearby trees, but not enough to start a blaze. Those that hit the magnataur only made him angrier as he brushed them away like so many gnats. Even then, the barrage continued, spreading as the other bulls also reached the river.

There was no signal to tell the titanic monsters to keep

moving. As Shandris had surmised, Garrosh had no desire to let the Alliance regroup anymore than it could. The warchief would crush his enemies here and now and take Ashenvale in one swift, sweeping victory.

Horde archers began firing the moment that they reached their designated positions. Their return fire forced the Alliance archers to shoot back at them and left fewer to try to turn back the magnataur with the fire arrows.

The latter mission was not progressing well, anyway, Shandris saw as she shot a grinning troll through the chest. They would have needed much more fire to turn away the beasts.

Moonlight suddenly shone in the faces of the magnataur, even though there was no moon to create it. Shandris smiled, but the smile faltered as the magnataur proved to be unaffected. They were creatures of Northrend and as such lived in a place where snow and ice could be even more blinding. They were adapted to survive such conditions, and now those made yet another potent weapon of the defenders moot.

The lead bull crossed the river. It did not take him much effort. As he came onshore, lancers charged at his legs, seeking to wound one and possibly cause him to lose his balance. They might as well have been more gnats. The magnataur grabbed two cats and smashed them and their riders into a stomach-churning, unidentifiable mess that he afterward tossed among the defenders.

Now a horn sounded from the Horde side. With wild, eager cries, Garrosh's warriors at last rushed forward.

"We have no choice but to meet them!" Tyrande called to her.

"I know!" Shandris gave the signal.

The regiments in wait surged toward the river. As they did, the archers up front retreated under cover from comrades behind them. More lancers joined the Alliance push.

The armies came together, the clash of arms playing over and over. Night elves fell. Orcs died. And though they were the dominant forces of the opposing sides, they were each joined in death by many allies: tauren, human soldiers from Theramore, dwarves of the three clans, troll warriors, and more. Shandris could not see the entire battle, but she knew that scores perished in the first few seconds alone.

But worst of all, the magnataur were unstoppable. They ripped through the Sentinels as if the seasoned warriors were stalks of wheat and the magnataur were reapers. Bodies lay everywhere and in every sickening condition. The night elves tried in vain to focus on the behemoths, Horde archers keeping any attempt to attack the magnataur from even beginning. Thus left unchecked, the fearsome creatures continued to wreak their havoc.

The priestesses of Elune both fought and healed, and because of that they and their leader were also special targets of any Horde archer. Despite the Mother Moon's blessing, Sisters were not indestructible, as Tyrande had almost proven herself. Their numbers were depleted quickly and those still left were forced to take greater defense and thus become less effective in aiding their comrades.

Although commander of the Sentinels, Shandris did not shirk from the struggle, either. When not making expert use of her bow, she threw her glaive again and again, and rarely did she miss with either weapon. She also had to shield herself from more than her share of arrows and other weapons intent on ending the life of one of those most essential to the hopes of the faltering defenders.

Tyrande also fought. She had faced demons, shadow creatures, orcs, and more in her long life, and fell into the rhythm of war with more ease than she cared to think about. Yet, for every enemy that fell, there seemed a dozen more.

And again, there were always the magnataur.

The Sentinel lines finally cracked.

"We cannot hold them here!" Tyrande shouted. "The riverbank is lost! Pull back!"

Shandris grabbed the lead trumpeter. "Sound the call! We move to the secondary position!"

The trumpeter blew hard, her notes picked up by the other surviving trumpeters. Tyrande and Shandris had decided on a backup position a little farther in, where the natural rise of the area would give them a bit of a defensive wall. Against the magnataur it would be nothing, but it would at least slow the Horde itself.

As best they could, the Sentinels and their allies moved. They did battle all the way, the archers trying to buy some distance between the defenders and the attackers. The magnataur, caught up in their eagerness for destruction, did not follow the Horde at first, buying the Alliance a few precious seconds.

But a few seconds were indeed all that bought, and as Tyrande and Shandris fell back with the rest, both were keenly aware that from their second position . . . there was nowhere left to go.

Ashenvale was falling.

• • •

Ashenvale falls, Garrosh Hellscream thought with growing anticipation. *Ashenvale falls, Father!*

Garrosh wondered how his father would have viewed this victory. Would he have been proud? Even eight magnataur had proven enough to easily crush the decadent Alliance. They had been all he needed to tilt the balance once and for all.

This land will help us grow, he thought as he surged forward with the rest of his loyal force. A Sentinel caught behind the collapse of her lines sought to bring more glory to her doom by suddenly leaping up from the dead to attack him. She proved to be a decent adversary, briefly stalling his advance, and so when Gorehowl ripped through both her breastplate and her torso, he wished her spirit well in the afterlife.

This would be a battle of which the young would be taught forever. Every family would have heroes to name in the festivals that would come after the war's triumphant end.

Even the legendary Thrall, Garrosh's predecessor— even Thrall, who had been reluctant to renew the struggle for Azeroth—would surely call Garrosh the champion of the orc race and of all the Horde.

Ashenvale is ours . . . and the rest of Azeroth will follow. . . . There is nothing more mighty than the Horde . . . nothing that the Alliance can do to change what fate demands of this new world. . . .

One had to be strong in the Azeroth that Deathwing had created. The Alliance had once been so, but it was of the past. The Horde was of the future.

Garrosh was the future.

He almost pitied the night elves and their ilk. They fought bravely but without a chance. They acted as if there were hope, when it was obvious there was not. Garrosh had used the very summit intended to bring his enemies together in order to catch them most off guard. The other factions of the Alliance had provided the night elf force with the handful of supporters that he had calculated. By the time Theramore and the others were able to send greater numbers, the Horde would have Ashenvale secured.

Ashenvale is ours, the warchief repeated to himself, savoring that fact. *Ashenvale is—*

An unearthly howl arose from the forest to the north. The warchief missed a step as he looked that direction. He knew wolves, dire wolves, and most of their cousins, and this sounded like none of those.

The howl repeated, this time much stronger, much more challenging, and Garrosh knew right away that it challenged the Horde. Moreover, he was not the only one. Everywhere, orcs and others hesitated, eyed the forest, and clutched their weapons a little tighter. Even the magnataur looked up in curiosity at this sharp cry.

And from the forest there answered a multitude of similar howls. Even from where he stood, Garrosh could hear the shaking of leaves and brush as something that seemed as massive in its own way as the magnataur closed on the battlefield.

Recovering, he raised Gorehowl and opened his mouth to shout orders.

Stunned yells arose from those warriors farther to the north, the ones who had been passing through the forest toward the night elves' position. Those shouts were followed by growls and screams.

"To the north, you fools!" Garrosh commanded. "To the north—"

Out they flowed, a river of dark death. Wave after wave of sleek, furred forms. The orcs, trolls, and tauren Garrosh saw in their path went down in a flash of weapons and claws. The fiends moved like the wind and spread out as they met the Horde.

But most amazing of all was that at their head ran a human. Yet, he moved like no human, but indeed seemed more a wolf than even the dread fighters who flanked him. He wielded a sword that glittered and that identified him to Garrosh from clear across the terrain.

"The sword Shalamayne . . . ," Garrosh snarled, his fury rising swiftly. "Varian Wrynn . . ."

28

THE SWORD
AND THE AXE

It had taken every resource for Varian to get himself, his crew, and, most of all, the worgen to Ashenvale in time. In truth, he had expected to come to find that all had been laid waste in the Alliance-held lands and that everyone he knew among the defenders was dead. Yet, as the ship had dropped anchor as near as they could and the worgen disembarked, he had suddenly been filled with a sense that, not only had he not arrived too late, but his belief that this had been his destiny all along was more true than he could have imagined. The moment that he stepped onto the shore of Ashenvale, Varian had felt the call of Goldrinn even more than he had during the ritual. It had grown stronger with each breath he took—so strong that he finally no longer resisted it but fully embraced it.

Clad in lightweight but durable leather armor and

with Shalamayne sheathed at his side, Varian started running, running with purpose.

Genn Greymane had seen him standing there, watching the forest. The aura of Goldrinn had grown around the king of Stormwind. All the worgen could see it, even if Varian's own people could not. Genn had realized what was about to happen and had been the one to tell those of Stormwind to follow as best they could later. Almost immediately after that point, Varian had disappeared among the trees.

Genn had followed . . . and the worgen had followed him.

Varian would recall little of the run through the forest. He only knew deep inside that somehow he ran faster than should have been possible, that he seemed to outrace time itself. The spirit of Goldrinn fueled him, the great wolf's fury touching his heart and enabling Varian to push on and on toward his destination.

At last, sensing something, he drew to a halt as Genn and the worgen came up behind him. Genn blinked, sniffed the air again, and muttered a single word that verified Varian's suspicions: "Horde . . ."

That word encompassed so many smells, so many aspects, of the enemy. Varian himself could smell the muskiness of the orcs and the tauren, the sweat of many trolls, the decay of the Forsaken, the smoke of many fires, and the stench that could only be attributed to goblin machines.

The other worgen raised their snouts as they, too, smelled the nearness of the enemy. Varian led them a bit closer and they caught their first glimpses of the battlefield.

At that point he had drawn Shalamayne and, seeing what he and the worgen must do, had thrust the sword forward and shouted a war cry.

The worgen had howled with him, and Genn, glancing Varian's way, had seen the aura around the king of Stormwind radiate stronger than ever. The snarling visage of Goldrinn had loomed over the wolf Ancient's champion.

Varian had leapt into the fray, the worgen spreading out as he had bidden them. The first of the Horde had been brought down with almost ridiculous ease, so disbelieving had they been of the sight.

Now, as the worgen spread out into the main battlefield, Varian decided on his next course of action. He wanted dearly to find Garrosh Hellscream, but such a personal battle had to take second place to the more imminent disaster.

"To me!" he roared to the nearest worgen. Without looking to see who followed, he ran—yes, ran, despite so much distance already crossed—and headed for the lead magnataur.

A shaggy tauren saw him and moved to intercept. The heavy axe created a dust cloud as it drove into the ground where Varian should have been. However, the king had moved far more swiftly than his bullheaded adversary had calculated. Varian was already to the side of the much bulkier, taller warrior. With Shalamayne, he slashed across the tauren's torso, cutting so deeply that the tauren was dead before he fell.

The Horde ranks no longer charged forward. They were already painfully aware of a new and powerful enemy in their very midst. Yet, the orcs and their allies were not used to the fluid movements of the worgen. Underestimation of the lupine attackers led to many Horde deaths in the first few moments.

That was not to say that worgen did not perish. The Horde had not thrived without being able to adapt. Two orcs combined to catch a worgen between them. What one axe failed to strike, the other caught in the spine. Other worgen dropped with bolts through their chests or throats.

But the Horde suffered much greater. Not only was this a foe that they had never met before, but it came at them from the side, forcing them to face both the west and north at once. After all, Tyrande and Shandris were not so slow-witted as not to realize that they once again had hope. Even with the magnataur still wreaking havoc, they managed to re-form some of their lines and counterattack.

But all of this Varian only vaguely registered as his view swept from the field to his prey. The bull had turned his attention to this new enemy of his masters. A huge hand grabbed at a worgen and, while not succeeding in snatching him up, did inadvertently swipe the unfortunate Gilnean, sending him hurtling to his death.

Two orcs attacked Varian, but a worgen leapt at one, pulling the green-skinned warrior to the ground, where they struggled. The worgen's claws tore through the throat of the orc.

Varian dodged the swing by the second orc, came under his shield, and thrust Shalamayne through the orc's midsection. Pulling the sword free, the king then had to jump to the side as one back leg of the magnataur came down.

The gigantic creature turned. However, the magnataur were not built for speed. They did not need to be: they were so huge that they covered distance readily. However, in close combat, Varian at least had the advantage in mobility, as long as he avoided the feet or the hands. That, though, would avail him nothing in the long run, and he had no intention of merely running.

As the behemoth instinctively turned after him, Varian moved toward the hind leg again. He came within reach.

"Varian Wrynn!" roared a voice the king recognized. "Varian Wrynn, I challenge you! Turn and meet your doom!"

Varian whirled. Garrosh Hellscream, Gorehowl raised high, grinned as the two faced one another.

The human said nothing, his expression answer enough for the orc. They converged, the axe wailing as the two weapons clashed and sparks flew. The force of their strike sent both combatants stumbling back a few steps.

The warchief grinned ominously. "Such a weapon! With Gorehowl, it will make the finest comrade an orc could wield!"

"Shalamayne prefers the taste of orc blood," Varian replied. "Yours especially. . . ."

He lunged.

The orc deflected his strike, the blade and the axe head again sending up a shower of sparks. Garrosh swung. The human countered. Again and again, the two champions found themselves as evenly matched as their fabled weapons.

"I've waited for this moment!" Garrosh grinned. "Our

fight in Ulduar was too brief and without satisfaction, especially since I did not then have Gorehowl to match against your sword. . . ."

"My sentiments exactly!" The king deflected another strike by Gorehowl, both fighters forced to squint as sparks from the clashing weapons flew at their eyes. "I promise not to disappoint you this time . . . except when I take your head. . . ."

The orc laughed. "Your skull will have a place of honor on the gates of Orgrimmar!"

He swung Gorehowl low, seeking to catch Varian by surprise and disembowel the human. The king turned Shalamayne down and, though the angle was awkward, kept the axe from his torso.

Ignorant of the battle waging below him, the magnataur continued his turn as he hunted for the puny human. Varian saw the great leg sweeping toward them. He rolled back as Garrosh, not yet aware of the danger, readied another blow from the wailing axe.

The leg struck the orc. It was only a glancing blow, but it was enough to send Garrosh sprawling.

Unable to see what happened to Garrosh after that, Varian chose to sheathe Shalamayne. He watched as the magnataur settled in place for a moment. When that happened, Varian jumped at the leg.

The moment he grabbed hold of the magnataur's fur, the monster roared and tried to shake him loose. But before the behemoth could, another figure clung to the other hind leg. The worgen began his climb at the same time as Varian, creating a distraction for the king.

A second worgen jumped onto the same leg as Varian. Several more quickly did the same. They were for the most part those he had commanded to follow him, but who had become momentarily separated by the battle.

Gritting his teeth, Varian pulled himself up. The first part of his plan had come into play, but now he had to follow through. Without the aid of claws, Varian still reached the back of the magnataur long before the first worgen.

The magnataur twisted as much as his upper torso would allow him. His hand came agonizingly near Varian, who drew Shalamayne and cut at the fingers. He was rewarded with the behemoth snatching the bleeding hand back, which allowed several of the worgen to make it to the king.

There was no need for words. The worgen knew their task. Like ants, they raced up and around the magnataur and, wherever their blades, maces, and other mundane weapons proved too unmanageable, began rending the flesh with their claws and even biting. The thick, tough hide of the gigantic creature protected at first, giving the magnataur the chance to try to brush off some of the vermin on him. A half dozen worgen went spilling off the beast, some managing to land well or snag hold of a leg, but others plummeting to their deaths.

But then a worgen managed the first tear in the magnataur, his success followed immediately by another. The bull howled in rage and shook back and forth. With his stocky build, especially his elephantine lower half, the magnataur could no more jump than the mammoth that part of his body resembled. Instead, he abruptly reared up on his hind legs, seeking with the unexpected motion to dislodge his attackers. Two worgen fell free, but Varian and the rest managed to maintain their grips despite this surprise.

More worgen joined those swarming the magnataur. They clambered over his back, his neck, and some of the most daring even tore into his chest. Alone or even if only a dozen or so, they would have been mere annoyances . . . but now they began to take a toll. The bull's rage took on a hint of frustration, then pain, as he bled from more than two dozen wounds.

Shalamayne proved even better than ordinary swords and claws at cutting through the rough hide. His feet braced, his balance careful, Varian slashed again and again, opening ravines in the magnataur's back.

Another angry bellow caught his attention. The next nearest magnataur had finally chosen to aid the bull. It was not out of any loyalty between the monsters, but rather a sense of survival. The other magnataur had realized that anything that could potentially harm their leader could next turn on the others.

Varian grinned. The reason for his grin became instantly apparent as more worgen suddenly crawled up the legs of the oncoming magnataur. No longer interested in assisting the dominant bull, the other behemoth tried in vain to clear his own hide of the rapidly increasing numbers of lupine invaders.

A battle horn blowing an Alliance signal made Varian look to the night elves' lines. Without the magnataur in direct conflict with them, the Sentinels were able to even better regroup. What had been a rout was now more of a balanced battle again.

Varian planned to take it further than that. The worgen, heedless of their danger, did not flinch from attacking the other magnataur. Others of the great pack continued their rush into the midst of the Horde forces and, from the monster's back, Varian could see the swath of death that the Gilneans had already made through the enemy.

The bull suddenly began to move toward the deeper forest. Varian knew what he planned: the magnataur intended to either seize a partial tree trunk and try to knock the worgen off, or begin rubbing against the standing trees in the hopes of doing the same.

Varian returned to one of the hind legs. There, he found, of all Gilneans, Genn Greymane. "Why are you here?"

"To make sure what you want done *is* done!" the other monarch roared back.

Varian was actually pleased to see him. "The other hind leg! We need to get down lower while he's distracted!"

Genn looked puzzled until Varian made a cutting motion. The worgen then smiled. "I'll take the lead with them!"

They separated without another word. Varian sheathed his sword, then began his descent. What he planned could not have been done until now. The magnataur needed to be focused on the worgen as a whole, not a few who climbed *down* now instead of up.

As he reached the point he desired, Varian drew Shalamayne. He glanced at the other hind leg. Despite the creature's movement, the worgen easily clung to the limb. Genn had just reached the same level as Varian.

Without hesitation, and with his other hand and his legs holding him as best they could, Varian Wrynn used Shalamayne to cut as deep and wide a wound as he could in the back of the magnataur's leg.

The beast roared in sudden agony. It stumbled to the side, nearly dislodging some of the worgen elsewhere. Varian hoped for the best for the brave Gilneans as he readjusted his aim and, instead of slashing, *drove Shalamayne* deep.

The effect was instantaneous. The bull's leg collapsed. Sword gripped tightly, Varian threw himself free.

He landed a short distance from the crippled leg. Blood dripped out of the wound, but that was not why the leg could not hold any longer: Varian had expertly severed the tendon.

The magnataur tried to keep moving, but the damaged limb slowed him too much. It gave Genn and the worgen on the other leg the opportunity they needed. With the lord of Gilneas guiding the others, the worgen thoroughly tore into the same area that Varian had. Genn cut deep with his longsword through what his claws could not rend. Already in terrible pain from the first leg, the magnataur belatedly tried to reach back and grab the Gilneans.

With one final cut, Genn finished the tendon. He howled sharply, then jumped from the ruined appendage.

Warned by Genn, the rest of the worgen fled the wounded magnataur. As the last of them leapt to safety, the struggling giant, in the act of trying to seize the king of Gilneas, lost his balance as the second leg gave out.

With an almost mournful roar, the dominant bull tumbled onto his left side. His collision with the ground created a shock wave that tossed many of the combatants in the vicinity from their feet.

But it was not over yet. Varian cried out a wordless challenge and bounded onto the struggling behemoth.

He ran toward the head even as worgen once more swarmed the rest of the body.

With fingers still bleeding from Varian's earlier strike, the magnataur swatted at whatever worgen he could reach. Some of the most eager of the worgen fell prey to the swinging hand, but Varian dodged it, then raced up past the shoulder to the neck.

The fearsome visage twisted in his direction, the magnataur's long, curving tusks sweeping toward Varian and nearly succeeding where the hand had failed. The baleful eyes glared at the puny human who had caused him so much pain. Varian felt the muscles leading to the arm move and knew that the wounded magnataur had come to realize that this was prey finally within easy reach.

With the hand rushing to him, Varian held Shalamayne downward with both hands and stepped off the neck.

As he dropped, he took the sword and jammed it into the soft part of the throat.

The fabled blade cut through as if the flesh there were water. The magnataur's life fluids drenched Varian as he continued a drop slowed only by how long it took Shalamayne to cut through.

A great gurgle escaped the bull. The behemoth thrashed about, in his death throes threatening to do to Varian what he could not before.

A furred form seized Varian before the arm could crush him. He and his worgen rescuer rolled in a heap, Shalamayne flying a short distance away.

Varian picked himself up. He discovered only then that his rescuer was none other than Genn. The worgen leader lay stunned. Varian knelt by his side and discovered that Genn had struck his head hard. Blood matted the fur there.

Genn's eyes opened. He stared up at Varian.

"Such fury! Small wonder you are Goldrinn's chosen champion. . . ." The worgen leader blinked, his humanity quite evident in his eyes despite his furred form. "I feared for a moment that we'd lose you due to your impetuousness."

"Your people almost lost you instead."

"A small price to pay. The worgen have found you. We have found our place through you."

Varian looked for his sword. "Our place may be the grave. This battle isn't over."

Genn sought to rise, then winced and sat back again. He took a deep breath, then tried once more. This time, the worgen leader succeeded.

Varian retrieved Shalamayne, but as he looked up again, he saw something amidst the chaos of the battlefield that made him bare his teeth.

"Don't follow me, Genn."

"What—"

Not waiting around to explain, Varian charged back into the struggle. An orc saw Varian and foolishly tried to take him. The lord of Stormwind barely noticed as Shalamayne sank deep in the orc's chest. A second warrior fell as quickly and just as unnoticed.

Varian only had interest in one opponent, the same one who had earlier hunted him with such obsession, but from whom the human had been separated by circumstance.

Garrosh Hellscream.

The battling armies once more obscured the warchief

from Varian's view, but Gorehowl's shriek was unmistakable, even from a distance. Varian paused and listened again as the axe sang its song of death, then altered his path.

A horn blared from the Alliance side and suddenly there were lancers on nightsabers everywhere. Horde warriors scattered as the huge cats brought new death among them. One of the lancers came to the rescue of a worgen surrounded by enemies, the lance running through one as the nightsaber ripped apart two others. The worgen readily handled the rest.

A magnataur bellowed, his body almost literally covered with worgen. Several worked at the legs and, even as Varian passed them, one limb gave.

The worgen were everywhere in the battle, darting in and about and slashing with either weapon or claws as the need arose. Ghoulish Forsaken retreated in the face of a foe too swift for them, the undead having already seen several of their number ripped apart or cut to wriggling, useless pieces. Hardened tauren sought to take a stand, but their very agile foes more often than not got under their defenses, striking true and finally pushing the tauren back. The top half of a goblin machine spun around and around as its operator frantically tried to keep two worgen at bay. The Gilneans calmly waited until they had the measure of the mechanism's movements, then one sprang past the whirling blades, landed behind the driver, and raked the goblin's back with his claws.

A glaive flew past Varian, the rushing weapon followed by two more. Sentinels on foot now entered the thickest part of the struggle. Some continued to toss their blades over and over while others used the glaives in hand-to-hand combat. With them came Stormwind's forces, who instantly surged toward where the worgen—and thus King Varian—fought. The outcome of the struggle was far from clear, save that now at least the Alliance had a chance.

Then lines began to re-form on the Horde side. Varian heard Gorehowl once more, this time exceedingly close by.

He picked up his pace, unaware that one of the mounted Sentinel officers saw him. Alerting another, the night elf had her force follow the king of Stormwind. Worgen also began to track behind Varian as he moved quickly across the field despite a path littered with bloody and mangled bodies from both sides.

Still ignorant of the charge he had begun leading, Varian closed on the area where he was certain that he would find Garrosh. Capture or slay the warchief, and the battle ended. That was all that mattered. . . .

A line of orcish archers suddenly rose up from hiding and fired at the oncoming enemy.

Somehow, Varian dodged those shafts that came near him. He had no notion as to what happened behind him. Some of those who followed perished, but others quickly replaced their numbers. There was a sense among the Alliance that a defining moment was upon them, that this charge led by the king of Stormwind would make or break the day.

But on the other side, the Horde was more than ready to meet this new challenge. The deadly flight of arrows preceded a rush of heavily armed and armored warriors both on foot and astride the great dire wolves.

Still paying no heed to those who followed him, Varian

saw the enemy ranks as merely impediments. When the first dire wolf reached him, he used Shalamayne to slice through one eye and pierce the brain. As the animal fell forward, Varian stepped up atop its head and all but cut the orc rider in two. A blood elf who grabbed for the lord of Stormwind pulled back with his hand lost. Axes and blades tore at his garments and bloodied his body, but none were more than nuisances, and they slowed him not a bit.

And though he himself did not notice it, did not feel it, both those who followed and those who faced him thought that they saw in the dust and smoke swirling in his vicinity the darting form of a great wolf. Who first shouted the name was a question none could answer. The worgen assumed it was one of their own, for had they not been the first to recognize the king of Stormwind as the Ancient's champion? The Sentinels believed it either the high priestess or her general, while those dwarves and humans who had accompanied the expedition from Darnassus thought someone of their ranks was responsible.

What mattered was that someone first shouted "Varian!" and then *"Goldrinn!"* and those names repeated over and over to become the new battle cry. It was a cry that reverberated through the Horde ranks and sent the first true hint of uncertainty through their minds. The victory should have been theirs long ago. The Alliance should have fallen. What was happening now was not how the magnificent plan had been supposed to play out.

And none knew the last more than Garrosh Hellscream. The future that he had envisioned coming to fruition once Ashenvale was in Horde hands now looked so very distant. His ultimate weapon, the crushing power of the magnataur, had now become a much-too-visible image of his master strategy gone awry.

Even as he thought that, another of the giants went crashing to the ground. Worgen swarmed over the fallen behemoth, seeking especially the throat.

One of the Kor'kron pushed close to Garrosh. "Warchief, you risk yourself here! We cannot lose you. . . ."

"*Lose* me?" Garrosh shoved the insolent guard aside. "I will not hide from battle!"

"But the Alliance—"

The warchief glared, causing the hardened guard to flinch. Garrosh roared another command, sending in reinforcements where the accursed worgen had weakened his forces.

The Alliance's new battle cry pounded in his head. Garrosh could not make out exactly what the enemy called, but he could see how it stirred them to greater effort against his warriors. "What is that? What words do they shout?"

Another guard answered. "They cry the name of the human king . . . and with it, *Goldrinn* . . . their title for the great *Lo'Gosh*!"

"The wolf Ancient . . ." Garrosh's gaze searched the struggle. "Lo'Gosh . . . and Varian Wrynn . . ."

And as he once more spoke the human's name, the orc leader spotted the Alliance's apparent champion among the enemy encroaching on his position . . . and Varian Wrynn spotted him.

In silent agreement, they pushed toward one another. Garrosh's personal guard protested, but he slipped in among the other fighters and left his would-be protectors struggling to reach him.

Shalamayne moved as a blur, cutting and slaying any who stood in the king's way. Brave though orcs, tauren, blood elves, and trolls might be, foolish they were not. There was better chance for glory—and life—against many others.

But one figure did come between the two, Varian his intended hunt, also. His impetuous thrust almost did what so many had failed to do. However, the cut in Varian's arm was shallow.

Briln, the edge of his axe blade stained with the human's blood, glared at Varian.

"My magnataur!" roared the former mariner bitterly. "My glory and honor! Look what you've done!"

His ferocity forced Varian into momentary retreat. Briln had not survived for so long without being skilled with the axe, as Haldrissa had discovered to her detriment. There were tricks that he could have even taught Garrosh—not that such a thing mattered at the moment to the distraught orc. The magnataur were to have been his way of redeeming himself for all the catastrophes of the journey, especially the lives lost. Now this human, this lone human, was undoing that.

Varian had no time for this insane orc. He knew that Garrosh was very close, even perhaps almost within striking range. Yet, the former mariner would not be denied.

Briln swung again, and in doing so reminded Varian of his one obvious weakness. The eye patch meant darkness was all that the orc could see on that side, and even though Briln knew that, too, he could still not change that fact.

Varian let the orc attack anew, and when the swing pulled Briln so that his lost eye best faced the human, Varian drove Shalamayne into his adversary's chest.

Briln dropped his weapon as Varian pulled Shala-mayne free. The orc fell to his knees. Still glaring at Var-ian, he gasped, "My . . . magnataur . . . my . . ."

The captain crumpled, and Varian swung Shalamayne behind his own back.

A shock ran through his body as the blade met metal. Half kneeling, he spun and blocked a second swing. Both times an inhuman wail preceded the clash.

"I knew you'd deflect both," Garrosh rumbled in hon-est admiration as he loomed over Varian. "You would not be who you are if you could not. . . ."

"I'd be dead," Varian answered lightly. "I'd be you."

The warchief chuckled . . . and attacked.

Shalamayne and Gorehowl bit at one another once, twice, three times. Their wielders brought them together so quickly that, rather than sparks, it was as if lightning played over the human and the orc.

Varian stumbled over a corpse. Garrosh chopped downward, intending to cleave him in two. The king rolled to the side, came up, and lunged.

Now it was Garrosh's turn to retreat. He kept Gore-howl up, saving his throat twice, then used the hefty reach the axe provided him to stave off Varian until the orc was able to regain his footing.

Once more, sword and axe joined together. Garrosh sought to catch the blade with the curve of Gorehowl's head, but Varian withdrew the point at the last moment. He then tried to drive under the warchief's defenses, only to have the orc block Shalamayne with the flat of the axe.

"You only delay the inevitable!" shouted Garrosh. "The day of the Alliance is at an end! The Horde is Az-eroth's future!"

"The Horde should fear the end of day! With the end of day comes the night . . . and with the night comes the worgen . . . ," Varian retorted.

The gap that had separated them from the other combatants around them closed at that moment. Warriors locked in desperate combat flowed into the pair, pressing them into one another. The eyes of the human and the orc met long, and both saw death in the other's gaze.

"Pray to your spirits," the king flatly stated.

"I shall do so. You'll need a proper guide to the afterlife, human. . . ."

With a roar, Garrosh shoved as hard as he could. Varian slammed into those behind him. The warchief cut a savage arc, Gorehowl's mournful cry sending those closest scattering again.

Varian cut off the cry with Shalamayne, first deflecting the axe, then using a twist of his wrist to enable the sword to bring the orc's weapon to the side.

With his fist, Garrosh hammered the human's shoulder. Varian gritted his teeth as his bones shook. Seeking to stop the attack, he brought his blade between his shoulder and the pounding fist.

The warchief swung at his other, now-unprotected shoulder.

Varian tossed Shalamayne to his other hand, then tilted the blade toward Gorehowl. But although he kept Gorehowl from crushing his shoulder, the axe still cut across the upper arm. The king grunted in renewed pain as he shifted away.

Shalamayne avenged him quickly. Varian had long ago learned to wield his sword with either hand, although one would always be favored over the other.

Garrosh reacted too slowly to the fact that his human foe could handle Shalamayne well even now. The tip of the sword drew a red line along the warchief's chest just below the throat.

Suddenly another axe entered the fray. One of the Kor'kron had reached the struggle and, in keeping with his duties, sought to protect Garrosh. The guard threw himself bodily toward Varian, his unexpected intervention leaving the king in desperate straits.

Another Kor'kron came at Varian from the opposite direction. Their axes were not Gorehowl, but they were well bloodied and wielded by expert hands. The Kor'kron slashed and swung, pushing Varian back.

Garrosh growled angrily at his guards, but his words were drowned by the battle. Both Kor'kron looked upon Varian with malevolent eagerness: with his death they would not only serve their warchief but also bring acclaim upon themselves.

The lord of Stormwind read their reflexes, recognized their moves. He let one guard press ahead of the other. As the first Kor'kron's anticipation of striking the fatal blow rose, Varian shifted his grip on Shalamayne and *threw* it like a spear.

Caught unawares by the unorthodox maneuver, the foremost guard left himself open. The force of Varian's throw sent the blade deep into his foe.

Before the second Kor'kron could make sense of matters, Varian had snatched away the dying guard's axe. With the full force of his might, he swung at his other adversary's leg.

The axe all but separated the limb. Screaming, the orc fell to one side.

Varian plucked Shalamayne free, then skewered the wounded Kor'kron.

Why Garrosh had not pursued his two guards became evident as the orc buried Gorehowl in the skull of a riderless nightsaber. The cat did not die immediately, its sharp claws seeking one last time to tear the orc to shreds. But with agility more remarkable due to his broad form, Garrosh evaded the feline's paw, then moved in and for a second time let Gorehowl bite into the nightsaber's skull.

The warchief turned his dripping axe to Varian. Without a word the pair renewed their duel. Blood from those who had gotten in their way splattered the human and the orc, but neither paid attention to anything but the other.

Horns sounded. Alliance horns. They grew more dominating, though Garrosh did not notice that. What he did notice was that his breathing was growing more ragged. He had expected to slay Varian Wrynn by now and raise the human's severed head for all the hapless Alliance to see. Because of that, he had exerted himself harder than he usually did.

But this human has come an impossible distance! the orc angrily reminded himself. *He should be the weary one! He should be unable to even lift his sword. . . .*

Varian, though, looked as fresh of energy as he had when first they had met. The human's eyes remained unwavering.

Garrosh realized that he had far underestimated the human. This king possessed the fury of an orc and, through him, the defenders seemed to have gained that fury as well.

And only then did the warchief truly see that the stories he had heard about Varian Wrynn were true. Lo'Gosh *did* smile with favor on this human . . . and why not? They were of a kind. Here was one who had the heart of a great and determined hunter, a great and determined warrior.

The heart . . . of a wolf.

I have been a fool! the warchief knew then. *I should've planned an even greater, more brutal thrust! With such a leader, the Alliance may even take eastern Ashenvale back!*

Unmindful of what went on in his adversary's thoughts, Varian further pressed his attack. He saw Garrosh give ground and knew that the orc did not do so as part of some sinister strategy. The advantage had turned to Varian's.

Varian slashed. It was an attack a weary Garrosh knew that he could parry, but his arm moved a fraction slower than it was wont.

Shalamayne dug into the upper arm, striking tensed muscle.

Garrosh's entire arm shook. The warchief's grip momentarily failed. Gorehowl slipped from his twitching fingers and fell to the ground.

Varian pulled back to strike—and an ear-shattering roar overwhelmed both fighters. Varian and Garrosh looked up to see another magnataur come rushing down on them. Worgen scurried over his body as he sought to escape their savage attacks. The worgen had taken Varian's tactics to heart and had improved on them, for as the behemoth reached the pair, his ravaged front legs gave out and he pitched forward.

Varian threw himself back. With his good hand, Garrosh risked life and limb to seize Gorehowl. As the shadow of the plummeting magnataur rushed over him, he leapt.

The stricken monster rolled to one side, but the worgen only clambered to safer ground, then resumed their relentless shredding. The hind legs kicked wildly, forcing Varian to back farther away.

Garrosh pushed himself to his feet. He searched for the human, but the struggling magnataur blocked his view.

Rage refueling his strength, the warchief began running to the back of the beast. He would find Varian Wrynn again and this time there would be a decisive—

"Warchief!" Another of his Kor'kron stepped in front of him. Garrosh tried to shove the fool aside, but suddenly other hands seized him.

"Beware!" shouted another guard. Two others stepped in to protect their leader as several worgen atop the magnataur took interest in fresher meat. "Get the warchief away!"

As some of his personal guard battled the worgen, a furious Garrosh roared, "Release me, you damned fools! I must find him! I *will* have his death . . . and claim the sword!"

"The battle is lost!" the first Kor'kron dared to say. "We must get you from here before we're overrun!"

Garrosh rewarded the speaker with the back of his hand. As blood dribbled down the guard's mouth, the warchief roared, "The next coward to speak such lies loses his dishonorable head!"

"No lies!" proclaimed another. Several heads bobbed in agreement. "All but one magnataur are down. Our lines have disappeared. On our south, we are among the enemy already. You but have to look and see. If I lie, my head is yours!"

"Mine also!" said the first, with the rest following suit.

Such offers were not given lightly, not with the great possibility that Garrosh would accept. The warchief frowned, then surveyed what he could of the struggle.

It took no imagination to quickly see that they were right. The banners of the Sentinels could be seen edging closer. His own warriors' banners were little in view, and most of those could be seen farther and farther east. The rest lay no doubt trampled under the enemy's feet.

"No! I will find him even if I must fight every foe on the field! I will not lose. . . ." He tried to go in hunt of Varian again, only to have his own guards seize him and begin to drag him to safety.

"We will win Ashenvale yet," the lead Kor'kron assured him as the guards continued their struggle to save Garrosh.

"The warchief himself says that one battle is not a war!" reminded another. "We will take Ashenvale! We swear it, Warchief. . . ."

Garrosh fought with himself to accept what they said. They were repeating what he had always proclaimed to them. Yet, the reality was bitter to swallow . . . especially after the unfinished duel with Varian Wrynn.

He shook free of his fearful guards, but, to their relief, headed to the mounts to which they had been steering him. In their wake, the battle still raged, though it was clear that the Alliance continued to gain ground.

"Sound the horns," Garrosh ordered. "Sound the retreat."

A relieved guard signaled a trumpeter, who did as commanded. As the hated sound reverberated in his mind, Garrosh mounted. He swung Gorehowl once, listened to it wail as he did, then hooked it onto a brace on his back. Just before Garrosh urged his mount on, he looked over his shoulder to where the first elements of the Horde were abandoning the lost cause.

"It *is* but a battle," the warchief finally agreed. "*Only* a battle. Ashenvale is our destiny. . . ." Garrosh envisioned again the realm he would build and, in envisioning it, once more knew that it would happen.

He led them off, already making plans. This was not over . . . not until he had won. . . .

And not until Varian Wrynn was dead.

Varian watched the riders fade in the distance, aware that he could have pursued but had chosen not to do so.

Genn Greymane found him near the great corpse of the magnataur who had separated the human from the orc. The worgen leader's fur was slick with blood and other gore, as was that of every other of his people.

"You let them go . . . ," the king of Gilneas muttered. "I saw you come around and watch the orcs take their warchief and all but carry him off. He fought them so much, we could've easily caught up and taken them. This would've all been over."

Varian continued to watch even after he could no longer see Garrosh. He shook his head as he replied, "Would it have? Not at this point. No . . . sometimes you have to let the prey run for a while. Then . . . then you'll know when the right time does come."

Genn's ears flattened as he tried to accept what Varian said. He was saved the trouble by the sudden arrival of a contingent of Sentinels led by both the high priestess and General Shandris.

"Varian Wrynn," Tyrande greeted, smiling. "Elune finally reveals her miracle."

"'Her miracle'?" Genn cocked his head. "No, my lady, Elune might have some part in this—as surely Goldrinn has—but both would without a doubt give the greatest credit to another!" He extended a clawed hand toward Varian. "A warrior now in balance with himself, a leader now in harmony with the needs of those he commands!" The worgen leader turned to the others. "Varian Wrynn!"

As the worgen leader shouted out the name, the other Gilneans began to pick it up. At first they murmured the name, but as their enthusiasm rose, they repeated it louder and louder. "*Varian Wrynn! Varian Wrynn!*"

Having already rallied to that name as a battle cry, the Sentinels and the other Alliance fighters readily joined in again. Varian Wrynn did not enjoy such acclamation, but he understood the need for those cheering him to have this outlet. Varian only prayed that it would die down soon.

If he hoped for help from the high priestess, he did not find it there. Still smiling, Tyrande nodded to Genn and said, "You speak right indeed." She bowed her head to the uncomfortable Varian, raised her hand, and said loudly, "Hail to you, King Varian! Hail to you, savior of Ashenvale . . . and perhaps Azeroth as well. . . ."

29

TO FORGE A FUTURE

Under the guidance of General Shandris, new and better-situated outposts were quickly arranged along the eastern edge of the territory under Sentinel protection. A much more tempered Denea was given command of one of these, and Su'ura Swiftarrow, while still battlemaster for Warsong Gulch, was promoted to replace the late, honored Haldrissa. A commission was also offered to Illiyana Moonblaze, but she preferred no higher rank, as it would mean more responsibility—and less independence.

The Horde had shored up its defenses beyond the river, but the Alliance had reclaimed Silverwing and quickly rebuilt it. The Sentinel outpost had been made the staging ground for supplying the Alliance's counterattack. Tyrande blessed the restored Silverwing in the name of Elune before she and Shandris returned out of necessity to Darnassus.

They did not return alone.

• • •

"It is a wonder we were able to call them all back," Malfurion commented as they watched the other representatives of the Alliance gathering for a *new* summit. "I commend you, my love."

"Do not commend me. With the Horde still active in Ashenvale, it is more necessary than ever that we all come together. Garrosh will not sit long. He bides his time: that is all."

"It still took much to get them to come. I know that they had already agreed to send troops to Ashenvale, but we both understand that there is more involved if we hope to keep the Horde in check for more than a short time." He hugged her. "As I said, you are to be commended."

She accepted his hug, only after that explaining, "But it was not I who truly convinced them . . . it was Varian."

"Varian?"

Before she could say more, both noticed a figure standing quietly in the shadows to their side. When he realized that they saw him, he finally stepped forward. It was Jarod, his wounds recently healed by the Sisters of Elune. However, despite now being in excellent condition again, the expression on his face was akin to a man who had just learned that he was to die.

"High Priestess, forgive me . . . if you can."

"I will not forgive you for calling me *high priestess*, Jarod Shadowsong . . . I am *Tyrande* to you. As for what I think you are apologizing for, do not." Her own expression saddened. "I am more at fault here than anyone. Poor Maiev! I should have seen how the madness was slowly consuming her! I am only grateful that you and my husband were able to prevent further catastrophe!"

"But she escaped."

"And no one holds that against you, Jarod," Malfurion interjected. "Especially us."

He stood straighter. "Nevertheless, I swear to both of you that I will find her. She must be brought to justice and it must be by me."

"Just be careful that you do not begin to follow the same path of obsession your sister did," Malfurion cautioned.

"I understand what you say. I will be careful in that regard, but I will not shirk from my duty."

The high priestess acquiesced. "No one can deny you that right, and you have proven your abilities, Jarod . . . which brings me to my first point. Not all of the Watchers were surely aware of Maiev's plot, and from among those proven innocent I intend to have a new leader appointed. However, the Watchers will play a different role than what we need from you, Jarod."

"Me? I do not understand."

"Once, you ably commanded warriors—and even *demigods*—in battle for us. With my husband's agreement, I would have you lead a new security force, one designed to deal with troubles . . . such as Maiev."

"I am honored . . . and will gratefully accept."

"Shalasyr would be very proud of you, Jarod," the high priestess added.

He tried to reply, but could not find his voice. Shalasyr's face filled his thoughts, and, for a moment, Jarod forgot that Tyrande and Malfurion stood before him.

"I . . . like to think so," he finally answered. "I can only hope so. She was so much more full of life than me. She should have been the one to live on."

"The choice is not ours. How we honor those who have passed on with the way we continue our lives is."

"You sound like Shalasyr."

The high priestess put a comforting hand on his shoulder. "In regards to Maiev, Shandris will assist you in choosing from among the Sentinels some possible candidates for your new force."

"I thank all three of you."

"We will talk more after this."

"I will not let you down." Jarod bowed, then quickly stepped away.

As Tyrande and Malfurion headed toward the summit, Malfurion leaned close and whispered, "Sending him to Shandris? What are you doing?"

"Thinking of the future . . . ," she replied with a thoughtful smile, "and when the time is more appropriate for them."

He held back any further comment as they entered among the representatives. Malfurion noted the swiftness with which the last emissaries sat and knew that it could only mean that Varian Wrynn had arrived.

Sure enough, Tyrande surreptitiously touched his hand. He glanced her way and in doing so found Varian striding to his place among the others as if he were not the one who had succeeded in bringing them together again. The king of Stormwind sat down, then looked to Malfurion.

The archdruid took his cue. Stepping forth, he raised his staff. Silence filled the gathering.

"We thank you for coming here and again being our guests," he told them as Tyrande stood next to him. "With the events in Ashenvale, time has grown more precious, and so, if there is no objection, there is one among you who would speak and who, I believe, should be heard." With one hand, he indicated Varian. "I present to all of you, King Varian Wrynn of Stormwind. . . ."

The other rulers and representatives began to applaud, but Varian waved them to silence. He studied them all, then shook his head.

"You shouldn't be applauding me. Not a man who is supposed to rule by reason but did so by rage instead."

His self-condemnation brought concerned murmuring from his audience. Malfurion looked to Tyrande, who smiled in reassurance.

"An unreasoning, unfocused rage that brought calamity on me and all I held dear and served only to divide the Alliance"—Varian's expression forbade anyone to deny what he said—"and for the latter, I apologize."

It was no small thing for Varian to apologize for anything, and no one there thought him any weaker for it. The story of his actions in Ashenvale was already becoming legend despite his desiring otherwise.

"The Varian Wrynn who reigned with such rage is dead!" he declared. "But in dying, he learned that it wasn't the rage that was at fault, only he! The fury, the anger, must have purpose! It must be the righteous anger of one defending his family, his home, and his friends! It must be the fury that keeps all he loves safe from those who would rip them from him. . . ."

"Hear, hear!" rumbled an enthusiastic Thargas Anvilmar. The other dwarves glanced in his direction, but out of what seemed more satisfaction with his response than annoyance.

"And now is the time to focus that fury!" the lord of Stormwind continued without pause. "Now is when we need the worgen most, not only for their own fury and fire, but to help guide all of us to safely and rightly unleash this side of us! This is our only way to defeat the Horde and, I will say it, perhaps even bring down the terrible black dragon *Deathwing* himself!"

Malfurion finally understood where Varian was heading and nodded. Tyrande leaned close and murmured, "You see? We had faith it would work out and it did."

"You had faith. I am still learning."

At that moment, the king of Stormwind slammed his fist down. "The Horde has tried once to take Ashenvale! They'll try again! If we let them do so without a fight, we've already lost! They see Azeroth as a new world and, because of their relentless energy, they see themselves as the only ones appropriate to tame it! But we will match that energy and more, and we will fight the Horde and all other foes at every turn until the Alliance and Azeroth can finally claim that peace prevails!"

This statement brought more murmuring, this time angry. Yet, beneath that anger was a growing agreement, a joining of purpose among the factions. Archmage Tervosh nodded to Drukan, who bobbed his head in return. Gelbin and the gnomes muttered together, their gazes continuing to return to Varian with obvious admiration—a rare display by gnomes for someone who was a warrior, not an inventor. Everywhere, Varian's words struck home, for the moment bringing together even all three dwarven clans.

Encouraged by their reactions, Varian thrust on. "Anger. Fury. You feel it now. This is what we need, if we're to match the energy of the Horde! This . . . and something more. . . ."

Varian signaled to someone unseen near the entrance through which the representatives had again marched. A horn blared . . . and the anthem of Gilneas played.

Led again by Genn Greymane and fully transformed to their astonishing lupine shapes, the worgen reentered. They spread out as they reached the center, displaying their might for all to see.

Fist on his chest in a salute, the worgen leader stood directly before Varian. He gazed up at his counterpart and waited.

Varian did not look back but instead addressed the audience as a whole again. "When last we were here, the archdruid sought a vote on full membership of Gilneas and the worgen by acclamation! I call on you today to recast your vote! What say the rest of you?"

"Aye!" shouted Kurdran.

"Aye!" the other dwarven representatives yelled immediately after.

A stately female draenei rose. "I am Ishanah, high priestess of the Aldor, chosen to speak in place of the Prophet! The draenei cast a vote of aye!"

Theramore and the rest of the Alliance factions followed, each repeating their earlier votes. Malfurion hugged Tyrande with one arm as they watched the acclamation build. They made no attempt to take command of the summit; this was Varian's gathering until he deemed otherwise.

The king surveyed the assembly, which watched him in anticipation.

"Stormwind votes aye!" Varian bellowed triumphantly. "Gilneas and the worgen are full members of the Alliance!"

The worgen let out howls of pleasure. From beyond the gathering, other howls arose from the direction of their encampment.

Only Genn Greymane did not howl. The worgen leader stood solemn before Varian. "You honor us!" the king of Gilneas declared. "But we also honor you, Varian Wrynn of Stormwind! We honor the champion of Ashenvale!"

Now both the worgen and the other assembled delegates cheered.

Malfurion finally left Tyrande to go to the lord of Stormwind. Varian gratefully let him take over, but first indicated that he had something to whisper to the archdruid.

"When we arrived, there was a missive brought by a draenei messenger from my son. He wanted to assure me that when he completed his own path with the Light, he would return to Stormwind. . . ." Varian eyed Malfurion suspiciously. "Is this some doing of yours or the high priestess's?"

"None whatsoever. This happy news is from Anduin himself, I assure you! I knew nothing about this until you now told me, and I can swear the same for Tyrande. She would not have kept such a thing from me, much less you. . . ."

The king exhaled. "Then that makes his promise all the more welcome!"

Varian continued to drink in the thought of his son's return as the archdruid, after a congratulatory touch on the human's shoulder, took over. However, if Varian thought his part at an end, he was sorely mistaken.

"Gilneas and the worgen are welcomed into the fold!"

the night elf called. "And the worgen are welcome to a new, permanent home here with the night elf people!" The worgen howled their gratitude and the emissaries and their retinues added their applause again.

When things had settled down, Malfurion continued, "But we must also welcome the man who has brought us together again and who has also brought the future of the Alliance sharply into focus at last! Varian Wrynn, king of Stormwind!"

There was no cry of disagreement, not even from the Dark Iron dwarves. To a member, the Alliance factions called out the king of Stormwind's name over and over.

Varian wanted nothing more than to step back, but instead it was as if his body responded in the reverse, for he found himself moving up next to the night elf.

The assembly continued to cry out, *"Varian! Varian!"* The subject of their acclaim shook his head in denial, but no one seemed to care about his opinion.

He did not see when Malfurion slipped away to Tyrande again. Varian stood staring back at those who thought of him as not only champion of Ashenvale, but also their very future. He stared at them . . . and knew that he could never be the Varian that he had been in times past. Never again would he be able to turn from his allies for the mistakes that they had made, not when Varian could at last see how theirs were so insignificant compared to his own.

"I will do what I can . . . ," he whispered. "I swear I will . . . Anduin."

And behind him, the archdruid and high priestess watched the events with more than a little satisfaction.

"You were right, Tyrande," Malfurion commented.

"This is potentially even more than I imagined. . . . He could very well guide the Alliance to new, fresh heights, just what it needs to compete with the Horde for this Azeroth we have all inherited from Deathwing's madness. . . ."

"New, fresh heights," she agreed. "Perhaps even . . . a new *age?*"

The archdruid frowned. "*If* the Horde can be defeated. And *if* Deathwing does not rise anew and unveil some even more heinous plot, as you and I both suspect the accursed dragon intends. . . ."

She touched his cheek in some concern. "You must find *some* gladness in today's events. I thought you did."

"I do . . . I do . . . I find—" The archdruid stopped, all thought of their discussion for the moment pushed aside. He stared at Varian Wrynn, who now had taken to heart the summit and spoke to the others of what they needed to do next in terms of Ashenvale and beyond.

At the same time, Varian Wrynn felt a presence surround him, a presence that stirred his confidence in his decision. He did not have to ask who that presence was. It could only be one being.

And from his position, Malfurion watched as, for the briefest of moments, the form of Goldrinn—Lo'Gosh—superimposed itself over Varian. Malfurion was no over-imaginative sort; he knew that the vision he had seen was neither a product of his troubled mind nor a trick of his eyes.

The archdruid glanced at Tyrande.

"Yes," she murmured. "You see true. Goldrinn chose well his champion. . . . They are of a kind. The wolf Ancient: it was said that in the early days of the world he used to howl his fury against the moons, against Elune.

Perhaps, through this choice, he has redeemed himself in the eyes of Elune as well." She studied the human. "Such a choice! Varian Wrynn truly has the spirit, the heart of the wolf... and all our hope for the future...."

Seeing that—and hearing Tyrande's words—Malfurion Stormrage felt a sudden weight lifted from his own soul. He was very aware that mortality would claim him at some point, perhaps even sooner than he prayed. Since that realization, the archdruid had not been able to shake his fear of the tremendous burden on those who would follow him ... those who would not have him to help protect them.

But now Malfurion saw his great hubris. He should not have worried. It seemed as if Azeroth itself would find the ones who would next take up the banner, doing what they could to preserve their world and even perhaps finally forging a true, lasting peace.

And whoever they were, wherever they came from, Varian Wrynn, scion of the wolf Ancient, would be there to guide them.

NOTES

The story you've just read is based in part on characters, situations, and settings from Blizzard Entertainment's computer game *World of Warcraft*, an online role-playing experience set in the award-winning Warcraft universe. In *World of Warcraft*, players create their own heroes and explore, adventure in, and quest across a vast world shared with thousands of other players. This rich and expansive game also allows players to interact with and fight against or alongside many of the powerful and intriguing characters featured in this novel.

Since launching in November 2004, *World of Warcraft* has become the world's most popular subscription-based massively multiplayer online role-playing game. The latest expansion, *Cataclysm*, sold more than 3.3 million copies within its first 24 hours of release, making it the fastest-selling PC game of all time and surpassing the previous record held by *World of Warcraft*'s second expansion, *Wrath of the Lich King*. More information about the *Cataclysm* expansion and upcoming content, which continues the story of Azeroth where this novel ends, can be found on WorldofWarcraft.com.

FURTHER READING

If you'd like to read more about the characters, situations, and settings featured in this novel, the sources listed below offer additional pieces of the story of Azeroth.

- Many of the trials and tribulations that King Varian Wrynn has faced throughout his life are recounted in *World of Warcraft: Arthas: Rise of the Lich King* and *World of Warcraft: The Shattering: Prelude to Cataclysm* by Christie Golden, *World of Warcraft: Tides of Darkness* by Aaron Rosenberg, *World of Warcraft: Beyond the Dark Portal* by Aaron Rosenberg and Christie Golden, *World of Warcraft: Stormrage* by Richard A. Knaak, and the short story "Blood of Our Fathers" by Dan Arey (on http://us.battle.net /wow/en/game/lore/). Varian also plays a major role in the monthly *World of Warcraft* comic book by Walter and Louise Simonson, Ludo Lullabi, Jon Buran, Mike Bowden, Sandra Hope, and Tony Washington.

- More information about King Genn Greymane and the lengths to which he has gone to protect Gilneas is revealed in *World of Warcraft: Tides of Darkness* by Aaron Rosenberg; *World of Warcraft: Beyond the Dark Portal* by Aaron Rosenberg and Christie Golden; *Warcraft: Day of the Dragon* by Richard A. Knaak; the *World of Warcraft: Curse of the Worgen* comic book by Micky Neilson and James Waugh, Ludo Lullabi, and Tony Washington; and the short story "Lord of His Pack" by James Waugh (on http://us.battle.net/wow/en/game/lore/).

- In *World of Warcraft: The Shattering* by Christie Golden, Thrall appoints Garrosh Hellscream warchief of the Horde. Other details concerning this proud and fierce new warchief can be found in issues #15–20 of the monthly *World of Warcraft* comic book by Walter and Louise Simonson, Jon Buran, Mike Bowden, Phil Moy, Walden Wong, and Pop Mhan; *World of Warcraft: Beyond the Dark Portal* by Aaron Rosenberg and Christie Golden; and the short stories "Heart of War" by Sarah Pine and "As Our Fathers Before Us" by Stevie Nix (on http://us.battle.net/wow/en/game/lore/).

- Malfurion Stormrage and his love, Tyrande Whisperwind, struggle against the shadowy Emerald Nightmare in *World of Warcraft: Stormrage* by Richard A. Knaak. Further insight regarding the relationship between Malfurion and Tyrande is offered in the *War of the Ancients Trilogy* (*Warcraft: The Well of Eternity*, *Warcraft: The Demon Soul*, and *Warcraft: The Sundering*) by Richard A. Knaak and the short story "Seeds of Faith" by Valerie

Watrous (on http://us.battle.net/wow/en/game
/lore/). The *World of Warcraft: Curse of the Worgen*
comic book by Micky Neilson and James Waugh,
Ludo Lullabi, and Tony Washington also docu-
ments Malfurion's efforts to deal with the worgen
curse long before it appeared in the kingdom of
Gilneas.

- In the *War of the Ancients Trilogy* by Richard A.
  Knaak, Tyrande Whisperwind reluctantly estab-
  lishes herself as the leader of the night elves. Other
  exciting events in Tyrande's life are portrayed in
  World of Warcraft: Stormrage by Richard A. Knaak;
  issue #6 of the monthly *World of Warcraft* comic
  book by Walter Simonson, Ludo Lullabi, and Sandra Hope; the *World of Warcraft: Curse of the Worgen*
  comic book by Micky Neilson and James Waugh,
  Ludo Lullabi, and Tony Washington; and the short
  story "Seeds of Faith" by Valerie Watrous (on
  http://us.battle.net/wow/en/game/lore/).

- You can read about Shandris Feathermoon's past,
  including her relationship with Tyrande Whisperwind, in *Warcraft: The Demon Soul* and *Warcraft:
  The Sundering* (books two and three of the *War of
  the Ancients Trilogy*) by Richard A. Knaak; *World of
  Warcraft: Stormrage* by Richard A. Knaak; issues #2,
  3, and 5 of the *World of Warcraft: Curse of the Worgen*
  comic book by Micky Neilson and James Waugh,
  Ludo Lullabi, and Tony Washington; and "Seeds of
  Faith," a short story by Valerie Watrous (on http://
  us.battle.net/wow/en/game/lore/).

- Jarod Shadowsong rose to fame for his heroic command of the night elf resistance forces against the Burning Legion in the *War of the Ancients Trilogy* by Richard A. Knaak. The last book of this series, *Warcraft: The Sundering*, also features Jarod's relationship with his older sister, Maiev, and Shandris Feathermoon.

- The mysterious origins of the worgen curse, which has afflicted King Genn Greymane and many other Gilneans, are disclosed in the short story "Lord of His Pack" by James Waugh (on http://us.battle.net/wow/en/game/lore/) and the *World of Warcraft: Curse of the Worgen* comic book by Micky Neilson and James Waugh, Ludo Lullabi, and Tony Washington.

- Legends abound concerning the wolf Ancient, Goldrinn. The great creature's Taur-ahe name, *Lo'Gosh*, has been used to describe King Varian Wrynn due to the human's ferocity in battle. You can learn more about Goldrinn in *World of Warcraft: Stormrage* by Richard A. Knaak; issue #3 of the monthly *World of Warcraft* comic book by Walter Simonson, Ludo Lullabi, and Sandra Hope; and issue #1 of the *World of Warcraft: Curse of the Worgen* comic book by Micky Neilson and James Waugh, Ludo Lullabi, and Tony Washington.

- Warden Maiev Shadowsong's role during the War of the Ancients, including her relationship with her brother, Jarod, is depicted in *Warcraft: The*

Sundering, book three of the *War of the Ancients Trilogy* by Richard A. Knaak.

- During the War of the Ancients, many of the arcane-wielding Highborne were bent to the fallen titan Sargeras's will. Only recently have the Highborne been allowed to take part in night elf society again. Their history, at times tragic, is explored in the *War of the Ancients Trilogy* by Richard A. Knaak and *Warcraft: The Sunwell Trilogy: Ultimate Edition* by Richard A. Knaak and Kim Jae-Hwan.

- The many challenges of Prince Anduin Wrynn's life, such as his difficult relationship with his father, Varian, are shown in *World of Warcraft: The Shattering* by Christie Golden; the monthly *World of Warcraft* comic book by Walter and Louise Simonson, Ludo Lullabi, Jon Buran, Mike Bowden, Sandra Hope, and Tony Washington; and "Blood of Our Fathers," a short story by Dan Arey (on http://us.battle.net/wow/en/game/lore/).

- Long ago, the wise leader of the draenei, Velen, led his followers from their homeworld of Argus to elude the fallen titan Sargeras. Their escape and subsequent time spent on the world of Draenor are portrayed in *World of Warcraft: Rise of the Horde* by Christie Golden.

- A glimpse into High Tinker Gelbin Mekkatorque's efforts to liberate the gnomish capital, Gnomeregan, from the forces of Sicco Thermaplugg is offered in "Cut Short," a short story by Cameron Dayton (on http://us.battle.net/wow/en/game/lore/). The brilliant gnome also makes an appearance in *World of Warcraft: Beyond the Dark Portal* by Aaron Rosenberg and Christie Golden.

- In *Wolfheart*, three dwarves journey to Darnassus as lead representatives of the newly forged Council of Three Hammers. Another tale concerning the Bronzebeard representative, Thargas Anvilmar, is told in issues #8–15 of the *World of Warcraft* monthly comic book by Walter and Louise Simonson, Jon Buran, Mike Bowden, Sandra Hope, and Jerome K. Moore. Insight into the Dark Iron representative, Drukan, can be found in *World of Warcraft: The Shattering* by Christie Golden. Lastly, the various exploits of the Wildhammer representative, Kurdran Wildhammer, are recounted in *World of Warcraft: Beyond the Dark Portal* by Aaron Rosenberg and Christie Golden, *World of Warcraft: Tides of Darkness* by Aaron Rosenberg, and "Fire and Iron," a short story by Matt Burns (on http://us.battle.net/wow/en/game/lore/).

THE BATTLE RAGES ON

In the wake of the Cataclysm, tensions between the Horde and the Alliance have ignited conflicts throughout the world of Azeroth. Yet these clashes have only sapped resources and diverted attention from an even greater threat, as the corrupted black Dragon Aspect, Deathwing, and his minions grow closer to plunging the world into darkness. . . .

In *World of Warcraft's* third expansion, *Cataclysm*, you can take part in the epic confrontations between the Horde and the Alliance and also work toward thwarting Deathwing's schemes. The previous two *World of Warcraft* expansions, *The Burning Crusade* and *Wrath of the Lich King*, take players to the ruined world of Outland and the icy wastes of Northrend, while *Cataclysm* allows players to explore once-familiar regions in Kalimdor and the Eastern Kingdoms forever transformed by Deathwing's assault on Azeroth. The battle lines between Azeroth's defenders and their adversaries have been drawn. All that remains is to decide whether *you* will join in the fight to save the world from annihilation.

To discover the ever-expanding world that has entertained millions around the globe, go to WorldofWarcraft .com and download the free trial version. Live the story.